WHERE THEY BURN BOOKS, THEY ALSO BURN PEOPLE

MARCOS ANTONIO HERNANDEZ

ISBN-13: 978-1-7368067-0-8 (Paperback edition)

ISBN-13: 978-1-7368067-1-5 (Ebook edition)

"That was but a prelude; where they burn books, they will ultimately burn people as well."

HEINRICH HEINE, *ALMANSOR*, 1821

CHAPTER ONE

The Catholic Church was dying and Friar Diego de Landa was stuck on a ship. He was a patient man, tempered over years of service in the Toledo monastery, in the center of Spain, and had had ample opportunity to demonstrate his superior waiting skills over the weekslong journey to the Yucatán Peninsula. During a brief stop for provisions on a Caribbean island, after crossing the Atlantic Ocean, his comrades—there were nine friars total, including him—wanted to explore the island, eager to begin their holy task of converting new members to inflate the ranks of their weakening religion. Friar Diego had stayed in his island lodgings, studying the Bible and preparing to meet the natives of the Yucatán, knowing the true enormity of their upcoming task and not allowing distractions to turn his gaze, even for a second, away from their shared goal.

The friars came from different parts of Spain. They were all part of the Franciscan Order, itself a part of the Catholic Church. They had been recruited by Friar Nicolás de Albalate for the express purpose of coming to the Yucatán and converting the Yucatán's native population. Every friar who made the trip believed that by saving more souls they provided the Catholic

Church the necessary strength to fight back against the onslaught from the Muslims in the south and east and the Protestants from the north. None of the friars had been born when Christopher Columbus discovered the New World in 1492; they grew up with the belief that his discovery of the New World for Catholic Spain was God's divine purpose, that they had been led to a fountain-spring of souls where Catholicism's seed could take root.

Beliefs about evangelism differed within the Franciscan Order, creating factions within factions, and Friar Diego came from a group who still believed in the coming of the third age, the age of the Holy Spirit—the first age, the age of the Father, had been the period before Jesus Christ, and the second age, the age of the son, had been after his crucifixion. The third age would see the Church governed by the Holy Spirit instead of the Church's hierarchy, making the office of Pope unnecessary. In a move that shocked no one, the movement had been condemned centuries before by Pope Alexander IV, after the prophesied date of the New Age's beginning came and went. However, it persisted as a groundswell of whispers passed down from mentors to eager pupils in the shadowed halls of the Toledo monastery.

Friar Diego knew, in the marrow of his bones, he would be the one to bring about this New Age.

The group of friars had been stuck on the ship for hours, watching the sailors, led by their captain, enjoy their first steps on the land that held their future. The New World had existed on the horizon of their lives for so long that when it had appeared in their sight the day before, they thought it was a mirage. During the countless hours of their approach, each recruited friar stood in silent awe of the immense power the untamed wilderness possessed. They continued staring after arriving in the shallow waters off the coast, though this time in impatience, wanting to go onshore and begin the gargantuan task they had accepted with bowed heads back in Spain.

"We stay on the ship until the escort arrives," Friar Nicolás had said when the ship first anchored, before the first sailors rowed ashore.

Every Franciscan but one nodded their assent. Friar Diego remained motionless, staring and plotting.

The sun beat down on the group of nine friars from a cloudless blue sky, permeating their brown habits and intensifying the pungency created by dozens of unwashed men and their cargo emanating from the ship. The new recruits stood on the ship's deck, hands or elbows on the railing, watching the men who had taken the trip with them lying in the sand, exploring the nearby foliage, or luxuriating in the clear blue waters of the Caribbean. Friar Nicolás, who had gone back to Spain for reinforcements after years in the Yucatán, sat on the quarterdeck, alone and uncaring. Most of the Franciscan group's tonsures had grown in, saving the tops of their heads from the sun's rays, but nature had decided that two of the men, one of which was Friar Nicolás, would be bald; they both wore their mantle, the hood covering their head, despite the stifling heat.

Friar Diego pulled himself away from the torture of watching the men onshore and sat on the deck with his back against the opposite railing. The beach wasn't visible from where he sat; instead, he watched the treetops swaying in the tropical breezes, noted the foreign, multicolored birds, and strained his eyes to catch a glimpse of the monkeys he had heard about but had never seen. His ears searched in vain for sounds of wildlife in the land that would become his new home over the continuous noise of waves crashing against the side of the ship, his temporary prison. He pitied his fellow new recruits for their inability to understand that time spent staring in jealousy at those on the beach brought them no closer to meeting and converting natives. The way he saw it, they needed to find a way off the ship without going against Friar Nicolás, their superior.

The order to stay on the ship had been given so the men wouldn't rush headlong into exploring the New World; in effect, it doused their passions before the novelty of the environment could pull their attention away from God's plan. The recruits were young compared to Friar Nicolás, all in their twenties, and still needed the patience age had bestowed upon him by years of service in the name of the Lord.

Convincing Friar Nicolás of the urgency of meeting the natives might be enough to change his mind. In Friar Diego's experience, elder Franciscans were logical and willing to listen, in particular with regards to the best way to spread the word of God. In Toledo, he had often come to his mentor with a solution the old man hadn't considered and was lauded for his input. One time, when a farmer announced his rejection of the Church, banning his workers from worshipping on his land, Friar Diego suggested they inform the man that any future marriage of his daughter, who was a child at the time, would be illegitimate, instead of pursuing legal action against the farmer through the local authorities, which is how the church elder had dealt with such matters before. The farmer was back in church the following Sunday, and even paid extra tithes to make up for his momentary lapse of faith.

For his plan to work, each man brought to the Yucatán for the first time would need to understand the purpose for going onshore; there could be no break in the ranks, no frivolous time spent relaxing in the sand. While Friar Diego stared into the horizon with a burning curiosity about life among the foliage, one of his comrades, who was a hair to the right of his line of sight, turned around.

Friar Francisco Navarro was the closest thing Friar Diego had to a friend on the trip. They were both twenty-five, both came from Spain's center, and both believed they were destined for greatness; many nights during the trip across the ocean, well after everyone else had fallen asleep, had been spent talking about the role they would play in the Church's future. Friar Diego displayed a thin-lipped smile and Friar Francisco returned the expression before walking over to his friend.

"Land in sight and we're stuck on this ship," Friar Francisco said, crossing his arms as he rested his backside against the railing. He looked up at Friar Nicolás leafing through the Bible.

"He thinks we'll go onshore and waste time like those sailors," Friar Diego said, without taking his eyes from the horizon.

Friar Francisco looked down at Friar Diego. "We deserve to relax, after so much time at sea."

Friar Diego met his friend's gaze. "Friar Nicolás knows there's no time to relax when the future of the Church is at stake."

A cloud of shame passed over Friar Francisco's face. His heavy eyebrows and deep-set eyes grew darker. "You want to stay on the ship?" he said.

"I didn't say that," Friar Diego replied. "I'm merely saying that Friar Nicolás read your hearts."

"And not yours?"

"Not mine, no. I don't want to waste time on the beach. I want to meet the natives and get to work."

"But the natives are onshore! You waste time up here."

"My point exactly. If we can go to our dear Friar Nicolás, as a group, and inform him how our time is best served onshore, looking for natives to convert, he might find it in his heart to change his mind."

"I see. And what part do I play in this?"

"Do you agree with my position?" Friar Diego asked. There was no point in talking to the others if even one didn't concur.

"I do . . ." Friar Francisco said, his voice trailing off.

"Then return to your spot on the rail and send another man over."

Friar Francisco walked back across the deck. Minutes later, he turned to his right and told another new recruit to speak with Friar Diego. His prudence was a welcome addition to the scheme—Friar Nicolás might think it odd that a single man summoned the others one at a time in quick succession.

After Friar Diego informed the second man about the necessary shift in perception, how Friar Nicolás was misguided in his fears they would waste time on the beach when they were in fact wasting time on board the ship, not converting natives, he confirmed with the man that his message was received and agreed with, and told the man to send over the next after a moment's wait.

Within the hour, the other six friars were on board with Friar Diego's plan. The contents of each man's stomach frothed with excitement at the thought of meeting a native and spreading the word of God, putting the noisy waves crashing onto the ship's exterior to shame. Friar Diego sat back, pleased, wondering who would be the one to urge Friar Nicolás to reconsider.

As A YOUNG MAN, early in his education, Friar Diego had learned the value of withholding his true opinions until he could be sure of the recipient's trustworthiness. It took him years to trust his mentor in Toledo enough to give his true opinions, and he was rewarded for his candor by admittance into the secret group who believed in the New Age's coming. Before then, it had been his habit to pass on his more radical ideas to classmates, who would then pass the ideas off as their own and suffer the punishment or receive the glory, according to the whims of the elders. In this way, Friar Diego had discovered which of the church's elders were open to suggestions and which kept their mind shut with lock and key.

Friar Nicolás was still an unknown. For Friar Diego, weeks weren't enough to get the measure of a man.

Friar Francisco took the plunge. It started with a whisper, passing from the left to the right, each man nodding his agreement. Then, with a final nod, seven men pulled themselves away from staring at the beach, turned to the left, and approached the quarterdeck.

"Friar Nicolás, can we have a word?" Friar Francisco said. His words rang clear as the surrounding sky, his tone subservient but firm.

Friar Nicolás stood from where he sat, his grimace of pain betraying his aching bones. With the mantle covering his bald head, he took labored steps towards the main deck and stood against the railing, looking down at the men he'd convinced to follow him from Spain. "What is it you want?" he said, prepared to repeat his earlier proclamation.

Friar Francisco cleared his throat. "We want to go onshore—"

"We have to wait for the escort," Friar Nicolás said, cutting the younger man off.

Friar Francisco picked up where he left off. "To begin, right away, meeting natives and spreading the word of God."

Friar Nicolás looked down at the men before him, second-guessing his own assessment of their intentions. They were young, inexperienced, and after being stuck on the ship, he'd assumed stretching their legs was their primary concern, unappreciative of the magnitude of the task before them. He looked at Friar Diego, still seated halfway across the deck, his back against the railing farthest from the shore.

"Friar Diego!"

"Yes, Friar Nicolás?" he responded, standing up.

"Do you not agree with the men here? Why do you sit by yourself?"

"I'm waiting for the escort, sir."

Friar Nicolás smiled. "Of course, of course." He turned his attention back to the other seven men of their party. "There won't be any natives this close to the shore," he said. "And even if there were, converting them takes more than reading the Bible to them. You do realize we don't share the same language, don't you?"

"Then we should get started learning it right away!" Friar Francisco said.

"It's not so simple a thing," Friar Nicolás responded. He turned his back on them and started walking back to where he'd sat in heat's silent misery before he was interrupted by the young men's eagerness.

"We're wasting our time on the ship!" the other bald recruit said, throwing his mantle back as if he were storming into battle.

"We. Wait. For. The. Escort," Friar Nicolás roared.

"Is that the escort?" Friar Diego said, pointing to a friar—identifiable by his habit—and a barrel-chested, dark-skinned man who emerged from the well-worn path leading into the jungle. The arriving friar inspected the sailors on the beach, nodded his greeting, then continued to the shore with slow, measured steps before raising a hand to his brothers on the ship. The indigenous man, a head shorter than the Spanish friar, was dressed like the sailors: dark breeches and a loose white tunic, open at the neck.

Friar Nicolás looked at the shore. "That's them," he said, without acknowledging his prior outburst. "Gather your things, men. We're going ashore."

Everyone scampered below deck, bringing their meager belongings up to the deck. The rowboat came back to the ship from the shore and took the friars to land in two trips. Friar Diego and Friar Nicolás were on the second trip. Friar Nicolás made sure he sat next to Friar Diego.

"You manipulated your brethren," Friar Nicolás said, looking back towards the ship so nobody but Friar Diego could hear his words. "God was watching."

Friar Diego didn't reply. His gaze was locked on the approaching shore, inspecting with pride the solemn men who forewent the expected jubilation at their arrival in the New World as they waited for the rest of the group crossing the stretch of sea between the shore and the ship.

Sailors waded through the shallow water as the rowboat approached shore. They offered to carry the friars' possessions so the holy men could hold their habits above the water, hoping God would see their good deed and remember their charity when they stood in front of Peter for judgment. The friars, like the group before them, denied the sailors the chance, carrying their own packs against their chest or over their head. Each man's habit was soaked to the thighs when they got to shore.

Friar Diego took slow, careful steps on the surface of the beach as he approached the rest of the men so sand wouldn't wind up in his sandals. It didn't work. He never shook the feeling there was something from the environment affecting his person during the rest of his time in the Yucatán; besides rocks in his sandals, he suffered foreign plant fragments scratching him through the fabric of his habit, small insects burrowing in his hair whenever it got too long, and leaf oils on various patches of skin, unknown until they produced the characteristic incessant itching.

When Friar Nicolás approached the escort friar, they both reached their arms out, grabbed each other's shoulders, and smiled before their embrace. They finished off their greeting with a light kiss on both cheeks. Friar Nicolás made the necessary introductions.

"I'd like you all to take a good look at the man who made our holy work in the Yucatán possible: Friar Lorenzo de Bienvenida."

His career was legendary on both sides of the ocean. Friar Lorenzo had come to the New World in 1542. After a brief time in Guatemala, he arrived in the Yucatán Peninsula in 1544, accompanied by indigenous men trusted by Spanish missionaries who helped him establish contact with the indigenous population on the Yucatán Peninsula: the Maya. He had spent the last five years learning the language and preaching to the Maya as best he could, according to the account provided by Friar Nicolás during their voyage.

Each man nodded when Friar Nicolás introduced them, one at a time, to the pioneer. Then, he revealed the identity of the native man to his recruits. "And this is Don Francisco de Montejo Xiu, Lord of Mani." Seen up close, the man had a flat forehead. There was evidence of wrinkles around the corners of his eyes and lips, but he otherwise could have passed for a man in the prime of his youth.

The indigenous man placed his palms together in front of his chest and nodded.

Friar Lorenzo spoke up. "We can thank him for the safety of the monastery at Mani, our very first establishment in the Yucatán and still in operation."

All of the friars crossed themselves.

"Speaking of the threats," Friar Lorenzo said, speaking to Friar Nicolás alone. "Montejo's no longer *Adelantado*."

"Who's been elevated in his stead?" Friar Nicolás asked.

"Another one of the colonists: Francisco Hernandez."

"The *encomenderos* are all the same," the Lord of Mani said in rough Spanish, spitting on the ground. "They think the Mayan people belong to them."

Friar Lorenzo addressed the stupefied friars just arrived from Spain. "The leaders of the *encomiendas* believe the native's spirit must be broken so they accept their forced labor and required tribute. Their methods are brutal: mutilating women, murdering children, branding and chaining men."

"I've told them," Friar Nicolás explained.

"We're able to convince the Crown to take away the *encomiendas* from the worst offenders, but removing Montejo from office had an unforeseen consequence: the colonists are unified against us. They'll learn, in time, to leave the souls of these poor people to our order. God is on our side."

The men crossed themselves once more.

Friar Lorenzo clapped his hands together after a moment's silence. "Your journey isn't over yet, brothers, but it's almost complete. Shall we get on our way?" Without waiting for a response, Friar Lorenzo turned to the Lord of Mani and asked him to lead.

"Of course," the Mayan man replied. He waited for the men's belongings to settle on their backs before leading them onto the path through the forest. The men all waved goodbye to the sailors, the bald recruit adding that he would pray for them.

Friar Diego lingered at the back, alongside the slow-moving Friar Nicolás.

"I do hope God was watching," Friar Diego said when he was certain nobody was listening.

"God's always watching," Friar Nicolás said. He was unsure

about what Friar Diego spoke of, their conversation on the rowboat wiped from his memory by the induced elation at seeing his old friend and being back on the soil God had called him to till.

"Then he saw me convincing my brothers about the need for expediency in converting the natives. We were wasting time on the ship."

A bright red blush crept up the neck and onto the face of the elder friar. He scowled at the young man. "You went against my expressed charge. The men didn't need to be tempted by indolence onshore."

"You have little faith in your men," Friar Diego observed.

"You forget your place!"

"I know exactly where I should be. The question is, do you?"

"Pride is the most insidious sin," a furious Friar Nicolás whispered.

Friar Diego started walking faster, leaving the old man fuming alone in the procession's rear.

"You will learn, this place isn't so simple."

"It's simple to me," Friar Diego said, turning around. "God has put me in a position to save the Church; I can't while I'm stuck on a ship."

CHAPTER TWO

Cortez Vuscar had expected to dread walking up to her in front of the type of people who would care enough about a burning library to stop and stare: the poised, well-dressed individuals in the part of the city where he didn't belong. Surprising himself, however, he was looking forward to it. As soon as more people were there to witness his bravery, he told himself, he would rush out to her and prove his worth once and for all.

The flames crackled high above him. He looked up, and the faint smell of smoke tickled his nostrils. The building was old, having hosted the city's repository of knowledge for over a century. Thick black smoke issued from the highest windows, passing through ancient seals the way water finds its way into a house during the worst rainstorms. It licked the stone masonry surrounding the roof before continuing its ascent into the atmosphere, obscuring the ornate carvings that lined the outside wall. Wisps of thin white smoke curled out from between the exterior columns surrounding the building, evidence of the flames spreading to the lower levels.

The books were burning.

Cortez turned his attention back to the object of his desire from the previous thirteen days: Alara Chel. Her black hair was pulled back from her face, tied in her typical braided ponytail, exposing her mask of horror and sadness. She was his burning obsession, his reason for searching within himself for the courage to be the man she deserved. His primitive instinct awakened with the memory of her hair smelling like roses from the one time he had gotten close enough to experience the fragrance himself. Coming from her, the smell—along with every other enchanting characteristic she possessed—was capable of both inspiring him and rendering him helpless to resist fulfilling her most frivolous wishes. As the fire gained strength high above him, Cortez lost himself in thoughts of her scent; the smoke created by the burning books was the vapor of Alara's pungent floral scent reaching out and brushing his cheek across space and time. Cortez's nose led him into a rose garden waiting for him, which he alone could access.

He couldn't tell if she was crying from where he stood on the side of the building, though he hoped she was. It was his right to dry her tears, hard-fought and well-earned.

The library's entrance was across the street from the vast park that separated the city in two, keeping the struggling, second-class citizens like Cortez away from the domain of the privileged. The library was on the line where property values became prohibitive for most of the city's inhabitants. The wide stone steps that led to the imposing dark wood doors created one final pretentious barrier for those from his part of the city who crossed the park for access to the space, detracting from the humble servitude of the tomes held within. The adjacent park was crosscut with paved paths shaded by dense clusters of trees of uniform height; the trees closest to the street projected their leaves over a path that ran between the park and the street in front of the building, under which onlookers—including Alara—congregated, watching the blaze. The mouths of each person in attendance hung open in astonishment as they witnessed knowledge's destruction, their collective breaths acting as bellows for the growing inferno.

A few individuals were watching the fire from the far side of the street that ran alongside the building where Cortez stood. They called out to him, urging him to get away from the burning library. He turned to them, flashed a smile the way his mother had taught him when spreading the Christian message, and waved. He kept his body as close to the library as possible so Alara wouldn't see him before his grand entrance. Their continued yelling induced a surge of burning panic inside Cortez's chest, the pressure escalating as the heat arrived in his throat. He turned his attention back to Alara. Her eyes were still skyward.

Noticing anything but a burning library that has stood as knowledge's guardian for over a hundred years takes more than yelling.

The distant blaring of sirens from fast-approaching fire trucks pulled Cortez back into the moment and provided the salve for the flames in his chest. He scanned the faces in the crowd around his beloved. Though he wanted more witnesses when he approached her, the few dozen already present were more than he had ever had the courage to stand in front of before. His lack of fear filled him with pride. The previous version of himself, the one before the fire, would have fought himself to abandon the plan, and he had been prepared to storm into battle in the name of love. Standing straight with confidence despite the sharp pain in his ribs—his mother would have been proud—he emerged from the side of the building, heading straight towards where Alara stood beneath the trees' protective leaves.

She didn't notice him. Nobody did. Their eyes were glued to the sky, watching the now-black smoke billowing from between the columns. The sirens were getting closer. Air rushed into the flames behind him through broken windows, creating a peculiar noise of consumption; the fire had emerged from its shell and was taking its first massive breath. Cortez had to say his piece before the firefighters had time to park, set up, and organize a plan of attack against the blaze. Their perimeter would be impenetrable once deployed.

His plan didn't budget time for him to get Alara's attention. The way it had played out in his head, she would see him and be grateful for his arrival. He was the knight in shining armor, she was the rescued princess from the movies. Her gratitude would multiply when she understood what he was prepared to do for her. In the deepest recesses of his heart, he hoped she would rush into his arms and plant a kiss on his lips. He could think of no better scenario for his first. When he was mere steps away, lost in a daydream that would never occur, she turned in his direction, facing him without a trace of recognition.

The truth dawned on Alara when Cortez's path became clear. Her features hardened. "What are you doing here?" she asked, understanding who stood in front of her.

"The library's burning," Cortez replied, as if this simple fact explained his presence as well as if she had asked the same question inside his own home and he replied that he lived there.

"I can't believe it," she said. Her voice carried immeasurable sadness and a hint of resignation.

The first fire truck arrived on the scene, skidding to a stop on the street between the park and the library now behind Cortez. It was in desperate need of a wash, the typical shiny red paint dulled with layers of grime. The attached white ladder had peeling rust spots littering its skin. The fire truck was from the side of the city where Cortez lived with his mother, on the far side of the park; it was the first on-scene because of how the fire stations were distributed throughout the city. It was a shoddy version of the two fire trucks that pulled to a stop soon after. These were red and polished to a high sheen—they were brand new and looked like they belonged in a magazine. As Cortez watched, the two gleaming fire trucks forced the one that had first arrived to back up so they could take the prime position in front of the blaze and receive the lion's share of the glory for saving the great sentinel standing guard against intruders from the far side of the city.

Cortez knew time was running out. He raised his gaze and stared at the fire for a moment, relishing the shared experience with Alara. The crowd, having grown, was large enough, everyone there ready, in his mind, to witness his great emergence from the shadows. He turned to Alara and said, "Remy's in there."

The information caught Alara off guard. She blinked multiple times and shook her head from left to right as she pulled it back, unable or unwilling to accept the news. Part of the confusion came from the way Cortez had shared the information. His tone of voice would have had the same matter-of-fact quality if he had said, "There are books in there." Most of the confusion, however, came from finding out her boyfriend was in the library. Remy Moncard didn't read. He was proud of the fact and owned it, a contorted badge of honor he displayed on his chest. According to him, reading played no part in his plan to further his own station in life. Discipline, charm, and his smile were his winning combination.

"Remy?" Alara repeated when she found her voice.

Cortez's eyes lit up. "Uh-huh," he said with a sweet smile and slight nod. It was a joke to him.

Alara was first repulsed, then grew frantic. "What's he doing in there? How do you know?"

"Relax," Cortez said. He stretched out the beginning of the word, the way it was said on the old sitcoms he used to watch for hours after school while his mother was at work. He adopted the nonchalant air of the show's most charming characters and told her there was nothing to worry about. "There's nothing to worry about. God brought me here for a reason," he said.

"Of course there's something to worry about! Remy's inside a fire!"

"I can save him if you want." His offer was served with a singsong quality, the final word dragged out.

Alara became enraged, her braid hovering above her back, no longer in contact with her body, a cobra preparing to strike. "And what are you going to do?"

Cortez looked at the crowd of people around them; there were plenty of witnesses for his great sacrifice. He imagined they were listening to his conversation with rapt attention without looking out of politeness, their gaze instead drawn to the stage where his production would unfold. Everything Cortez had done for her was coming together just as he had planned. Getting Remy inside the library and starting the fire had given him the chance to prove his devotion.

"I'll go in and get him," Cortez said, imagining he was Jesus accepting his fate for the good of mankind. He stared into her eyes and was shocked to discover disgust where he had expected, and believed he'd earned, admiration.

Part of Alara wondered if Cortez was lying. She knew he didn't like Remy, and wouldn't like any boyfriend of hers, but his absolute conviction in Remy's presence inside the fire was the first time she had heard Cortez speak in a confident, commanding way. The cold power behind his words frightened her. She brushed him aside and walked away, looking for someone who could help her trapped boyfriend. Cortez shuddered at her touch, goosebumps radiating out from the point of their contact.

Pulling himself from his reverie, Cortez grabbed Alara's arm, stopping her before she took her first steps into the street. "I'll be right back," he uttered, his own sudden seriousness evident in his voice. He was silent while he waited for the response to his grand gesture, which he had played on repeat in his mind: the kiss, his first, the one that he knew would bring him into direct contact with God's grace.

Alara froze. As she stood still, Cortez reached a hand up and caressed her cheek, the way he had seen it done in the movies. A crash rang out from inside the library, causing a collective gasp from the onlookers. He imagined it was the crowd in a theater, watching his performance. Cortez was a man possessed by something far greater than himself, and once he realized the kiss wouldn't materialize, he turned his back on the flames of his own passions and prepared himself to rush headlong into the raging inferno inside the library.

Once past Alara, Cortez turned and, walking backwards, said, "If God has put me in a position to help, I can't look the other way."

CHAPTER THREE

THE NEW FRIARS were encouraged to roam the countryside and learn all they could in the months between their arrival and the upcoming council in Merida, where they would receive their orders detailing which monastery they would reinforce. Friar Diego de Landa walked for days on end, first through the *encomiendas* surrounding Merida, then going farther to the east, southeast, and south, looking for natives to convert. The *encomienda* Maya were a known quantity and therefore of little use to Friar Diego; the understanding among the Franciscans was that saving their souls was inevitable because they were already well within the Spanish sphere of influence. Friar Diego was searching for untouched Maya the same way Cortes searched for gold, with the certainty that the precious substance was in the New World's wilderness and awaiting discovery.

When the roaming friars first began exploring the peninsula, they went out in small groups, discussing the Bible, their holy mission, and the future of the Church. The first examples of ancient structures they encountered were at the site of the home monastery in Merida. The Spanish town had been built upon a giant square site paved with stones, the vast open space in the middle surrounded by stone cells with stone doors—stones that were used in future years to create Merida's colonial buildings. The friars also saw the site of Chichen Itza with its numerous buildings made of carved stone. The main pyramid fascinated Friar Diego; it had four stairways that faced the four cardinal directions, each with so many steps it was tiring to climb them. Each corner was made with rounded stones, so the building narrowed with an elegance of craftsmanship that called out to the new recruits from an ancient time long since past.

While they walked through the stoneworks, Friar Diego listened for hints that his brothers knew about the New Age prophecy as well. He couldn't outright ask if the men believed in the potential of the converted Maya to bring about the age of the Holy Spirit, knowing the belief was outlawed by the soon-to-be-useless Pope. Instead, he listened for statements that compared the Maya to the Old World's Jewish population.

The original prophecy of the coming New Age claimed the Jews' conversion to Christianity would be the initial domino that would result in the entire world following the one true religion: that of Jesus Christ. Drastic measures were taken when the Jewish conversion didn't materialize as expected. The Disputation of Paris in 1240, which resulted in twenty-four wagons full of Hebrew manuscripts—ten thousand volumes—being burned, was instigated by Friar Nicholas Donin of La Rochelle in an inspired attempt to force the Jews to accept the Christian God. Everything changed when Columbus discovered the New World. While Franciscans as a whole made strides towards the native population's conversion, those in Friar Diego's line of mentors believed the natives' conversion was the catalyst that would lead to the whole world believing in Christ's grace, Jews included. So, if any of the other friars discussed their mission in the Yucatán Peninsula and brought up the Jewish faith, there stood a chance they were members of the same whispered sect.

To his disappointment, Friar Diego discovered he was alone.

The novelty of roaming fell for the other friars after the first few weeks. They swore off walking vast distances into the wilderness, telling Friar Diego he was crazy for braving the untamed jungle with little more than the meager rations, hammock, and Bible he carried and the clothes on his back. The other new friars visited *encomenderos* who were friendly to their cause, preaching to the natives held in forced service by the Spaniards. Friar Diego opposed their lethargy, and his solitary wanderings grew in scope until each excursion took him a day's worth of walking away from Merida.

Friar Diego's communication with the Maya he encountered grew more difficult the farther he got from Merida. The satellite monasteries of Conkal and Izamal, both established with the expected arrival of Friar Nicolás de Albalate with reinforcements, each included a school and infirmary, but the establishments hadn't had enough time or manpower to teach the surrounding natives Spanish customs. Friar Diego received a smattering of Mayan words handwritten on parchment, the result of years of work by Friar Luis de Villalpondo of the Campeche monastery, the man with the greatest mastery of the Mayan language. While Friar Diego walked, he dedicated himself to memorizing the various terms, committing to memory the words for greetings, various types of food, water, and the plants and animals of the jungle. The repetition of the Mayan words for his surroundings calmed the hypervigilance every sound of the jungle induced in Friar Diego's senses, born from the ancient fear of unseen predators hungry for human flesh; identification removed the unknown aspect of the jungle, and his spoken words provided solace in the face of suffocating silence.

The Izamal monastery was a full day's walk to the east of Merida. Friar Diego took the trip alone a month after his arrival on the peninsula, trusting the instructions given to him by Friar Lorenzo de Bienvenida. When he arrived, the Izamal friars were engaged in prayer; he joined them, was fed, then passed the night in one of the infirmary beds. The next day, he continued east, off into the jungle. The Spaniards he encountered were few and far between, the brave souls forced away from the prime locations on the coast and surviving in the interior of the Yucatán through sheer determination.

Friar Diego faced a decision at midday: he would have to turn around if he was going to return to the Izamal monastery. The sun was high in the sky as Friar Diego walked through narrow paths in the underbrush created by the Maya, too narrow for any horse or wagon. He had just passed by a fledgling *encomienda* and stopped to pray with the Spaniard, who claimed his location was the most remote. In return, he received a small portion of food for lunch before refusing to take further provisions for his excursion.

Like any good Franciscan, he prayed for guidance, urging God to show him the path forward. He heard a rustling on the path ahead of him while his were eyes closed. He tried ignoring the sound and focusing on his prayer, but the noise persisted. Thinking it was perhaps a native, the first he'd encountered outside an *encomienda*, he opened his eyes, searching for the source.

It was a monkey. Dark fur covered its face, with light fur on its torso leading to darker fur on its arms. It hung from a tree branch, staring at the seated friar.

Friar Diego had seen flashes of the creatures before. Each time, they were high in the trees, obscured by leaves. This was the first time he had seen one in full, and the experience left him certain of God's instruction: continue forward. He stood up and kept walking.

As the sun set, Friar Diego found a suitable spot for his hammock, then prayed, his conversation with God enough sustenance for his body. The bugs kept him awake all night. They swarmed his body each time he closed his eyes, tormenting discovered bits of skin despite the friar's attempts at protecting himself with his habit. Dawn was a blessing. He rose from the hammock, scattering the various insects into the wind, and broke camp after relieving himself of the night's water. He set off after his morning prayers, following the path worn down by years of traffic from countless sandaled feet.

Lack of sleep made every footstep heavy. The jungle around him faded away by midmorning, replaced by an acute awareness of his own ragged breathing. Years of conditioning in the Church had taught him the fortifying strength possessed by the Bible, and he called forth the story of Jesus Christ carrying the cross. The knowledge of the sacred man putting one step forth at a time, despite his previous torture, gave Friar Diego the needed strength to pull the world around him back into focus. He saw the world with blessed eyes. Rays of sunlight filtered through the variety of bright green leaves above, leaving pockets of God's golden touch at occasional points on the path. Traversing among illuminated patches removed the weight of travel from Friar Diego's shoulders; they were small bread crumbs leading him deeper into the jungle.

After the sun passed through its zenith, Friar Diego thought he heard chanting in the distance to his right. He paused, unsure. There wasn't a monastery this far into the interior, and the *encomendero* he'd encountered the previous day had told him, with pride, his was the farthest into the peninsula. Friar Lorenzo had reminded all the new recruits of the danger of leaving the path. He told them the Maya wouldn't dare harm a hair on their head, after the Great Maya Revolt of 1546 left them sure of their position in the hierarchy, but that the real risk came from getting lost in the jungle and the resulting exposure to the elements. The chanting intensified while Friar Diego contemplated. He knew the possibility of imagined sounds sprung forth from his exhaustion, but a tingling in his stomach convinced him the opportunity of encountering natives was worth the risk.

Friar Diego left the path and the surrounding foliage swallowed him whole. Short shrubs and young trees grabbed at his habit as he passed them, and all manner of terrestrial insects found their way into his sandals. He apologized to God for killing one of his creatures each time a small exoskeleton snapped beneath the skin on the bottom of his feet. The chanting grew louder as he approached. Gratitude swelled within his breast when he realized the sounds of his own clumsy path through the undergrowth were drowned out by the unified cries. His progress slowed when he got the first glimpses of humans through the trees. These were the natives he was looking for, the first steps to saving the Church and bringing about the age of the Holy Spirit! He located a thicket of the densest brush and crouched behind, watching.

Hundreds of Maya were in a vast clearing. Their dark skin was painted red, and they danced around a naked girl tied to a post. They all possessed a robust physique, muscular and lean—clear evidence of their physical strength. Each member of the group had a flattened forehead. Many of the group wore piercings in their ears and noses, and most were covered with tattoos.

Both men and women had long hair. The women wore theirs parted in the middle, and the men braided theirs and wore it ringed on the crown of their head, leaving an untouched portion hanging down to their shoulders.

The girl tied to the post had a crown of flowers, reminding Friar Diego, who had earlier had Jesus on his mind, of a crown of thorns. She was surrounded by clay vessels that reached her knees. Next to her, presiding over the ceremony, was a man with feathers sticking up from his head, covering his cape, and attached to the strips of cloth that hung from his waist, covering both front and back. None of the others in the clearing wore the cape or adorned their heads, but all of them had similar strips of cloth covering their genitals, with various amounts of decoration. The women also wore pieces of fabric that ended at their ribcage, attached beneath the armpits, covering their shoulders and breasts.

Friar Diego watched the complex choreography taking place in the clearing. They danced in unison as if they had been performing the ritual their entire lives. Dancers moved to spaces occupied moments before by another member of their group, seamless transitions that happened all over the clearing.

The girl tied to the post watched without a trace of fear. She was, in fact, delighted by the pageantry. The feathered man next to her had his own part to play in the ceremony, shaking and rattling on one foot, then both, then from his knees. His part was all in the same cadence as the rest of his troupe, along to an inner music available to them that Friar Diego couldn't hear.

The dancers all stopped at once, without a single member of the group continuing a moment longer than the others. They were frozen, not blinking; the sole evidence of life was the slight rising and falling of their chests, which Friar Diego thought wasn't substantial enough for their level of exertion and gave testament to their quality breeding. When Friar Diego took measure of his own breathing, he noticed his own chest and shoulders moved more than those of the Mayan men and women in the clearing, even more than the heavier and older members of the group.

At a preordained moment, every member of the group looked at the feathered man and the girl tied to the post. Friar Diego's gaze followed. The girl was young, hadn't yet hit puberty, and her hair was pasted on her head with a shiny substance. The feathered man jumped forward and yelled to the group, who responded with a unified shout. There was a flurry of back-and-forth shouting, during which Friar Diego swore to himself he would learn the Mayan language so he would never be ignorant of their customs again. The feathered man grabbed one end of his cape and began twirling at a steady rate, and after a number of turns every person in the clearing took a knee.

Now that everyone was half as tall, Friar Diego could see a knife on the ground in front of the girl. A prescient awareness gripped him, his eyes opening wide. Every hint of exhaustion was forgotten. Out of nowhere, a sharp pain erupted from his right foot. He looked down and saw a collection of red ants swarming on the skin left exposed by the sandal. Shaking the insects away, he turned back to the ceremony. Several of the Maya closest to him were looking in his direction, staring into the brush. The feathered man had the knife in both hands, holding it up to the sky.

Once Friar Diego decided the time for the Maya conversion had arrived, no force on earth or in heaven could convince him to stray from his course. He stormed through the thicket, ripping his habit and suffering deep scratches on his arms and legs, and emerged from the undergrowth while yanking the cloth from the grasp of reaching plants. He stood tall, brushing himself off and straightening his garment while hundreds of kneeling Maya studied the intruder.

Without hesitation, he stormed forward and untied the girl from the post. The Maya in the clearing—the feathered man holding the knife included—watched him with curious stares. Even the girl he saved from sacrifice was surprised; she stood still as Friar Diego untied her and didn't move even after the rope holding her in place was removed. It took a nod from the feathered man for her to step away from the post, jumping over the clay vessels in a graceful bound.

Friar Diego couldn't reconcile his anger with the unaroused Maya. The thought of their idolatry, and the affront to God, coursed through his veins. He smashed one of the vessels before turning around, inspecting their reaction.

All eyes were on the feathered man, who didn't pay attention to his multitude. He looked at Diego, smiled, and walked forward, picking up one of the clay vessels and throwing it down on the ground, smashing it to pieces. After urging those closest to him to join, they stood up and started smashing the vessels, none of them smiling, unlike the man who granted them permission. They kneeled again after the destruction.

Diego couldn't believe how simple it had been to convince them to abandon their ritual. Now calm, he thought there could be no better time for the people to hear the word of the Lord. He would have to earn their trust first, using the words Friar Luis had provided. Friar Diego began with a greeting.

He discovered the feathered man's name was Ahkinmai.

Ahkinmai had seen friars before, in passing, but none had come to him with such clear animal characteristics as the man who burst forth from the thicket. His first thought after seeing the friar was that the man must be under attack from bees, who were seeking revenge for the honey-based alcoholic drink beloved by the Mayan gods. Then, when the angry little man stormed to the front of the ceremony, one lone man among many, Ahkinmai knew there was a bee in the house. The best thing to do, he thought, was what they did every time an enraged bee stormed into their living space seeking revenge: stay still and wait for it to fly away. He pitied the friar's sting, the smashing of the vessel, knowing the stinging bee doesn't have long to live. Ahkinmai thought that whatever possessed the young man with short hair on the crown of his head to act in so brave a manner, the beehive he was protecting, was worth learning about so he could use its power to inspire his warriors before they went into battle. So, he joined in the destruction and spilled the alcoholic offering onto the earth, trying to understand.

Of course, Friar Diego didn't know any of Ahkinmai's reasoning, didn't realize the feathered man pitied him, and he blazed forth in his practice of the Mayan language. After the greetings, he went through various other vocabulary, working out the correct way each word was said. After a few confusing moments, when Ahkinmai didn't understand the point of saying random words, he understood Friar Diego wanted to practice his pronunciation. The list wasn't long, and the rest of the Maya in the clearing stayed in place while the two men in front of them spoke basic words. The girl who had been tied to the post stood off to the side, still naked.

Friar Diego took out his Bible. With a rough gesturing of his fingers against the words, he informed Ahkinmai he wanted to read from his sacred text. Ahkinmai, familiar with reading and writing himself, knew right away what the young friar wanted, and he led the girl away, leaving Friar Diego alone in front of hundreds of Maya. The girl's mother stood up from where she knelt, rushed over to her daughter, and led her away into the jungle. While Friar Diego read from the Bible, one of the men closest to Ahkinmai asked him why he didn't get upset with the foreigner.

"The Spaniards are ruining our way of life," the Mayan man muttered.

"This isn't one of the colonists. This is one of their priests," Ahkinmai replied.

"Without feathers?"

"They all wear the brown cloth."

"Why are you making us listen to him?"

"You aren't listening now," Ahkinmai said with a sly grin.

"You know what I mean."

"His God inspired him to run, alone, into a group of this many men," he said, using a finger to point at the masses. "If he teaches us his ways, we can worship this God too and use the provided bravery."

"What about the god of the harvest? He'll be upset with us after today."

"There's always tomorrow."

Ahkinmai gestured for the man to return his attention to Friar Diego. He stood off to the side for the duration of Friar Diego's sermon, one in which the friar urged the natives to abandon their false idols and follow the one true God.

During his most impassioned moment, Friar Diego smashed a nearby idol made of soft stone into two. He looked at Ahkinmai when he was done, and the feathered man returned to the front of the crowd.

"Praise be to God!" Friar Diego shouted.

Ahkinmai turned to his people. "This man speaks the language of bees!" he shouted.

Friar Diego assumed Ahkinmai had translated the benediction. He concluded by saying, "Serve the Lord."

Ahkinmai grabbed an idol, made of clay, and smashed it on the packed earth. "And he's here to teach us his ways!"

Friar Diego smiled, with tears of joy dampening his eyes.

Ahkinmai swiped from left to right with an open palm, and the crowd all stood up, then dispersed into the trees. He turned back to Friar Diego and made a vertical circle with his index finger.

"I'll come back," Friar Diego said. It was the second time they'd understood each other, after the initial introduction.

The sermon and conversion made the solitary walks and sleepless nights worth every moment, and Friar Diego looked forward to preaching to the natives in the future. For years after the mass conversion, he told anyone who would listen that the Maya had begged him to stay and teach them further because of the quality of his initial speech, that they smashed their idols because of his persuasion to follow the word of God, and that they didn't walk away and leave him alone in the clearing.

CHAPTER FOUR

THIRTEEN DAYS before the library fire, Cortez had left the house for work at the same time he did every weekday. He descended the stairs from the seventh floor two at a time with his mother's reminder to have a good day still echoing inside his head. The bright blue backpack hanging from his shoulders carried his daily supplies: a packed lunch in a brown paper bag from his mother, a pencil and notebook that had been blank since its purchase months or years ago, and an assortment of medications he carried with him everywhere. His asthmatic lungs required an inhaler if he overexerted himself or was struck with enough panic to affect his breathing. Blue pills were there to catch him if he fell victim to a panic attack. The white pills helped him whenever he needed an extra dose of courage, like when he was faced with too many social interactions; unbeknownst to him, they were sugar pills not prescribed by a doctor but included in his arsenal by his mother. As a devout Christian woman, she knew the power of belief.

The sun blazed outside his patchwork building, and with it came the smell of baking garbage that flooded Cortez's nostrils as soon as he walked outside. The black trash bags in the alley he passed had been put out the night before and hadn't had enough time in the sun to create enough vapors to account for the stench. Instead, the smell emanated from the concrete and asphalt itself, in the forgotten part of a city where those with less were able to scratch out a corner large enough for them to exist.

Cortez kept his head down as he walked by his neighbors. There had been a time, when he was younger, when he would have greeted those that lived around him, or even looked them in the eye, but after he'd mentioned to his mother that one of them had shown him a handgun, she forbade him to interact with them without her watchful eye there to protect him. He had memorized the cracks in the sidewalk and knew every place water entered the sewer system. He looked forward to walking over the grates that would blow air up from the subway system below but was careful to stay off them in the presence of his guardian, in case she also forbade him to tempt fate.

The walk to the ice cream factory was eleven blocks and took him ten minutes. He always arrived five minutes before eight. When the boss arrived, he always found Cortez sitting on the concrete step in front of the door, waiting to be let in. The boss was a surly man by nature, but he started the morning with an inspiring hope that each day would be one worth living before the inevitable small inconvenience ruined his mood and made him look forward to beginning the next.

"Cortez," the boss said when he parked near the factory's entrance. He wore khakis, a yellow polo, and was supported by off-white sneakers that had survived decades of abuse. If Cortez had been more observant, he would have noticed that the different-colored polos his boss wore throughout the week corresponded to the different days. Red on Mondays, to start the week hot. Yellow on Fridays, in anticipation of the weekend and spending time outside in the sun, even though his pale skin turned bright red on the few occasions each year when he followed through with his plan and made it outside. He wore green, blue, and purple polos on the remaining days of the week, according to an internal logic he would take to his grave.

"Morning, sir," Cortez replied. He stood up, waited for the boss to unlock and open the double doors, and followed him inside. After walking through the reception area together—unused save for visits from vendors once a month—the boss turned right and went into the office he still insisted on locking every night, while Cortez turned left and went through a set of swinging double doors and walked onto the factory floor. He liked being the first one there so he could hang his backpack on the third hook from the left, which corresponded to the position of the locker where he kept his coat. Since nobody else paid attention to these things, on days Cortez wasn't the first one to arrive he ran the risk of leaving his belongings disjointed. This would result in a mild sense of dread and panic that sat just below his throat and would last the entire workday, making it difficult to concentrate and requiring many white pills. He had learned long ago that people didn't like their things moved from his hook without their consent, and that consenting to something they didn't understand wasn't an ability anybody he worked with had ever demonstrated.

With his belongings left hanging in their proper place, Cortez turned and went back to the building's entrance. He sat down on the step in front of the door once more to wait for his friend's arrival. Other workers streamed in as the clock approached eight thirty, the time everyone was required in the building so production could begin at nine. Some of his fellow employees shook his hand, some nodded their head in his direction when their eyes met, and one leaned over and patted his back. On some days, Simeon would be waiting for Cortez as soon as he walked back through the front entrance, but this wasn't one of those days.

Cortez was getting anxious by the time Simeon Blough rolled up three minutes before eight thirty. His friend was also Hispanic and had been born without the use of his legs. His black hair was matted on his head, the sides tickling the tops of his ears. As he explained it, showering wasn't something he was concerned with, and what little smell his body generated from sitting in a chair all day was no match for deodorant.

"Hi Cortez," Simeon said, coasting across the final portion of the parking lot. He couldn't wave because both hands were busy monitoring his locomotion, ready to stop on a moment's notice.

"Good morning, Simeon. Long time no see." It was his morning's standard greeting phrase, comforting in its regularity because they saw each other every day during the week.

"Not long enough," Simeon said with a smile, his typical reply. He stopped in front of the step and turned around, his back to Cortez.

Cortez grabbed the handles of his friend's wheelchair, tilted him back, and lifted him over the step. In theory, anybody could perform the minor task, but after Simeon had been left outside in the rain one morning, the boss had told Cortez it was his job from then on. He also helped Simeon get around when they were both inside the factory, a task that left Cortez and Simeon tethered together until the end of each workday. After Simeon was rolled to his locker, he opened it and placed his lunch down on the bottom. According to the chart on the wall near their station, the team would be making orange sorbet pints that day. The pair was responsible for putting lids on the sealed pints. During production, the pair took up stations on opposite sides of the conveyor belt, and each person would be responsible for putting the lids on alternating containers. It was possible for one of them to take over putting lids on every pint if necessary, but they weren't allowed to do it for long because the boss didn't want to risk backing up the entire line. When Simeon's employment had first begun, there was talk about lowering the conveyor belt and allowing Cortez to sit down as well. In the meantime, a wooden platform had been provided where Simeon could apply the brakes to his wheels and be within reach of the belt. It had been over a year since the stopgap measure was instituted.

The pair began getting ready for the morning's production. Cortez grabbed two boxes of orange lids and placed one on each side of the conveyor belt. Then, they both put on hairnets and aprons before Simeon washed his hands and put on gloves. Once Simeon was ready, Cortez got him in position on top of the wooden platform before taking care of his own hands. The pair was ready to go when the boss came to make sure they were in position. Soon after, the conveyor belt started moving. Within minutes, the first pints came down the line.

Simeon and Cortez fell silent as they began putting lid after lid onto the pints of orange sorbet after they had been sealed. It was easy, mindless work. Cortez's skill set was limited, and he was grateful for the job.

"Are you interested in making some extra money?" Simeon asked Cortez with a mischievous glint in his eye once they got into a rhythm.

Cortez knew the struggles his mother had to go through to pay for their home, food, and lives. Every dollar counted, and he gave her every paycheck without questioning where the money went. Still, he was skeptical of his friend's random question because, in his experience, making money was never easy.

"What do you mean?"

"I mean I've got a way for us to get some extra cash in our pockets." Simeon looked around even though the two of them were alone. "I know someone who wants to buy some of those little blue pills you take."

Cortez froze and missed placing lids on two pints that were his responsibility. Simeon covered for him but yelled at him to snap out of it before he became overwhelmed and couldn't cover for his friend.

"It's against the law," Cortez said after they got back into a shared rhythm.

"So? Nobody will find out. It's easy money."

"But I need them."

"So do these guys! They're college students and have big exams coming up. They're stressing out. You can help them. Just say you lost your bottle. New medicine and money in your pocket."

Cortez stayed silent while alternating lid placement with Simeon. After a while, Simeon let out a sigh loud enough to be heard over the low hum of the conveyor belt.

"I'm just trying to help you out, OK?" Simeon said. "We don't have to talk about it."

THEY DIDN'T SAY another word to each other until lunch. Their half hour began when the belt stopped. Cortez took Simeon down from his wooden platform and rolled him to his locker. Simeon took his hairnet, apron, and gloves off during the short trip and put them in his locker. While Simeon grabbed his lunch, Cortez took off his protective clothing and swapped it with his backpack. He then took hold of the handles on Simeon's wheelchair and wheeled him towards the entrance.

"I thought you'd want to eat lunch alone today," Simeon said, upset at being the victim of the silent treatment even though he had created the conditions for the retaliation himself.

"We eat lunch together every day," Cortez said without further justification.

Cortez rolled Simeon off the front step and continued down the street to where two picnic tables were set up beneath a cluster of trees a block away from the factory. The other employees at the factory all went out to eat, or ate their lunch inside the building, so on days it wasn't raining the two friends responsible for lidding pints came to this spot and ate lunch alone. Within minutes, Cortez had spread out his sandwich, small plastic bag of chips, and banana on top of the brown paper bag they'd come in. Simeon drank a can of Coke with a straw and downed three-hours-old taquitos.

By the time Simeon finished, Cortez had polished off his sandwich and chips and was about to work on his banana. He didn't notice Simeon roll backwards so he could get a better look at the street.

"Hey! Over here!" Simeon yelled.

Cortez turned and saw Simeon waving to a group of men down the street. He ate his banana as fast as he could and found himself with a mouthful of fruit when they arrived at the lunch spot.

"This is the guy," Simeon told the three newcomers while pointing at Cortez. They were about the same age as Cortez, hesitant to engage, and carried an air about them that they were on the lookout for what other people said was fashionable instead of creating fashion themselves.

Cortez looked at the group and nodded. He wasn't sure what Simeon was talking about. Everyone looked at Cortez, waiting for him to finish chewing and say something. The last bits of banana went down, and he searched their faces for a sign of what came next.

Simeon took charge. "Show them the pills."

A slap in the face wouldn't have been as surprising as Simeon's command. Cortez didn't move.

"Give us a moment," Simeon said to his three guests. He used his head to gesture for them to walk away. When they were far enough away, he turned to Cortez and unleashed his wrath.

"Look, we both know you need money. Stop being weird about this and get it over with. You can get more pills from the doctor."

"I need those."

"Exactly why the doc will give them to you! These guys are struggling in school. They told me they need to graduate before they can go on their mission trip. You don't want to be the reason they can't spread the word of God, do you?"

Cortez took a good look at the three visitors. They didn't look like any Christians he knew, and something told him they were more interested in curing hangovers on Sunday mornings than going to church. He dashed these thoughts right after they crept into his head, reminding himself judgment was reserved for the Almighty.

"No, I don't," Cortez acquiesced.

"Get them out," Simeon commanded, pointing at Cortez's backpack. Then, he turned to the buyers. "Guys, come on over here." When they got close, he told them the price was ten dollars a pill.

One of the buyers pulled out five twenty-dollar bills and held them out, unsure whether to give the cash to Simeon or Cortez. Simeon reached out his hand and was handed the money.

"Give them ten pills, Cort," Simeon said.

Cortez counted out the pills and handed them to the closest of the three. He looked down into the bottle, shook it, and grew anxious at how much his stockpile had dwindled. After shaking one pill into his palm, he downed it without water, closed the bottle, and closed his eyes.

Police sirens pierced the air. The buyers looked at Simeon, terrified. Simeon called the three buyers rats. One of the alleged college students turned to his companions, told them to run, and all three of them fled.

Inspired by the quick exit of the purchasers, Cortez grabbed his backpack, dropped the bottle into the open center portion, and ran away without zipping it shut, traveling in the direction of the factory. A pang of guilt struck him at having left his trash on the picnic table. It didn't cross his mind that Simeon was a sitting duck until he looked back at their lunch spot from behind the corner of an adjacent building, after taking a puff of his inhaler.

Neither of the two officers bothered giving chase to anyone who fled. Cortez watched as they sauntered up to and engaged with Simeon. The three of them talked for a few minutes before the officers got back into their car and left. Cortez went back to his friend when he was sure the police had gone.

"You left me," Simeon said. He didn't try hiding the anger and disappointment in his voice.

"I wasn't thinking," Cortez replied. "What did they say?"

"They said I should get better friends." Simeon held out four of the twenty-dollar bills. "These are yours," he said.

Cortez accepted the cash. "I thought there were five," Cortez said after counting his cut.

"I get twenty for arranging the deal," Simeon said. "Let's go back to work."

Cortez stuffed the trash from his lunch into his backpack before rolling Simeon back to the factory, where they spent a wordless afternoon lidding pint after pint of orange sorbet.

CHAPTER FIVE

The first chapter of the Custody of the Yucatán was days away. The leaders from every satellite monastery in the Yucatán were on their way to Merida, where they would listen together for God's guidance about the roles each man would play in the Church's leadership. The new recruits at the Merida monastery waited for the arrival of their Franciscan brothers from the Campeche monastery in particular, among them Friar Luis de Villalpondo, because of the hushed tones veteran friars used when talking about the man.

Friar Diego de Landa looked forward to Friar Luis's arrival more than most. He had heard about the elder friar's mastery of the Mayan language and success in earning the natives' trust since they'd first set sail from Spain, and during his time in the Yucatán the reverent whispers grew so fervent that Friar Diego became convinced the man was a living saint. Friar Diego had managed a tenuous grasp on the language in his three months of living in the New World and he was eager to pick Friar Luis's brain for the next step in his progression, having mastered the listed terms and displayed his skill during the mass conversion in the jungle.

After preventing the human sacrifice, Friar Diego had gone back to the Izamal monastery to recuperate. He then went back out into the wilderness, searching for Ahkinmai, and when he found the feathered man he was again placed in front of a kneeling crowd. Before the Maya disappeared into the jungle, he communicated that they were welcome at the Izamal monastery. He went back wondering if any would show up. The Maya began trickling in right before Friar Diego went back to Merida, and reports from the satellite monastery detailed the dozens of natives who had arrived and the success the friars had had in preaching the word of the Lord. There was still no word of the feathered man's making the trip to the monastery, but Friar Diego held out hope, as did the men at Izamal.

Friar Diego hoped his successful preaching would catch the attention of Friar Luis and gain him a private audience. More friars arrived in Merida each day, none of them from Campeche, joining them in prayer as if they had been there all along, with little attention given to their time away from the central location of Merida other than a short embrace and blessing.

The Campeche friars arrived during morning prayers the day before the scheduled conference. The noise on the packed-earth street leading into the town—integral to both the Franciscans and the colonists—died away, leaving a vortex of noiselessness that urged every praying man to abandon his station and investigate. To the credit of every man of God engaged in prayers at the time, none of them moved, each man finishing their communication with the Lord before leaving the sanctuary. Friar Lorenzo de Bienvenida greeted the arriving friars, asking them about the journey.

"Age has made me slow, but other than the ache in my knees

I have nothing to complain about," Friar Luis said, speaking for all. He wasn't the oldest Franciscan in the Yucatán, but years of hard living had aged him beyond his years. His back was bent, forcing his head forward in perpetual subservience, and the hair on the sides of his head was stark white. The tanned skin between his jaw and cheekbones was as tight as a drum until he spoke, when crinkles appeared throughout the space. His dark eyes were the sole part of him untouched by age, still possessing the sparkle of youth fascinated by the world around him.

Friar Diego noticed the man's first words didn't include a mention of God.

Friar Lorenzo smiled. "Age takes its toll on all of us," he said.

"Me more than you," Friar Luis responded, his eyes catching the sun.

The two old friends embraced before Friar Lorenzo asked if the men would join them in prayer.

"Of course," Friar Luis said.

For the second time that morning, Friar Diego found himself participating in morning prayers.

Introductions came after the men lifted their bowed heads and walked back outside. Friar Lorenzo knew all the men who came from Campeche, but he said their names for the benefit of the new recruits. Then, he went around and told the men from Campeche about the men brought by Friar Nicolás de Albalate, each man nodding his head as his name was spoken. Friar Diego was the last name said.

"So this is the man responsible for the conversion at Izamal," Friar Luis said with curiosity. He inspected the young Franciscan, taking measure of the sharp nose, weak chin, and sorrowful eyes.

Friar Diego closed his eyes and nodded his head once more.

"Were you scared?" one of the men from Campeche asked. He had somehow maintained his heavyset frame, and his face was puffy from never submitting to the thirst most in the Yucatán had learned to accept. Water was a scarce resource outside close proximity to the *cenotes*, and his supple skin was evidence he spent all his time close to and within the monastery.

"Scared? I knew God was on my side," Friar Diego replied.

"I was scared when I first arrived in the Yucatán," Friar Luis said. "Weren't you?" he added, addressing Friar Lorenzo.

"Even with God's grace guiding me," Friar Lorenzo responded.

Friar Diego didn't notice the men modeling humility. "I was too upset with the thought of human sacrifice. Nobody told me the natives perform such acts," he said, looking at Friar Nicolás.

"There's a lot we don't know about the native population," Friar Luis said before a startled Friar Nicolás could respond.

"You can hold conversations with them, correct?" Friar Diego said.

"After many years of practice," said Friar Luis.

"With your permission, I'd like to speak with you about learning more of the language."

Friar Lorenzo put a hand on Friar Diego's shoulder. "Friar Diego's picked up the language remarkably fast. I'd dare say he'll be as good as you one day," he said with pride.

"God willing," Friar Diego and Friar Luis said at the same time. Friar Luis smiled at the young man. The expression was met with a flexing jaw when Friar Diego realized his request for a personal audience had been ignored.

"Why don't we get you situated," Friar Lorenzo said, breaking the silence. He dismissed the new recruits with a nod and walked away with the Campeche men.

Friar Diego began the typical tasks of a day at the Merida monastery, this time later than usual because of the double dose of prayer. He transplanted wine from the barrel into a chalice and a larger carafe, covering the chalice with a thin white cloth before carrying both containers from storage into the sanctuary and placing them atop the altar for the evening mass. The numerous lamps within the living quarters, school, infirmary, and sanctuary all needed topped off with oil after their use the night before. These tasks completed, he went to the man responsible for feeding the Franciscans, Friar Alonso, a greasy man with ears big enough to hear a whisper across the room, and asked what needed to be done.

"You're late," Friar Alonso said. Then, softening, he grumbled, both to himself and to Friar Diego, "The arrival of the Campeche group threw everything off. But they'll still want their meals at the same time!" He then told Friar Diego to fetch enough water to fill two enormous clay pots. The cooking equipment, clay pots and wooden utensils, surrounded a stone oven an arm's length in diameter with a short space at floor height thin enough for feeding wood without exposing the flames to the elements and a circular, sunken space where the cookware sat above the heat.

The new recruits, all younger and stronger than those they reinforced in the Yucatán, took turns retrieving water. Keeping enough water on hand was a laborious process, requiring numerous trips throughout the day. When Friar Diego first arrived in Merida, he'd tried to fill the large clay pots at the *cenote* and bring them back one at a time, but their immense size made them too unwieldy for easy transport, so he learned to fill them the way Friar Alonso suggested he do the first time: multiple trips with smaller buckets.

When each of the clay pots was filled three-quarters of the way up—what Friar Alonso meant when he said to fill them up —Friar Diego cleared the sweat from his forehead with the fabric of his habit. The rough fabric scratched his face if he wiped, so he blotted instead.

"You'll be sweating more in a bit," Friar Alonso said with a chuckle. He then dumped massive quantities of cut vegetables and pork into the water. "Provided by the colonists," Friar Alonso said when he saw Friar Diego staring at the meat.

When Friar Diego was dismissed, all of Merida, except for himself and Friar Alonso, was escaping the midday heat by relaxing in the shade. Friar Diego, drenched in sweat, took off his habit and hung it on a peg next to his hammock before lying down and drifting off for an afternoon nap. He woke up at the exact same time as the rest of the snoozing friars—though he got less rest than any of them—and put his habit back on, with stares from the others as to why he was naked while the sun was still up.

Friar Alonso led everyone in prayer before they ate. In addition to the Franciscans, the Lord of Mani was also present, as was the colonist who'd donated the meat and his family. They were all seated at a long table, the same table Friar Alonso had used to prepare the meal, and when Friar Diego bowed his head he saw still-moist bloodstains on the wood before he closed his eyes. Friar Alonso thanked the Lord for their bountiful feast, thanked the colonist for donating the meat, then invited the rest of the friars to join him in the Lord's prayer.

Everyone joined hands.

"Our father, who art in heaven . . ."

Friar Alonso urged them all to eat after the final "amen." Everyone was provided a bowl with their portion and a chunk of bread, and it was understood the rest of the stew would go to the sick in the infirmary and the children who were learning Spanish customs at the same time they were learning about God but were too far from home to go back and eat.

Friar Luis sat three seats down from Friar Diego, on the opposite side of the table. Friar Diego didn't want to force another interaction, still smarting from the ignoring of his earlier request to discuss his further education in the Mayan language. He ignored the older man, and everyone else, staying silent while those around him filled the time discussing the various trivialities about days spent in the company of the same group of people, doing the same things.

Friar Diego was the first man done with his meal, since he didn't utter a word while eating.

"You seem to have liked it," Friar Luis said to Friar Diego. His words commanded everyone's attention, though some continued talking to people who were no longer listening.

Friar Diego looked at the wizened old man. "The day's work inspired my appetite," he said, nodding.

Friar Luis looked down at his own bowl. "I don't eat as much as I did when I was younger," he lamented. "Especially meat; it doesn't agree with my stomach."

Friar Alonso stood with his mouth full and rushed to Friar Luis's side, asking what he could provide. "Perhaps more bread?"

Friar Luis waved the chef away. "No, no, I've had quite enough. Sit back down, enjoy your meal." He looked at Friar Diego. "Would you help me finish my portion? I don't want it to go to waste."

"It won't go to waste," Friar Diego said. "One of the boys will eat it."

Friar Lorenzo, in arm's reach of both men, grabbed the bowl and set it down in front of Friar Diego. "But he wants you to have it," he said, in a way that Friar Diego knew the arrangement was beyond questioning.

Friar Diego uttered his thanks then took a bite.

"If it's all right with you, I'd like to discuss the conversion of the natives outside Izamal after this evening's mass," Friar Luis said.

The eyes of every Franciscan at the table widened, the whites of their eyes like nocturnal creatures peering out from the jungle.

"It's all right with me," Friar Diego said. He tried to pull the bowl of soup given to him by Friar Luis closer to him and continue eating like nothing had changed, but the bowl had grown too heavy to move and didn't budge. He resigned himself to leaving it where it sat, not wanting his dining mates to doubt his strength.

EVENING MASS STARTED SOON after the conclusion of their meal. Colonists trying to save their souls sat shoulder to shoulder with the Franciscans listening to Friar Luis, who was taking over for Friar Lorenzo. In the back, both standing and seated, were numerous converted Maya from the *encomiendas*. Some were dressed in breeches and a tunic, like the Lord of Mani, and some were dressed similar to the ones Friar Diego had seen outside Izamal, the men covered front and back by cloth hanging from the waist, the women wearing the same and in addition covering their breasts. Scarred backs, courtesy of the *encomenderos'* whips, were common, and one young man's scabs still oozed clear liquid from recent lashings.

Friar Diego was mistaken when he thought Friar Luis would be available right after mass. The old man took the chance to talk to the natives in attendance, ignoring the colonists, greeting the elder Maya like old friends and the younger ones with a delight unseen by Diego among any Franciscan on either side of the ocean. Friar Luis, seeing Friar Diego watching him, waved the younger man over with his hand, gesturing for him to stand by his side. Friar Diego was fascinated by the ease with which Friar Luis spoke the native tongue. He recognized a smattering of the words Friar Luis had provided on the written sheet, and a few others he had picked up during his time since landing in the New World, but watching Friar Luis stringing them together, with little use of the hands, was like watching a master musician play their instrument: effortless from years of practice. Friar Luis was even able to participate in their humor, making them laugh with a quick retort, something Friar Diego hadn't seen anyone do since he first arrived.

When the natives left, Friar Luis asked Friar Diego to join him on a walk. They went towards the part of town frequented by the colonists, walking through the rudimentary marketplace where, hours before, carts sold everything from vegetables and meat to fabrics and tools. The friars strode through the discarded remains of the day, Friar Luis with his hands behind his back, while Friar Diego told the story, in exacting detail, of the jungle conversion outside Izamal. Friar Luis took particular interest whenever the feathered man, Ahkinmai, was mentioned.

"He's a Mayan priest," Friar Luis said when Friar Diego finished his tale.

"I gathered."

"They are learned men. There are rumors they can read and write."

"In their language?" Friar Diego said, astounded.

Friar Luis nodded. "None of their books have been shown to me, but I have reason to believe in their existence. It took me a while to understand the word, but they refer to their 'records' as if everything has been written down."

Friar Diego looked at the sky, lost in thought.

"The conference tomorrow. Have you given any thought to where you want to be placed?" Friar Luis asked.

"No. I'm prepared for wherever God calls me to serve."

"None at all? Not even Izamal?"

"Why Izamal?"

"The natives are arriving there because of you. I thought you might want to be there to see to their conversion yourself."

"Izamal needs an experienced leader. I'm too new."

Friar Luis stopped. Turning his head, he looked at Friar Diego. "And what makes you think you'd be there as a leader?" he said.

A sheepish Friar Diego stumbled on his words. "I misspoke," he managed.

Friar Luis started walking once more. "Let me guess: you think that, because of your early success with the natives, you deserve a leadership role tomorrow during the conference."

"I didn't say that," Friar Diego replied.

"You don't have to. I am. There's no denying the quality of your work, or the importance of getting Izamal traction among the natives. Your actions laid a solid foundation for the monastery's success."

Friar Diego thanked the elder.

"But you're too young to be a leader. There are many who have been here longer, who know the difficulties of dealing with the colonists. You'll learn that dealing with the natives is just one part of our job in the Yucatán. We also need to protect them from the other Spaniards here who want to turn them into slaves and servants."

Friar Diego knew about the mistreatment of the natives at Spanish hands but didn't consider their situation his problem. Still, the number of conversions he alone had accounted for couldn't be ignored, and he couldn't abandon hope for a leadership position within the Church.

The topic of conversation turned more lighthearted on the walk back to the Merida monastery. "You've been able to pick up the language quickly," Friar Luis said.

Friar Diego nodded his agreement, still lost in thoughts of the potential results of the next day's conference.

"Well, we need to work together to get you to where I am now. I could use some help teaching the others."

Friar Diego's feet left the ground at the implication that he was going to be responsible, alongside Friar Luis, for teaching the rest of the Franciscans the Mayan language. He managed to bring himself back to earth before the elder friar noticed his levitation. They made plans to discuss his further progression in the future, with Friar Luis promising to provide Friar Diego with a copy of the *arte* of the Mayan language—an overview of the native tongue he himself had made—before retiring for the night.

An exhausted Friar Diego fell asleep as soon as he lay down. His dreams that night transported him forward several decades, and he saw himself at his desk in a castle in Spain, writing out all he'd learned about the Mayan language, informing the rest of his countrymen about the New World's culture.

AT THE FIRST chapter of the Custody of the Yucatán, held in late September 1549, Friar Diego was passed over for every leadership position within the Franciscan Order. Friar Luis de Villalpondo was elected *Custos,* leader of all Yucatán monasteries. Friar Lorenzo de Bienvenida was named Guardian of the Izamal monastery, and Friar Juan de la Puerta, who'd come from the Campeche monastery with Friar Luis, was chosen to go back to Spain and recruit more friars, the same position Friar Nicolás held when he came back with Friar Diego de Landa in tow.

Friar Diego was assigned to the Izamal monastery, with instructions to continue working on gaining the trust of the natives under Ahkinmai. Friar Francisco Navarro, his friend during the voyage, was stationed in Campeche, and it would be years before they saw each other again.

Friar Luis stood in front of the Franciscans as *Custos* for the first time. The decision had always been between him and Friar Lorenzo, but the whispered undercurrents suggested that Friar Lorenzo had longer to live, and would have his chance to lead in the future. Friar Luis informed the men of a similar meeting being held among the colonists.

"We don't know what *Adelantado* Francisco wanted to talk about, but we can be sure it's going to put the natives in harm's way," Friar Luis said. "His goal is to wring every cent from these people. God willing, we can put a stop to his cruelty." The Franciscans all crossed themselves. "Let's keep our eyes and ears to the ground; their footsteps can be heard from miles away."

CHAPTER SIX

"CORTEZ! WAKE UP!" his mother yelled from the kitchen. She had no way of knowing he had been awake for almost an hour, listening to her make breakfast without any regard for how much noise she was making. Their Sunday breakfast was the one time each week when he ate a meal before leaving the house. Its composition never changed. Two fried eggs, two sausage links, and two tortillas would be waiting on his plate when he came out and began his day. In the event he was still hungry after this portion, he could fill his belly with more tortillas. They were store-bought, came in a bag, and didn't require his mother spending more time cooking than she already had.

"Cortez!" she yelled again.

"I'm up," Cortez grumbled. He didn't have to yell; their apartment was so small they could hear each other at a conversational speaking volume. His mother yelled for the benefit of the neighbors, as if demonstrating the control over her dominion that her son had never threatened. The neighbor women all yelled on different schedules. The Sunday morning slot belonged to his household, Monday through Friday at six Mrs.

Wyatt yelled to her brood to come eat dinner, and Ms. Roberts down the hall screamed around midnight on Friday and Saturday nights whenever she hosted male company. If there was ever a time that every woman happened to yell at the same time, the resulting cracks in the walls could bring their building crashing down.

The white short-sleeved dress shirt he wore each week to church hung in his closet, ironed to sharpen the creases. His blue slacks, also sharpened, lay folded over the bottom portion of the same hanger. The creases his mother had made in the fabric were for the benefit of everyone else who attended their church. According to her belief, the sharper the crease, the more one believed in God, and she did all she could to convince others that her household's level of devotion was on par with the Pope. Cortez put on his clothes, careful to preserve the remnants of the Holy Spirit in the cultivated lines in the fabric. He selected one of his two pairs of blue dress socks and wore them beneath brown loafers that clung to existence from a time before he was born.

Cortez went into the bathroom without greeting his mother, even though he could sense her watching him as he crossed the hallway. After relieving himself of the water stored up overnight and brushing his teeth while paying full attention to keeping his clothes pristine, he combed his hair to the side in the same direction he had every morning since he hit puberty. Combing his hair was the ritual that had the greatest impact on his ability to engage with other people; the act of arranging his hair was the finishing touch on a mask that hid his sinner's nature. Greeting his mother had to wait until he felt ready, but once he left the bathroom, he walked right up to her and planted a kiss on her cheek while she cooked eggs.

"Good morning," he said. The standard greeting.

"Good morning, my son. Are you hungry?" Her standard

reply. She wore a light pink full-length dress and wore a white head covering over her braided hair.

Cortez nodded, and his mother pointed with her spatula to the plate that held the typical Sunday morning meal, just as expected. He grabbed a fork, took the plate, and set it down on the coffee table before taking a seat on the couch. Grease issued from the sausage when he stabbed it, and he leaned over his plate and bit off the end of a link so no grease would fall onto his clothes.

"Wait!" his mother scolded. He set his fork down and sat with his hands folded in his lap.

She finished making her own plate then took it with her before sitting in the reclining chair where she spent every night. Early in the evenings, she watched game shows and the news. As the night progressed, she switched to dramas, the channel and show depending on the night of the week. The tray where she ate her meals was never folded up and put away; instead, she moved it to the side when she wanted to lie back, as sleep crept up on her. With a plate in her left hand, she grabbed the folding tray with her right, setting both down in front of her station before turning her attention back to her son.

Cortez picked up his fork, eager to take another bite of sausage. His pork dreams were dashed when his mother reminded him, in tones harsh enough to chastise sailors, that they needed to pray before they ate, and prayers were more important on Sunday than on any other day of the week. Cortez set the fork down, bowed his head, and folded his hands once more.

"Father, we thank you for this food we are about to eat. May the blessings you have given us extend to everyone we know, and everyone we meet, as we go into the city in your service. Please keep a watchful eye on Cortez as he navigates becoming a man and all the trials and temptations that come along with it.

Teach him that there are people in this world who want to take advantage of his sweet soul, and protect him whenever your path for him puts him in the company of these kind. In your name we pray. Amen."

As the prayer drew to a conclusion, Cortez was sure that his mother knew about him selling pills at lunch on Friday. Did she know that Simeon had forced him? Had Simeon told the police about him, and had they contacted her? As the possibilities of his discovery swirled through his guilty mind, he missed saying "Amen" in time with his mother, and he said it well after she was done speaking.

She began her meal by rearranging the food on her plate using her fork, taking measure of the most appetizing bite, similar to the way birds peck at a crust of bread a few times before flying off with the entire piece in their mouth. Once she determined the moment's perfect bite, she placed it into her mouth and chewed a set number of times, a number only she knew and that varied depending on the food.

Cortez dove into his food with a hunger strengthened by fear. By focusing on his meal, he hoped to forget his mother's prescient prayer. He was done with breakfast well before his mother, and he had to wait for her to finish chewing every last bird bite before she informed him it was time they left for church.

THE CHURCH WAS a fifteen-minute walk from their apartment. They walked together, with personal Bibles beneath their arms, at a slower pace than Cortez would have walked alone. His mother wasn't too old to walk fast; she was one of those people who took great care when they walked to make sure anyone looking wouldn't think she was in a hurry. Their congregation met in the auditorium of a public middle school. The prevailing sentiment about their choice of space was that God could be worshipped anywhere, and they could be more effective in their evangelism if they weren't viewed as having an ornate, imposing structure looking down on nonbelievers. In reality, their financials had never allowed them to consider meeting anywhere but the large spaces of public buildings, a fact the church elders took great care to spin in a way that made their situation favorable.

After church, the majority of the afternoon would be spent out on the streets, trying to spread the word of God to anyone who would listen. Each week's service spent a large portion of the time extolling the virtues of converting sinners, and the members of the church each accepted their holy mission to find the most converts. Over the years, spreading God's word had become an unspoken competition among the parishioners. Every one of them belonged to a tree that traced its roots back to the member who was responsible for the chain of conversions. A hierarchy had formed; Cortez and his mother occupied its bottom rungs.

Cortez had yet to convince a single person to join him on Sundays. He'd had hopes for Simeon when they first met, but after weeks of excuses Cortez had dropped the subject and was still waiting for the right time to bring it up once more. His mother was on the same step of the church's unspoken ladder as him—the lone soul she had brought into the church for saving was Cortez.

The church service faded to the background as Cortez lost himself in daydreams of finding a rich seam of precious souls he could mine. His body carried him through the familiar motions of the service: the hymns, the communion, the congregation's vocalized responses to the priest's prayers. After the final "Amen" was said, he shook himself out of his stupor and prepared to stand next to his mother while she made the rounds of her weekly small talk. The women and men stood apart;

Cortez never joined the other men. The congregation's children split into two groups: the younger children played together in the hallway, and the teenagers sat in the empty, still-warm chairs. Cortez was the only child who never left his parent's side.

The reunions lasted half an hour and ended when the priest, his robe removed and now sporting a light blue shirt and navy pants, announced the arrival of lunch. After the sandwiches were wolfed down, the priest asked his flock if they were ready to go fishing, the preferred metaphor for finding new church members. A more enthusiastic group might have responded with a loud collective "Yes!," but the members of Cortez's church murmured their agreement. He didn't repeat the question, wanting to avoid another lackluster response and knowing his inability to generate more excitement himself.

"Now remember, you have all the tools you need in your hand," the priest said, holding up the Bible. "We want to spread the Lord's message and find more people to join us in worship. Good luck, everyone, and God bless!"

With that blessing, the members of the congregation were released. A wave of excitement washed over Cortez when he walked outside, a combination of no longer being trapped indoors, the removal of the social yoke he'd never quite figured out how to carry, and the promise of winning the respect of the rest of the group through his evangelism. Although he had yet to convince anyone to join him on Sundays, each week he was convinced this would be the one when his luck would change. His mother had always told him he was destined for greatness and that once his father heard about what a fine young man Cortez had become, he'd rejoin their little family. Evangelism was his chance to fulfill his destiny and make his parents proud. It was also when his mother allowed him to leave her side, and he was determined to show his worth by completing his holy task alone.

It was no secret that some of the members of the congregation went home instead of looking for souls to save. These people stayed for the free lunch after worship but were never seen in the streets. Cortez saw their absence as an opportunity: he had less competition for glory. Together with his mother, he walked for blocks in the opposite direction of their home, into new parts of the decaying city. As they passed beneath aboveground railway tracks, Cortez announced he was turning left into a part of the city he had flagged as a potential fishing spot the week before.

"Be careful, and good luck," his mother said. "I'm going to a restaurant this way to see if I can talk to people leaving lunch." She pointed in the direction they were already walking.

"See you soon," Cortez said. He took a white pill for courage.

WHERE OTHER PEOPLE saw spoilage in the abandoned storefronts on the road that ran alongside the tracks, Cortez saw opportunity. He got the feeling he was walking the right path, as if destiny herself had made the decision for him long ago and he had discovered her plan for him. Every nook had the remnants of a homeless person's presence from the night before, and every corner had groups milling about without purpose—none of them were the ones he was looking for. Block after block passed by while he walked, searching for destiny's next sign.

He passed a woman wearing a skirt and halter top. Her clothes looked like they had been worn for days, stretched out and looser-fitting than designed, and parts of her unkempt hair stuck out at odd angles. "Are you lonely, honey?" she called out to him.

Cortez would have ignored her if he wasn't infused with the Holy Spirit. Instead, he asked if she had friends.

"I do, they're right over there." She pointed across the street, to another street that ran to the left.

"I want to talk to them," Cortez said. An excitement built in his stomach, a certainty that he was on the right track.

"We'll do more than talking," the woman said, trying her best to force her dull eyes to twinkle. "Let's go."

Cortez followed her as she led the way, his Bible tucked under his arm. He didn't notice the confused looks of people that drove past with their windows rolled up. The woman was aged beyond her years. She wasn't much older than him, but her body spent more time healing the bruises and sores on her arms and legs than fighting back the wrinkles on her face. She walked tall, having made peace with her position in life. They found the woman's four friends standing in an alley.

"What do you have in mind?" the messy-haired woman asked. She said it loud enough for her friends to hear.

When their attention turned to him, Cortez knew the time had come to face the most difficult part of his mission. Whatever uncertainty he had harbored about talking to the group was suppressed by the certainty that he was a messenger from God, with help from his pill. "I'm here today to speak with you about our Lord and Savior Jesus Christ." These were the exact words the church had drilled into his head over the years about how best to begin the conversion.

In unison, the women rolled their eyes and shook their heads, each one a marionette controlled by the same set of puppet master's strings.

"Why'd you bring him over here," the oldest-looking woman in the group said.

Cortez ignored their reaction. He opened his Bible using the bookmark he had inserted for this moment. He began to read, "It is not the healthy who need a doctor, but the sick. I have not come to call the righteous, but the sinners." He closed the book, keeping his thumb inserted to the spot in case the women wanted to hear more. He looked at them with an expectant smile on his face.

The smile disappeared when he saw the anger in their eyes. "So you're calling us sinners? Like we don't know that already?" the woman who had brought him said. She pushed him back in the direction of the street. "Do you think you're better than us? What the hell is the matter with you?" she demanded to know.

A car door opened across the street and a large man got out. He stood tall, his gold rings and necklace sparkling in the sunlight. "Hey!" he yelled out. "Quit bothering the girls!"

Cortez looked at him, confused. Didn't these people realize he was there to save them? "I'm not bothering them," he said.

The man walked right up to Cortez and grabbed him by his shirt's collar, wrinkling it and driving out the Holy Spirit contained within. "Get out of here," he snarled. Crumbs littered the collar of his black shirt.

Memories of Daniel in the lions' den gave Cortez strength. "Our church meets at ten on Sunday mornings. Would you like the address?"

"No, I don't want the damned address!" the imposing man said. "What part of get out of here do you not understand?"

Cortez was convinced he had found the big fish he had been searching for. If he could convince this man to join him in worship, the others might follow. He was about to try again when he heard his mother yell out from the direction he had come.

"Cortez! It's time to go home!" she said.

Everyone turned to watch the woman fly down the street, carried by angels. Her white head covering trailed in the breeze as she approached, and it settled on her back when she stopped.

"Good afternoon, everyone," she said, with a polite nod to the bejeweled man. "Thank you for finding my son." She grabbed Cortez's arm and pried him loose from the man's iron grip. "Let's go," she said.

"But these people need God," Cortez pleaded.

The women all laughed. The man, still angry, didn't find it funny.

"And you'll meet God soon enough if we don't go home," his mother said, her tone firm. Cortez knew not to push back when she spoke this way.

"God bless," his mother said as a farewell.

The women repeated the phrase, sneering, as they waved goodbye.

"What are you doing here? I was going to get them to come to church next week," Cortez said to his mother as they started the trip home.

"I followed you, to make sure something like this didn't happen." She had calmed down now that her son was no longer in danger, though her shoulders still rose with each of her deep breaths.

They walked in silence for a long time before Cortez spoke again. "They need our help. They need *God's* help."

Cortez's mother stopped, grabbed Cortez's shoulders, and looked into his eyes. "The Church doesn't want those kinds of people."

CHAPTER SEVEN

THE NEVER-ENDING work at the fledgling Izamal monastery took what little meat Friar Diego de Landa had from his bones, leaving him thin as a whip and with skin twice as tough. Working for Friar Alonso in Merida had provided the young friar a taste of the type of work necessary for the successful operation of a monastery; he soon missed the Franciscan chef's jovial urgings after experiencing Friar Lorenzo de Bienvenida's biting orders. The elder Franciscan was a taskmaster of the highest order—he could put any Spanish matriarch to shame with the ruthless organization he maintained over his domain.

Friar Lorenzo took Friar Diego aside when they first arrived in Izamal, after their first prayers with the three friars already stationed at the remote monastery. He informed the new recruit that preaching to the natives, and thereby converting them, was one small part of their role in the New World. The majority of their duty, the elder friar explained, rested in creating a sustainable way of life for the natives while protecting them from the colonists: a taste of the Spanish technology and way of life without the bitterness from too large a swallow.

"In this way," Friar Lorenzo explained, "we can keep gaining their trust by improving their living conditions."

The *encomenderos* and the Franciscans were in a perpetual battle for the fate of the natives. Each *encomienda* was a plot of land given by the Spanish secular authorities, and within that plot of land the Spaniards were given free access to any Maya within in exchange for protecting the borders in Spain's name. The Franciscans benefited from the *encomienda*'s protection as well, since they didn't have any methods of protection available to them, but believed the colonists went too far in exercising their absolute authority. According to them, the natives could provide labor and pay tribute in exchange for protection, but the ultimate fate of the men—their souls—belonged to God. Their job was to show the Maya the path to heaven. *Encomendero* lips curled in disdain at the thought of any threat to their agricultural endeavors, both from Franciscans and from potential native revolt. The Franciscans received faraway protection from the Spanish crown, the Old-World government recognizing the power of the Pope. The natives had no such overarching protection, and it fell to the Franciscans to take the native charges under their wing.

The first step in the broader Franciscan plan was the establishment of monasteries farther into the interior of the Yucatán Peninsula. With this greater reach, they could be in better contact with the Maya that needed their protection from the ever-advancing *encomiendas*. Each monastery included a school and an infirmary along with a designated place for worship.

Friar Diego's first assignment was teaching the sons of local chieftains. The young men, varying in age from five to thirteen, arrived at the monastery soon after dawn, coming from nearby lodgings provided by their fathers and accompanied by retainers from among their people. They waited for the friar each morning while he finished his morning prayers. Their customary greeting, taught on the first day through demonstration with Friar Lorenzo, was a slight bow with hands folded in front of their chest. Existing students demonstrated the process for new children, and the children all stood in a line outside the sanctuary as Friar Diego greeted each one in turn. The children were then led to the school, an open space with a thatched roof supported by stout wooden pillars in each corner protecting the class from the sun.

The first lessons made full use of the smattering of words Friar Luis de Villalpondo had given to Friar Diego. Friar Diego's initial teaching consisted of training the native youth on correct behavior while in the monastery—bowing the head, kneeling, and staying silent during prayers. The students first learned to hold their previous way of life, and the way of life of their families, in contempt during this training. Following a baseline level of manners, the friar then taught the Catechism of the Catholic Church, forcing the memorization of the various prayers. Each monastery's attached school followed the same first instruction, then future instruction was left to the teachers and depended on the attendance, capability, and reception of the students. The boys all made quick progress because they never missed a class, a fact that amazed Friar Lorenzo because in all his years in the Yucatán he had never heard of such consistency. Friar Diego didn't mention the whispers he'd heard among the students that led him to suspect Ahkinmai's involvement in the continued support of their studies, and he allowed the elder friar to believe it was in fact his own quality instruction. The number of students began swelling after the initial cohort's success, and Friar Diego's class approached one hundred students by the end of the following year.

Friar Diego learned as much from his students as they did from him. He was insistent on learning their language, not wanting his students to learn Spanish so their thoughts wouldn't be poisoned by the *encomenderos* with bitterness against the missionaries. Friar Luis's handwritten *arte* arrived at the tail end of 1549, two months after Friar Diego first began teaching in Izamal. The younger friar discovered he had a better grasp of the language's nuance than his older counterpart, though the tome contained a much wider array of vocabulary. The *arte* was similar to a dictionary but included phrases and bits of theory about the Mayan language. Friar Diego studied the *arte* alone at night, memorizing as much as he could by candlelight and listening for scraps of practical examples from the children whenever they spoke their native tongue among themselves.

One day, early in 1550, Friar Diego interjected into a conversation in the children's native tongue, telling them it wasn't proper to make fun of Friar Lorenzo. His too-large tongue fumbled some of the pronunciation, but the message was received.

The children all stared at Friar Diego in amazement. One of the seven, the fourth oldest and fourth in height, told his best friend, the oldest student, that Ahkinmai had been right when he said they had a lot to learn from the friar.

"I have a lot to learn from you," Friar Diego said.

The student looked at his feet, blushing.

THE IZAMAL MONASTERY was dealt a surprise a month after Friar Diego's arrival, before the *arte* arrived and when the boys still spoke their native tongue without worrying about being understood. A native woman and her daughter, thin and ragged, showed up at the monastery looking for Friar Diego, calling him "the bee." None of the Franciscans could translate the word. Friar Luis knew what the word meant, and perhaps would have probed the meaning of the name if he had been in Izamal, but Friar Lorenzo didn't possess the same mastery of the language and so didn't inquire further when he met her at the edge of the monastery's land. The entire class, teacher included, saw the arriving natives from where they sat beneath the thatched roof.

The children's eyes grew wide and a murmur rippled the air between them. Friar Diego clapped his hands to draw their attention, a move that became his standard during all the years he taught. When Friar Lorenzo led the woman and her daughter past the school to the sanctuary, in full view of the class, Friar Diego recognized the young girl he had untied from the post.

The girl and her mother had been missing since the failed sacrifice. It wasn't uncommon among the Maya for people to leave for weeks or months at a time and return without explanation, but the girl was still required for sacrifice to the harvest god. The boys in Friar Diego's class couldn't contain their shock; they all knew the girl and her mother had been missing.

Friar Diego tried to continue his lessons in vain. The boys kept turning to look where the girl and her mother had gone, and whispered in their native tongue at every opportunity. Friar Diego, realizing further instruction would be wasted, dismissed them all with a wave of his hand, telling them he'd see them again tomorrow. The boys all walked to the edge of Izamal then broke into a run, wanting to be the first to inform their retainers about the reemergence of the girl.

The girl was alone with Friar Lorenzo by the time Friar Diego found them seated in the sanctuary.

"The mother left her here with us," Friar Lorenzo said. The girl was dressed in the traditional Mayan clothing, including a covering for her flat chest, and was looking around the sanctuary in awe.

"Left her?" Friar Diego said, astonished. It was the first time he had heard of a native child being handed over to the Franciscan Order in the Yucatán. If the youth had been a boy, they could have raised him to be a priest, but they had no prior experience with a girl and no nunnery where she could go.

"I don't know why."

"It's the girl who was supposed to be sacrificed," Friar Diego said.

"Is it now?" Friar Lorenzo thought for a moment. "That makes sense. Her mother said something about how there's no food for her even though I know this year's harvest was plentiful."

"What is she supposed to do here?" Friar Diego said.

"The mother pointed at you. I think she's saying the girl is your responsibility now."

"My responsibility! How so?"

"She was supposed to be sacrificed to their gods. Perhaps this is an offering to our God."

The young girl looked at Friar Diego, her calm, brown eyes reading his face. There was a stirring in his gut, an uncertain fear of his responsibility that he'd never experienced before, even when accepting his assignment in the New World.

"If she is rejected by her people, she needs our help. We can't let her go to one of the *encomenderos*. Who knows what kind of perverted games they'd play with her," Friar Lorenzo said. "She stays here."

Friar Diego got down on one knee. "What's your name?" he asked in her native language, one of the phrases he knew by heart.

"Ix Cuatchel," the girl replied with firmness.

"Take her to the infirmary. She can sleep in one of those beds until we can figure out what to do with her," Friar Lorenzo said.

Friar Diego extended his hand. After a moment's hesitation, the girl took it and allowed herself to be led to the infirmary, a building protected from the elements by four walls and containing six beds. Friar Diego told her to stay inside, and she sat down on one of the beds farthest from the door. He found her in the exact same position when he gathered her for evening prayers, motionless and staring at the wall.

Ix became a fixture within the infirmary. The friars never found a different place for her to lay her head, not wanting a young girl inside their living quarters. They couldn't prevent her from learning Spanish, since her life depended on figuring out the ebbs and flows of the monastery. Most of the sick people who took advantage of the infirmary were colonists working for local *encomiendas*, without land of their own, and this gave her the chance to practice speaking her new language with men, women, and children who were forced to stay in close proximity. They arrived with all sorts of ailments: stomachaches from the New World's food and water that their bodies weren't used to, which caused eruptions from both ends of their digestive tracts; headaches from too long spent in the sun with too little water; and all sorts of broken bones obtained while trying to bend the land to their iron will. The friars took turns caring for those in the infirmary, and each of them learned to rely on Ix Cuatchel's reports on the previous treatment of their patients.

Whispers of Ix Cuatchel's healing skills trickled from colonists in the town to the *encomenderos* in the fields and went a long way towards establishing trust between the Spaniards who were in the Yucatán for land and those who were there for souls. The *encomenderos* began sending their own natives to the Franciscan infirmary, still wary of the potential for indoctrination but more certain in the value of a healthy laborer. These native workers, still in communication with their counterparts not under *encomienda* rule, told the natives under Ahkinmai about the healing powers of the Mayan woman in the infirmary. When the first untethered Maya came to the infirmary, a woman who brought her young son to the Izamal monastery with a fever that took weeks to break, she arrived with word for Ix from Ahkinmai that Friar Diego's God was a powerful addition to their pantheon. His instruction for her was to learn all she could from the habit-wearing men. This was said in their own native language when the friars had left for evening prayers, so none of the men suspected Ix Cuatchel was anything other than a helper sent down from God to accept some of the weight from their already stooped shoulders.

Friar Diego's entreaties to Friar Lorenzo to allow him to go back into the jungle and preach to the natives never ceased; the leader of the Izamal monastery stood firm in his rejection of the idea. In his opinion, there was too much work to be done inside the land occupied by the church. They still had to contend with threats against their work from *encomenderos* who were in favor of using the infirmary but didn't want their natives worshipping the Lord on a regular basis, fearing the Franciscan mindset about who the Maya belonged to would undercut their control and affect their ability to generate wealth. Friar Lorenzo maintained his belief that the fight was against their fellow Spaniards, and that winning over their fellow countrymen would lead to greater rewards in the future.

Friar Lorenzo baptized colonists and natives in solemn ceremonies that used mere drops of water after it had been blessed. The colonists were always young, since the older inhabitants of the New World had come from Spain and been baptized before they left, while the natives he baptized ranged in age from older children to young adults. The older Maya were obstinate in their belief in Ahkinmai and the power given to him by their array of gods, despite the feathered man's urging that they take up Friar Diego's God as well, but they never stopped their younger brethren from visiting the monastery at Izamal.

The baptisms were on the first Sunday of each month. A line formed while Friar Lorenzo completed his morning prayers, and he baptized one at a time with the help of the other friars. The colonists were always first. Each native was given a Christian name. The Maya came to see the ritual as necessary and repeatable; for a while, Friar Lorenzo baptized them over and over again. Some received the same Christian name, while others were given a new one. Soon, there were dozens of Juans, scores of Isabels, and a vast number of Miguels throughout the jungle around Izamal. The Maya said their numerous names with pride, as if they were titles bestowed upon them by a king. Friar Lorenzo called a stop to the repeated baptisms when he knew for a fact it wouldn't create a schism between the Franciscans and the natives, tasking both Friar Diego, who by then had shown a mastery of the native tongue, and Ix Cuatchel, who knew most of the people coming month after month and could speak Spanish with the friars, with making sure the people who came to be baptized were there for the first time.

The torrent of baptisms turned into a steady flow of new converts.

In addition to the baptisms, Friar Lorenzo also performed marriages and funerals for the people around the Izamal monastery, though neither ceremony with any regularity. The colonist marriages were few and far between, the result of young Spanish colonists, having arrived as children in the early 1540s, coming of age and wanting to cement familial alliances. The native marriages were a novelty, since they had their own customs regarding partnering, which the Franciscans spoke against but couldn't prohibit. The Maya married young, around twelve to thirteen, and allowed divorce within their culture. They never married family on their father's side, but all relations on the mother's side were available matches. Men who slept with married women were handed over to the offended husband for him to pardon or kill by dropping a large stone on his head. Adulterous women were disgraced, which to the Maya was worse than death. If a married man or woman's partner died, they were free to partner again after one year.

Since these customs were part of the Maya's traditions, those who were married by Friar Lorenzo didn't place much extra stock in the union under God. The Franciscan funeral traditions occupied a similar space: an additional security measure but in no way the law of the land. While dying colonists received elaborate burials, paid for by their families and presided over by the Franciscans, the Maya would permit the friars to visit the dead bodies after the Franciscans requested access. The Catholic rituals were never the primary death ceremony, and the friars were ushered away before the ultimate burial inside, or in close proximity of, the house. The living space was then abandoned, the jungle reclaiming the land.

The disputes between Friar Diego and Friar Lorenzo never escalated beyond simple questions posed by the younger to the older, but all five men at the monastery knew the intentions hidden in the shadows of the young recruit's words. It was frustrated impotence against the calculated foresight of the Guardian of the monastery. The simmering Friar Diego never spoke an ill word to any of the other men, choosing instead to bide his time and wait for an opportunity to prove the correctness of his methods.

His chance came with the arrival of a group of over seventy natives. They'd fled from their land after learning it fell under the jurisdiction of a new *encomienda* created by *Adelantado* Francisco Hernandez for one of his close friends. Having heard about the man's brutality from fellow natives, they abandoned their homeland and traveled to the closest Franciscan establishment, hoping to settle under the protection of the friars.

Friar Diego leapt at the chance for a second mass conversion. With Ix's help, he convinced them to set down their belongings and join him in the sanctuary. There, he proceeded to give them the same sermon he'd given to Ahkinmai's group, complete with the same Bible readings.

The natives looked at him, confused but attentive. They modeled their behavior after Ix, who listened to each word as if she were a starving girl looking inside a kitchen window to a prepared feast. The just-arrived natives didn't have a leader like Ahkinmai telling them to absorb Friar Diego's faith so they could use it for their own purposes; all the group of refugees wanted was a place to call home, somewhere they would be protected, away from the *encomienda* system they knew would leave them whipped and in chains.

Friar Diego led them to a clearing beyond the infirmary and told them they could live there until a more permanent arrangement was determined. Friar Lorenzo watched Friar Diego's feverish attempts at recreating his prior mass conversion from the infirmary, where he had taken over care of the patients from Ix and told her to help Friar Diego. He watched as Friar Diego strode over to him as tall as he'd ever been and with an extra lightness in his step.

"Another large group of converts," Friar Diego boasted.

"They seemed to pay attention," Friar Lorenzo observed.

"We should be preaching to them more often," said Friar Diego. "They were like thirsty soil, ready to accept water."

"I see that." Friar Lorenzo paused while looking at the Maya setting up camp, waiting, thinking.

"I told them they can stay there for now," Friar Diego said.

"We can feed them for a day or two," Friar Lorenzo replied.

Friar Diego gulped, his eyes wide as if he had swallowed an insect. "A day or two? They came here for our protection . . ." he said, his voice trailing off.

"Where do you think we get food? The *encomiendas*. As

mad as they get at us, they know we're a necessary part of society. But they won't appreciate us housing their labor."

"But they don't want to labor for them!" Friar Diego said, pointing to the natives. "They want to join the Church, to worship. They need our protection!"

"How long do you think we can survive without supplies? A few weeks, at most."

"So where should they go? Into the jungle?"

"They could, but that's going to rely on the goodwill of other Maya. In my experience, those divisions run deeper than the hate the Maya feel for the *encomenderos*."

"So they can't go into the jungle and they can't stay here. Where are they supposed to go?"

Friar Lorenzo took a long, tired look at a frantic Friar Diego. The young man should have learned to listen without subjecting dozens of natives to the flames of his passion, but he was proving to be a difficult learner. "They must go back to their land. You can let them know that we will make sure the *encomenderos* treat them in a decent manner, but that we have no resources to provide them with any further assistance."

"How can I tell them all that? Their language is still new to me!"

"Have Ix tell them." Friar Lorenzo turned to go back into the infirmary. "She's turning out to be more useful than I ever thought she'd be."

CHAPTER EIGHT

THE BOSS ARRIVED at work Monday morning wearing his red polo. He waved from inside his car when he saw Cortez waiting in front of the factory's entrance. It was raining, a light drizzle that made one wonder whether it was worth it to go through the hassle of carrying an umbrella. Cortez had opted for a navy-blue rain jacket to combat the elements. He had learned to keep his backpack beneath the jacket years ago on his trips to school, but he didn't account for the lack of coverage when he sat down on the wet concrete step. That was why he found himself with a wet bottom while watching his boss take a few deep breaths before getting out of the car.

"I swear people don't know how to drive," the boss said.

"It's the rain," Cortez replied. It was something he heard people say. He didn't have his license and had never driven a car. People in the city didn't have the same pressure to drive, since everything one might need was within walking distance. In the event someone needed to travel farther distances, they could always take public transportation: ancient buses and rickety underground trains crossed the city at all hours of the day and night. The boss drove a car because he commuted into the city from beyond the outskirts. Even though his car was an older model, the fact that he drove at all provided the elevated status he needed to look down on those around him.

"And the day started so well too."

Cortez stood up, giving his boss access to the main door. Once inside, he took off his rain jacket in order to take off his backpack and hang it up in its proper location, then he put the jacket back on before going back outside to wait for Simeon. The sky couldn't decide whether it was done raining or not. Its color didn't change, but pockets of clear weather emerged, on one occasion leaving Cortez untouched while droplets of water hit the puddles around him. He didn't have to wait long for Simeon to roll up to the factory. As soon as Cortez spotted his friend passing the neighboring building, he walked forward so he could push the wheelchair the remaining distance, which would keep his friend's hands from touching more rainwater on the wheels.

"Morning, Cort," Simeon said. He was cheerful in a way Cortez had witnessed a handful of times before. His hair was matted against his head, this time because he didn't have an umbrella or a rain jacket. The shoulders of his shirt were soaked through, the moisture fading away towards the still-dry parts around his stomach. Sunken eyes surrounded by dark circles crinkled at the edges when he smiled, as Cortez hurried to get behind his wheelchair and push him the remaining distance.

"How was your weekend?" Simeon asked.

"It was good. Went to church," Cortez replied. He turned the wheelchair around and pulled the wheels over the concrete step with a grunt.

"Of course you did," Simeon said. He continued when Cortez didn't say anything more. "My weekend was good too. Sat around mostly." Simeon turned around and looked at

Cortez out of the corner of his eye with his mouth hanging open.

"That's nice," Cortez said, wheeling his friend towards the factory floor.

"Nothing? You get it, don't you? I'm *always* sitting!" Simeon said.

Cortez thought for a moment, still didn't understand, then let a chuckle escape his lips because something in the way Simeon looked at him informed him it was the right thing to do.

Simeon shook his head, a switch flipped, and he became irritated. "My jokes are wasted on you. You don't appreciate anything."

Cortez ignored Simeon's erratic mood and took a look at the board with the day's production schedule. They were in for a busy one. There were two different flavors being made in the morning, and three in the afternoon. He had to get two different boxes of lids on each side of the conveyor belt before morning production started, and it would be helpful if he located the lids they would need that afternoon. It was a good thing Simeon had arrived a little earlier than normal. There wasn't much Simeon could do while Cortez gathered boxes from where they were stored, carried them to their station, and took care to arrange them within Simeon's reach.

The pair were on their respective sides of the conveyor belt when production began. The morning was dedicated to water-based flavors because it was easier to transition to milk-based flavors than going from milk to water. Raspberry sorbet got red lids, and they worked for an hour before the conveyor belt stopped. When it started back up again, mango was coming down the line. Cortez hadn't been paying attention and began placing red lids on each pint, and when Simeon pointed it out, he had to hurry and switch the few mistakes he'd made with the necessary pale orange lids while Simeon lidded the oncoming pints alone. The team making the pints was working faster than normal in order to get the orders completed, leaving both Cortez and Simeon so busy that they were slightly out of breath, with no air left to chat.

They welcomed the arrival of their lunch break. Simeon had never dried out; the rain had been replaced with sweat, his hair still matted to his head. Instead of the moisture originating from his shoulders, it now spread out from his armpits. Cortez ripped off his hairnet and plastic gloves. His hands welcomed the cool air of the air-conditioned room after being trapped and unable to breathe. The pair caught each other's eye, and Simeon said, "That was a lot."

"Busy day," Cortez replied. "And there are three this afternoon."

"Bet you're looking forward to lunch," Simeon said.

"Of course. I think I have a sandwich today."

"Cort. You always have a sandwich."

"That's very true." Cortez walked to Simeon's side of the belt, undid the brakes on his wheels, and rolled him off the wooden block. He left Simeon while he went back and moved the boxes they'd used in the morning away from their station, so he had space to bring the new boxes in after lunch. Then he rolled Simeon back to where they kept their belongings. While there, he took a puff from his inhaler before throwing his backpack over his shoulders and turning to his friend. Simeon hadn't taken his lunch from his locker. In fact, he hadn't moved from the spot where Cortez left him.

"I'm going to skip lunch today," Simeon said, looking disappointed. "I need to talk to the boss."

This had never happened before, and Cortez didn't know how to feel. He had never considered whether he liked their shared lunch time, but it was a consistent part of his day, a sure thing he knew was coming and had navigated many times before. He wasn't even sure he would be able to eat in their normal spot—it depended on if the sky had decided to call it quits after depositing enough water for the day. Would his sandwich taste the same when eaten alone again after so long with Simeon for company?

"Do you want me to roll you to the boss's office?" Cortez asked.

"No, I think I can manage." Simeon rolled himself away, and Cortez realized he was still wearing his plastic gloves.

The sun was shining when Cortez went outside. It was bright and hot enough to dry off the world while he had been working inside, and if he hadn't been in the morning rain, he wouldn't have believed the bad weather had passed through. Black birds were perched on the wires that ran between telephone poles, so many that they covered the span and their friends were left flying around looking for somewhere to land. On the way to his picnic table, he thought he saw someone in the driver's seat of an unmarked police car staring at him through the windshield. He remembered his mother's wisdom, told to him after being caught hiding candy he had been forbidden from gathering on Halloween: guilty people act guilty. Acting innocent wasn't hard—Simeon had sold the drugs, against his wishes—but he imagined the cops might want to talk to him if they recognized him as one of the people who had run the previous Friday. Finding strength in his most innocent thoughts, he walked towards the picnic table with his head held high, sat down, and took out his lunch, then began to eat.

Nobody approached him during his meal or while he sat waiting for the end of his lunch break. He forgot Simeon wasn't with him. They ate in silence most days, each lost in their own thoughts. The flames of their conversations never burned bright;

instead, they were the coals at the bottom of a hot fire, always ready to ignite if given fuel. Cortez was comfortable alone, and, despite his misgivings, his lunch that day had tasted the same as it always did. He never figured out that the part of his routine that was most soothing to his soul was getting outside and sitting among the trees. They watched over him with their steady gaze, unaffected by the day-to-day happenings of the people who walked among their trunks, growing and marking periods of time in a way not perceivable by humans. The trees, the consistent friends he never knew he had, kept Cortez company while he ate.

Cortez gathered his lunch's trash into his backpack and went back to the factory. Simeon had positioned himself in front of his own locker and sat with the evidence of his eaten lunch on his lap. He was finishing his Coke when Cortez arrived and didn't turn around when Cortez hung his backpack back in its usual spot. Instead, he stared into his open locker, as if hoping to find the answer to the meaning of life in the emptiness of the locker's dark interior.

"How was lunch?" Cortez asked.

Simeon pulled his head back, blinking multiple times in rapid succession, as he was pulled from his reverie. He turned to look at Cortez. "It was good," he said. He drank the rest of his beverage in one long pull on the straw, then placed it on his lap with the rest of the trash, rolled to the trash can, and deposited everything from his lap inside.

Cortez watched his friend through the stifling air of being ignored. "Everything all right with the boss?" Cortez said.

"Everything's fine." Simeon said. He turned his wheelchair around to face Cortez. "Don't you have to get ready for production?"

Cortez nodded and hurried off to gather the lids the pair would need for the afternoon without a second thought about

Simeon's attitude. He had been raised to believe that if someone was upset, the best thing to do was whatever they expected for as long as necessary in order to get back in their good graces. One time, his mother had been upset with him for an entire week. Cortez never knew that the pressure of being his mother, caring for him day after day, year after year, had gotten to her. All he knew was that the house needed cleaning and the mail needed gathering, and he managed to feed himself while she stayed in her bedroom and ignored him. She emerged from her withdrawal without mentioning her disappearance, and this was how he learned that acts of service would lead to a return to normalcy, as long as he could hold up his end of the bargain.

He took the four boxes of the two types of lids they'd used in the morning, now far lighter than before, and carried them into the warehouse in four trips. Simeon was still near his locker when Cortez looked at the board and determined which color lids they would need for the afternoon. Six trips were needed to bring the lids for the three flavors they were making—two boxes of each color, one for each side of the conveyor belt. By the time everything was arranged for them to begin, Simeon was already next to the wooden block with his hairnet, gloves, and apron on, waiting for Cortez to put him on the riser. Cortez hurried to put on his own gear and tied his apron as he went over to Simeon and helped him into position before putting on his gloves.

They were standing in silence when the conveyor belt began moving, and they performed their duties in silence. Simeon didn't acknowledge Cortez during the color change, when Cortez moved the box of white lids for vanilla out of the way and brought the brown ones for chocolate chip into Simeon's reach. The final switch of the afternoon involved bringing the green lids close for the mint chocolate chip, and they continued working for the rest of the afternoon, finishing a half hour past the normal end of their workday.

. . .

Simeon ripped his hairnet and gloves off when the conveyor belt stopped for the final time and waited for Cortez to help him off the riser. He rolled away at the first chance he got. Cortez was left alone while he packed up the boxes and carried them to the warehouse. During his second trip, the boss stopped him on his way back to the factory floor and asked Cortez to come to his office before he left for the day. Cortez nodded, then went back to grab another box and return it to the warehouse. While carrying it, he saw Simeon rolling himself towards the front door. He called out to Simeon, telling him to wait.

"I'll help you down the step, just wait for me to put the lids away," he said to the back of his friend's head.

When Simeon ignored him, Cortez set the box down and hurried to catch up. They were in the reception area at the front of the factory, with the front door across the room. "Hold on, let me help," Cortez said, reaching out and grabbing one of the wheelchair's handles.

Simeon twisted his torso as if Cortez had grabbed his shoulder and needed to be shaken off. "I don't need you to do everything for me," Simeon spat out. "There are other people here, you know."

Cortez looked around. He didn't point out that they were alone as he took his hand off the wheelchair. "I'll see you tomorrow then?" Cortez said, his voice rising as he came to the end of the phrase, implying a question.

"Whatever," Simeon said.

Cortez watched as his friend wheeled away, opened the front door, and went through it. He waited to hear if there was a commotion past the front door, but all was silent. He took a deep breath then returned to carrying boxes. He arrived at his boss's office with a sheen of sweat covering his face and a fresh puff from his inhaler in his lungs.

"You wanted to see me?" he said after sticking his head through the door. The boss was leaning back in his chair, his head back, staring at the ceiling, looking like he hadn't moved in a while. His desk was cleared of paper, the day's work already filed away to be dealt with tomorrow.

"Come in," the boss said. He didn't offer Cortez a seat.

Cortez shut the door behind him and turned to face his boss. His heart was pounding. Years of conditioning by the public school system had taught him to fear one-on-one interactions with men in power, and he struggled to focus when every fiber of his being screamed to do whatever was necessary to remove himself from the situation.

"I'll make this quick," the boss began. "Today was your last day working here."

Those words took the air from the room, leaving Cortez breathless and suffocating. His vision narrowed, and he realized too late that the pills he had for these situations were in the backpack still hanging on his hook. He scanned his boss's face, searching for a hint of sympathy. The Church had taught him the power of prayer to bring about salvation but had never mentioned how someone could save themselves if they forgot every prayer they'd ever been taught.

"Are you going to say anything?" the boss said.

Cortez stared at his boss. He had a hard face lined by years of imposing his will on people whom he had decided were not, and would never be, good enough. His too-dark hair, dyed for years, was beginning to show hints of gray at the roots.

This wasn't the first time the boss had had to give someone their walking papers, but it was the first time the recipient hadn't said a word. The first thing others had inquired about was why, which was followed either by a fierce defense and a promise to change or a proclamation that the job wasn't what they wanted in the first place and they'd be happy to leave. Cortez reminded the boss of when he had visited his uncle's farm as a boy—times he thought he'd forgotten. Years ago, he had tried to save the calves reared for veal as they were led to slaughter. His uncle had put one hand over his shoulder and squeezed tight as they watched the animals march past at a relaxed pace. In a show of compassion, his uncle didn't make him watch their ultimate demise. The creature in front of him now, just told about his termination, didn't know enough to fight for his life.

The boss looked past Cortez, sure that not looking at him would be the best way to fight the urge to save him. "A tip for your next job: don't sell drugs on company time. Simeon told me all about the way you let him take the fall when the police arrived. What you do on your own time is nobody's business, but during lunch? That's not smart." He forced himself to look at Cortez, not knowing that this act of bravery paled in comparison to the courage it took for Cortez to not run away.

Cortez looked down at his shoes. He knew, without ever being able to put it into words, to do what those with power wanted until he was back on their good side. Don't fight back; it could make the situation worse. Acquiesce until you're forgiven. Worship until your salvation. He managed to say, "I'm sorry," the two words he kept tucked away for every time he faced someone else's disappointment, before turning and leaving the boss alone in his office.

CHAPTER NINE

Nachi Cocom arrived at the monastery early in the year 1550, during the peak of the dry season. He emerged from the jungle one afternoon wearing breeches and sandals, carrying a once-white shirt slung over his shoulder, leaving his bare chest exposed. His skin was covered in tattoos, dozens of small square glyphs arranged in clustered neat rows on his chest and back, with enough space between each cluster for even the friars, who couldn't read the ancient language, to understand different concepts were represented. His long hair was gray with streaks of black, tied up in a bun with an exposed portion lying straight on his back, reaching below his shoulder blades. Deep creases lined his dust-covered face.

Nobody could escape the dust. A thick layer covered every surface in the monastery, and on the worst mornings the friars were forced to wipe the air in front of their faces clear when they woke up so they could sit up without traversing through the extra weight of the particles. The Yucatán colonists accommodated the extra weight of the dust when calculating how much their donkeys could carry, and the eggplants in the gardens grew long and flat from the extra weight forcing the direction of their growth.

The gathered dust exposed the various lizards, snakes, and scorpions on the monastery grounds by betraying their movements to the friars. Friars followed thin lines to a snake's hiding place beneath buildings; caught serpents were then taken into the jungle and released. The scorpions left thousands of tiny dots all around the living quarters and were never found in the light of day. The lizards' trails were a combination of the two, with their four feet leaving fewer—though larger—dots than the scorpions and their tails leaving a thinner line than a snake's. The lizards came into the monastery during full moons, and their trails extended into every part of the monastery, including up every wall and onto all the ceilings. The sole specimen the friars caught had confused a cloudy day with the light of the moon, and strode from the jungle as if it had made the monastery itself.

The spiders and ants were a bigger problem. Their footsteps were so tiny they were hidden by the windblown particles, and they hid their bodies in the dust while they waited for their prey. Ix Cuatchel taught the friars to watch out for two types of venomous spiders: a small jet-black variety and a large tarantula who stored its venom in delicate little black spines that resembled down covering its exoskeleton. One type of large ant had a bite more painful than any scorpion with swelling that lasted twice as long; Friar Diego de Landa learned about the effects firsthand when one bit him in the foot while he squatted over the hole they used for a toilet. Ix, when she saw the size of the crushed insect before it was swept away by a dust storm, gathered a number of small red worms from the jungle, crushed them into a yellow ointment flecked with red, and applied it to the friar's bitten heel. He never knew the extent to which it relieved his pain, because he never received the full force of the bite without the ointment.

Friar Diego had just begun walking without a limp when the Mayan man called Nachi emerged from the undergrowth. He was teaching the native youth when he saw, across the courtyard, Ix stop where she was and turn around while holding a bundle of clean habits against her chest. A moment later, the Mayan man walked by without acknowledging Ix, who was presenting her back to the man with her head bowed. The schoolchildren turned around and began whispering amongst themselves in their native tongue. Friar Diego saw Friar Lorenzo de Bienvenida walk from the living quarters to meet the man, who put on his shirt before the friar arrived. After a brief consultation, he waved Friar Diego over.

"This man is here to speak with you," Friar Lorenzo said. "His name is Nachi Cocom."

"Hello," Nachi said in awkward Spanish.

Friar Diego nodded his greeting.

"I'll take over for you in there," Friar Lorenzo said. "Where did you leave off?"

"They're practicing writing," Friar Diego said, turning to look at his students. The children all turned back to their work at a glance from their teacher.

"They're disciplined," Friar Lorenzo observed. "This should be easy."

The youngest student of the cohort, just five years old, dared another glance at the visitor. Nachi, his attention also drawn to the school, raised his eyebrows three times in quick succession, drawing a smile from the young student. Friar Diego's stern glance made the student turn back around.

Friar Lorenzo left the two men alone. Friar Diego invited

Nachi to the covered patio in front of the sanctuary where the friars sat and recorded those who arrived for baptism each month before they entered into the sacred space. Ix was trying to invoke the spirit of a mouse and sneak away unnoticed, but Friar Diego called out to her, in Spanish, and told her to drop off the habits and join them in the shade.

The two men exchanged a thin-lipped smile before sitting down on identical three-legged stools, their expressions needing no interpretation. A light breeze cooled the sweat on the lower part of Friar Diego's legs, the sensation transporting him back to an exchange that had occurred weeks before, during the previous baptism event.

He had been seated in the same spot, with a table in front of him, as he recorded the names of all the natives who came to be baptized. Friar Lorenzo had been inside, performing the ceremonies. The morning had been long; the sun was high in the sky when the last group was let inside. Friar Diego had been looking over his notes, correcting spots where his penmanship was unclear, when a Mayan woman had appeared in front of him. He had flipped to the last page of his notes, prepared to make another entry, when the woman launched into a tale about a man who had been baptized by the Franciscans.

"He's enamored with me," the woman had said in her native tongue.

Friar Diego knew enough of her language to understand, in broad terms, what she was saying. He could see why a man wanted her: the woman was beautiful by any standards. Her curves emanated feminine genius, and her skin had the supple tenderness of fruit at the perfect stage of ripeness. God had given her a face worthy of preservation in statues, and old masters long dead were the only ones who could have captured the spark contained within her eyes. For the first time, Friar Diego had questioned his dedication to a life wearing the habit;

his confessions revolved around her for the next few days and would pop up again years later.

She had continued before Friar Diego could speak. "My husband is away and last night this man came to my house. He declared his intentions with many flattering remarks, and tried to give me presents. When I still didn't welcome him into my home, he tried to force himself on me. We struggled all night. He was large, much larger than me, but I refused to give in," she had said with pride.

Friar Diego could tell the woman was furious at the transgression and expected him to do something about the misguided convert. He had told her, in a rough rendition of her own language, that the man was wrong and that God would punish him for what he did. Folding his hands against his chest and bowing his head, then demonstrating that the Mayan woman should do the same, he had prayed with her in Spanish while Friar Lorenzo finished baptizing the group inside the sanctuary.

"Amen," Friar Diego had said, lifting his head. Friar Lorenzo was walking the baptized group out, and he said each person's Christian name for Diego to record before taking the beautiful woman into the sanctuary; she was the last baptism of the day. Friar Diego fell asleep while waiting, and was woken up by Friar Lorenzo reporting that the woman's new name was Maria.

Friar Diego had watched the Mayan woman walk away. He never discovered her native name because the name no longer existed within the monastery. This was the first time he'd realized the quality of the native women; to him, these were the first true rivals to the Spanish examples of the same sex he knew in the Old World.

Ix's arrival pulled Friar Diego from his memory. Nachi greeted her with a mischievous grin, a smile that she returned with trepidation as she sat on the floor between the two men.

"I'll need you to talk to him for me," Friar Diego said in Spanish.

"I can understand some of what you're saying," Nachi replied, leaving out some of the words but still managing to get his point across.

"How did you learn?" Friar Diego asked, astonished.

"I have many years of experience with the Spaniards . . ." Nachi began. With Ix's help, Friar Diego learned about the man sitting with him and the role he had played during the Spanish conquest of the Yucatán.

Nachi told his tale from the beginning. Not just his beginning, but his family's beginning. One hundred and twenty years before Nachi sat in front of Friar Diego, a rival family of the Cocom, the Xiu, convinced the rest of the lords to join forces with them and kill the governor Cocom and his family where they lived in Mayapan. Their plan worked; the entire clan was murdered except for one son, who was away trading. The Cocom line waited over a hundred years for their revenge. A great drought followed the exit of the first wave of Spanish conquerors fifteen years before, in 1535, when the foreigners realized there was no gold. At the height of the dry spell, the Xiu traveled to Chichen Itza—in Cocom territory—to make sacrifices to the god of rain. Nachi's father, the previous leader of the Cocom, allowed the Xiu safe passage into their land, where they stayed in one large house. Before the sacrifice that would end the drought was performed, the Cocom lord set fire to the house and killed anyone who escaped the blaze.

"Great wars were fought after, and locusts made sure nothing green was left," Nachi said with sadness. Friar Diego discovered Nachi blamed his family's actions for the resultant plague.

When the Spanish returned in 1540, intent on settling the land, the Xiu allied with the invading Spanish, seeking the destruction of their rivals, the Cocom. Nachi's father had died by then, leaving Nachi lord of the clan, ruling from Sotuta. He struggled against the yoke of servitude the Spanish tried to impose, leading the Yucatán provinces to the south and east against the combined forces of the Spaniards and the provinces of the north and west. The fighting came to a head at Tiho in 1542, where Nachi lost the majority of his forces. The following three years were spent in guerrilla warfare, making Spanish life as miserable as possible. They burned many villages and *milpas,* their corn plots, so the Spanish wouldn't get their hands on them. Once the Maya realized their destiny lay in the *encomiendas*, that they were fighting the inevitable, Nachi disbanded their resistance movement.

"I presented myself to the *Adelantado* Montejo, expecting to die," Nachi said. "Instead, they baptized me, told me I should continue as chief of Sotuta, then gave me the entire province, telling me to make sure things run smoothly—meaning, they want peaceful labor forces and consistent tribute. The Xiu didn't like that one bit." Ix translated a large majority of this information.

"Why didn't they reward their original allies?" Friar Diego asked, through Ix. He was astounded to be seated across from the man placed in charge of the natives. Here was one of the three men vying for power in the Yucatán: Nachi oversaw the Maya, Friar Luis de Villalpondo was in charge of the Franciscans, and *Adelantado* Francisco ruled over the colonists.

"Because they said I was better at bringing together the men," Nachi explained. "To them, the Xiu are lapdogs. They even gave me a Spanish name! Don Juan," Nachi said with a laugh.

The sun was setting by the time Nachi finished the history of his people. Friar Lorenzo had dismissed the students long ago, and the other friars were in the middle of evening prayers. Somehow, everyone in the monastery knew not to disrupt the discussion between Friar Diego and Nachi Cocom.

"Are you a member of one of these families?" Friar Diego asked Ix.

She shook her head no, looking down at her feet.

"She knows her family history. Every child does." Nachi then explained that the Cocom, the Xiu, and the Chel were the three principal houses in the Yucatán. The Chel line had been started when the daughter of the most respected member of the twelve priests of Mayapan married a young nobleman from a lesser house named Achchel. They settled on the coast, amassing many followers who took the name Chel for themselves, naming their province Ahkinchel. The Chel had been a rising power when Montejo first arrived.

"The Chel use their connection to the highly regarded priest and the fact that they were able to make themselves equal in prosperity to the Xiu and Cocom as reasons why they are greatest of all," Nachi explained, which Ix translated. "There were squabbles between the Cocom and the Chel over food, but none of that matters anymore," he added.

Nachi nodded towards Ix, still seated on the ground. "A Chel is the reason I'm here in the first place. I want to thank you for allowing her to stay here; it's gone a long way in keeping the priests happy. They believe you show our customs respect by accepting your responsibility for her well-being. The gods are pleased."

A repulsed Friar Diego stood up, rearranged his habit, then sat back down, folding his legs and leaning forward. "They think I'm participating with them, in a way?"

"Helping maintain order," Nachi clarified, after the question was told to him by Ix. "Plus, after hearing about you from Ahkinmai, I wanted to meet you myself."

Friar Diego didn't know what to say in response; he invited the man to dinner to fill the silence.

"No, thank you, I'm expected nearby," Nachi said, pointing into the jungle.

Their conversation dead, Friar Diego walked the Mayan visitor to the edge of the monastery's land with his hands behind his back in the same manner as Friar Luis, an idiosyncrasy he would keep until the day he died. He liked Nachi, and appreciated the firsthand account of the history of the Mayan people. The man had plenty of experience with Spanish customs and their way of life, and his mastery of Spanish was enough for them to communicate if Ix wasn't there, although her presence did speed up the process. Neither man knew the outsized role they each would play in the life of the other, but they parted ways after their first meeting with hopeful prospects for the future.

THE STUDENTS ASKED Friar Diego about Nachi during their lessons the next day in a brazen round of questioning that left the Franciscan frustrated at their lack of decorum. Each child knew who the man was and marveled that the friar had received a solo discussion, ignoring the presence of Ix at the meeting.

"Are you friends now?"

"When is he coming back?"

"Does he want to worship your God too?"

Friar Diego told the children they weren't allowed to speak the rest of the day and that the day's lessons would all involve reading and writing. Before he assigned their work, he made sure he clarified that his God was the sole God in existence; all others were false.

"There are lots of gods," the oldest boy said. "There's one for the harvest, one for water—"

"There's no God but the Christian God!" Friar Diego roared. The birds in the surrounding trees flew into the sky, casting hundreds of squawking shadows onto the dusty ground among the monastery's buildings. The insects in the undergrowth, who emitted a consistent hum regardless of the time of day, grew quiet, as if they suspected a larger presence nearby and didn't want their position betrayed.

Friar Diego came up with a new lesson plan for the day after hearing the child's belief, which he knew was shared by all —he commanded the children to copy the Bible. Ink and paper were in constant short supply, their use reserved for letters back to Spain, important communications with the Franciscans in Guatemala, and notes to the friars in surrounding monasteries. So, the children took turns copying the Bible in the front of the room, under Friar Diego's exacting gaze, while the rest of the class wrote the same passages with sticks in the dust as they were read aloud, doing the best they could to both spell and remember the characters without having the source material in front of them.

Their work continued until lunch, which was a piece of buttered bread for each, brought to the classroom by Ix. Friar Diego told the children he was going to lie down for an afternoon nap, and that their work would resume when he was refreshed. The children dispersed and Friar Diego found his hammock waiting for him.

The friar slept longer than usual. On most days, he stayed somewhat aware of his surroundings while his body digested his lunch and rose when his body demanded he relieve himself. This time, his body's processes never called out; instead, his dreams transported him back to Ahkinmai's ceremony in the clearing. A multicolored glow in the air above the chanting Maya crackled during Ahkinmai's fevered calls. The feathered man opened his mouth as wide as a snake, drank in the glistening air, and became a bird. His hawk's eyes looked at Friar Diego, who still stood hidden in the thicket, and his beak released a series of rapid words in the Mayan language that Friar Diego didn't understand.

A beating heart woke up the dreaming Franciscan. He knew right away he had slept too long. The words spoken by the transformed Ahkinmai echoed in his head, and he repeated them as he went in search of his students, torn over whether to ask them what the human-bird had said.

The students were in the clearing behind the infirmary. They all sat squatted with their backs turned to the monastery, looking at something on the ground. Friar Diego didn't announce his presence as he inspected what drew their attention.

It was a small rodent, split from the base of its neck down through its stomach. The entrails had been pulled from the cavity and sat in red-stained dust, folded with a deliberate neatness that came from human hands. The students had taken a lamp from one of the buildings, lit it, and were lighting small sticks on fire before shoving them into the mammal's cavity, dousing the flames in blood.

Friar Diego forever lost the Mayan words floating in his head. He crossed himself before rage took over every fiber of his being.

"What are you doing?" he screamed.

He flew forward on anger's wings, his habit ruffling in the created wind. Though his flight hadn't taken him high off the ground, he had to reach down with his foot to kick the mutilated carcass. The wind kicked up dust and covered the spilled blood, leaving the sole remaining sample on Friar Diego's foot—it crept up his skin until his body was covered in red streaks.

The oldest boy, the last one Friar Diego saw douse his stick, was within reach. Friar Diego grabbed him by the shoulder with his left hand, then struck him across the face with the back of his right, passing the advancing red streaks onto the student's face. The skin of the other students all became streaked with red, though they hadn't been touched, and Friar Diego found himself facing a group whose combined fury matched his own.

"I teach you about God and this is how you repay me!" Friar Diego said, seething. A faint stirring of memory passed through his mind of a time in the Toledo monastery when he was told the same statement after being struck by his mentor.

The boys all stared at him, looking like they wanted to perform the same ritual on him that they had on the rodent.

"Strike your false idols from your memory! You'll go to hell." And, he knew, if they didn't become Christians and therefore usher in the New Age, the whole world would soon follow.

The youngest boy started to cry at the mention of hell. The underworld was one of the first things Friar Diego had taught them, making sure they knew the importance of staying away from the eternal flames. His fear infected the others, and their red streaks all receded.

Friar Diego told them all to go home before anyone could offer words of explanation. "I expect you here tomorrow," he said. "Don't make me tell Nachi you aren't following the rules."

Friar Diego watched the seven sheepish boys disappear into the jungle, wondering what cavity he could crawl into to douse the flames of his burning heart.

CHAPTER TEN

THE WALK back to his apartment was spent waiting for the blue pill to work its magic. Cortez had first been given the pills years ago, the latest in a string of medications prescribed by various doctors all attempting to aid him with conforming to society. There was no telling when he would need them. Weeks would go by without a single thought of the little blue pill that would make human interactions less stressful, then a trigger would begin a series of days where nothing was possible without their support. He was told they weren't habit-forming, but his mother could always tell when he had been on them on a consistent basis for too long; she would beg him to try existing without their help. She claimed it took away his spark, his unique ability to light up the world, the certainty of this ability bestowed upon her by angels the moment he left her womb.

The sun was setting. In the blocks between the factory and Cortez's home, rats were waking up after sleeping all day inside hidden places the best exterminators could never find. The people whose waste products sponsored the rodents' existence congregated on porches, steps, and street corners. Whether they sat or stood depended on their years of hard living. Older people sat with their contemporaries, talking about the past and hoping that each word would prevent the decay of their memories. On the rare occasions Cortez's mother joined in the evening outdoor community, always with Cortez by her side, he was able to glimpse each person's idealized version of heaven. His mother's never included him. The younger people stood, always ready to greet a newcomer or go off on an adventure to a new gathering place. Cortez never talked to the other people his age in the neighborhood, even though he had attended school with all of them. He had trouble remembering their names even when he saw them every day, and now that they weren't in school together anymore, their faces were hazy reminders of memories from a time he wished to be forgotten. It was a curse familiar to all who can't relax enough in their own skin to enjoy the company of anyone else.

Normalcy returned by the time he got to his building's block. The dread of confrontation constricting his heart had passed, allowing blood to flow back to his arms, legs, and lungs. The fresh air had helped. His hand reached out for the few trees he passed, lone sentinels at random intervals along the street, and the feel of the last one's bark grazing his hand reminded his nervous system that he was close to home. The awareness of his proximity to his room brought a fresh surge of anxiety, stemming from his mother's constant proclamations of his untapped greatness. He had lost his job and didn't know how to keep from disappointing her with the news. The feeling of inadequacy was familiar. It had occurred often when he was still in school and would come home with grades in the bottom third of the class. It wasn't for lack of trying—he was afraid to disappoint even before assignments began, which gave him the strength to use every ounce of his meager resources, but still his results would come up short. He wondered how he should break the news to his mother, whether he should include Simeon's deception. She had met Simeon a few times and liked him, and Cortez believed that she wouldn't see the sinner's heart of his former coworker and would take offense to laying the blame on someone without the use of their legs.

A headache was on the horizon. He got them whenever dread overwhelmed him, as if his head couldn't sink any lower and his neck wasn't able to fulfill its responsibility without causing pain further up the chain. The white pills helped, and he took one as the back of his eyes started to ache during his climb to the seventh floor—the elevator always smelled like a flatulent dog had come in from the rain and slept there overnight. To Cortez, taking the stairs was his chance to thank the Lord for providing him with two good legs, one more chance to communicate with a higher power each day. When the first six floors were left behind, he stood preparing himself in the stairwell behind the door that led into the seventh floor's hallway. He never lied to his mother, and he didn't have any intention of doing so, but he decided to keep the information about the end of his workday to himself unless she asked about his employment status. If he divulged he had a headache, he might be able to get away with short replies to any question she asked.

Somehow, Cortez discovered a floating plank of optimism and clung to it for dear life. Even though his mother had found him both jobs he'd ever had, starting the next day, he could go out and find a new one. The sting of having lost the job at the ice cream factory would hurt her much less if she knew his employment had already been addressed.

As soon as he walked into their home, Cortez could tell his mother was confronting another depressive episode. Trash had been left on the counter right next to the garbage can, uneaten food still on a plate on the tray next to her recliner. The television was on mute, a telenovela where the actress's mouth was wide open in surprise and shock after a soundless revelation by a man dressed in all black. He knew his mother was in her bedroom, lying on her bed, in all likelihood staring at the ceiling and hoping a fly would walk across an eyeball. Even if she acknowledged his existence, there was no way she was making him dinner that evening. Cortez set his backpack down on the couch and began cleaning up after her, hoping she'd appreciate what he'd done when she returned from the gloom. He discovered that the oven was still on, and when he looked inside he found a blackened pizza. He took it out and the oven door shut with a loud slam.

"Did you see I made you dinner?" his mother called out from the other room, her voice carrying over the sea of her sadness.

"I did. Thank you," Cortez said, before tossing the burnt pizza in the trash. There was no time to worry about having lost his job earlier that day, of being accused of selling drugs. It was his mother's time of need, and he was called into the same supportive role he'd filled since the first time it had happened mere days after she'd given birth to him. As a days-old newborn, he had figured out how to feed himself, go to the bathroom, and fall asleep alone. The energy it took had left his brain without the foundation it needed to thrive, resulting in his stunted mental abilities after a stellar first few days of life that suggested he would end up as one of humankind's shining examples of what was possible. He had faith, as he had throughout every moment of his mother's previous depressive episodes, that as long as he provided value in her time of need, he would be in her good graces when things went back to normal.

Cortez spent the evening eating canned beans, stale tortillas, and scoops of peanut butter, not knowing if the tears making his food salty fell because of the telenovela still on the television or because of the perceived hopelessness of his situation. Money was an ever-present concern for his household, a specter that stood next to the grim reaper just outside their door, each waiting for their time to collect. He had just given her his prior month's earnings a week before. He wondered what would happen with the wages he'd earned in the week and one day he'd worked at the ice cream factory since then. As much as he knew they needed the money, he also didn't want to ever come into contact with his former boss again. Doing so was an invitation for an avalanche of shame to come down from above. Plus, he couldn't imagine seeing Simeon ever again. A small pit of anger tried to sprout deep in his stomach, but Cortez's desire to avoid confrontation burned stronger than his desire for revenge, incinerating the pit and its pale green shoot before it could take root.

He awoke on the couch during the middle of the night, cleared the coffee table, and turned off the television, then went to his room after setting his alarm. His mother was still asleep when he awoke the next morning at the work week's usual time. The hotel where she worked was aware of her periodic need to sequester herself, and the other maids worked together to make sure the rooms she was responsible for were kept clean. In turn, she never took vacations, making it a point to pick up the slack whenever one of her coworkers wanted to take time off. Her son's termination, evidenced by his changed routine, was the last thing she needed to discover while she was bedridden. Cortez made a peanut butter and jelly sandwich that smeared its contents on the inside of the plastic sandwich bag because he could never quite figure out how to keep the fillings confined to the bread. He drank a glass of water while packing the rest of his standard lunch, placing the too-ripe banana covered with brown spots at the top of the paper bag. The paper bag got placed into his backpack, and he took one last look at the apartment before he left, making sure it was clean. His mother deserved a spotless home if she did manage to pull herself out of bed.

Cortez didn't know where to go in his search for work. He started in the direction of the factory, then stopped on the corner before crossing the street a block from his apartment. The only other place he had gone during the previous months was the church. Craving the familiar, he walked towards the place of worship. He forgot it was used as a school during the week until he arrived, and he stood outside the familiar building with unfamiliar occupants unsure of his next move. He paced back and forth in front of the entrance with slow, unhurried steps while he thought. As the minutes passed, he wondered if there was a job for him at the school. He knew he couldn't be a teacher, since school had never been easy for him in the first place and he didn't want to pass along his struggles to the future generation. If there were any boxes that needed moving he'd be the man for the job, but a school wasn't a warehouse, and he dashed the idea of their need for those services as soon as the inspiration arrived. He knew someone had to clean the place, and while he weighed the chances of their need for a janitor, the front door opened and the priest strolled out with a box in his hands.

"Hello, sir," Cortez said when the priest descended the final step.

"Hello," the priest said. He didn't recognize Cortez, having only seen him on Sundays, and even then the young man was always in his mother's shadow. The priest's eyes were close-set, and a pair of thin wire-framed glasses rested too far down the bridge of his nose.

Cortez could tell the priest wasn't going to stop and talk to him, but he couldn't resist the compulsion to confess. "I wasn't able to convince anyone to come to service next week," he said, divulging yet another of his failures.

A flash of recognition passed over the priest's face. "Ah, yes. That's why the Lord has taught us patience," he said. His voice had changed, going from a disinterested citizen to a knowing elder, a switch more prominent than if he had changed into his robe with a snap. He looked down at the box in his hands and blushed. "I don't normally come here during the week," he added.

Cortez took the statement as a question. "Me neither," Cortez said. The priest waited for Cortez to continue. "I had to pick up something down the street for work." The grip of panic set into Cortez's stomach when he realized he had lied to the priest. He looked up at the clouds, certain lightning was about to strike him down.

"Something for work," the priest echoed, his voice trailing off. He looked down at the box again. "Me too, just grabbing some things I need," he said. He adjusted the weight of the box, his thin arms stretched to their full length to accommodate its size. The two of them stood still for a moment, each unwilling to share more information. "I'd better get going," the priest said.

"Me too," Cortez replied. "Lots to do!" He had adopted the getaway phrase years ago, when he first understood that people expected everyone else to be busy. It was his way of getting out of conversations while still being friendly. In his worst daydreams, the people he walked away from would continue judging him long after he left, going over his peculiarity in their minds. He would die without ever realizing that people have far more important things to do than scrutinize the actions of a somber, forgettable individual.

Before the priest could get too far away, Cortez yelled to his back. "See you Sunday!" The priest didn't even nod.

. . .

Cortez forgot his plan to inquire about working at the school, instead wanting to leave the space and the memories of the interaction behind. He started walking in the opposite direction of the priest and soon found himself staring at a vast park at the edge of his side of town. It appeared out of nowhere; one minute, he was between dilapidated housing, and the next he was staring at green that loomed over everything for blocks to the left and right. There were tree-lined paths hosting the occasional walker, the leaves above them swaying in the breeze. Through the trunks he could see a wide-open space where a group of mothers, each with a stroller, stood talking. The few clouds overhead posed no threat of rain and let intermittent rays of sunlight through their cover. He had never had any reason, or opportunity, to travel so far from home before, so the park had been unknown to him before that revelation. The trees called out to him, begging him to crash his boat among their shores. He listened to their song, stepping one foot into the street, and was pulled from his enchantment by the honk of a horn and the whoosh of air as a vehicle sped past.

He lost all track of time as he strolled through the trees. It could have been minutes, it could have been days; all Cortez knew was that he was among friends. The path he followed took him straight across the green space in the center of the city, and by the time he regained his senses he stood staring at a different city altogether, with the library that held his fate in the distance on his left. The skyscrapers shone regardless of whether the sun's beams tickled their faces, each car was new and well-washed, and every person walking the streets came from another world, dressed in everything from suits to exercise clothes, all more modern than anything he had seen outside of television. Torn between his desires to continue his timeless existence among the trees or dive headlong into a new world, Cortez chose to step forth and explore the second new landscape he had encountered that day. He made the same mistake he'd made on the other side of the park, stepping off the curb and into the street without checking for oncoming vehicles. A gleaming blue sports car, its engine soundless, stopped on a dime a fraction of second before colliding with him. This time, instead of honking in anger, the driver met Cortez's eyes and waved him on, encouraging him to continue. Cortez was about to retreat back into the safety of the trees when the other cars, following the blue car's lead, stopped and waited for him to cross. The Jews following Moses out of Egypt couldn't have been more surprised at the parting of the Red Sea.

The concrete underfoot in the new part of the city was cleaner than any Cortez had walked on before, with no caked gum, no stains, and no cracks. He looked back at the park and it shrank away. He turned into the city, following the urge to explore, but then turned again, walking parallel to the park so it would always be one block away from him. He passed a series of small shops that included a deli, a convenience store, and a dry cleaner's, all on the first floor of towering skyscrapers. He couldn't resist entering a coffee shop called Decant, a decision that led to the first and last time he fell in love.

He didn't see her at first; she was standing behind the counter making drink after drink for impatient customers. Instead, his eyes were drawn to the sparseness of the interior: the white walls lacking any decoration, and wide-open spaces between tables standing on concrete. He was enthralled by the level of absence the people in this part of the city could afford, because on his side of town everything was crammed into every available space in an attempt to validate the consumption of already scant resources. The customers demanded his inspection. Seen with his unfamiliar eyes, they were all unhurried, elegant, and methodical, as if the one place they should be on a workday's morning was the corner coffee shop. It wasn't until he had absorbed the swirling water that his eyes focused on the center of the vortex: Alara Chel. Her black hair was pulled back into the braid he would learn was her preference and covered in a branded hat, and the dimples on her cheeks flashed whenever her mouth moved. He let himself be pulled into the whirlpool of her presence, each footstep inspired by a higher power he assumed was the Lord himself. She smiled when she saw him.

"Line's over there," she said, tilting her head to the register on her right.

Cortez looked down at his feet. He was ashamed of being caught staring and knew he had been warned by the Bible about the class of thoughts now running through his head. He took a deep breath, then remembered his mother's admonition whenever she caught him retreating into himself. "Be polite." It had been her catchphrase as he was growing up.

"No, thank you," Cortez said.

Alara made no indication that Cortez's response was disjointed from her own statement. In fact, she used the opportunity to beckon him closer. She leaned over the counter. "It's your first time, isn't it?"

Cortez nodded, ashamed, thinking she was asking if it was the first time he had been struck by love's arrow.

"What do you want? It's on me."

The suggestion of a free drink caused Cortez's financial-sensitive brain to wrest control from his heart. "I don't know what you have," he said.

"Do you drink coffee?" she asked. Cortez knew he would never experience another sound as sweet as her voice if he lived to be a hundred and one. He shook his head no.

"I'll take care of you," she said, retreating back behind the espresso machine.

Cortez stepped back, ignorant of the annoyed looks from the rest of the customers. Among the regulars sitting down, the men in particular took issue with Cortez, all of them having tried speaking with her in the past, unable to get her to respond with anything beyond the demands of her job. Her one-word answers were aimed at ending conversations and hit their mark with legendary precision.

She handed out two drinks before catching Cortez's eye and handing him a frozen vanilla beverage with whipped cream. "Before you take this, you have to promise to come back," she said with a wink.

In that moment, Cortez would have promised to go to the far side of the world and retrieve the retreating moon. All she had to do was ask. He nodded, then tasted his drink. He had never before tasted anything as good as that drink, and never did again, because in each sip was the certainty that he had come in contact with one of God's angels. By the time the drink was finished, he was the world's newest sufferer of its oldest addiction: the high one received from obsessive love.

CHAPTER ELEVEN

Reports of *encomendero* brutality were commonplace in the Yucatán, but a marked increase in frequency during the planting season's beginning worried the friars. Nachi Cocom was still telling the friars, and the *encomenderos*, that no mass revolt was on the horizon, indicating that the Maya's position in the hierarchy was accepted, but Spanish fears weren't assuaged by his declarations. He was, after all, the man who'd led the last Maya holdout against Spanish rule, and what he said to the Spaniards could very well be different from the tune he sang among his people. The increased native complaints affected everyone, and their potential to shatter the tenuous existence of the Yucatán society cast a worrying spell on the region's members.

The harvest would suffer if the Maya chose to push back against the claimed brutality; there was a real chance of food shortage by the end of 1550. The *encomiendas* would have the least to worry about, since they held control of the food supply, but the local magistrates and religious authorities could see a future where their already meager allowances evaporated and their currency bought less than before. An even greater increase in the savagery of *encomendero* tactics, to spur production in an attempt to capitalize on the food shortfall, wasn't beyond the realm of possibility; this would leave the most savage, and therefore the most productive, *encomiendas* able to garner the most profits.

Friar Lorenzo de Bienvenida knew the system well from his years in the area and prophesied how the future might play out for the rest of the friars at the Izamal mission. He made frequent reference to Friar Luis de Villalpondo at the Merida monastery, the *Custos* of the Yucatán, and in doing so illuminated his increased correspondence with their sister location.

The reports started when a number of Mayan women, all from the same *encomienda*, showed up in Izamal for Sunday mass missing an ear. The holes in the sides of their heads still oozed thin red blood, leaving dried trails of serum to their collarbones. Friar Diego knew this was a favorite tactic of the Spanish overseers, and he shook with rage while he read from the Bible for the congregation. The women, to their credit, didn't act as if anything was different—they still stood tall when they walked, and their voices still smoothed the Mayan men's rough edges during the spoken portions of memorized prayers. They left mass without talking to any of the friars, who served as the mediators between the *encomenderos* and Maya.

The following week, three of the children's backs were whipped raw. They weren't the sons of local chiefs lucky enough to attend school; these were children of the native populace who were forced to accept the yoke of servitude. Thin slashes of exposed flesh covered their skin. They sat with locked jaws, without their backs touching any surface, bowing their heads at all appropriate times during mass. The Izamal monastery was called out to a local *encomienda* to give funeral rites to a child during the following week; every Franciscan had a terrible feeling it was one of the whipped boys. They were right. Friar Lorenzo himself went out to perform the funeral. When he came back, he told his brothers the *encomenderos* were getting out of control.

"They are doing whatever they can to break the native will," he said. His head grew heavy with sadness, and for the entire next day he struggled to take a full breath.

He was asked if he saw any native mistreatment while he was there.

"No, he was smart enough to keep them out of my sight," Friar Lorenzo replied.

The number of funerals of murdered children requiring oversight grew each week until the friars had to miss the burials because the corpse's decay demanded more immediate disposal. Numerous times they arrived to pray over a burial site and discovered more than one body needed God's word.

Branded native men was a common sight among the populace; the chieftains and their families were spared because of the potential for mass uprising if the ruling class wasn't kept satisfied. The most popular spot *encomenderos* chose to mark their property was the upper arm. Some used initials, others geometric shapes—whatever worked, as long as the metal could be molded into the correct form. The arrival of planting season saw many updated brands, fresh burns left exposed to the surrounding air. Friar Diego had come to learn the marks and knew which *encomienda* each Mayan man belonged to, so when he saw men with the same marks in the same position, he asked Friar Lorenzo why they were being branded again.

"The *encomenderos* don't want them to forget who they belong to," Friar Lorenzo said. Ix Cuatchel was listening to their conversation under the lamplight outside the sanctuary. When Friar Diego looked at her, she scurried away into the night.

Some of the most religious native men, notable because of their consistent attendance, started missing Sunday mass. Their absence was noticed by the friars, who remarked among themselves about the missing men like schoolteachers discussing the progress of shared students.

"Under normal circumstances," Friar Lorenzo said, "I'd assume they were busy with planting. But now I'm not so sure they're even alive."

They were alive, and they did return. The friars found out part of Friar Lorenzo's suspicions had been correct, the part concerning planting, but the men came back to the Izamal monastery with fresh marks on their bodies: strips of raw flesh on their wrists and ankles.

"They chained us up and made us work. Mass is our reward for the last few weeks," the men said.

They prayed with extra fervor that day, staying long after the final benediction. Each man received a personal blessing, complete with a heaping dose of holy water, before they left to return to their imprisonment.

"THE *ENCOMENDEROS* MUST BE COMMUNICATING with each other," Friar Diego told the rest of the Franciscans in the living quarters that night. "Those men came from different *encomiendas*."

The friars all nodded their heads.

"We have to do something," Friar Diego said to the group, hoping Friar Lorenzo would heed the call. "They need our protection."

"Agreed," Friar Lorenzo said, a plan formulating in his head. "I'm too old for these battles. And my job is here, with the monastery. I've considered sending you, but since you're the best at speaking the Mayan language I've selfishly kept you here to teach the schoolchildren, not wanting anyone else to take the task."

It was the first time Friar Lorenzo had mentioned how much Friar Diego's language skills had improved since coming to Izamal.

"But maybe you've gotten a grasp on the language because you teach the children . . ." Friar Lorenzo said, his words trailing off as he lost himself in thought. "That's beside the point. Why don't you go to the *encomiendas* tomorrow and see if you can intercede on behalf of the natives?"

Friar Diego accepted his assignment with a solemn nod, despite his own internal glee at the thought of being seen by the Maya confronting one of the *encomenderos*. He knew the kind of goodwill the action would create and trusted their communication networks to send word to the entire surrounding area, perhaps the entire province. He hoped even Ahkinmai would hear, the man he hadn't seen in person since before he was assigned to Izamal but who visited him in the occasional dream as a man-sized bird.

The next day, with a Bible, a hammock, and two flasks of water, Friar Diego set out to where he believed the worst offenses were occurring: the house of none other than *Adelantado* Francisco Hernandez. He believed that if he spoke up against the leader of the colonists, showing Franciscan strength and imposing the will of God in his protection of the natives, the rest of the *encomenderos* would follow suit and reform their brutal ways. The *Adelantado* lived in an opulent mansion outside of Mani, which was a two-day walk to the south of Izamal.

He walked as long as he could on his first day of traveling, ignoring small *encomiendas* and their presumed brutal treatment of the Maya. His thoughts turned to the night's shelter when the setting sun started casting shadows that covered his path through the jungle. Before the world was blanketed in darkness, he encountered a fledgling *encomienda*—evidenced by its meager main house and lack of secondary facilities—where he could spend the night. The man in charge of the operation was a short, broad-faced man with a thick mustache and stubbled beard. His wife and three young children, a boy and two girls, were in the main house when the friar approached.

In general, *encomendero* attitudes towards the friars were tepid. While they detested the Franciscans' meddling in their affairs with the Maya, they also respected the holy men after being raised on a steady diet of Catholicism from a young age in Spain. The *encomendero* Friar Diego approached about hanging his hammock in a corner of the man's property was honored the priest would be blessing his home with his presence for the night. He introduced himself as Don Antonio, his wife was Doña Maria, and the children's names were Diego, Isabel, and Francisca.

"We are at your service," the wife said. These five words were all she spoke to Friar Diego, and she made sure the priest didn't see her or her children again for the duration of his stay, out of respect.

Despite Friar Diego's extreme exhaustion, he listened to the *encomendero* as the two men sat in front of the house fire after dinner drinking wine. The *encomendero* had a sense of the local issues the other colonists were having with the natives, and he went to great lengths to assure Friar Diego knew the respect with which he treated his own Maya population.

"If you want, I can call them in to tell you themselves," he said.

Friar Diego looked into the ink-black darkness outside, wondering who would be the one to gather the native witnesses. He told the man it wouldn't be necessary. "I believe you," he said.

"Then I have a request," Don Antonio said as if he had stored the words in his heart all evening.

Friar Diego released a prolonged exhale through his nose and stared at the man with patient eyes. "I'm at your service," he said.

"Can you pray for the health of my wife and children?"

Friar Diego was struck by the man's simplicity. He thought the *encomendero* would ask for a blessing of his house and operation, or to a prosperous relationship with the natives. He was happy to oblige the man's request. Together, they bowed their heads and prayed to the long lives of everyone in the house, the patriarch included, and Don Antonio had tears in his eyes after the prayer.

The two men sat in a momentary silence before Don Antonio told the friar he was going to bed, urging Friar Diego to do the same after his long day of travel. Friar Diego didn't need further insistence; he collapsed into his hammock and didn't move a muscle until the sun's rays tickled his face the next morning.

Don Antonio was the sole member of his family awake in the home when Friar Diego reported he was leaving. He offered to feed the friar, who declined, saying he had a long day ahead of him and no time for breakfast. The two men shared a quick morning prayer before the friar set off.

ADELANTADO FRANCISCO'S *encomienda* was another seven hours' walk away. Friar Diego thought about the prophecy he was determined to fulfill, bringing about the Church's third and final age. The progress he had made with the natives outside Izamal was promising, but an impatient insistence on bringing about the final destiny and the anticipation of its arrival warmed his blood. The Spanish Council of the Indies banned severe treatment of the natives to bring about their conversion, fearing these actions would be counterproductive. Friar Diego had had his own doubts about the validity of this sentiment before he came to the New World, but after seeing the readiness with which the Maya took up Christianity, he'd determined their childlike innocence in the nuances of faith needed gentle guidance, not a firm hand. Each step brought him closer to the belief that the subversion of the native priests would bring about the mass conversion of the Maya population. He thought about Ahkinmai, how the feathered man appeared whenever and wherever he wanted, even in the friar's dreams, and wondered how he would convince the natives to turn against him.

Friar Diego didn't realize he was on the *Adelantado*'s property until he was surrounded by rows of organized crops. He turned around when he recognized the difference in the surrounding landscape, taking one last look at the trees in the distance before continuing to the main house.

The mansion stood in a clearing on a small, raised plot of earth that overlooked the *encomienda*'s vast lands. Its front door was surrounded by decorative white stone masonry that went straight to the pointed roof, standing in stark contrast to the building's red walls. The six windows, three on each side, were also decorated in the same way. The surrounding buildings were built from the same red stone material but without the decorative flourishes. Dark streaks ran down the red stone walls of every building from where water trickled down—the houses were ready to bleed again with the arrival of the rainy season.

Both natives and Spaniards bustled around the property. Each time someone noticed the friar they lowered their eyes and rushed away. An animalistic roar came from beyond the house. Friar Diego investigated, turning the corner right as a massive Spaniard struck a native man in the face with a club.

"You're their chief!" the club-wielding man screamed. "Make them work!"

Friar Diego had never seen *Adelantado* Francisco before,

but from the rumors surrounding his treatment of the natives he had no doubt the man swinging the club was the head of the province. His belt was the same leather used to saddle horses, and numerous rings matching his assortment of necklaces glinted in the sunlight.

The Mayan man, dazed and with blood streaming from his head, looked around in desperation as he crawled away from the angry man. His fellow Maya all turned away, not wanting to invoke the Spaniard's wrath. The chief caught the eyes of the one man who dared witness the scene without blinking: the thin friar, in his brown habit, near the edge of the house.

Adelantado Francisco saw the friar at the same moment as the native. He laughed as the Mayan chief half crawled, half ran towards the priest, stumbling into his arms for protection. The native man had defecated from terror sometime during his flight. The chief was covered in dark red blood from head to waist, sulfuric from fear, and dark brown excrement from waist to foot, reeking of dismay. Friar Diego turned around with the man in his arms and ran away.

The *Adelantado* caught up to them before they got past the side of the house. He ripped the native man from Friar Diego's arms by the hair in front of several Mayan laborers and a Spaniard who'd stopped to see the result of the Franciscan's intervention.

"You're not going anywhere," *Adelantado* Francisco said before bringing the club down with all his strength on the man's exposed shin. A sickening crack of bone rang through the air right before the chief screamed.

Friar Diego stood aghast as the *Adelantado* beckoned the lone watching Spaniard to his side and handed him the club, telling him to wipe it off and place it with the others. The Mayan man's eyes searched for the friar's, imploring him to do something with his gaze. The chief then pointed with his little remaining strength into a space between two buildings, now visible from where they stood on the side of the house. A naked native woman, her body limp, was tied to a pole. Blood from hundreds of lashes covered her from her back down to her heels, where it seeped into the thirsty ground.

Adelantado Francisco wiped his sweaty brow with the back of his forearm before running his fingers through his greasy straight hair. "She's dead," he said, as if it were a joke.

"No one deserves that," Friar Diego said, flexing his jaw.

"She didn't listen to me. I used her to teach the rest of them a lesson," he said.

Friar Diego had never experienced such a level of rage in his twenty-six years on the planet. It seeped into his bones, infected his teeth, and surged through the hairs on his head. The anger was infused with a deep disgust at this wanton attitude towards human life, and regret for the ways in which *Adelantado* Francisco was undermining the Franciscans' molding of positive native attitudes towards the new arrivals from the Old World in the Yucatán. He turned and left without another word to the cruel man.

INSTEAD OF GOING to another *encomienda* or walking back to Izamal and reporting to Friar Lorenzo, he decided to report his observations to the man in charge of the entire province: Friar Luis. The walk was supposed to take a day and a half, including a stay overnight somewhere along the path, but Friar Diego made the entire trip without stopping, arriving in Merida before noon the following day. His hunger and thirst were the furthest things from his mind, his habit was torn and filthy, and his sandals had torn sometime during the night.

He strode onto the monastery's property and demanded an audience with Friar Luis. The old man came from the living quarters, led by the bald friar who'd come with Friar Diego to the New World, and as soon as Friar Luis saw the crazed look in the young friar's eyes he led the visitor straight into the sanctuary. Friar Luis told Friar Diego to sit down and prayed before asking him the reason for his unannounced visit.

Friar Diego told Friar Luis how Friar Lorenzo had told him to investigate claims of brutality among the *encomenderos*, and how he'd gone to confront the man in charge of them all: *Adelantado* Francisco. He then relayed all he'd seen on the Mani mansion's property without omitting a single detail.

"We need to help them. They're like children—they don't know any better!"

"Their innocence is beyond question," a pensive Friar Luis said.

"We need to tell the Spanish crown!"

"And then what? Montejo was removed for the same reason. It's always more of the same."

"Let Spain decide! Right now the *encomenderos* receive no punishment whatsoever." The release of this message, and the reality it described, forced Friar Diego to acknowledge his body's exhaustion.

"It costs more to kill a cow or horse in Yucatán than to kill a native," Friar Luis observed. He led Friar Diego to the living quarters, forced him to clean up while the young friar described every detail once more, then made him lie down on one of the spare beds. Friar Diego fell into a deep sleep that lasted until the following day. When he woke up, he found Friar Luis walking back and forth in a small study, his hands behind his back and looking at the ceiling while speaking his thoughts out loud. Another friar was huddled over a desk, transcribing.

"I'm almost finished," the elder friar said.

Friar Diego sat down and waited for the *Custos* to finish dictating the letter. He heard the elder friar recount what Friar

Diego had seen with surprising precision. A short time later, the old man announced he was done. The scribe set down his pen and left. Friar Luis took the seat and leaned back in the chair.

"Take a look," Friar Luis said.

The letter was a detailed account of the transgressions of ten *encomenderos.* Each example included the exact *encomienda*, along with listing the villages and number of native inhabitants each establishment possessed.

Friar Luis had been hearing reports of various examples of brutality, and kept each one filed away in his memory, but the actions of the *Adelantado* were the last straw. Friar Diego read about various hangings and killings of the Maya in everyday life, chilling because of the way brutality had seeped into their Yucatán existence. Friar Luis outlined, for the Crown, how local administrators released their neighbors without punishment for these actions, with the expectation of receiving the same treatment in the future when their roles were reversed. His final example before relaying the *Adelantado*'s damning offense was the tale of a native man who was killed in front of a tax collector because he didn't provide transportation for cargo fast enough. Of course, the man's penalty was nominal: a small quantity of beads for the dead man's wife and family.

"We'll send it to Spain right away and see what they'll do," Friar Luis said when Friar Diego had finished reading.

Both men crossed themselves.

CHAPTER TWELVE

The tides of the coffee shop ebbed and flowed throughout the day amidst the all-encompassing smell of roasted, ground, and brewed coffee. At some points, when the tide was out, there was a mere trickle of customers, and the baristas would resume paused conversations. This ability, speaking on a different timescale than the one displayed by clocks, was the first thing new hires learned, and was the reason Alara never thought twice when Cortez responded with an odd statement after his momentary retreat into himself. When the tide was in, wave after wave of customers came crashing down, overflowing the space and spilling out onto the streets. The employees stood tall against the onslaught, immovable pillars until the end of their shift.

Cortez couldn't find the strength to leave Alara's orbit even after he finished his drink. He had no urge to escape from the public and head back to his part of the city, even as the day dragged on and the other customers questioned how someone could sit so long without doing any work. He snuck glances at Alara, taking great care not to stare, though the one thing he wanted was to inspect every aspect of her face free from social expectations to look away. As the sun began to set, Cortez realized he hadn't eaten. He took his bagged lunch from his backpack and ate in small, distracted bites. The banana, which he saved for last, had been compressed at some point in the day, leaving a third of it soft and mushy. During meals at the picnic table, he would toss the soft parts of the banana on the ground and watch the birds fly down from the overhead wires to inspect the rejected food. On the day he met Alara Chel, each bite of the fruit was cooked until soft by the heat coursing through his veins, so he didn't notice when part of it was softer than the rest. The burning questions in his heart threatened to turn his shirt into ashes. He wanted to know what foods she liked to eat, where she'd grown up, how many times a week she went out to eat. The most trivial details were, to him, the most pressing, because they were the ones nobody could find out without being allowed into her gravitational pull.

There were still a few hours left in the day when Alara said goodbye to her coworkers, took off her apron, and left her station behind. She emerged from behind the counter with parts of her apron visible over the top edge of her shoulder bag. The bag hung loose from her shoulders, a relaxed fabric that reminded Cortez of the hammock in the picture his mother kept on display of her homeland, Mexico. Alara wore all black: a tight-fitting polo and pants that highlighted the curves running from her hips to her thighs. Cortez, along with every other male in the space, noticed her robust femininity, though Cortez was the only one to drop his gaze before crossing the chasm into lust. Looking down at his shoes served a double purpose, because although he hadn't been able to think of anything but Alara since the moment he saw her, he also didn't want her to pay attention to him when there wasn't a counter protecting them from each other, and looking at his shoes ensured he wouldn't have to reciprocate her potential acknowledgment.

Alara knew Cortez had stayed in the coffee shop all day. She'd thought he was lost when she first saw him. They were both Hispanic and around the same age—facts that inspired a particular kinship with him. Her decision to give him a free drink had fulfilled the urge to help him find his way. The employees gave away free drinks all the time, so she didn't think twice about it. She thought it odd that the young man had combed his hair with obvious precision without having the clothes to match. In her experience, men who cared that much about their hair wore suits, drove expensive cars, and had an outsized view of their importance in the world. It was one of the perks of her job that she could ignore men like that when they tried to learn more about her; it was her purpose to put them in their place. She had kept tabs on Cortez out of the corner of her eye and knew he hadn't been working while in her dominion, instead sitting and watching the rest of the world around him as if he was born yesterday.

She held her head high while she walked out of Decant. An older lady sitting by the door, a regular who came in for a latte each afternoon before caring for her grandkids, commanded her attention by looking at her face as she approached. "Heading home?" she said.

Alara looked down at the lady and smiled. "All done for the day."

"Enjoy the sunshine."

"I plan on it."

It was the sort of clipped conversation Alara preferred. There was no divulging of information, no questioning of motives. She was the master of trite, memorized statements that were simple acknowledgments of existing in a shared space.

Behind her, Cortez packed his bag. He waited until she left

the coffee shop before standing up, telling himself he should be heading back to his side of the city. "Excuse me," he asked the young man still seated next to where he'd spent the bulk of his day. "What time is it?"

After the man glanced at his watch, he told Cortez it was minutes after four. Cortez didn't thank him for the information and left. Deciding he had seen enough of the city, he walked towards the park instead of going back the way he came. The trees in the distance promised both shade and security from the judging eyes of the people he passed. At the end of the block, he looked left and right for oncoming cars before he crossed the street and turned right. Ahead of him, on the park's edge, Alara was visible for an instant before she turned inside and was lost among the trees. Cortez's heart leapt into his throat as hurried after her. He had heard about the miracles Jesus performed but never in his life thought he would be on the receiving end of such a gift. Destiny was once more smiling down on him by placing her in his path. Mindful of appearances, he tried his best to walk at a relaxed pace when every fiber of his being urged him to run to where he last saw her. When he arrived at the spot where he saw her enter the park, he followed her into the shadows.

Alara frequented the park on the days she got out of work early enough to enjoy the sunshine. On days it was raining, she would sit in the library instead, reading until there was just enough light left in the day to avoid walking home in the shadows. She'd learned long ago not to go into the park during the night. The first and last time she stayed after the sun had gone down, she had emerged from the park and was waiting to cross the street when a car rolled to a stop and the male driver asked her how much for the night. He grew angry when she ignored him, putting on his hazards and stepping out of the vehicle. When she informed him she had no idea what he was talking about, the man asked her what she was doing at the edge of the park at night if not looking to be purchased by the hour. She ran until she got home and, collapsing through her front door, promised herself never to get caught in that situation again. The danger of the encounter didn't affect her as much as the man's belief that she was available for a price. Though it didn't last for more than a minute, and the potential customer now knew better, his momentary belief had wounded her delicate pride.

She walked to her favorite spot—a bench with its back to the trees that overlooked an open lawn—sat down, and began to read. Books had been her obsession for as long as she could remember. When she'd first learned to read, it was a way of signaling her independence. Now that she was older, it was her escape from the demands of the modern world. Her financial troubles were left behind, the questions about her purpose in life put on hold, and her insatiable curiosity about the experience of others were all remedied by ink on paper. She was reading *Love in the Time of Cholera.* Before work, she had read about Fermina Daza's rejection of Florentino Ariza, and it had haunted her mind while her body continued the familiar motions of her job. It was the saddest thing she had ever read and had created an atmosphere inside her soul where any act of witnessed injustice stirred tears she hid with stubbornness. If she had been one of the trees behind her, her leaves would have wilted, indifferent to the seasons of the year, instead under the spell of the seasons of her heart. On that park bench, alone with her book, Alara Chel existed in perpetual autumn.

Cortez hopped off the paved path when he spotted her in the distance. Between leaving the road and finding her he had walked without thinking, allowing his heart to lead his feet. He'd walked with the certainty he would find her, and he had taken a few turns that made no sense to his brain. His belief in destiny was justified when he found his nymph on a bench where the trees met an open lawn. He watched her from behind a tree. Walkers and joggers passed by without her lifting her eyes from the page. Children played in the open space ahead of her and she was deaf to their shouts. Cortez walked deeper into the woods, away from the path, careful not to step on any twigs, a sound that might betray his position. In truth, he could have yelled and Alara wouldn't have noticed. As he stood bewitched by the slow rise and fall of her shoulders with each breath she took, a group of young men came to the open area in front of her and began playing soccer. The leanest and most muscular of the group took off their shirts with glances in her direction without any reaction from her. While she read, she shared with Cortez an absolute focus on the task at hand—they were both lost to the rest of the world around them.

Without consulting her watch or phone, Alara closed the book, put it into her backpack, and stood up. She looked at the sky, confirming her decision to leave by the position of the sun. The soccer ball rolled to a stop as every player watched her walk away. There were other, closer spaces where they could play, but none held so beautiful a prize. They came for her and she had no idea they existed. It was a curse many men who came across Alara Chel fell victim to, but none bothered to study her the way Cortez did. He was watching for ways he could fill a role in her life, an access point that would provide a way to prove his worth. His first role, however, was to make sure his heart didn't combust before he got the chance.

Cortez was torn when Alara walked back towards her side of the city. Questions about her emerged in his soul. He wondered what she was reading, if she always read in the park, and what type of men she liked if not the athletes on display. More pressing, he wanted to know where she was going. It was also past the time he should be home. His mother would be waiting for him if she had managed to pull herself from her depressive episode, though her low points never lasted for just one day. Never having been consumed by love before, and therefore never learning how to navigate the situation, he gave into his curiosity and followed Alara back to her side of the city. In his mind, destiny had put her in his path, and it was his role to follow through. Her beauty did make him wonder about his true intentions, and in an effort to assuage his guilty conscience he convinced himself he would try to convince her to come to church.

Yes, his role was to save her soul. The best way to do so was to learn more about her, including where she lived, and to protect her, making sure she lived long enough to hear the word of God next to him on Sundays.

There was a half-block minimum between them at all times. He had never followed someone before but had seen enough movies for a rough idea of how it should be done. Ducking into entrances, stopping to window shop while keeping the target in the corner of his eye. It wasn't difficult to follow her because she never thought she was worth following, so she took the simplest path home. Alara's path went straight into a part of the city Cortez had never seen before, past buildings that reached for the sky with unnatural determination. Cortez's anxiety increased at the same rate as his distance from the park, and by the time Alara left the skyscrapers behind and turned into a residential area with tree-lined roads, Cortez had taken a white pill to combat the certainty he had gone too far from home, a sailor on concrete seas who had lost sight of land for the first time.

The streetlights flickered on as the lack of light from the setting sun triggered their sensors. Cortez gave himself two more blocks before he would turn around. He was questioning whether he remembered the way back. He stayed farther away from her now, more than a block behind, taking greater care to stay hidden now that there were fewer options for him to utilize for cover on his stealthy mission. It was an unnecessary precaution; she never looked behind her. Cortez was about to turn around, planning on returning to Decant the next day to see her again, when she turned off the road, too soon to be another intersection. Cortez quickened his pace, closed the distance, then slowed before coming to where Alara had turned. She had crossed a concrete courtyard with a series of weed-filled planters. More weeds were poking up through the cracks between concrete slabs. Cortez was comforted by the overgrowth. Its presence meant that the people living on this side of the city still had to deal with life seeping through the cracks of their pristine exteriors. The buildings around the courtyard were made of brick, and all of them stood three stories high. Movement flashed from across the space. It was Alara, climbing the exposed stairs that ran between units. Cortez exhaled, grateful he hadn't stormed into the space in pursuit. If he had, she would be staring down at him right then, and there was no way to explain why the man who had received a free drink earlier in the day was standing outside her home.

Cortez saw her turn into a unit on her left on the third floor. Some of the units had windows facing the courtyard, but the one she entered was on a corner between the far building and the one on his right. There would be no window where she could see him approach, but that also meant there was no window where he could see what she was like alone. Even if he crossed the courtyard and took the steps she had just climbed—which he had no intention of doing—there was nothing for him there but a door. He kept walking past the courtyard and turned, walking along the back side of the building on the courtyard's right. He could see inside the units on the ground floor through vertical blinds. Some were occupied by families, some by lone individuals, but each space gave off the particular blue light indicative of turned-on televisions. Cortez saw some shows he recognized, and one person was watching the news. He stopped beneath where he believed Alara's unit was located. There was a dull yellow light, instead of the typical blue, on in one of the third-floor units. The rest on that level were dark or had the blinds shut. Cortez stood beneath the tree that stood outside the lit window and took stock of its ability to support his weight. Deciding it could support him, he began to climb.

Cortez had never been with a woman. He was old enough to understand that the body had its own needs, but without ever experiencing them himself, he had never learned to think about how his own actions might be interpreted as driven by sexual desire. He climbed with an innocence born out of his sheltered existence, out of mere curiosity, because he did in fact just want to see how Alara lived when she was alone. He got high enough to see the ceiling above the kitchen when the loud clearing of a throat drew his attention from below.

"And just what do you think you're doing, young man?" a middle-aged woman with short hair, taking her dog for a walk, said to him with one hand on her hip. The dog continued walking, following its nose, and turned around when it reached the end of the leash, staring at its human for the rude interruption.

Cortez had been yelled at before by his mother, and various other women in school or church when he was a child, but each one had been either Hispanic or Black and never used the language he associated with old sitcom reruns. He almost laughed at the perfect replica the woman was able to produce, and he was certain that if he opened his mouth the chuckle would escape his lips. Instead, all he did was stare.

"Well?"

Cortez began climbing down. When he got back to ground

level, he discovered the woman came up to his armpit. He ran away before she could utter another word and didn't stop until he had crossed the park once more and climbed the seven flights of steps to his own home.

From inside her dark apartment, Alara witnessed a young man with a backpack running away from a lady walking her dog. She had just gotten out of the bathroom and was at the window to close the blinds—which she always did before turning on the light—when the rapid movement down on the street in front of her neighbor's unit drew her attention. She never imagined that the man fleeing was there because of her. A call to the police would have been Alara's next step if the lady, whom Alara had assumed had been robbed, hadn't continued walking while shaking her head with disappointment. Alara closed the blinds, warmed up leftovers from the day before, and dove headfirst into the pages of her book once more.

CHAPTER THIRTEEN

Word of Friar Diego de Landa's visit to *Adelantado* Francisco Hernandez's *encomienda* traveled to Izamal and was waiting for him when he arrived, sitting cross-legged in the dirt. The Maya he passed on his way into the monastery caught his glance with knowing eyes before looking away in deference. Ix Cuatchel stared at him from the infirmary as Friar Diego walked to the living quarters before dashing off to the sanctuary. The returning friar put his few belongings down and sat down on the bed before taking his shoes off and rubbing his aching feet.

He had stayed in Merida for two nights before making the trip back to his assigned location. The friars under Friar Luis de Villalpondo made sure their brother was fed, watered, and rested before he set out. Despite their best efforts, the accumulated days of travel took their toll on his body; being home was a welcome relief. His bed called to him, but he ignored its pleas, knowing work never stopped, that students still needed instruction. Their lessons were his continued practice of their language, the mastery of which was even more imperative now that Friar Diego had witnessed the treatment of the Mayan people firsthand. His sense of paternal love for the natives had deepened after witnessing the *Adelantado*'s disregard for human life. His sense of duty went beyond saving their souls; their bodies were on the line. He wouldn't have the chance to add any natives to the ranks of Christianity if the *encomenderos* killed the natives before they converted.

Friar Diego was retying his sandals when Friar Lorenzo de Bienvenida walked in. The older man took slow, deliberate steps, not because he couldn't walk faster, but because he was convinced of the need to save his strength for the years ahead. He sat down on a bed and faced Friar Diego.

"I didn't think you'd go clear to Mani when I told you to visit local *encomiendas*," Friar Lorenzo said with a hint of reproach.

"I know. But I thought that if I could confront the *Adelantado,* the rest of the *encomenderos* would understand our oversight extends over all."

Friar Lorenzo nodded. "Well-thought-out reasoning," he said. "You're learning the importance of politics in the region. It's a fight I've been waging since I arrived almost ten years ago."

Friar Diego said he was a slow learner.

"We both know that isn't true," Friar Lorenzo said. "Did you visit any other *encomiendas* on your way back? According to what we heard, you were in Mani days ago."

"I went to Merida and spoke with Friar Luis."

"To report on *Adelantado* Francisco?"

Friar Diego nodded.

"And what did he say?"

"He sent a letter to Spain, asking for them to intervene on behalf of the natives."

Friar Lorenzo looked up at the ceiling's palm leaves. "The *encomenderos* aren't going to appreciate that," he mused.

"They'll have to learn," Friar Diego said with a certainty the elder friar found unsettling. The young man would move heaven and hell for the natives, even at the risk of his own safety.

"We can't have them retaliate against us," Friar Lorenzo said, again looking at the young friar.

"Go against the Church? No Spaniard would dare."

"You're right . . . as long as they consider themselves Spanish."

Both men then discussed the potential of the *encomenderos* breaking away from Spain. Friar Diego announced they wouldn't because they still relied on the Crown for their rights to the Yucatán land.

"They have no choice but to accept whatever Spain requires," Friar Diego said.

Friar Lorenzo curled his lips under and squeezed them together. "You're right," he said. "But I'm still worried about how they'll respond."

"Let's pray God shows us the path," Friar Diego said. He folded his hands and bowed his head.

Friar Lorenzo joined him, proud his underling had suggested guidance from above before he arrived at his own conclusion.

Friar Diego stood up and announced he was going to the school.

"Rest today," Friar Lorenzo replied. "Twenty-three new students arrived when you were gone. Let them learn our customs from the others before you get involved with the memorizations of the prayers."

Friar Diego asked where he was needed.

"I know someone who's been waiting for you to come back," Friar Lorenzo said. His eyes darted to the left and his head tilted backwards, calling Friar Diego's attention to the front door.

A pair of eyes, too close to the ground to belong to any full-grown man, pulled back from the opening.

"Ix," Friar Diego whispered with a smile.

Friar Lorenzo nodded. "Go," he said.

Ix was pretending to fill the oil lamp hanging outside the structure's entrance. Friar Diego asked her what had been going on in the infirmary.

"It's been slow," she said, focused on not spilling a single drop of lamp oil.

"That's good," Friar Diego said. "It means people are healthy."

Friar Lorenzo walked between them on his way out. Ix watched him walk away before exploding in a torrent of words.

"Is it true you stood up to the *Adelantado*? Were you scared? The others say you're here to protect us!"

Friar Diego ignored her first two questions. "Who says I'm here to protect you?" Pride's warmth seeped into every corner of his body, from his fingertips to his toes, resulting in small beads of sweat forming on his forehead, which he blotted with his habit's sleeve.

"The new students. Their fathers sent them when they found out about your visit to the *Adelantado*," Ix said. A sudden awareness of her enthusiasm, which stood in contrast to the measured consistency of the monastery's solemn atmosphere, forced her back into herself and she grew quiet once more.

Friar Diego was delighted his actions had led to another large swath of natives joining the Franciscans. He wondered if Friar Lorenzo knew about the reason for the swelling of the school ranks and, if he did, why the Guardian of Izamal didn't mention the fact during their conversation.

"He's afraid of my pride," Friar Diego whispered in a flash of understanding. He made no effort to tamp down the feeling. "Did you hear anything else?" he said, addressing Ix.

Ix opened her mouth but something pulled her back.

"What is it?" Friar Diego urged.

"I heard the students say they have to tell their companions in their village when you return. Nachi wants to speak with you."

NACHI COCOM ARRIVED the next day. He had set off from his home in Sotuta when he received word of Friar Diego's visit to the *Adelantado* and was staying among the small village of retainers and support the chiefs had sent along with their sons when Friar Diego arrived back at Izamal. The friars never discovered that Nachi's insistence was the reason the new students had arrived in the first place: on his trip from Sotuta to Izamal, he had gathered the children and deposited them at Izamal like a shepherd herding sheep to new lands.

Friar Diego was walking to the school after morning prayers when he saw Nachi standing on the edge of the monastery's land. He looked at the two friars who were helping teach the basics of Spanish behaviors; they had seen Nachi as well and told Friar Diego with a nod they would take care of the lessons until he returned.

Nachi smiled at Friar Diego and extended a hand when he approached. Friar Diego shook his hand without missing Nachi's ease of using Spanish customs.

"Glad to see you're unharmed," Nachi said in Spanish.

"Tired, but in one piece," Friar Diego replied in the Mayan language.

"Can you still walk some more?" Nachi said, reverting to his mother tongue.

"Of course," Friar Diego replied.

Their walk that day was the first in a series of meetings that occurred over the course of months. Nachi led Friar Diego into the students' temporary village, talking about his people's organization and culture. The students all lived in a sprawling, multifamily house, split in the middle with a wall down the length of the structure; the front half was exposed, without walls, and the back half was sectioned off. The boys all slept in the open area, and their companions occupied the space in the back, along with the belongings brought from their home villages. Nachi explained every facet of their way of life that stood in obvious contrast to the Spanish method of living. The information wasn't shared in an apologetic way; he wasn't asking for patience or even explaining why the older Maya had trouble accepting the Old World's ways. Rather, it was as if Nachi had found someone he trusted enough to show the inner workings of their culture.

Once Friar Diego realized Nachi was willing to teach him about the people he'd vowed to save, he began asking all manner of questions about their family structure, their religion, and their daily lives. He discovered the importance of maize and all the manners in which they prepared the crop, both witnessing the production and tasting the results. The women softened the maize by soaking it in lime and water overnight. In one method, they ground the maize on stones the next morning until it was a rough, course flour, then rolled it into balls that could be stored for months without spoiling. Friar Diego learned maize stored in this way acquired an added sour taste. Another preparation used fine-ground maize; they thickened it over a fire and drank it hot in the morning.

The *milpas* where the Maya grew corn were worked by all within a community. They gathered in groups of twenty and planted seeds in one *milpa* at a time until all were completed. They sowed in different places, so that if one of the harvests was short, the others could make up the difference. Whenever nutrients of one area's soil had been depleted, their entire community moved to a new central location, always within easy reach of a *cenote* from which they could draw water.

Friar Diego grew to understand the wildlife in the Yucatán from the native's perspective. He learned about the salt, fish, and manatees that came from the coastal waters, the tapirs and large cats present in the peninsula's interior, and the various birds and their calls. Nachi pointed out numerous trees, flowers, and fruits, providing the friar with more information about their utility than any previous Spaniard had ever known.

The Maya prided themselves on their skill in pottery and woodworking. They made idols of clay and wood while fasting and following many ancient rites; these were traded throughout the Yucatán. In addition to these sacred objects, traders exchanged salt, cloths, and cacao. Certain red shells were used as currency, along with particular, beautiful stones Friar Diego thought looked like other jewelry the Mayan women wore—Nachi insisted the traders could tell the difference.

Nachi explained the importance of the tattoos on himself and others. The more tattoos one had, the more valiant and brave he was, because the process was painful and time-consuming. Those without tattoos were ridiculed. Nachi's tattoos told the stories of the various battles he'd fought. His symbols were the first glyphs Friar Diego learned to read, and he discovered a record of the dates Nachi had fought against the Spanish. This knowledge opened up an entire world for Friar Diego.

The Maya had two ways of keeping time. One way used twenty glyphs and a count from one to thirteen that resulted in a two-hundred-and-sixty-day "year." The second way measured a year with eighteen months, each twenty days long. Friar Diego never grasped a complete understanding of the ways in which these calendars worked, but he was amazed the second Mayan calendar also included a period of five extra days at the end of each year, which brought them into complete consistency with the Old World's calendar. The Maya considered the period of five additional days outside their calendar year unlucky. They moved as little as possible, fearing evil waited for them outside the safety of a complete month.

In July of 1550, during these five unlucky days, Nachi announced he was taking Friar Diego to a remote village to witness the festival marking the start of a new year, based on the calendar with three hundred and sixty days: 1-Pop. Friar Diego had learned each month had its own associated festival but had never been invited to witness one, and a request wouldn't have been proper.

They traveled for two days, past where he had first encountered Ahkinmai. During their walk, Nachi informed Friar Diego that everyone celebrated the first day of the new year and that all the idols were worshipped. The sole work that the Maya performed during the five unlucky days prior to 1-Pop was in preparation for the festival that marked the new year's beginning. This included renewing and cleaning every item in their home: plates, bowls, stools, mats, and old clothing were either refreshed or thrown away in great heaps in the middle of the village. Friar Diego stared at the discarded items as he followed Nachi through the village, wondering where the pile would end up.

"Do people come take what they need?" he asked Nachi, in the Mayan language. Friar Diego had learned so much of the Mayan language from Nachi that he never used Spanish outside the monastery.

"No, those can't be touched," Nachi said. "It would anger the gods."

Friar Diego nodded, reminding himself of the need for

patience with their misguided fear. He had faith he would convert them and, when he did, they would understand the folly of their beliefs.

The village was similar to the small settlement where the students lived but larger, with multiple sprawling multifamily structures, and with a wider variety of age groups represented. Everyone was covered in black soot; Nachi explained this was common during periods of fasting. Friar Diego was taken to a small home that stood apart from the other structures. Nachi invited him in, telling Friar Diego this was one of his many houses throughout the province.

"We'll stay here tonight. Tomorrow, the men will go to the temple."

He explained that women weren't permitted at the temple, but that they could participate in the feast afterwards. According to him, all the men had abstained from their wives in preparation.

"At least for thirteen days. Some for months," he said.

Friar Diego thought the *encomenderos* could learn something from the natives about the importance of going without.

"No salt or pepper for thirteen days too," Nachi added, as if foregoing flavor was on par with rejecting the flesh.

Nachi gave Friar Diego a hammock before joining the other Maya in the festival's preparation, telling the friar he would cover himself with the same black powder. Friar Diego lay down and soon fell asleep. He woke up the next morning to a clean Nachi covering himself with red ointment—the exact same color Friar Diego had seen at the previous ceremony he had interrupted. He looked down at his own brown habit, feeling at once both overdressed and as if he was wearing rags.

"No one's expecting you to wear anything different," Nachi told the friar, chuckling.

The two men emerged from Nachi's temporary lodgings

and found a group of men already waiting for them. They were painted red as well, washed free of the black soot that had covered them the night before. Right after Nachi asked if anyone was missing, a thin young boy, around twelve, ran up to the group. Everyone then said no.

Nachi led the way to the temple, less than an hour's walk away. Other native groups of men were already in the temple courtyard when they arrived, and more arrived after Nachi's group. Friar Diego guessed thousands were present for the ceremony. At a word from Nachi, Friar Diego stood on the edge of the courtyard, still beneath the surrounding trees. Many sets of eyes inspected Friar Diego, but nobody dared challenge his presence because he'd come with Nachi. Other than the way they stood separate from each other—because of familial ties—there was little to distinguish the men from each other. They were from the same area, after all, and most of them had fought against the Spanish under Nachi before the previous *Adelantado* gave him charge over the entire province.

The temple was a miniature of the large one at Chichen Itza, cut in half, with a raised waist-high rectangle made of stone. The rectangle, about the size of a man, stood on the exposed square, which was higher off the ground than the tallest man. Around the edges of the exposed square stood dozens of idols facing outward—sentinels watching the world around the temple. The square stone base was smooth on all sides except for a staircase on the side facing the courtyard. The land around the temple was devoid of trees but had a number of small shrubs and grasses, none of which reached farther than halfway up the structure. The courtyard where the men stood was dirt.

Each group of men produced a large quantity of food, maize-based beverages, and wine, setting them down between themselves and the temple. They all knelt down on one knee and bowed their heads, exposing a man covered in feathers seated in the middle of the courtyard: the priest, Ahkinmai. Friar Diego's breath escaped him, lost in the terror inspired by the large bird from his dreams.

In front of Ahkinmai was a wide, shallow clay pot with a small fire. Around the brazier were a number of small wooden boards, each dotted with incense. Friar Diego had seen one of the men carrying a board but hadn't seen when it was placed near the fire. Ahkinmai uttered a series of incantations, working himself into a frenzy that culminated with him retching thin yellow bile. Four men with feathers in their hair and on the fabric hanging from their waists, but not sporting the same cape as Ahkinmai, emerged from the undergrowth at the four corners of the courtyard. They lifted a thin rope in each arm, creating a square that surrounded all the men in the middle. The men inside the ropes each took turns approaching Ahkinmai, picking up a small ball of incense and tossing it into the fire—producing an eruption of sparks—before returning to their kneeled position. This continued until every ball of incense had been removed from the boards, which had been the exact number of men inside the square. At a nod from Ahkinmai, one man gathered the four ropes and the clay pot that contained the fire, taking them in the opposite direction of the temple.

Friar Diego learned after the ceremony that this ritual purged the temple.

There was another clay pot beneath the one that was removed. In this, Ahkinmai lit a new fire while the men chanted in their native language. The new flame for the new year. One man from each group came forward and tossed a large amount of incense into the flames, waiting until the sparks died down from the previous addition before adding their own. Once this was completed, Ahkinmai threw a small portion of his own incense into the flame. This was met by a jubilant cry, revealing to Friar Diego their excitement at the arrival of the new year.

Nachi approached the priest, took a small portion of the feathered man's incense, and tossed it into the fire, staring into the flames until they returned to their normal state. Every man did this, a process that took so long that Ahkinmai had to feed the flames with the boards used for incense until they were all gone.

The burning of the last incense started the feast. The men all started eating with a hunger cultivated for days beforehand, and their depleted bodies became roaring drunk with the shared wine. The men all returned to their villages and began feasting with the women and children.

Friar Diego spent the rest of the day on the edges of the village, eating as much as he wanted, drinking wine without ever approaching drunkenness, and certain he had just witnessed the natives calling forth the devil.

Ahkinmai arrived in the village as night descended on their celebration. The center of the feast shifted. Prior to the priest's arrival, the people had gravitated towards Nachi where he sat next to the fire. They would bring him food and drink, both men and women studying his face in hopes of gaining his audience. This attention transferred to Ahkinmai, with increased solemnity despite their drunkenness. What surprised Friar Diego the most was that Nachi didn't mind. In fact, Nachi himself brought Ahkinmai wine, sitting down next to the priest who never moved. Friar Diego watched him from a distance, observing the large quantity of wine the priest drank without ever becoming the least bit drunk. Ahkinmai met Friar Diego's gaze from where he sat next to the central fire; each man looked at the other with pity.

When Ahkinmai waved Nachi away, making room for a native woman and her young son next to him, Friar Diego realized the feathered man was the true leader of the Mayan people. The Spanish colonists had created a hierarchy without appreciating the one that already existed, thinking they knew better because of their Old-World education. The Maya played along with the Spanish desires, all the while hiding their true beliefs from the *encomenderos*.

Friar Diego left the feast before anyone else, retiring to Nachi's house to say his evening prayers before lying in his hammock. He stared at the thatched roof, listening to the festivities outside with the story of Daniel in the lion's den in mind, knowing he was surrounded by the devil's agents and trusting in God's holy protection. The last thing he thought of before drifting off to sleep was the large bird. He hoped the creature was content with visiting him in person and wouldn't bother invading his dreams.

CHAPTER FOURTEEN

WEDNESDAYS MEANT CHURCH. Their faith's midweek refresh. Cortez didn't look forward to it, and he didn't dread it; rather, it was just another part of the routine, a task to be completed. He had gone to Decant earlier in the day, looking for Alara. It must have been her day off, or she was working at a different time, because she wasn't there. He didn't know which drink to order, and when he sat down to wait for her empty-handed, one of the baristas told him to get out by informing him that tables were for paying customers only. She had been terrified of breaking the news to Cortez and apologized with a shaky voice. Cortez left without a word, followed by the stares of the customers in the shop, and spent the rest of the afternoon sitting on Alara's park bench, imagining which of the smells that reached his nose lingered from her presence in the same spot the night before.

The question of whether they would attend the Wednesday night service at all plagued Cortez during his walk home at the same time he used to get off work at the factory. His mother's depression had showed no signs of abating. She had been missing from his life since Sunday, and when he left that morning she was still trapped in her room, not going to work.

Cortez never questioned why her job didn't fire her. Thinking about job loss forced Cortez to recall his own, this time accompanied by a sickening possibility: his mother had found out about the events at work without him telling her. A sense of shame welled up inside him, one that caused him to use a tree for support and retch, though nothing came out. The knowledge that his mother would confront him if she did know, wanting to hear his side of the story, comforted him, and he was able to continue home after taking a white pill. The story of the Virgin Mary popped into his head while he walked, and he came to believe that her depression had been caused by him without her ever having learned the information. The immaculate conception of his mother's depression.

His mother had managed to pull herself from the bedroom's darkness and was in the kitchen frying plantains when Cortez arrived. She was wearing her light blue dress and had foregone the head covering, saving it for Sunday. "Hello, my son," she said when Cortez walked in. "How was your day?"

"It was good," Cortez said. Whenever anyone asked, his day was good, no matter how it had been in reality. Nobody ever asked him to elaborate. Even though that day hadn't been good —he knew that for the rest of his life a day without seeing Alara could never be good—the phrase prevented him from having to talk about it with his mother, and she kept moving forward like a train after it had left the station.

"Mine too. After you left, I got out of bed and went into work. They were mad, but they'll get over it," she said with a laugh. Cortez wondered what it would be like to be untouchable at a job.

She sat the spatula down on the edge of the frying pan and looked at Cortez as if seeing her son for the first time. The gaze made him uncomfortable. "You know you're my inspiration, don't you? Waking up and going to work each day, without interruption." Cortez looked at her mouth while she spoke, not wanting to look in her eyes. Understanding she was making her son uncomfortable, she picked up the spatula and poked at the frying fruit. "You remind me so much of your father."

"You've told me," he replied.

Bringing up his father was the worst part of his mother's depressive episodes. She did it every time she emerged. The man had abandoned them when Cortez was born. His mother was convinced that if she and Cortez were able to make it on their own, to demonstrate their worth, he would come back and they could be together again. Cortez did all he could to help with her mission, but it had been over twenty years and there had been no sign of him, not even a postcard. As a boy, Cortez had hoped he could impress his absent father through school. It hadn't taken long to realize it wasn't going to happen. Then, with his first job delivering newspapers, he wondered what financial empires he would create to entice his father's return, but those dreams had been dashed when he became overwhelmed and had to rely on his mother's help to get the work done in the early morning hours. That was how he had come to believe the one avenue available was the Church, though now that he had met Alara Chel, he wondered if a quality woman by his side would be enough to impress the man he'd never known.

"Get a plate," Cortez's mother told him. Cortez retrieved one from the cabinet and stood next to his mother while she put the plantains from the frying pan onto it, creating a stack that multiplied with each scoop. Jesus feeding thousands with a few loaves of bread. She grabbed another plate, put some food onto it for herself that didn't make a dent in Cortez's pile, then commanded him to eat.

. . .

THE PAIR CLEANED the kitchen and left for church when their meager meal was finished. His mother talked the entire walk, releasing every word she had saved up during her two days in darkness. She talked about the gossip at the hotel, she talked about the things she wanted to do the following weekend, and she discussed the storylines of her favorite shows like they were old friends she hadn't seen in a while. Cortez pretended to listen the whole time, interjecting various expressions he knew would make her believe he cared what she was saying. Out of nowhere, she turned to him and declared that she hadn't heard anything about him recently. "How's Simeon doing?" she asked.

"He's been good. Sitting a lot," Cortez said. He smiled at his joke, the same one Simeon had made about himself.

His mother hit him in the arm with the back of her hand. It wiped the smile off his face. "What's the matter with you? Making fun of that poor boy's condition is mean! He's had a hard life."

Cortez looked down at the sidewalk. "I know."

They walked the rest of the way to church without saying another word.

His mother blossomed as soon as they entered the school building where service was held. Cortez stood by her side while she pretended her life was worthy of envy, as if she hadn't spent the intervening days between her last appearance and this one in a cocoon of blankets. The service was led by an older member, one of the church's first. He was on the church council and stood in front of the few dozen members of the congregation wearing a suit that looked like it had been worn all day and for many years beforehand. When he began, he informed the congregation that their priest had become their former priest, having left on a mission trip to Mexico. Cortez's mother beamed with pride at the information. She was from Mexico, had been born there before coming to their current city, and Cortez had heard about his ancestor's position in the Church for as long as he could remember. The way she said it, he was born to lead people to Christ: it was in his blood.

"And so, I'll be leading us for the time being," the new leader said. Wednesday services were less formal than Sundays, and they spoke about real-life experiences instead of dissecting the Bible. The suited man was notorious for wiping his nose with a light purple handkerchief he kept in his right pants pocket, and he did so multiple times while he spoke about giving to the poor. Soon after he began his story, Cortez stopped listening, instead focusing on how many times the man withdrew his handkerchief and wondering why he was talking about his own charity when it was supposed to be between the giver and God. The entire talk took less than half an hour, far short of the typical length, and Cortez was grateful when they were told to go out and spread the word.

The real reason the Wednesday service was held was so that the congregation would have a reason to gather before going back out onto the streets in search of more parishioners. Whoever had begun the practice, which had been in place since before the previous priest had arrived, didn't trust the people to go out on their own without worship beforehand. There were few reunions after the short service, since most had taken place when people first arrived. It was still a work night, after all, and everyone wanted to finish their holy task with time to relax at home before bed. Cortez's mother led the way to her chosen spot for the night's work, a Mexican restaurant they went to twice a year, on each of their birthdays.

"We'll be the ones to save the Church," she said with certainty when they arrived.

. . .

THE RESTAURANT HAD BEEN in the city for as long as anyone could remember. Its owners had claimed to be the first Mexicans to arrive, and legend had it they'd created the restaurant so the arriving diaspora would have somewhere to congregate. The food was nothing spectacular, but the atmosphere had created a Mexican religion whose adherents chose their country as their deity of choice. Cortez and his mother took up position outside, determined to talk to the people waiting for one of the coveted tables. With a wait that could go over an hour each night, there was plenty of time for them to discuss the power of God's grace.

The air was heavy with the smell of frying meats, fresh tortillas, and perfume. The plantain in Cortez's belly had been delicious but was no match for the smells emanating from countless Mexican dishes. When his stomach rumbled, he reminded himself that some things were more important than meals. In particular, the sustenance his soul would receive if they were successful in bringing new people to Christ.

Mexican music could be heard from outside. Cortez, who had learned Spanish from his mother but never spoke it, listened to his mother talk in her native language with the people waiting to eat dinner. At first, the people assumed she was waiting for a table as well. They would chat about where in the country they came from, if they knew this or that person, and when they'd first arrived in the city. Once they were deep in conversation, she would switch and begin talking about the Church, extolling the virtues of her particular place of worship, and would share how instrumental faith had been in her successful transition into the English-speaking city. Most of the people listened until their table was called, but some adopted looks of disgust when they realized her ploy. There were people who belonged to other churches who would want to discuss matters of faith with her, but when she realized they already belonged to a church, Cortez's mother would find a way out of the conversation.

Diners began avoiding the lingering pair when they realized the woman and her son weren't waiting for a table until a man and woman, both old enough to be retired, sat down and took more interest in Cortez than in anything his mother was saying. It started when they asked if he was Mexican as well, after hearing his mother came from a city in the Yucatán Peninsula.

"Well, he's my son," Cortez's mother said as an explanation.

"Full Mexican?" the older woman clarified, in English. She had white hair and the air of a patient librarian. Her husband was bald and thin everywhere except his belly.

"Full Mexican," Cortez said.

"Where's your father from?" the woman asked.

"Mexico City," Cortez answered. His mother shifted in her seat. She had a habit of shutting down whenever Cortez's father was brought up, but her earlier emergence from her room and subsequent comparison of Cortez to his father had prepared her for the interaction. She was silent, but present, and paid attention.

"We're from Mexico City," the man growled. He wasn't mean, just serious from a life of scraping by to support his family while struggling to master a foreign language.

"What was his name?" the wife asked.

Cortez looked at his mother. She never spoke his name, not wanting to invoke the associated pain the man had caused by his exit. It was as if his name had the power to break her attachment to Cortez and suck the strength she received from her son's continued existence. "It's not important," Cortez said.

"Well, what if we know him?" the man said, defending his wife's question.

"Even if you do, we don't," Cortez said. He was a moment away from ignoring them when he remembered why he and his mother were outside the popular restaurant in the first place: to find more people to worship alongside them at church. It was this duty that gave him strength, even though he wanted the conversation to be over. In a flash, he imagined the old couple had children, each old enough to have their own families. They might have friends, or siblings, who would all have descendants of their own. Sitting next to him, asking him questions he'd rather not answer, they could be the big fish he had been hunting, the prize that would elevate him in the Church, bring back his father, and end his mother's torment whenever the man was discussed.

"My father is the Lord," he said, inspired. In that moment he became his mother's angel, emerging from heaven to save her from the pain of rejection.

The wife and husband looked at each other. "So you're Jesus, and this must be Mary," the man said.

Cortez's mother's jaw went limp, her mouth open. "His name was Diego . . . Albalate," she said when she pulled herself together.

"We knew a Diego Albalete," the white-haired wife said. She had the devil's wicked smile. "He came here about twenty years ago."

"Doubt it's the same one," Cortez's mother said, exhausted.

The wife turned her attention to Cortez. "You kind of look like him," she continued, turning the knife. She looked at her husband. "What ever became of him?"

"After he dated Rosalín? I'm not sure."

"Rosalín was our daughter's best friend," the wife explained to Cortez and his mother. "Beautiful girl."

Cortez didn't expect the anger on his mother's face. He knew he had to take action, to save his mother from the past and, with any luck, convince these two they were the seeds in the soil that would produce fruit in the church's orchard.

"Do you pray?" Cortez asked, trying to change the subject.

"What's it to you?" the husband answered.

"Our church meets on Sunday. There's always room for two more."

The couple laughed. Just then, they were informed their table was ready. Cortez's mother spat on the ground when they got up and walked away with the small steps typical for people at their advanced age. "They'd better pray the Lord doesn't strike them down for their wickedness," she said. Cortez held out hope they would show up on Sunday, even though they'd never inquired about the location, not knowing the couple would be dead before the start of the following Sunday's service.

The hostess studied Cortez and his mother, then frowned. Within minutes, the restaurant's owner was outside telling them to leave.

"I can't have you sitting out here scaring the customers!" he bellowed.

Cortez looked past the rage and saw another opportunity. The owner of the most popular restaurant in town would be a wonderful addition to their congregation. Maybe, if they were lucky, he would provide the food for their after-service meal. "Our church meets every Sunday at nine," he said. "Would you like the address?" He used his sweetest voice, one he reserved for asking favors from his mother.

"No, I don't want the address!" the man yelled. He looked at Cortez's mother. "What the hell is the matter with him?" he asked.

"He's trying to save your soul, that's what's the matter with him! He's out here, among you sinners, trying to save you. One day, all of you will be sorry when you realize you dismissed a great man!" With that, she grabbed her son, and together they walked away.

Cortez waited until the music from the restaurant had faded into the distance. "Do you really think I'm a great man?" Cortez asked.

"Not yet, but you will be," his mother said. All the hope she had in the world rested on him, and she lived off the sustenance its sweet nectar provided.

CHAPTER FIFTEEN

Friar Lorenzo de Bienvenida returned to Spain late in 1551, leaving Friar Diego de Landa in charge of the Izamal monastery while he was away.

The promotion within the Franciscan ranks to Guardian of the Izamal monastery would be a temporary one; there was no question Friar Lorenzo was coming back. He was returning to Spain to gather more friars and supplies for those stationed in the Yucatán. Their letters hadn't garnered sufficient support from the Old-World priests, so they sent one of the men who had been in the New World the longest, hoping his experience would inspire greater action. Friar Lorenzo was known throughout the world as one of the most pious and devout members of the Franciscan Order. Perhaps the one man who was more respected was Friar Luis de Villalpondo, but his advanced age made an ocean crossing impossible.

The dwindling supplies at the Izamal monastery was a problem noticed by all throughout the Yucatán. Their habits were thinning, spots worn through the fabric. The younger friars joked about the breeze, but the older Franciscans abhorred the thought of their neglected appearance. Wine was needed for mass, and oil for lamps. These items could be purchased in the Yucatán, but at great cost—it was up to Friar Lorenzo and the Franciscans in the Old World to decide the best method of acquiring these supplies.

There was talk of Friar Nicolás de Albalate going back to Spain for reinforcements once more, but this was shot down by Friar Lorenzo because he sensed he could garner more funding himself from the men across the Atlantic. What was unspoken, but suspected by all, was that he wanted to bring back hand-picked friars to join him in the New World. Nobody outright said Friar Nicolás had chosen poor candidates, but outside of Friar Diego, not a single one had emerged as willing or able to accept the leadership roles that would be vacant when the aging friars expired. Friar Nicolás was also floated as a potential candidate for Guardian of the Izamal monastery while Friar Lorenzo was away, but Friar Luis decided the shuffling was unnecessary when an eager replacement was already on-site.

The decision to leave Friar Diego in charge was made after months of hand-wringing. Friar Luis suggested the young man take over for Friar Lorenzo based on the immense love the Maya had shown to the young Franciscan. Friar Lorenzo's pushback, in no way absolute but voiced as a concern, was that Friar Diego had shown a reckless streak with his willingness to convert the natives at any and all costs. The open communication among the friars, encouraged by Friar Luis as *Custos* of the Yucatán province, created a scenario in which Friar Diego knew the Guardian of the Izamal monastery was the one man standing in his way.

Friar Diego struggled with his wounded pride for the months prior to Friar Lorenzo's departure. Friar Luis's judgment won in the end, resulting in Friar Diego's taking over as Guardian of the Izamal monastery.

Any opinions about sweeping changes Friar Diego had

harbored during his two years in the Yucatán were buried deep inside his soul. As he watched Friar Lorenzo set out on the voyage back to the Old World, Friar Diego made it his mission to operate the Izamal monastery in the exact same manner as Friar Lorenzo had, with as few changes as possible. He soon discovered how much time the extra responsibilities took from his day. The amount of correspondence alone made finding time for additional prayers difficult, and the sheer volume of meetings with local Spanish colonists, none of them in possession of an *encomienda*, meant meals were often taken with added ceremony among company or wolfed down in solitary meals while seated at his desk.

The school had swelled in size; hundreds of students now learned to read and write the Mayan language in European script, sing in the choir for the various services each day, and learn about the more nuanced aspects of the Christian faith—the curriculum had been created by Friar Diego himself. Along with these students came an increased strain on the monastery's already depleted resources, and another part of Friar Lorenzo's trip back to Spain involved obtaining more educational materials for the wide age range represented in Izamal.

Construction of larger versions of the monastery's three main buildings was undertaken after a long period of consideration and prayer by Friar Diego. His chief concern was that Friar Lorenzo would view the buildings as tangible proof of Friar Diego's outsized pride. When he shared this sentiment with Friar Luis in a letter, the *Custos* told him to pray on the matter. Friar Diego did, and he wrote back that it was a practical matter, that their ranks were swollen past the point of what could be considered reasonable.

"The sanctuary holds less than half the churchgoers. The natives gather outside to hear what they can," Friar Diego wrote.

Friar Luis wrote back that Friar Diego had his blessing.

THE SCHOOL WAS the first building to be rebuilt. There was no shortage of labor, with so many young men enrolled in the school. Friar Diego spoke with Nachi Cocom, who still visited the friar with regularity, and asked him to convince the local chieftains to donate supplies, since their sons were the ones benefitting from the space. Nachi said the harvesting season was fast approaching and that he couldn't convince anyone to abandon their *milpas* before then. Diego had to wait until the end of 1551, but during one week of furious work, scores of Mayan men descended on the land outside the Izamal monastery and prepared the thick wooden support posts, thinner wooden poles for the roof, and piles of bundled palm leaves for the thatched roof.

When they were finished, the native man in charge of the operation found Friar Diego and reported the materials were ready.

"Great, we'll begin construction next week," Friar Diego said. He allowed his thoughts to wander while considering schedules, labor, and the construction process.

"You're building this?" the man asked. "Nachi just said you needed help with the supplies."

"We built all the other buildings," Friar Diego said. It was a lackluster explanation; the existing structures were multiple sizes too small, with patchwork roofs and various leanings.

The Mayan man laughed. "Wait until I tell the others," he said as he walked away.

Friar Diego thought the rest of the laborers would enjoy a good laugh before going back to their homes the next day. Instead, he woke up to the industrious men digging multiple holes surrounding the existing school pavilion.

"What are you doing?" Friar Diego asked the closest man. He was one of the older workers, wearing the typical piece of fabric hanging from his waist, which exposed his wrinkled skin to the elements.

"We're building this school!" the man replied, showing off multiple missing teeth.

Friar Diego found the man in charge. He was near the raw materials, telling the swarms of men where they were needed.

"We hadn't decided where to put the new school," Friar Diego said.

"Did you want to move it?"

"No, we just assumed the students would spend half the day in class and half the day working on the new facility . . ."

"Those kids can barely go to the bathroom without getting some on their leg!" the native man said with a laugh. Turning serious, he said, "Plus, they are here to learn, not to build roofs. Let us take care of this."

Friar Diego turned and looked at the holes being dug around the existing school. Looking back at the posts, he realized the massive size of the new facility: the existing school would fit underneath without any issue whatsoever. The length of the new pavilion required the undergrowth behind the existing school to be cleared, and teams of men were undertaking the task with ferocity born from competition with each other. He heard the man in charge speak from behind him.

"It takes no time at all if we all work together," he said.

Friar Diego nodded. He turned, took both of the man's hands in his own, and prayed. He went to morning prayers with tears in his eyes.

The students had trouble learning when there were dozens of men around their school shuttling back and forth as they erected giant support pillars. Their lessons were interrupted whenever a man scampered to the top of a support pillar to work on the roof, because they kept leaning over and looking past their own roof to witness what the men above them were doing.

From the outside, the men all looked like ants on, around, and beneath an anthill. They worked from dawn until dusk with a fervor any Spanish *encomendero* would have been amazed to witness. There was a competitive nature to their task, each man wanting to contribute more to the church. The *encomienda* system could never capitalize on this way of life because the community was the sole recipient of this labor force's benefits; the improvement to the community, not padding one man's pockets, made the work worth completing. Without this, the work was meaningless. Friar Diego appreciated their society for the way they looked out for the whole of the community; he viewed them as similar to his own Catholic Church.

A buzzing industry was created around the men, supporting them with food and places to rest each night. Their encampment was similar to that of the students but with less permanence, and the laborers' support included women; each man's wife made sure he was fed before and after the day's work.

The new school was completed in two weeks, on a Thursday. The lands cleared for the Izamal monastery extended farther into the undergrowth, providing enough room for one edge of the large pavilion. The building was long enough to fit three of the former schools in side by side, and wider than the previous school was long. The former school sat nested in a way that both structures had a front edge right along the street, and their pointed roofs aligned between the earth and sky.

Friar Diego and the other friars held a simple ceremony to bless the structure, during which the Mayan men stood on the fringes of the space and watched with curiosity. To a man, they were sure the rituals performed by Ahkinmai would have been far more effective. Friar Diego then led everyone in an impromptu mass, blessing the students and the laborers. The children knew all the parts of Friar Diego's service and modeled the correct behavior for their elders.

The Maya who built the school evaporated into the trees after Friar Diego's last words, taking all evidence of their habitation with them. The students took to destroying the old school with a palpable excitement that infected the friars, who helped with the labor and clearing of old materials until the new space was as ready for instruction as the new students.

The infirmary was built the same way, just before the planting season in 1552. Friar Diego had mentioned the need for another new facility to Nachi, who in turn told the native men, who arrived one day with their supporting entourage and stayed until the work was complete.

"We won't be able to make any more buildings until after the harvest," Nachi said when he visited Izamal during the start of the planting season. As the leader in the province, he could rely on donations of food and therefore didn't have to engage in the same planting and harvesting cycles as the rest of the natives not on an *encomienda*. This was why he had the time to visit Izamal in the first place.

THE YEAR HAD a lot more in store for the Yucatán Franciscans besides the new facilities at Izamal. Soon after the infirmary was completed, Friar Diego received word from Merida that Friar Luis's health was on a steep decline. Friar Nicolás urged the temporary Guardian to come to Merida at the first opportunity; Friar Luis had asked for him by name. The other friars at Izamal didn't want him traveling alone, despite his repeated resistance and numerous prior trips. The day after Friar Diego received the letter, he set off for Merida with two of his star pupils; the trip, and meeting Friar Luis, was their reward for their success in the classroom.

The students never got to meet Friar Luis. The old friar's condition had deteriorated too far for anyone but the most important guests to visit by the time the group arrived from Izamal. Friar Diego left the students with Friar Nicolás, who took them to Merida's school. Their institution had been founded years before the Izamal location, and their school had over two thousand students. The students' various frequencies of attendance meant that the older children, now young men, displayed a wide range of aptitude in the Spanish customs and Christian traditions. Friar Nicolás discovered that the two young men taught by Friar Diego had, in the span of just over two years, exceeded all of the Merida students. Every Franciscan in the Yucatán knew Friar Diego was responsible for the schooling of the children in Izamal, and he thanked God for blessing him with bringing the young man over from Spain.

Merida's infirmary was heavy with the smell of expected death when Friar Diego entered. There was a curtain hung around a corner of the room, with two friars standing outside. The other patients in the facility didn't make a sound—coughs were choked down, flatulence held until it barely escaped, and they covered themselves with blankets before relieving themselves in clay pots to muffle the sounds of their body's waste hitting the receptacle. Both natives and colonists watched as Friar Diego crossed the space and greeted the two sentinels before one opened the curtain and allowed him inside Friar Luis's corner.

The aged friar was wide awake when Friar Diego walked in. His yellowed skin stretched tight across his cheeks, making him look like one of the Maya's wooden idols, and his greasy hair stuck flat against his head. The man was thin as a skeleton beneath the blanket; if it wasn't for the head sticking out, resting on a pillow, the bed could have been empty.

"I thought it was you," Friar Luis said.

Friar Diego assumed the premonition had been passed down by God. In truth, Friar Luis thought every footstep was the young friar, and he had been prepared to utter the phrase whenever he heard someone enter the infirmary, regardless of whether or not they passed through his curtain.

"Sit down," Friar Luis said.

Friar Diego took a nearby stool and set it next to the bed. Taking Friar Luis's hands in his own, the two men prayed.

"I don't have much longer," Friar Luis said, withdrawing his hands from Friar Diego's grasp.

"Only God knows when we'll pass," Friar Diego replied. "Let's hope for your recovery."

Friar Luis laughed with a heavy wheeze, which resulted in a fit of tortured coughing. "Learning to let go of my life is what led me to this place," he said when his coughing subsided, looking around the makeshift room. "I've been here a long time."

"You have," Friar Diego agreed.

The two men sat in silence.

"Do you know why I've called you here?" Friar Luis asked.

"Because with Friar Lorenzo gone, Izamal is my responsibility."

"No. Even if Lorenzo was in the Yucatán, I'd request your audience. Your skill with the native tongue and your fearless efforts have put you in a position to be their champion," Friar Luis said. "It's a role I've felt called to occupy myself, since I was the man who knew their language best, but it's time I relinquished my hold on the position."

With a great effort, Friar Luis reached up and took off a necklace with a small wooden cross. "I brought this with me from Spain," Friar Luis said. "I've had to replace the rope, but the cross belonged to my mentor. I want you to have it."

Friar Diego took the necklace and put it on. He was filled with a sense of far-off destiny, a land on the horizon he could feel in his bones but couldn't see.

"These people are the future, and they need our protection from the *encomenderos*. I don't know how the Crown plans to respond to my letter, but I want you to be their ally in whatever they do. For the good of the natives."

Friar Diego didn't hear a word beyond the mention of the natives as their future. He was filled with thoughts of his mentor in Toledo, of the coming New Age the conversion of the natives would bring. Did Friar Luis believe in the same whispered secret?

"With your mastery of their language, and the trust they have in you, it's going to be your responsibility to preserve their culture. Remember all you can and write it down so the believers in the Old World know the type of people we bring into the Christian realm."

Friar Diego told Friar Luis about the festival Nachi had showed him at the start of the new year. Friar Luis nodded as if he already knew.

"They already trust you more than they ever trusted me. I've known Nachi for years, had him as a guest at my dinner table, and never once was offered the chance to see any of their ceremonies firsthand." Friar Luis grew saddened by the news, resigning himself to never seeing the natives' celebrations for himself. "Learn as much as you can about all their festivals, about their calendar, and their way of life. The better you understand them, the better you'll be able to preach God's message in a way they'll accept."

Friar Diego couldn't bear his curiosity about Friar Luis's belief in the coming age of the Holy Spirit. Under normal circumstances, the question would have been inappropriate: the coming New Age removed all requirements for a hierarchy. Belief in it would mean Friar Luis's station would be on equal footing with his own. Now that the aged *Custos* was on his supposed deathbed, the question could be asked without fear of future reprisal.

"Conversion of the natives will bring about the third age of man," Friar Diego said. He locked eyes with Friar Luis, his gaze boring into the sick man.

Friar Luis looked away. "I had a feeling you'd been told about the prophecy. The belief in the age of the Holy Spirit held by the Toledo priests is the worst-kept secret in Spain." He looked back at Friar Diego. "You know it's heresy?"

"Of course. I haven't told another soul since I left."

"And don't. I agree, the conversion of the natives will save the Catholic Church, but I don't think it will bring about the conversion of the rest of the world. People's beliefs are too varied, too absolute. Look what happened to the poor Jews and Muslims in Spain: they were punished because they believe in their god as much as we believe in ours."

"Some might say your words are heretical as well," Friar Diego said, his seriousness unwarranted.

"Then we'll keep both our beliefs a secret," Friar Luis said with a tired smile. "You do know the same prophecy views the Church's wealth as scandalous?"

"If you don't agree, why join the Franciscan Order? The prophecy urges the Church to accept our austerity."

"Without the Church's resources, how could we have come to the New World? How would we teach the natives?"

Friar Diego thought for a moment, then grew frustrated. "We would have come here eventually."

"And yet those who believe in the prophecy tried to force the Jewish and Muslim conversion because they felt they were running out of time. How much time do you think was saved by using the Church's resources?"

"Use the resources until the third age arrives," Friar Diego said, more to himself than to Friar Luis.

Friar Luis shook his head. "Converting the Maya will spread the Christian message, but it won't lead the rest of humanity to suddenly believe in Christ's message," he said. "In any case, I won't be around to see it."

Friar Diego admired the man's resignation, thinking it was one of the braver acts of faith he'd ever seen.

"Learn as much as you can about these people and teach the incoming friars about their ways. Through knowledge comes understanding, and with understanding comes the compassion that will allow us to gain their trust."

A sudden shame filled Friar Diego for pushing the old man into an argument when the *Custos* wanted him there to bestow his blessing. He nodded, saying he would undertake the task.

Their conversation was interrupted by Friar Nicolás telling them the two native boys from Izamal were preaching to the Merida students.

"You are going to do great things," Friar Luis told Friar Diego with a heaping dose of paternal pride.

Friar Luis de Villalpondo, the man with the greatest mastery of the Mayan language, died three days after his encounter with Friar Diego, having never told a soul that the young man believed the Catholic Church outside the Franciscan Order must fall in order for it to be saved by the birth of Christianity's New Age.

CHAPTER SIXTEEN

CORTEZ TOLD his mother he was leaving and let her assume he was headed to the ice cream factory. The morning was overcast, creating a shadow over the city that confused the night creatures and convinced them to stay in the streets until well after their daytime neighbors had emerged. In addition to passing men selling contraband and women selling sex, Cortez walked by two traffic accidents caused by the increased number of people out of their homes, neither serious, which clogged traffic in both directions and caused stranded drivers to lean out of their windows shouting at the unfortunate souls who'd suffered through the collision. Police were present at both scenes. Cortez kept his eyes trained straight ahead, in case any of those he passed had been present at the drug deal that cost him his job.

The park was a welcome relief from the congestion. Inside its borders, there was plenty of space for all who chose to enter. Since it was still cool, few people had the desire to enjoy the open space. Some of those present were the ones who had been out the night before, stranded in the daylight. There were homeless people on benches and groups of young men looking for trouble; in more than one gathering, Cortez saw a replay of the drug deal he had experienced because of Simeon's greed. Humans weren't the only confused animals. Bats screeched as they shot through the air, opossums walked about on their two hind legs, raccoons looted garbage cans, and deer gathered together in the park's open spaces. The park, on that overcast morning, stood at the intersections of nature and civilization, night and day.

Cortez walked on a ray of light, above the detritus, inspired by the certainty Alara would be working that day. His night had been sleepless, filled with tossing, turning, and thinking, stuck in the space between full wakefulness and dreams. Thoughts of Alara had filled his head, and he feared the day in their future when he would be recognized by her neighbor after being invited to her home. She was still in his head on the rare instances he managed to dream. All he could remember from them was her smell. He couldn't place it, but he knew that he enjoyed it, was addicted to it. It was nature, sweetness, and pride, all rolled into one, and if he could find the scent he'd find a way to surround himself with it wherever he went. When he'd woken up, he'd known that the day would bring him into contact with her, with a certainty born from never having his heart broken before.

Nothing bothered him as he crossed the park. Both animals and people recognized he was a man on a mission bestowed upon him by a power they couldn't understand or experience. Older individuals out for their morning walk, awoken by various body processes each morning and never getting enough sleep, held a faint sense of recognition when they saw the way he walked, but it had been so long since they had witnessed a young man in the grips of love that they forgot his affliction and assumed he was suffering from chronic narcissism.

The clouds' shadows ended at the edge of the park. Cortez attributed their disappearance to the power of Alara Chel, certain in the knowledge that her radiance was even bright enough to chase away a storm. Controlling the weather was just one more attribute she possessed—he knew her power had no limits. If he ever managed to convince her to join him in worship, to save her soul, he knew she would be the one to save his church, the spark that would ignite the flame and light up the world. A moment of panic set in when he imagined the world discovering her magic for the first time. He had no doubt they would be as enamored with her as him. For her sake, he should keep her to himself, to keep her safe.

He laughed, knowing that saving her and, as a result of her conversion, helping save the Church was what he had been put on the earth to accomplish. Still, the darkness of stifling her had entered his heart as he crossed into her side of the city, and he would struggle to keep it contained until he took his last breath.

HAVING LEARNED his lesson the day before about needing to purchase a drink in order to sit inside the coffee shop, Cortez had taken a few dollars from the money he shared with his mother. She trusted him, never having a reason to doubt his good sense, and left it uncounted in a jar high up in the cabinet next to their refrigerator. Financial matters gave her a headache, and going to the bank made her constipated, so she reserved these tasks to one day a month, when she would have a plan in place to suffer in peace.

Decant was filled with people when he walked in. The line was to the door, and every seat was filled. Alara wasn't behind the counter. Cortez took his place at the back of the line behind a bicyclist who still wore his helmet and specialty shoes, which made a metallic snap with each step he took. A young woman wearing a dark gray skirt and matching sport coat stood behind him a moment later. She talked on the phone the entire time, her conversation filled with legal jargon as she told her assistant what needed to be done. The line creeped along at the same pace the drinks were handed off to customers who had already paid. It was a delicate balancing act, one the employees working the register had experience navigating, knowing they shouldn't try to move faster because on days they themselves made drinks they expected to be shown the same courtesy.

The young man at the register had long hair tied in a ponytail. It was obvious he was young from the red blemishes on his skin. When Cortez got to the front of the line, the young man asked what he wanted.

"What's the cheapest thing you have?" Cortez asked. The menu hanging overhead had numerous offerings, with names Cortez had never seen before, each priced higher than he had expected. His hand was in his pocket, gripping the cash with a sweaty palm.

"Um." The young man turned around, looked at the menu, and pointed to a section of small font in the lower right-hand corner. "A small coffee."

"I'll take one of those." He counted out the dollars and handed them over. Beneath their hands was an overflowing tip jar. While the young man working the register counted out the transaction's change, Cortez's mind contracted when he thought about the concept of leaving a tip himself. He didn't want to stand out from the other customers, and judging from the amount already in the jar, he guessed every previous customer had placed their change inside. In reality, the Decant employees, knowing the power of peer pressure, placed money from the cash register in the tip jar before the start of the shift. So, when Cortez received the coins that constituted his change, he placed them inside the tip jar before moving to the exact spot Alara had handed him the drink, hoping that his presence at the location of their previous encounter would somehow make her appear on the other side of the counter.

"I have your coffee right here," the young man called out to Cortez. Cortez went back to the register and accepted the drink.

The coffee Cortez had sampled before now was better classified as brown water. It was served at church and left sitting for hours. On the rare occasions Cortez had a cup, he added two sugars and enough milk to change the drink's color to a light brown. Decant's coffee didn't change color at all with the equivalent amount of milk, but he tasted it anyway, finding it much too bitter even with two sugars inside. He poured some out, then added more milk before tasting again and still finding it not to his liking. The process was repeated three more times, and in the end half the original coffee was in the trash, replaced with the same amount of milk. Content with his concoction, Cortez put the lid back on and scanned the room for somewhere to wait for his beloved.

She must have entered when he was busy adding milk. Alara sat in one of the two corner chairs, leaning over and engaged in conversation with a clean-cut young man. Cortez's heart entered his throat when he realized he, along with the rest of the people in the room, didn't exist for the couple. Her conversation partner was handsome, with a square jaw and long eyelashes, and tan skin that was the result of mixed parentage. His clothes were cut just for him, the shirt highlighting the size of his arms and leaving space for the vein on his biceps, and his pants ended right above his ankle.

The couple never noticed his stare. Cortez watched them for a full five minutes, not blinking, not moving a muscle, torn between jealousy and an appreciation that she hadn't been a figment of his imagination. She was real, was in the same room as him, breathing the same air, and that knowledge gave him the strength to stand tall against the torrential storm of hatred he held for the man next to her. His stupor lasted until they stood up. He scanned the room, found an open seat with a table, and sat down in time to watch them walk, together, to the open spot in the counter Alara would pass through to begin her workday. She was wearing the same outfit as the last time Cortez had seen her, with the same shoulder bag, but this time her black hair hung down below her shoulder blades. It was the most beautiful hair in the world, and he was struck by the sudden urge to hide inside her locks and watch her exist, the same way he'd hidden in the trees when he watched her in the park.

Before she went to work, Alara gave her companion a hug and a kiss. She didn't see the person doubled over, a sharp pain gripping his stomach, at one of the tables. Her boyfriend, Remy Moncard, walked her to work a few times each week. Every time he did, he made sure they were there early, so they could sit down and talk for a while before she had to clock in. What she thought was a sweet gesture was, in truth, a way for Remy to display his trophy to the men he knew watched her at the coffee shop. Before Remy left, she offered him a drink, but he refused, the same way he always did. Alara enjoyed their dance routine, performed in front of everyone in the room, lost in their own world for the few moments before she had to face the day's customers. Remy enjoyed the performance.

After Remy left, Alara twisted her hair into the braid Cortez came to associate with her, put on her hat and apron, and got to work. From the table against the wall, Cortez watched her move with a dancer's grace as she made drink after drink. His coffee had become cold by the time the pain in his stomach subsided, and he drank with each large gulp spaced out, making the drink last as long as possible—it wasn't hard, because coffee wasn't high on his list of preferred beverages. When the line died down to a trickle, and the employees were able to catch their breath, Cortez got the urge to approach her. There was a long internal struggle—and a white pill swallowed—before he worked up the nerve to stand up, and the war continued with each step on his approach to the counter.

He stood opposite Alara, waiting for her to acknowledge his presence. When she didn't, he worked up the courage to say the first word by reminding himself the Church depended on his action. "Hello," he whispered.

She didn't hear him.

The first barrier of speech was the hardest to cross; after that, the words trickled out. "Hello," he said, loud enough to be certain she heard. She looked up at him from over the machine she stood in front of and all air left Cortez's lungs. He longed for his inhaler, still in his backpack where he was sitting.

"Hi," she said. She didn't recognize the pale, timid-looking man standing before her.

"I came back," Cortez said. The advice of the Church, to smile when greeting new people, reverberated through his skull, and he forced his lips to display his teeth.

"Good for you," Alara said, smiling back at him. Their smiles, though the same classification of gesture, were leagues apart in quality. Similar to the way a chihuahua and a great dane are both dogs, but on different ends of the size spectrum. Cortez's smile displayed small teeth and bright red gums, and nervous lines formed where his lips met his cheeks. Alara's smile, on the other hand, showed perfect, straight, bright white teeth, and was so well practiced from years of charming customers that she was able to flash it without a second thought.

When Alara went back to her task behind the machine, Cortez tried to think of something to say that would keep her attention. His mother had spent years drilling into his head the etiquette when introducing oneself, and he blurted out, "My name is Cortez," in a sudden flash of inspiration.

Alara looked up at the miserable creature. He looked lost and inspired her pity. Something about him reminded her that she had given that same individual a drink two days before. "I made you promise to come back," she murmured, more as a reminder to herself than an attempt to continue their communication. It wasn't the first time a man had believed she wanted to see him again, but he was the most pitiful individual who had followed through.

"And I did," Cortez said. A dog expecting a treat for performing a mastered trick.

Alara chuckled. "My name's Alara."

No man had ever been as inspired by a single word as Cortez was when he first heard her name, standing in a coffee shop in a part of the city where he didn't belong. It was a breath of fresh air, filling his lungs with vitality, and in that moment he realized she was more effective than any prescribed inhaler.

"Did you already get a drink? The first one was free, the rest you have to pay for," Alara informed him.

"I did." Cortez pointed to the empty cup on the table. His backpack was on the ground next to the chair.

Alara abandoned her task and leaned with a hand on the counter. She enjoyed getting him out of his shell. "What did you get?" Alara said.

"A coffee. I already finished it though."

"Well, you know refills are free."

Cortez lit up. "Free" had been his favorite word, before he discovered Alara's name.

Alara could read the young man like a book and enjoyed his delight. She leaned farther forward, as if divulging a secret. "Just take your cup to the register and tell them you want a refill."

Though Cortez still held a library of words in his heart, he knew their interaction had drawn to a close. He retrieved his cup, got his refill, and spent the rest of the afternoon content with being in Alara's presence. Knowing nobody could ask him to leave, since he was a customer, was the best part.

CHAPTER SEVENTEEN

IZAMAL NEVER GOT a new sanctuary after the harvest. In fact, the entire Mayan way of life was turned upside down before the maize even reached knee height.

Spain's response to Friar Luis de Villalpondo's letter outlining the *encomendero* brutality arrived in 1552. His name was Tomás López Medel, a judge-administrator from Guatemala. The royal official began reshaping Mayan culture before the envelope holding his letter could be thrown away.

His declarations were meant to remind both colonists and Franciscans who was in charge of the Yucatán: the Spanish Crown. The unspoken agreements about tribute and service, to both the *encomiendas* and the monasteries, were turned into law, and the wages for the human carriers who transported goods around the peninsula were fixed on a predetermined scale, no longer up to the whims of the Spaniards. The natives were caught in the cross fire; his most sweeping changes concerned their continued existence in the Spanish colony.

López Medel handed down proclamations about every aspect of Mayan life he could imagine as a ruling elite from a faraway province. The number of recognized nobles in each village was reduced. From then on, there were no such things as nobles and lords; chiefs were the only ones allowed to keep their status. Any secret gatherings of the former nobility were banned. All typical village gatherings were forbidden, including the festivals in each of the Mayan calendar months. Their multifamily households, the type used by those studying at the Izamal monastery and common throughout the Yucatán, were banned, replaced by single-family units. Any man who lived with a woman as man and wife was forced to make the union official under God. Men who refused would be flogged until submission.

The royal official even described how the Maya were to eat their meals. Despite their lack of chairs, tables, and tablecloths, he demanded they sit around the table, fold their hands, and say grace before the first bites were taken.

His final proclamation was the most condemning, and caused lasting repercussions for all parties in the Yucatán: the friars, the *encomenderos*, and the Maya. López Medel sensed how his momentous edict would affect the region and set aside money to pay for colonists without land to enforce its completion, paying them before the change was put into effect. The announcement struck a thunderbolt through the fragile society, striking the ground above Friar Luis's grave, traveling down through the dirt, then striking his right hand, not knowing the friar had dictated the letter to the Crown that had led to López Medel's meddling.

The natives were to be gathered in villages centered around monasteries.

Friar Diego de Landa knew how pointless the previous edicts had been—they were unenforceable. But the last, with mention of money for the male colonists who weren't *encomenderos* to enforce the proclamations in the Yucatán long after López Medel went back to Guatemala, changed everything. For one, it disregarded the Maya's need to move their village to different areas of their provinces after depleting the soil. Within a few years, the *milpas* would yield next to nothing, creating terrible conditions for their food supply. The second problem: the *encomenderos* would be livid, if they weren't already, because moving the natives meant they would no longer live in the *encomiendas,* unless the *encomienda* was lucky enough to be near a monastery. In essence, the Franciscans, already a nuisance to the *encomenderos,* developed a target on their back.

School was canceled within days of the announcements. Friar Diego told all the friars at Izamal they were going out into the Mayan lands with the support of local Spanish men, those without *encomiendas* who were looking for easy money, to tell each village they must move closer to the monastery. He sent word to Merida and Campeche, urging them to do the same—a unified front from the Franciscans that took the opportunity to seize power from the *encomenderos.*

Friar Luis's words rang in Friar Diego's head: "Be their ally in whatever they do." The friars could have chosen to ignore López Medel's decree about Maya relocation, ascribing it to an overreaching of power by Mother Spain, but Friar Diego saw a chance for the Franciscans to take power over the fate of the natives, and he didn't want to squander the opportunity. Trusting in the vision Friar Diego put forth to the other friars in his letters, the friars in Merida and Campeche were preparing to march into the villages across the Yucatán and force the Maya from their homes, making them abandon their property with their meager possessions and leave their cultivated land behind.

THE IZAMAL FRIARS arrived in the first village outside the acceptable proximity to the monastery, one that was held under *encomienda* rule by a Spaniard, the head of three dozen Spanish men. Friar Diego marched into the center of the village alone, yelling for everyone to pay attention to him.

"By order of the Spanish Crown," he began in the Mayan language, in a clear voice that echoed through the silent Mayan settlement. "This entire village needs to move closer to the monastery."

The Maya who heard him stared at the friar, not comprehending what he was saying. They knew his words, because at this time Friar Diego was comfortable speaking in their language, but they couldn't understand the concept of being forced from their home. A lackluster harvest and a period of deliberation had always preceded their relocation in the past, before they left to capitalize on new soil in new *milpas* for their maize. Moving their village now, halfway between planting and harvest, made no sense and would leave them without food before the end of the Spanish year.

Friar Diego stared at the confused faces. He knew they didn't understand. He reminded himself that the relocation was for their own good, that he was saving them from the *encomenderos*' brutality. Speaking to two young boys, he told one to gather the men from the fields and the other to watch what was about to happen so he could relay the news to the other villages. Friar Diego then turned to one of the Spanish colonists who'd come with him, the thugs who would see the Crown's wishes carried out. He pointed to a cooking fire then to a thatched pavilion with nothing beneath: an open space where the natives congregated at the end of the day. The colonist, a flash of understanding lighting a spark of glee in his eyes, strode forward, lit a piece of wood lying near the fire, and put the pavilion to the torch.

The natives emitted a collective gasp. The friar thought they might attack out of agitation, and was grateful López

Medel had had the foresight to mention money for the muscle in advance.

"This whole village will be set on fire by the end of the day!" he declared.

The Mayan children started crying and were consoled by the women, who began gathering their belongings right away. The men returned within hours, berating the friars with questions and terrified of the *encomendero*'s response. Friar Diego answered the men, saying the Spanish Crown had taken steps to protect them from the *encomenderos,* that they would no longer have to serve those dreadful Spaniards who broke their backs for profits, and the sole condition for protection from the Old World was living in villages closer to the Franciscan strongholds.

The Mayan men were torn. Living in closer quarters meant a strain on the already thin soil, and they knew from generations of experience the land couldn't support such a concentration of people. They could fight back, against the friars, but fighting to maintain their status as part of an *encomienda* meant they would go against the one group of people who looked out for their well-being: the Franciscans. With heavy hearts, they aided the women in preparing for the move.

The Maya in the village were ready by the afternoon. They took one last look at their village before setting off with one of the other Izamal friars, who would announce their arrival to a village closer to the monastery. The entire village was then set aflame, not sparing the fruit trees they had cultivated with care during their years in that particular location. Their tears stained the dirt as they walked, serving as guides back to the Izamal monastery for other displaced Maya that lasted for generations.

Friar Diego and his troop of friars and hired colonists scoured the countryside, destroying villages one by one—both in and outside of *encomienda* control—in the name of protecting the natives. He was careful to send Maya to villages close to monasteries within their clan's own historical boundaries, trusting Nachi Cocom's information about the rival families and imagining a strained existence for the natives if they were sent to villages belonging to adversarial families. Each day was marked by the abandonment of a new village. Whenever one friar left with the natives as a guide, another returned; Friar Diego was the Franciscan present for each village's emptying, and he made the pronouncement himself from the center of each village.

Ahkinmai appeared when the Franciscans started clearing the villages near the location of the Maya's new year's festival. Friar Diego was in a hammock, just beyond the reaches of the smoke from the burning village, when he was woken up in the middle of the night by a dream of the Mayan priest in the form of a large bird. In his dream, the bird was pecking him in the lower back while he lay facedown in the sand on the beach where he'd first landed in the New World. One arm was sunken deep into the sand; whenever he used his other arm to free the trapped limb, he lost it to the sand's grip. When the friar opened his eyes, the Mayan priest, complete with his feathered cape, was seated beside him.

"You could've stopped this," Ahkinmai said, an infinite sadness weighing down every word.

"I have no choice in the matter. This is what the Crown wants," Friar Diego replied.

"This could have been dismissed," the Maya countered. "It was within your power."

"This is for your people!" the friar pleaded. Though he couldn't tell if he was awake or still in a dream, he did know that if he made an effort to get the attention of the members of his group, the feathered man would disappear.

"They will die."

Friar Luis's last conversation crept into Friar Diego's mind at the mention of death. "My mentor told me to be the Crown's ally. That it was for the good of your people."

Ahkinmai looked at Friar Diego. His face was obscured by shadow, but his eyes pierced through the darkness. "Your people have brought us nothing but death. Both holy men and farmers have blood on their hands."

Friar Diego sat up in his hammock and discovered Ahkinmai had gone. The sound of gentle snoring came from the other hammocks surrounding him.

No students were educated in the Yucatán during the months of the Maya's relocation. Throughout the Yucatán Peninsula, thousands of Maya were forced from their homes and made to walk hundreds of miles to new villages. They swelled the ranks of the villages lucky enough to be close to the monasteries or created new villages altogether. While Friar Diego saw little resistance—since the Maya surrounding Izamal knew his name and his association with Nachi—the other monastery's friars weren't so lucky. The colonists with them forced the resisting natives by killing those who pushed back against the decree, killing hundreds in order to ensure the compliance of the survivors.

Nachi arrived in Izamal days after Friar Diego returned from scorching the earth. Friar Diego was surprised to see him then; he had assumed the Mayan leader would find him during the relocation efforts. Nachi exchanged pleasantries with the friar as if nothing had happened since they last saw each other.

"I thought you'd try and find me while we were out in the villages," Friar Diego confessed, broaching the topic before Nachi had the chance.

"The order came from across the water. I've seen worse from your people."

Friar Diego's face grew hot from being lumped together with the rest of the Spanish. "Not all of their orders will be followed!" he said, arguing his case. "I don't care how you eat."

"So you chose the order that will kill the most people," Nachi said. He bit his thumbnail.

"Can't you see this was for the protection of your people? If they had followed the instruction, none had to die."

"Ripping people from their homes and it's their fault when they die," Nachi said with an icy stare. "Taking their homes isn't enough? They deserve the blame as well?"

Friar Diego grew silent after absorbing Nachi's words.

Nachi continued. "The death hasn't even begun. The harvest will be nothing this year. Then the true death begins."

Feeding the population close to the monasteries was something no Spaniard had considered during the months of relocation. Friar Diego began to argue they would purchase the required food but realized there would be nothing to purchase after the *encomiendas* had their output slashed by the loss of their labor.

"I didn't force Sotuta to move," Friar Diego said, hoping to earn Nachi's approval. The decision wasn't as charitable as Friar Diego implied: Sotuta was on the boundary between the Mani and Izamal monasteries, and neither location was close enough to make a determination about where the inhabitants should go.

"If you went there you would've found it empty," Nachi said.

"Empty? Where did they go?"

"Farther into the interior. My people will struggle, at first, but they'll have a better chance at life away from the Spanish."

"Is that where you were this whole time?" Friar Diego asked.

"No," Nachi said. "I was going from village to village too, trying to get them to abandon their home and go farther south, away from the Spanish."

Friar Diego thought about the empty villages he had burned. He had assumed they were satellite villages of main ones, the inhabitants hearing about the relocations and making the trip closer to the monasteries on their own volition. There had been so many traveling Maya that tracking where they came from would have been impossible.

"You're only delaying the inevitable," Friar Diego said. "We'll create more monasteries once Friar Lorenzo returns with more friars. They will have to move closer to one eventually."

"And when the time comes, I'll figure out what's best for my people."

"You'd rather they live in *encomiendas*?" Friar Diego said. "At least the friars treat the natives like humans, instead of pack animals."

"And yet you herd them like animals. *Encomenderos* and friars aren't so different: one aims to control our bodies, the other aims to control our souls."

Nachi promised Friar Diego he would make sure the natives wouldn't retaliate and left, leaving the friar wondering what it would take to earn his trust once more. He didn't have to wait very long, because the *encomenderos* made it clear during the harvest that the friars were still the lesser of two evils.

The complaints from the *encomiendas* began with the relocations, but increased once the men, who had once had a stranglehold on natives for labor, realized the extent of their losses. Their reports claimed they lost seven out of eight natives, to both relocation and deaths from their resistance, and no man who lodged official complaints claimed he lost less than fifty percent. These *encomenderos* forced the remaining natives to work even longer hours in an attempt to match their enterprise's expected output, leading to more native deaths in the process. This treatment of the Maya still in the *encomiendas* reached the ears of the natives now living near the monasteries, inspiring them to give thanks to the friars for their protection despite the fact that the actions of the Franciscans, taken under the command of the Spanish Crown, were the cause of those injustices in the first place.

The one saving grace from the entire affair, the one that saved the friars from a unified front of *encomendero* revolt, was that *Adelantado* Francisco Hernandez's property was deemed close enough to the monastery in Mani that his natives weren't taken from his possession. Every Spaniard in the Yucatán knew this would have been an untenable situation, and the friars thanked God for his foresight in making the man's *encomienda* near the Mani monastery. *Adelantado* Francisco didn't raise a finger to stop the other *encomenderos* from striking back though, and twice the monastery in Valladolid, the farthest to the east and one of the Franciscans' smallest establishments, was burned down in response.

The foretold deaths materialized as 1552 faded to a close. The relocated Maya had no food to eat since the crops belonging to the displaced had all been incinerated following López Medel's proclamation. Those who were taken to an existing village were turned away when they tried helping their hosts work the land—if they helped with the harvest, they would deserve some of the results, and no village could spare enough for the extra mouths. The existing villages needed to take care of themselves, leaving thousands of Maya without access to food. The landscape around the monasteries became dotted with decaying settlements, the structures intact but the people inside succumbing to slow, starving deaths. These phantom villages existed both on their own and attached to existing villages, and the Maya who were lucky enough to have food warned their children to stay away from the starving people within. They compared it to the castration of bulls—a band wrapped tight around the scrotum, choking the testicles of blood until they withered and dropped off. The starving people were the same way, parents explained, and soon enough they'd wither away and not have to worry about food anymore.

Ahkinmai was the one person who didn't abandon the dying villages to their fate. He flew between the dying villages around Izamal with his cape trailing behind him, circling the monastery so many times and with such feverish intensity that he kicked up dust behind him, which encircled the Izamal monastery and choked out the sun. Rumors of dust storms came from other monasteries in letters sent among the Franciscans trying to divine God's message in the signs from nature. Friar Diego didn't disclose that the Mayan priests were responsible, not because he didn't believe in their ability, but because he didn't want to admit to himself or others that there might be other priests in the Yucatán with the same capabilities as Ahkinmai.

The feathered man touched down at the Izamal monastery on the Spanish calendar's New Year's Eve. Friar Diego was preparing for bed after presiding over mass for the members of the local villages who had the food and the associated strength to attend the service. Together, they had prayed for those starving in the ghost villages—Friar Diego had prayed they would be accepted into heaven despite not being baptized, and the Maya had prayed death would come quickly.

Ahkinmai got right to the point of his visit. "The displaced are dead," he said.

Friar Diego crossed himself. "Their suffering has ended," he said.

"Suffering you caused," Ahkinmai replied.

Friar Diego saw past the feathers to a tired, decrepit man. His eyes were sunken hollows, pools of proud misery refusing another's pity. "I am keeping them safe," Friar Diego whispered.

"Some, yes," Ahkinmai agreed. "While leading the rest to death. Your eyes are covered with honey while you trample the flowers."

Friar Diego couldn't understand why the Mayan priest was talking about nature. He heard the words but couldn't remove himself enough to appreciate the lesson hidden within. "Were you with any when they died today?" he asked.

"Yes, I was with all of them."

"All of them?" Friar Diego said. His eyes narrowed in suspicion.

"Each and every one." Ahkinmai choked through a lump in his throat. "Your garden is pruned; the remaining flowers will grow. Take care of them."

Friar Diego sat down on his bed, folded his hands, and prayed. "How were you with so many at once?" he said when he raised his eyes.

Ahkinmai took a deep breath, allowing the exhale to trickle through his nose. "I killed them all myself," he said.

CHAPTER EIGHTEEN

Remy Moncard came back around the time Cortez started thinking about going home. Cortez's stomach dropped to his feet, and it lingered there until he curled his toes within his shoes to force it back up. Remy had changed into a suit and walked in carrying a bouquet. Everyone stared as he walked up to the counter on the opposite side of Alara, the spot Cortez had stood, and informed her they were going out to dinner for their anniversary. The other employees smiled to themselves, delighted at having a new topic of conversation that would last for days. If there's one thing a group of young people in close proximity will do, it's gossip.

Alara told Remy she had planned on going to read in the park. "I didn't even remember it was our anniversary!" she said. Finding out Alara was in a relationship didn't dampen Cortez's resolve; in fact, he thought of the man as another thing she needed saving from.

"You go there after work every day," Remy said, rolling his eyes. Cortez took note of the information. "One whole year," Remy continued, saying it loud enough for everyone, including Cortez, to hear.

Alara's short shift ended minutes after Remy arrived, and soon Cortez watched the two of them leaving, Alara no longer wearing her job's required accessories. She complained about not having anything to wear.

"I look terrible next to you!" she said.

"Like you belong on the other side of the park," Remy said with a laugh. "Don't worry, we're going to buy you a new dress. It's part of the date."

Alara laughed, and heat crawled up Cortez's neck. He wanted to be the reason she laughed, and he wanted her with him in a new dress when they walked into church together. His bed called out to him from across the city, beckoning him home to the embrace of escape. It was the same call his mother succumbed to that began her disappearances, one he was able to ignore. His melancholy at seeing Alara leave with Remy was overpowered by wanting to continue existing in her presence, and for the second time that week he found himself following her after she got off work.

The pair went to a multilevel department store. Its exterior was white marble, one part of a larger building, and the name was written in indecipherable cursive. Cortez managed to stay hidden from their view while following them up one level. He hid in the men's shoe section while Alara tried on a dress and matching shoes. Another man, balding and wearing thick glasses, slid next to Cortez while he watched.

"She's gorgeous, isn't she?"

Cortez hadn't noticed the man approach. He was startled, his heart beating loud in his ears. "What are you talking about?" he said.

"You know. Did you think you're the only one who notices her?" The man showed Cortez his employee identification card. "They come in here every so often. Do you see the man helping them? It was his turn to take care of her."

The salesman next to Remy turned to Cortez and the balding individual and flashed a quick smile before returning to the customers. "I'll get the next time they come in," he said with a lizard-like lick of his lips.

Cortez shook his head. "I'm going to save her," he said, resolute.

"You'll need saving from her boyfriend if he ever catches you," he warned Cortez before leaving his side.

Remy paid for the change of clothes with a swipe of his card. Alara wore low black heels and a simple black dress that left little to the imagination. A bag provided by the store held her work clothes and shoes. Cortez saw Alara shake her head when Remy pointed to the makeup section of the store. He grew angry with her companion, not just for being the man by Alara's side, but for suggesting her face required compounds to enhance her beauty. The celebrating couple left the store without noticing the six eyes watching them, two from behind a rack of shoes.

Their actual date was at a restaurant next to the largest fountain Cortez had ever seen. He watched from outside the entrance as they were led to a table right next to the water. After hurrying to the opposite side of the fountain and taking his post on a stone bench with a good view of their table, he watched for the next hour while they enjoyed their meal. Cortez hadn't eaten since lunch but confused the hunger for the longing in his heart. Worrying about his mother never crossed his mind, and at that exact instant she was wondering where her son could be, fearing the worst, with a frozen pizza cooked and sliced for when he arrived.

"She's a beauty, isn't she?" an old man said. He was seated next to Cortez on the bench.

Cortez, sure this was another man who had fallen for

Alara's beauty, said that she was the most beautiful woman he had ever seen.

"The fountain, boy, I mean the fountain. The way the light sparkles around the edges of the water droplets before they come crashing down to earth. It's mesmerizing."

It sounded to Cortez like the man was describing an angel. His angel, Alara. They sat facing the fountain together, the old man watching the water and Cortez watching the couple, until Alara and Remy finished their meal. Their check paid for, they set off in the direction of Alara's house. Cortez followed from a distance, pleased with how well he tracked them without being seen.

They stood outside Alara's apartment for a few minutes, saying goodbye. Remy was asking to be let in, expecting to spend the night, but Alara told him she had work in the morning and didn't want to share her bed. She promised him she would come over tomorrow. Remy, not used to anyone telling him no, pushed back, but Alara was firm.

"I'm going to sleep as soon as I get upstairs," she said. The truth was, she had stopped reading her book at a pivotal moment, and she'd spent the majority of their date looking forward to what happened next. She had waited long enough, and she knew that if Remy came upstairs she wouldn't have a moment's peace. Most nights, she appreciated the company, but when she wanted to be alone there wasn't anything that could convince her otherwise. One of her fears was how she would handle moving in together, if it ever got to that point, but the scenario was far enough away that she didn't bother herself considering how she would navigate the situation.

Once Remy realized how pointless it was to push back against Alara's obstinacy, he kissed her, gave her a hug, and told her he'd see her tomorrow. He watched her walk up the stairs from inside the concrete courtyard before turning to leave.

Cortez ran down the block and turned onto the next street when he saw Remy turn around. There was no good reason for him to be in the area. He panicked when he realized he didn't know which way Remy would walk, knowing that Alara's companion might catch him lingering at the corner. He peeked around the corner and saw Remy walking right towards him. Cortez was lucky Remy was too lost in thought to notice the pair of eyes cutting through the darkness. Cortez started walking away from the corner, hoping that even if Remy was going in the same direction he'd never recognize the back of his head or his backpack. He turned around at the end of the block and saw Remy walking in the opposite direction. He was headed back towards the coffee shop and the high-rises. Cortez turned around, hurried forward, and followed Remy until he disappeared into a luxury apartment building.

LIFE in the city after the sun went down reminded Cortez of life he had seen in movies. He hadn't noticed while he was following the couple, but now he couldn't notice anything else. There were well-dressed people in restaurants, walking back from or going to late dinners, and shiny cars reflected the headlights of their fellow vehicles. Cortez took the scene in from outside Remy's apartment building and didn't see when his quarry reappeared at the entrance, letting in another woman.

Remy recognized Cortez from the coffee shop and was shocked to find him outside his building. They were about the same age, but a lifetime on different sides of the city had left them with little else in common. After he let the woman inside the building, he told her to wait inside the entrance. "There's something I have to take care of," he said. "I'll only be a minute." He left the building and approached Cortez, unnoticed.

"Have you been following me?" he said while standing next to Cortez, staring at the city alongside him.

Cortez had never been so terrified in his life. He had been yelled at before, and was scared each time it happened, but something in the coldness of Alara's friend's voice made his hair stand on end. It was all he could do to shake his head.

"Then why are you here?" Remy asked, without looking at Cortez, after seeing the denial out of the corner of his eye.

"I was in the area," Cortez responded.

Remy turned to face Cortez. He grabbed him by the front of his shirt. "Look, I don't know what kind of weird thing you have with Alara, but she's taken," he said. "Don't let me see you around here again." With that, Remy turned and started walking back into his building; Cortez downed a blue pill.

Seeing Alara on a date reminded Cortez of his own inexperience with spending intimate time with a woman. Once he'd recovered from Remy's threat, reminding himself that Alara's friend couldn't keep him from the coffee shop, he spent the rest of the walk home lost in thoughts of how he could keep a conversation going if he was alone with her. His first mistake was assuming the entire responsibility rested on his shoulders. As he walked back through the park, he scanned his memory for questions he had been asked when first meeting people, knowing he could never ask the specific questions about her peculiarities he wanted answered. Though he remembered meeting people at the factory, at church, and at school, he couldn't come up with a single piece of useful information. The nighttime people in the park didn't dare approach the young man who was muttering to himself; they thought he had been let loose by some benevolent caretaker, allowed to roam the paths at night because he couldn't be allowed out during the day for fear he'd scare anyone who saw him conversing with his own shadow. Cortez thought about the various television shows and movies he relied on for cues about proper social interaction. He remembered the characters dressed in their Sunday best, how they put their napkins on their laps to signal their politeness and smiled while looking their companions in the eye. For the life of him, he couldn't remember what they said.

His second mistake was assuming any strategy he came up with would even be effective in the heat of battle.

His mother was waiting for him when he got home. She was in her recliner, watching a telenovela, and Cortez knew right away from the angle of her chair that she was still wide awake. Still hoping for a miracle, he closed the door without making a sound.

The truth was that his mother had spent the entire night staring at the television without registering what was happening on-screen. Her son, the lone bright spot in her gloomy world, hadn't come home at his usual time. She knew he didn't make friends, and didn't have hobbies, so his disappearance was a mystery she couldn't ignore. In hopes his nose might lead him back, she had made a second dinner and left it on the counter, chicken and onions with enough spices that the smells of the dish permeated their neighborhood and left an indelible scent trail Cortez could follow back home. It would have worked if he hadn't been on the far side of the park.

His mother's disappointed stare bored into Cortez's head before he turned around from closing the door. When he turned to face the flames, he braced for the onslaught of heat from her words with a smile.

"I'm home," he said.

"I see that," she responded. She waited, hoping the heat would melt her son's exterior and reveal the secret he held inside. When he walked over to the counter and inspected the prepared meals—the chicken dish and the pizza, now cold—with a long sniff, she forced the issue.

"Where were you?" she said. "You never come home this late."

Cortez grabbed a plate, pretending it was the same time he arrived each day after working at the factory, and helped himself to two chicken thighs. He didn't want to lie, but he didn't see another way out of the situation. In a flash of inspiration, he told her he'd gone to a coffee shop.

"Alone?" she asked.

"No," he replied. He took his plate, sat down on the couch, and began to eat. The meat fell off the bone, and the chicken's soft tissues were indistinguishable from the flesh. "This is good," he said.

His mother ignored the compliment. "Are you going to tell me who you went with?" she said.

"I met a girl there," he said. It wasn't a lie—he had met Alara—but it wasn't the truth.

Cortez's mother changed in an instant. An angry, worried mother hen was replaced by a docile, patient bird worthy of display in an poultry show. "A girl?" she said. Never, not once, had Cortez even bothered to feign interest in the opposite sex. She had resigned herself to dying without grandkids long ago. Now, the potential continuation of her line made her look around her meager apartment, taking stock of what was suitable for children. She determined her collection of statues depicting the crucifixion were both too fragile and too violent to continue existing in the living room. A shrine for all her religious ceramics appeared in her bedroom the very next day.

Shaking herself from her daydream, his mother asked the girl's name.

"Alara," Cortez answered.

His mother spit out a rapid slew of questions. "Does she

have a last name? Where's she from? What does she do?" The questions continued for a full five minutes, without a moment for Cortez to answer a single one.

Cortez stopped eating and paid attention to her interrogation, not so he could answer her but because he realized these were the types of questions suitable for a first date. He remembered as many as he could. When his mother stopped, Cortez told her he didn't know the answer to any of them and informed her that he would find out as much as he could and report back as soon as he discovered more. The conversation inspired Cortez to come up with a few questions himself. He wanted to know whether anything she had done had caused a rainstorm, how often she worried about saying the wrong thing, and if she preferred to cry in the shower because it was an easy way to hide her tears.

"Here, let me get you more food," Cortez's mother said when she saw his empty plate. She returned with two more thighs and three tortillas. She knew, from her own experience, that children couldn't be made without the proper amount of fuel. It was the first time her son's thinness bothered her, and she resolved to remedy the situation the best way she knew how: from then on, she decided, there would be three full meals a day, and four on Sunday.

Nothing Cortez could say or do could dampen his mother's excitement at the mention of Alara. She stole glances at her son, each one bursting with maternal pride, for the entire half hour they watched television together before going to bed. When he went to bed and she reclined her seat, she stared through the ceiling, past the neighbors above her, and into the heavens, thanking God for bringing her the chance to prove her worth as a grandmother.

CHAPTER NINETEEN

Friar Lorenzo de Bienvenida didn't approve of the Maya's relocation. He had returned in late spring 1553 with fifteen friars in tow, ready for the expansion of the number of monasteries in the Yucatán. His plan, he informed Friar Diego de Landa, would have created enough monasteries to fulfill Tomás López Medel's order from the Spanish Crown, without the forced relocation and subsequent strain on the area's resources.

"You should've waited," the returning friar told Friar Diego during their first meeting after he arrived back in the Yucatán. They were seated together in the sanctuary at Merida, in the altar's shadow after their morning prayers.

"How was I supposed to know you would bring any men at all?"

"I sent a letter last autumn."

"To Merida, not to me," Friar Diego said, pouting. He couldn't help bringing up his lack of inclusion in the communication chain, still smarting from Friar Lorenzo's lack of support in his appointment as Guardian of the Izamal monastery.

"In any case, I've come back to a mess. Almost half the

population is with the Lord now," Friar Lorenzo said, crossing himself.

"But the ones still alive are now closer to us and away from suffering at the hands of the *encomenderos*."

Friar Lorenzo sighed. The relocation was complete, and no amount of discussion could change the situation. He changed the subject to the upcoming Franciscan council. "Your position will become permanent soon, I suspect," he said, looking around the sanctuary.

"As do I. You'll be elected *Custos*."

"Friar Luis's passing affected me greatly," Friar Lorenzo said. "I wish I could've seen him during his final days."

"He never doubted your friendship."

Both friars grew silent, preoccupied with memories of their friend and mentor.

A timid voice spoke up behind them. "Excuse me," one of the new friars fresh from Spain whispered. Finding his voice, he spoke again, louder. "Excuse me," he said.

"We heard you the first time," Friar Diego replied.

Friar Lorenzo smiled at the young priest, urging him to continue; it was a deliberate juxtaposition to Friar Diego's curt reply.

"The others are ready to come in," the young man said.

"Thank you. We'll gather them when we're ready," Friar Lorenzo said, closing his eyes in an elongated blink and lowering his head.

The new arrival turned and left the priests in their shared solitude.

Friar Lorenzo broke the renewed silence. "Before they join us, tell me about Friar Luis's last days."

Friar Diego told Friar Lorenzo about their final conversation—leaving out their discussion of the prophecy about the coming age of the Holy Spirit—while their companions waited outside.

When the tale was told they prayed together, asking God to guide their actions in the upcoming council, before Friar Diego retrieved the rest of the Yucatán friars and brought them into the sanctuary.

At the council, Friar Lorenzo's role as *Custos* was made official, as well as Friar Diego's charge as Guardian of the Izamal monastery. Friar Nicolás de Albalate was sent to Izamal by order of the new *Custos*—Friar Lorenzo wanted a veteran presence balancing out the young priest because the Izamal monastery's strategic importance required the additional resources.

Friar Diego took the additional oversight without worry. Friar Nicolás had years of experience, but he was no match for Friar Diego's fire-whirl energy. There was little the old man would do when faced with the resolute speed with which Friar Diego made decisions.

Friar Lorenzo made another announcement regarding Izamal and Merida: he had secured funding for new facilities. Money was allocated for the two locations to receive a complete overhaul.

"I know you took steps to create a new infirmary and school," Friar Lorenzo said to Friar Diego in front of every influential Franciscan in the Yucatán. "These were good and proper steps."

A flush of pride crept up Friar Diego's neck.

"But with these additional resources we can build something more permanent in both locations. In Merida, we'll use the stones from the neglected portion of the ancient settlement this city was built on to create our new facility."

Friar Diego already knew where to get stone in Izamal. On the opposite side of the monastery's adjoining settlement—the portion of Izamal where the colonists lived outside the Church's direct rule—sat an ancient Mayan temple. Nachi

Cocom had explained its use was important during droughts, that the Maya kept the temple cleared of vegetation so that whenever the next drought came they could pray to their gods for rain. The Franciscans had left the site untouched in hopes the natives' conversion would lead to the temple's abandonment.

Friar Lorenzo looked at Friar Diego. "In Izamal, try and find a source of stone already harvested from the earth by the natives that isn't in use. Not forming the building materials ourselves will save a lot of money and time."

Friar Diego nodded, making no mention of his plans.

The friars stayed in Merida one more day, praying together and catching up with old friends. Friar Diego spent much of his time with Friar Francisco Navarro, his friend from the ship, discovering he was still stationed in Campeche. Their lives were similar in all respects, the lone difference being their attitudes towards the Maya's relocation. While Friar Diego still held resolute in his belief that it was a necessary step for the preservation of the natives, his friend believed the natives had suffered because the Franciscans wanted to teach the *encomenderos* a lesson.

"The natives are caught in our power struggle," Friar Francisco said during one of the two men's walks after lunch. "Many died so we could strike a blow to our fellow Spaniards."

"It was imperative," Friar Diego said.

"I'm not so sure. Did many die at Izamal?"

"Nearly half," Friar Diego said.

"How can you justify that?" Friar Francisco asked. His time in the Campeche monastery had taken no toll on his face; he still had the same heavy eyebrows and deep-set eyes Friar Diego remembered.

"The ones who believe will repopulate the region, then the earth. Christianity depends on it," Friar Diego said.

Friar Francisco looked sideways at his friend. "The Old World is a long way from here," he said.

"And they depend on our success with the natives. Relocation was another step towards their salvation."

THE NEXT DAY, Friar Diego walked back to Izamal with Friar Nicolás, six other friars, and the two natives from Izamal. He stayed in Izamal with Friar Nicolás and two of the friars; the four remaining continued on to Valladolid, where Friar Juan de la Puerta took up his post as Guardian of the monastery.

The four Izamal friars found Ix Cuatchel and the two natives, who they'd left in charge of the monastery, in the sanctuary. One of the young men was wearing a friar's habit and was preaching to Ix and his fellow student. The preacher lost all color in his face when the friars blocked the sun streaming in from the open entrance. Ix and the other turned around, then stood up when they realized the friars had returned. The preaching Maya took off the habit, folding it with care before placing it on the altar, then all three of them left without a word spoken by any.

Friar Nicolás laughed when they had gone. "What are you teaching them?" he said. "They soak up the Lord's word like a sponge!"

The other two friars laughed. Friar Diego was lost in thought. He turned and walked out, going into the living quarters. He sat down and wrote a letter to Friar Lorenzo, inspired by the new Yucatán veteran's talk of a drastic increase in the number of monasteries. He outlined a rough plan where natives would serve as schoolteachers in the remote areas of the Yucatán to the Maya who had escaped relocation. His initial thought about the natives whom Nachi helped live outside both *encomienda* and monastery rule was to wait until the reinforcements from Spain arrived; with the additional men, they could go farther into the country with their outposts. Instead, the young natives could serve as both an introduction to the Spanish way of life and as a bellwether for their inclusion into the church. He found Ix and told her to tell the preacher he wished to see him.

"Then, go to the students and tell them classes resume tomorrow," he said.

The preaching native found Friar Diego showing the grounds to Friar Nicolás. He waited while Friar Diego explained the construction of the new facilities. Friar Nicolás was amazed at the extent to which the natives had helped.

"They still look to us for every little thing in Merida," he shared, adding compliments about Friar Diego's productive relationship with the natives around Izamal.

Friar Diego agreed, then turned to the young man he had caught in a habit.

"Let's walk," he said before dismissing Friar Nicolás.

Friar Diego and the preaching native set off through the settlement without saying a word to each other. The tradesmen all stared at the friar, hoping he would stop by their establishment and spend some of the Church's coin, wondering if the young native with him was there to carry his purchases. The pair walked straight through.

"You know the temple, right?" Friar Diego asked, in the Mayan language.

The young man nodded.

"What would you say if I wanted to use its stone for another building?"

The young Maya thought for a moment. "I'd say God found a purpose for the stone," he said.

"And you'd be correct," Friar Diego said.

The temple, built from large stone cubes, was a short walk

past the settlement's end. There were three tiers, and fifty steps rose from the ground to the uppermost platform. It was as wide as the entirety of the existing Izamal monastery, providing plenty of stone. A large face was carved into the rock near the top of the temple; it was the height of two full-grown men and faced the settlement. The staircase was split in two at this height to accommodate the face, rejoining before the final ascent to the top level.

"I'm going to build a monastery to rival the one in Rome," Friar Diego said.

The Mayan student had heard of Rome from the friars, knowing the city's significance because of the hushed tones used when invoking the city's name. He didn't realize the sheer scale of the project. For all the native student knew, the men who'd taught him about God were the leaders of the entire church, and he couldn't imagine the religion's reach across the ocean. But the young Maya couldn't shake his uncertainty about the repercussions for preaching to Ix and his friend.

"Are you mad I took your position on the altar?" the student asked.

Friar Diego was pulled from his reverie. "What? No, not at all. In fact, I intend to send you out to preach to the natives who are hesitant to come to the monastery."

The young student was speechless. He wanted to drop to the ground and kiss the friar's feet, but he stayed content with following Friar Diego while the priest inspected the temple.

The power of Friar Diego's destiny took hold of him in the space. He envisioned the largest monastery in the Yucatán, built with the natives' industriousness and the Church's gold, unaware of how spending ran antithetical to his beloved austerity.

"We might need more stone than this," he said.

"More than this?" the student replied, his eyes wide.

"Yes. What I have in mind will last throughout the ages."

"Well, there's plenty of stone here." The student then scraped his heel against the ground, exposing stone bricks beneath a thin layer of dirt. "All of Izamal sits on this."

Friar Diego's eyes grew wide and his exaltation made his feet lose contact with the ground. "The monastery doesn't," he said, descending back to earth when he remembered the construction of the school and the holes dug for the support beams. "The natives dug into the ground, no problem at all."

"The settlement sits on stone walkways, and there's more here." The student turned perpendicular to the path and walked into the surrounding trees, telling Friar Diego to follow. They soon found an overgrown stone wall, which the student climbed up, followed by Friar Diego.

"This runs down the length of the path. It continues behind the town and ends at the monastery. Is this enough stone?"

Friar Diego grabbed the boy's cheeks and kissed him on the forehead. "God has put you here for a reason," he said. "We will sanctify a place once used for an abomination!"

The pair dashed off back to the monastery. Friar Diego wrote another letter to Friar Lorenzo, outlining his excitement about the temple that could be used for stone and asking for guidance about receiving the necessary funding. He also mentioned that Friar Lorenzo hadn't divulged the existence of the Izamal temple when he first arrived in the monastery, saying he'd discovered it because of the natives' willingness to help their cause. The letter was sent with the same man who was tasked with taking the letter about natives teaching other natives, since the man chosen to take the letter to Merida had been waiting for early the next day to set off—a solo trip could be taken in a day but required little rest and setting off before the sun rose.

. . .

Friar Diego had to wait a month for Friar Lorenzo's reply. The *Custos* first apologized for the delay in his response, then commended Friar Diego on the worthy idea of sending his top students farther into the Yucatán to teach the unreached natives. He waited until the end of his letter to address the building of the new monastery. His first mention of it was about how the presence of the temple wasn't important, and that he'd assumed the young friar had discovered it during his wanderings in the initial months in the Yucatán. He said the stone on the paths and on the walls outside the settlement were perfect for the task, since they weren't in use, but that the temple would best be spared as a gesture of goodwill to the natives. He warned that tearing down a temple could stoke flames of anger towards the Franciscan cause. His final words were to tell Friar Diego to try and find an alternative source of stone if more was still needed.

The letter fell to the desk after Friar Diego read it. He stood up and paced behind his chair, seething. The natives had no questions about who they allied themselves with. Wasn't the quality of his relationship with them enough to ensure their goodwill towards the friars?

Friar Diego sought out Friar Nicolás and found the older friar seated at the table, talking with natives and the other friars after a shared meal. The letter was thrust into his hands. Friar Nicolás read the letter and stared at Friar Diego.

"Why should you need more than the walls and pathways? Shouldn't that be more than enough?"

Friar Diego ripped the letter from his hands. "No. It's not. I intend to build the biggest monastery in the New World."

"And there's nowhere else to get the stone?"

"The *Custos*," Friar Diego began, the title said with disgust, "said they had to be unused. What do the natives need a temple for once they know God? Its use has ended!"

Friar Nicolás stood and asked Friar Diego to walk with him. When they were away from the others, he said, "Are you going to go against Friar Lorenzo's wishes?"

"He didn't expressly forbid it," Friar Diego said. "And I know the natives better than him."

Friar Nicolás's face softened, and he looked at Friar Diego like a father would a son. "I don't doubt that, judging by the relationship you have with them, but you can't discount Friar Lorenzo's experience."

"I rebuilt the infirmary and school, why can't he trust me with rebuilding the most important part of the monastery as I see fit?"

"You didn't build anything, the natives did. And if all you want is a new sanctuary, why do you need so much stone?"

"The temple is an abomination!" Friar Diego roared. The friars and natives seated at the table, still within earshot, stared at him. "Why are you supporting their worship of idols?"

"Friar Lorenzo is urging caution. You'd be wise to heed his advice."

"I know what's best for the Izamal natives."

Friar Diego stormed off. The next day, he sent a letter written in anger the night before, informing Friar Lorenzo that construction would begin the following day, without mentioning the temple.

When the students arrived for class that day, Friar Diego informed all one hundred and forty-seven of them that they would be going to the temple. Some of the older students knew why, because their friend had told them the night before, but the majority of the students had no idea why a Christian priest wanted to visit the place where their relatives worshipped ancient gods. The colonists in the Izamal settlement watched the strange procession, the Guardian of the Izamal monastery followed by hundreds of Mayan boys, curious about their destination. When they went straight through the town without stopping a single time, the traders all closed their establishments and followed the group, intent on finding out their purpose.

Friar Diego marched his group right up to the base of the temple. Friar Nicolás, with the other two friars behind him, hurried to Friar Diego's side. They were out of breath from catching up to the group after not being told about the short trip and struggled to regain their composure.

"We should wait for word from Merida," Friar Nicolás said, knowing Friar Diego had sent another letter.

"Our word already arrived. Friar Lorenzo said to use stones not being used. The natives have no use for their old gods. Problem solved."

One of the other friars stationed at Izamal spoke up. "Let's pray for guidance," he said. "The Lord will show us the correct path."

"I'm showing you the correct path," Friar Diego said. "You three are the ones who don't want to see the path God has laid out, plain as day." Friar Diego then turned away from the friars and turned to the throng of students. "We were handed a holy task," he began, speaking loud enough for all to hear.

The tradesmen had heard about the Maya's human sacrifices, and to them it appeared Friar Diego was beginning a mass sacrifice with the native youth.

"A new sanctuary will be built on this ground. These stones will provide the materials for the building, and you will provide the materials for the congregation!"

The student who had shown the friar the hidden available stone let out a whoop. The rest of the students followed suit, their hands raised in joy.

Friar Diego then talked about their duty to serve God, that they had all been called to play their part in the fight against the devil by tearing down the blasphemous structure. The students worked themselves into a frenzy in response.

One of the tradesmen, a leatherworker who had arrived from Spain less than a year before, walked over to the other friars from Izamal. He spoke to Friar Nicolás, the oldest among the group.

"They're going to tear down the temple?"

"Materials for a new monastery."

"Their parents aren't going to like this one bit," the leatherworker said. In the short time he'd been in the Yucatán, he'd watched the Franciscans, urged on by Friar Diego, take steps to anger those in power among both the colonists and the natives. He had no way of knowing, and Friar Nicolás never mentioned, how Friar Diego was also taking steps contrary to the leaders within the Franciscan Order.

The students were foaming at the mouth, eager for their chance at attacking the devil by destroying the temple. Friar Diego stood over the group, confident and proud. He looked at the other friars from Izamal with the smugness of an untouchable petulant child. While focusing his gaze on Friar Nicolás alone, Friar Diego lifted his hands.

The native students grew quiet. They wriggled in place with their fevered energy, like maggots in rotting flesh.

Friar Diego posed a question to the group. "Who will be the first to dislodge one of the temple's stones?" he said, letting his arms open wide.

One hundred forty-seven Mayan boys, ranging in age from four to seventeen, scrambled up the temple. Their fingers dug at the spaces between the stones until blood oozed from beneath their fingernails and sweat poured from their faces. It took half an hour for the removal of the first stone by the group of the oldest students, led by the young man who Friar Diego had caught preaching to the others. When there was enough space behind the stone for a body, two boys squeezed in and shoved the massive square stone with their knees. It toppled down the edifice, piercing the thin layer of dirt above the courtyard stones and displacing the thin rectangular slabs so they stuck out at odd angles.

The children all cheered. Friar Diego smiled, and Friar Nicolás sighed. Not a single person saw the steady stream of water trickling from the eyes of the face carved into the temple.

CHAPTER TWENTY

Cortez woke up the next day with the certainty that Alara was well within his grasp. He didn't remember a single dream he'd had overnight but knew, for no reason whatsoever, that his sleeping mind had spent the previous night calculating the best way to wrest her affection away from her boyfriend. The first thing he resolved to do was to find out the name of his competition. Again, he went through the motions to keep up the appearance he was headed to the factory, but this time he was forced to eat a breakfast of four eggs and tortillas before leaving.

"You need your strength," his mother said with a twinkle in her eye. The food was swallowed down with minimal chewing.

Cortez retraced his now-familiar route back to Decant, talking to himself the entire time. While walking through the park he practiced the questions he would ask Alara, remembering a handful provided by his mother. He practiced how he would smile, how he would look at her, imagining the mannerisms of the characters on old sitcoms and hoping his own reproductions would encourage the same results. Instead of hearing the sounds of the park, he heard the laugh tracks at his jokes, the various oohs and aahs from the nonexistent studio audience. In a moment of weakness—since he knew the actors never broke the fourth wall—he waved to the trees around him, acknowledging them as if they were the imagined audience. The other people in the park who witnessed him that day never forgot the man who laughed among the trees and engaged in conversations with himself, all the while with a faraway look in his eyes, never knowing anyone else in the world existed.

Alara was working when Cortez arrived. She looked up the moment he walked in the door and gave him a nod before returning to the task at hand. Cortez believed his immense love for her had forced her to look up when he first walked in, his own body creating a magnetic field that called out to her. Even if he had been told the truth, that she was annoyed at the number of customers on that busy morning and was looking to see if there was a break in their arrival, he would have decided the strength of his love had caused the customer conditions that led to her annoyance. His love determined everything around him, the life force early philosophers tried to imbue upon everything in the world.

The line was filled with impatient people waiting for their chance to order. The lone person stationed at the register was brand new—this was her first time handling the orders without someone watching over her shoulder. To her credit, she kept her cool in spite of the angry glances from the line of people in front of her. Cortez wasn't in a rush, since he didn't have anywhere to be, but he was eager to stand opposite Alara and use some of the questions he had been practicing. He couldn't decide which one was best for the situation, and by the time he stepped to the front of the line and got his coffee—since it was the cheapest thing on the menu—no clear victor had emerged. He moved to the spot and stood opposite her, separated by the counter, and waited for her to acknowledge him.

Alara knew Cortez was in front of her, but she was too busy

to spare any energy leading him in conversation. She hoped he would move if she ignored him long enough, but it soon became clear that it wouldn't happen. She sighed, looked up, and said hello.

"Good morning, Alara," Cortez said with a smile.

The way Cortez said her name sent a chill down her spine. He said it like he knew something about her, a deep secret he kept hidden away, something he thought they shared but in fact he possessed alone. "Good morning," she said before looking back down at the next drink she had to make.

Cortez waited for divine inspiration to strike him about what to say. Instead, he was hit by the devil's jealous flame. "I saw you leaving yesterday with that guy. Is he your boyfriend?" he said. A fist-sized knot formed in his stomach, and he got the urge to crawl beneath one of the lounge chairs in the corner and die like the cockroach he was.

"Remy? Yes, he is." The look on Cortez's face was pure anguish, a tortured soul who'd just found out that his one-way ticket from hell to heaven was a fake. She loved it, which scared her. Nothing gave her more pleasure than to dash men's egos on her rocky shore, but this was different. Cortez had no ego—his presence on earth barely made a ripple—but seeing him suffer gave her great satisfaction. Unknown to her, Alara's seed of revenge had lasted for generations. Her ancestors, the Maya from the Yucatán Peninsula, had been victims of overeager missionaries, the leader of which was Cortez's ancestor. The history was lost to time, but it existed in Alara's hands, and with a cruelty she'd never experienced before she grew determined to twist the knife in the stomach of the man who stood across from her.

"It was our anniversary yesterday," she continued. Children frying an ant with a magnifying glass would be familiar with the fascination coursing through her veins. "He's a great guy. Best

I've ever met." It was a lie, but worth saying, because Cortez placed a hand on the counter for support. The truth was, Remy made it easy to be with him by paying for everything. Being treated like a decoration was something she was willing to put up with for the time being, but she'd never considered the arrangement permanent.

Cortez was struggling to breathe. The weight on his chest had increased ever since he'd asked the ill-advised question, made heavier with each word Alara spoke. He managed to hold up his coffee while mumbling something about sugar, then turned around and walked to the condiment bar so he didn't have to look at her for a second longer. Along with the belief that everything happened because of his love for her, he also believed her responses were a direct result of his poor questioning, not knowing generations of anger were being released, aimed squarely at his soul.

He spent the day lingering in Decant, getting refill after refill and attributing his beating heart to the pulses of love instead of the doses of caffeine running through his veins. Alara took the opportunity to make him squirm every time he approached, mentioning the ways Remy was a great guy, the money his family had, and the quality of his education. In truth, Alara was certain Remy would be a mediocre student if he didn't have access to the highest-quality resources. Her own parents, thinking they were doing the right thing, had kicked her out of the home as soon as she turned eighteen, forcing her to work while trying to get through school. By the time she met Cortez, the demands of both occupations had become too much, and she had dropped school to focus on working full-time. She continued reading in an attempt to further her education on her own, propelled by the desire to prove to her parents she could make it in this world. Remy's money was a benefit she didn't like to acknowledge but couldn't ignore, providing access to a way of life different from anything she had ever known.

Alara had two breaks during her seven-hour shift—a short one, ten minutes long, and a longer one so she could eat lunch. During both, she toyed around with the idea of sitting next to Cortez and continuing her torture of him. In the end, she decided to take a seat in the lobby and read. Cortez studied her while she was lost in Colombia at a time when telegraphs were still in use. The first thing he did was memorize the book she was reading: *Love in the Time of Cholera*. He deemed it fate that she was lost in a book about love; he'd never heard of cholera, pronouncing the "ch" in his head as it's written. The question he was going to ask her was seared into his brain, but the nerve to ask it never materialized. "What's your favorite book?" he imagined himself asking over and over again, in various positions and with an array of facial expressions. He'd asked it to her imagined ghost so many times, in so many ways, he forgot he had never asked the question in the first place, and when she opened the book on her second break that day he believed fate, in the form of Alara, was giving him the answer to his question by showing him the book in her hands.

He stayed for the entirety of her shift. In the late afternoon, her coworker approached her, tapped her on the shoulder, and, using one hand to point to the wrist of the other, indicated the time. Cortez had to act fast. His plan had been hatched during the hours he had watched her, and he knew that there was little time to waste. He threw away his coffee cup—along with the trash from his lunch—and closed his backpack before darting out the door, hoping Alara didn't see his quick exit. A woman with a stroller, out for a walk with her baby, almost fell victim to his hurried exit as they stood in his path. With an agility that rivaled God's winged creatures, he swerved, missing the stroller by the width of a feather. The distance between Decant and the park was covered in a handful of full-length strides as he sprinted down the street, weaving among the other people on the sidewalk. Turning, Cortez ran down the street alongside the park and dove into the shadow of the trees at the same spot he hoped Alara would enter within minutes.

His plan was simple: to wait for Alara at her favorite bench.

Alara's favorite bench had seen better times. It was made of wood riddled with wounds from the spaces left by large splinters. Some of the trenches were the same color as the bench itself, and the fresher wounds were the light brown of new wood. A trash can nearby overflowed with plastic bags and various colored wrappers, and there were water bottles placed along the rim, some of which had fallen onto the surrounding grass. Cortez took a seat and watched the soccer game taking place in the open grassy space ahead of him, nervous at the prospect of sitting next to Alara. His list of prepared questions swirled through his head. Determined to ask one that would lead to a more fruitful conversation, he decided to ask about the book she was reading; he knew the title but little else. He stared ahead, lost in thought, while the team without shirts scored.

Alara laughed to herself when she saw Cortez seated in her spot. She considered finding another spot to read before he saw her, not wanting to share her space, but instead she exhaled and emerged from beneath the trees, walking straight to where she planned to spend the rest of the winding-down afternoon. There was no way she would allow him to rain on her parade, not when she'd spent all day cooped up indoors and craved the sunshine. When she got close, Cortez turned and looked at her. He looked both scared and fascinated, making her feel like a beautiful, poisonous creature. She sat down and kept her eyes straight ahead, aware that Cortez was staring at her.

The silence tore Cortez apart. He couldn't command his tongue to speak words and for the first time came to hate his body, a repulsion that separated his mind from his flesh. The split never healed.

"You've followed me before, haven't you," she said after a moment had passed. She was not aware of Cortez's inner turmoil.

Cortez knew he had to say something. He didn't want to acknowledge her question, hoping that ignoring it would erase his duplicitous actions. It occurred to him that she must not know about him following her home, a fact that provided little relief from the flames surrounding him. He mustered every ounce of strength he had and asked, "What book are you reading?" though he already knew the answer.

Alara withdrew her book and showed him the cover. "This is my third time reading it. He's my favorite author."

Cortez was elated at the correctness of his instincts, making no distinction between favorite author and favorite book. He had never heard of Gabriel García Márquez, but he decided then and there to find out as much as he could about him. Alara turned to face him before he could think of a response.

"Leave me alone so I can read," she said.

Cortez scurried away, knowing he had just gotten a glimpse of the lock around her heart, and certain he knew the exact place where he could find the key.

The Saturday after he learned Alara's literary preferences was unlike any Cortez had ever known. He leapt from his bed at the same time he did during the week, this time without an alarm, because he hadn't slept the night before. His night had been spent in the hazy half-light of darkness familiar to those who live in the city, his eyes wide open and staring at the ceiling, certain that no dream could be as comforting as the memory of sitting next to Alara the previous day. Saturdays were his chance to sleep late each week, instead of waking up to go to work or church, and his habit was to transplant himself from the bed to the couch and watch television until it was lunchtime. Not having slept a wink, he abandoned the task, eager to put the plan that had kept him awake all night into action.

His mother was still in her room when he got ready for the day, and he ate some of the leftovers overflowing from their refrigerator that had appeared after he shared there was a woman in his life. He closed their front door, careful not to make a noise, and descended the building's steps. The world outside his apartment had been awaiting his arrival. Birds launched from their perch and flew in clusters of ever-changing shapes, calling out to each other through the cloud-free sky. His neighbors, who ignored him most days, went out of their way to say hello. Each step he took was lighter than the one before, and by the time he got to the library he was floating on a pad of air as thick as the Bible.

CHAPTER TWENTY-ONE

THE TEMPLE's destruction took weeks. The students were responsible for the initial dismantling. Then, at Friar Diego de Landa's insistence, they made their entourages in the temporary villages take their place at the temple so they could return to their studies. At first the natives resisted. The temple belonged to their god of rain, and they feared destroying it would bring about a drought that would ruin their already strained food supply. The students convinced their fathers, the lords and chiefs Tomás López Medel had stripped of the bulk of their power, that destroying the temple would bring them into the Christian God's good graces. The Maya already relied on the Franciscans for protection against the *encomenderos*, where labor was the currency, and another transaction for their labor without the associated Spanish brutality made sense, according to the students.

The Mayan workers gathered massive piles of stone in the courtyard in front of where the temple once stood. Rolling a square stone building block took three men heaving on one side. Friar Diego allotted enough resources for each man to receive one meal each day, since the funds provided by the Church didn't cover the costs of feeding so many souls more.

The students learned from Friar Nicolás de Albalate while the temple was being destroyed and Friar Diego busied himself making plans for his crowning achievement. Drawing inspiration from Rome, he made the open atrium the second largest in the world, behind the one in the holy city. His initial plans had called for it to be the largest in the world, but Friar Nicolás urged the younger friar's reconsideration, saying the natives should look to Rome for guidance and that a more imposing structure in the New World might undercut their responsibility to the Old. Friar Diego, knowing the prophecy of the coming New Age would soon make Rome inconsequential, didn't want anyone suspicious of his own motives, so he agreed with the advice rather than explaining the reason why the size of the atrium in the Old World would soon be irrelevant. All churches would be obsolete once the age of the Holy Spirit arrived because of Friar Diego's conversion of the natives. His chief concern was a meeting place large enough for the masses—it could be twice as large as Rome for all he cared, provided there was enough stone. But older heads prevailed, making Friar Diego realize how such a massive space would be interpreted by those higher up the hierarchy he believed would soon come toppling down.

The atrium's grass would be kept well-groomed, an Eden for believers among the dangers of the Yucatán wilderness. The permanent stones would serve as a lasting reminder for generations of Maya about the friar's protection from the *encomenderos'* brutality. He planned for the main building to rise higher in the sky than Chichen Itza, the cross at the top looking down over God's dominion in the New World. All natives would become Christian believers when looking to the cross high in the sky, bringing the third age of man into existence.

Friar Diego waited for Ahkinmai in his dreams during the temple's destruction and his months of planning, certain of the coming rebuke. He worked late into the night and rose early each day, week after week, minimizing his chances of dreaming of the large bird. His body was so exhausted each day that he collapsed into the hammock, lying dead for a few hours before fear woke him.

Despite his every precaution guarding against the Mayan priest's entrance into his life, Friar Diego wound up walking straight from the monastery to Ahkinmai under his own power. Nachi Cocom was his guide.

The spokesman for the Maya from Sotuta showed up at the Izamal monastery one Sunday early in 1554 for mass with a group of devout native Christians. He didn't seek out the friars, instead choosing to blend in with the crowd. During the sermon, Friar Diego was struck speechless when he saw his old friend among the worshippers. Self-conscious for a brief moment, he collected himself and charged onward with his preaching, telling those in attendance about the letters Paul the Apostle sent to the Corinthians.

"He wrote the letters as someone who was converted. Not unlike all of you here today," he said, making a point of looking past the first rows of colonists to the natives.

Friar Diego sought Nachi after the final benediction. The procession of friars leaving the sanctuary—still too small to hold the entire congregation—and their standing at the rear of the building signaled the congregation's dismissal. The four friars stood perpendicular to the line leaving the sanctuary. As worshippers left, each would stand in front of one of the four Franciscans and receive a cross on their head from the priest's thumb, with a short directive to "serve the Lord."

Nachi received his blessing from Friar Nicolás. Friar Diego looked sideways at the man, wondering when he was going to be acknowledged. The glance never came. Nachi walked away and rejoined the men he'd come with.

Friar Diego gestured for the next congregant to wait for one of the other three friars and walked over to Nachi. The other natives with him watched Friar Diego approach Nachi's back, gesturing for Nachi to turn around.

"When did you get back into the area?" Friar Diego asked when he had the Mayan man's attention.

"The other day. I wanted to see the destruction of the temple myself."

"And did you?"

"I did."

Friar Diego waited for Nachi to continue. The man stayed silent.

"What do you think?" Friar Diego ventured.

"I think you were sent here to destroy us," Nachi said.

Friar Diego fumed. All of a sudden, his habit grew too heavy and constrictive, his mantle too hot, and the sun too bright. Nobody in the Yucatán but Nachi and Ahkinmai dared confront him in such a way—even the other friars spoke with measured care when addressing him.

Nachi realized he'd invoked the friar's hornet-spirit and took steps to reduce the coming sting. "I was going to visit you after my visit with them," he said, pointing to the men behind him. "We can talk about this then." He turned his back on the seething friar and left him alone in the dirt outside the sanctuary.

Friar Diego waited the rest of Sunday for Nachi's return. Despite reminding himself that it was a power struggle, that

Nachi wanted to maintain some semblance of authority over the situation, he couldn't slow the beating of his heart. He spent a sleepless night in the hammock, quitting his efforts in the early morning hours and praying until his anger subsided. When he emerged after morning prayers, the sun was peeking over the rooftops and Nachi was waiting outside the sanctuary.

"I thought you were coming back last night," Friar Diego said, trying his best to mask his anger.

"The meal lasted all day," Nachi said. He cracked a small twig in two, then each piece in two once more.

"Let's talk about your accusation from yesterday," Friar Diego said, getting straight to the point.

"Am I wrong? Hundreds died from the relocation, and now you're destroying our people's temple."

"I had to do these things!" Friar Diego said in defense. "I was saving the Maya from the *encomendero* brutality. They would've had to move, Nachi. The Crown ordered it."

Nachi understood; every Maya knew the *encomenderos* treated the natives like animals. The Franciscans at least tried to save their souls while exploiting their labor. "And the temple?"

"Did you see how many people were listening to mass from outside the sanctuary yesterday? We need a permanent place for worship. The facility I have in mind will be large enough to fit everyone in the Yucatán. It's for your people too."

Nachi squinted at the friar, who stood between him and the sun. "So your destruction of the temple has nothing to do with trying to erase us?" Nachi said. "Your Spanish Crown already banned all of our festivals."

"If it was up to me, your festivals would continue until you saw how pointless they were in the eyes of the true God."

Nachi appreciated the friar's candor. They had spent a long time together, and if the friar had claimed anything less than the eventual end of their rituals, Nachi would have known the man was lying. He did believe the friar didn't care in the interim, that the steps taken by López Medel were overkill for what the friars believed they could accomplish within the coming years of their persistent evangelism.

Friar Diego seized the moment of consideration. "I still want to learn everything I can about your people. For example, I don't know anything about the god that temple is built for."

"If you knew you wouldn't be so careless in its destruction," Nachi spat out.

Friar Diego sensed he was getting close to breaking the man's resistance. "Then why don't you tell me?"

"It's not my place to tell. Ahkinmai knows."

Friar Diego's stomach turned at the mention of the feathered priest. "And how did he learn?"

"From the books," Nachi said, without a second thought.

Friar Diego's eyes were opened to a room of darkness. A sense of the vastness of the Yucatán condensed before him, encapsulated in the texts Nachi mentioned.

"Well, if I could read these books, I could learn what the temple does and would understand your beliefs. How can you be upset with me for something I don't understand? I wasn't brought up in your way of life."

Nachi took measure of the friar's words and decided the friar made a valid argument. The friar was a man of faith, he thought, so he had done him a disservice by showing him the outward-facing display of the Maya's faith without giving him a solid foundation of understanding in the principles.

Friar Diego knew the moment he had won, and, wanting to seal the victory, he mentioned how he had shared his people's sacred text with the Maya. "It seems fair to me that your people share their sacred text with me."

Nachi agreed. "You have loud footsteps for someone who

doesn't know where they're going," he said, referring to Friar Diego's destruction of the temple.

Friar Diego understood the metaphor. "Then show me the way. Do you have a copy of the book yourself?"

Nachi shook his head, laughing. "They're rare, and I can't read them! Only the priests can."

"No one can read your language? How do they read the book?"

"I just said the priests can. And there's not one book, there's many, many books, dealing with the gods, the calendar, and the land. They are all interconnected."

"So everyone listens to the priests but can't read the book? Why?"

"We listen to you, don't we?" Nachi said. A thin smile emerged on his face, knowing he had Friar Diego pinned.

Friar Diego took the reconciliation without pushing back, trying his hardest to come up with a way his own spread of religion was different from that of the Mayan priests.

Nachi told Friar Diego they could get started with the education right away. Friar Diego considered the offer. During their previous excursions, Friar Diego had been able to leave the monastery with little notice. Now, as Guardian, he wondered which tasks would fall to Friar Nicolás and which should be delegated to the other two friars. It hit him that, as Guardian, he had even more freedoms, and could leave if he wanted without consulting anyone. He called out to Ix Cuatchel.

"Tell Friar Nicolás he's in charge while I'm away," he told her when she arrived at his side. "I'll be back in a few days."

Ix had heard about Nachi's displeasure with the temple's destruction from overheard whispers during mass. The students all said Nachi's opinion shouldn't matter, since he was on the wrong side of faith, but the students' support camps all agreed with Nachi:

Friar Diego was wrong to destroy the temple. She was confused when she saw an eager, excited Friar Diego leaving with a calm, smiling Nachi, but she nodded and said she'd tell the other friar.

Nachi took the road south, towards his own hometown of Sotuta. He explained that Ahkinmai's residence was never in the same spot for more than a few weeks at a time but that the traveling priest wound up back at his favorite spots multiple times each year. The priest had left Sotuta, headed for Mayapan, at the same time Nachi had left for Izamal.

"He feels close to the priests who came before him in that city," Nachi explained, reminding Friar Diego about the creation of the Chel—Ix's ancestors—by the daughter of one of the twelve priests.

THEY ARRIVED at the overgrown Mayapan stoneworks at midday. The sun bore down on them from above, creating thin shadows that stayed close to the travelers' bodies. A number of stone pyramids reminiscent of Chichen Itza rose from the vegetation, each of them overlooking the space with ancient nobility. Myriad dirt paths, created by both humans and animals, wound through the abandoned city.

"Ahkinmai won't be found unless he decides to show himself," Nachi said.

Friar Diego wondered if the feathered man's skill translated to dreams as well. Were Ahkinmai's nighttime visits a choice? The thought of Ahkinmai possessing some ancient knowledge that gave him the ability to hide in the shadows was banished by the friar as being blasphemous to God.

Nachi led Friar Diego to the top of the highest temple. There was nowhere to hide from the sun. Nachi raised his hands to his face and put both index fingers into his mouth. He emitted a series of loud whistles, the various notes weaving a tapestry on the wind.

"Let's go rest until he finds us," Nachi said after the call.

They climbed back down and took refuge in the shade of a large banana tree. They ate some of the maize ball Nachi had brought, drank sips of water not knowing when they could replenish their supply, and washed it down with fruit from the tree they sat beneath. Mayapan exerted a strong downward pull on the men; they both succumbed to the increased gravity and lay down. Their afternoon was spent dozing and waiting, neither man worried about staying alert for potential threats with the city keeping watch.

Nachi woke the friar after the sun was beneath the trees. The last rays of sunlight were still visible above the branches, casting long streaks of pink and purple into the sky above them.

"Hurry," Nachi said, standing up.

Friar Diego gathered himself and got to his feet. He followed Nachi to the top of the temple once more.

Ahkinmai emerged from the eastern edge of Mayapan, walking along the advancing line of shadow. As he did so, the space behind him was transformed into the city as it had been more than a century before. Silver specters of natives walked between houses with thatched roofs. The vegetation overtaking the stone temples disappeared, exposing the sacred structures and dozens of smaller stoneworks the way they had been during Mayapan's peak. Ahkinmai took two steps then stopped, waiting for the shadow to catch up, before taking another two steps. When he reached the temple where Nachi and Friar Diego stood, half the city was reanimated with apparitions of the old city and half remained as it had been in the daylight.

At first, Friar Diego thought he was dreaming. The magic possessed by the Mayan priest both fascinated and terrified him; he expected to wake up at any point. It wasn't until Ahkinmai had climbed the temple, hugged Nachi, and stood in front of the friar as a man covered in feathers, not a large bird, that Friar Diego knew he was awake. Friar Diego reached up to the cross hanging around his neck that had been given to him by Friar Luis de Villalpondo, clutching it as if it was the sole object strong enough to keep him anchored in the real world despite the advancement of the devil's realm.

A bird flew over the ghost city, making larger circles as it rose higher in the sky. Its path crossed over the line of shadow that marked the line between the real and spirit worlds, disappearing from view as it passed the three men on the temple before reappearing once it crossed back into the reanimated space.

Ahkinmai smiled as Friar Diego watched the bird. "What brings you to Mayapan?" he said, both to Nachi and to the friar.

"I brought him to see the books," Nachi said.

Ahkinmai blinked twice. The city's shadow apparition shuddered. "What have you told him?"

"That the knowledge belongs to the priests."

Ahkinmai stared at Nachi for a moment before speaking. "Why did you put me in this position? He doesn't want to understand, he wants to destroy."

"I thought the same thing. But he doesn't know any better. If we show him our knowledge"—Nachi gestured to the half of the city brought back from history—"he'll understand why destroying the temple damns everyone in the Yucatán."

The shadow had advanced well past the temple as the sunlight continued to disappear. Without Ahkinmai's accompaniment, the shadow past the temple covered a still-abandoned Mayapan, in the process of being reclaimed by nature.

Friar Diego begged Ahkinmai to show him the texts. "I want to learn," he said. This wasn't a lie, because he did want to learn, but his misguided curiosity was about the strength of the devil, not an appreciation of native secrets.

Ahkinmai looked from Friar Diego to Nachi. "I hope you know what you're doing."

Friar Diego and Nachi followed Ahkinmai down from the top of the temple and back to the edge of the city where they first saw the Mayan priest emerge. The silvered city from the past disappeared with Ahkinmai's advancement, leaving them in darkness while they walked through the abandoned city. The friar was both relieved and disappointed; he worried that entrance into the devil's realm would damn his soul, but his own interest in their composition made him want to reach out and touch the specter of a person or building. He never got the chance, because he never crossed the line between Ahkinmai and the apparition: it stopped before engulfing him on the temple, and receded as he followed Ahkinmai back to the city's edge.

Ahkinmai went into a small building near the edge of Mayapan. It didn't have the same silver glow as the other buildings in the apparition, instilling in Friar Diego the sense that the structure existed outside of time. Ahkinmai emerged with an armload of books and gestured for the two men to follow him.

The city from the past disappeared where the jungle began. Ahkinmai's camp was just past the edge. It consisted of a single hammock and a small fire burning without wood. With a hand gesture from the feathered priest, the fire roared to life, growing as tall as the three men. Ahkinmai set the books down in his hammock, picked one, and turned back to the two men.

Nachi was in awe—he'd never seen so many books in one place. Friar Diego was terrified.

Ahkinmai unfolded the book he held and showed Friar Diego a long series of the Mayan script. It was a continuous horizontal sheet, and as he opened the left side he folded the right.

"You can read all this?" Friar Diego asked. To him, the square symbols looked like writing handed down from the devil himself.

Ahkinmai nodded.

"What does it say?"

"This one is about harvesting and planting, the best ways to care for the plants, and is a record of the harvest times each year," Ahkinmai said.

"There are dozens of these books, all over the province," Nachi said with pride. "The priests take care of keeping the records of our lives."

Ahkinmai stared at Nachi, shocked his ally couldn't see the true nature of the friar's intentions.

Nachi continued. "Every priest has a number of these stashes. We can help them carry the books but we can't enter the spaces where the books are kept."

"That's enough," Ahkinmai said. Though the volume of his voice never raised, the strength in the command was evident, even to the friar.

A crestfallen Nachi looked at the ground.

"Do you have anything relating to the temple at Izamal?"

"The one you destroyed?" Ahkinmai spat back.

"I didn't know what it meant to your people," Friar Diego lied, doing his best to appear remorseful.

"A massive stone temple, requiring years of labor, didn't convey the message?"

Inside his heart, Friar Diego thanked Nachi for teaching him the nuances of the Mayan language. "It belonged to the past," Friar Diego said.

"There is no past or future. Time is contained in these

books," Ahkinmai said. "What passed will come again. We record our lives so our descendants can prepare for the future."

"Do your books mention the Spaniards?"

"Every priest has left record for the coming generations. The invasion was foretold in a previous cycle."

"Every priest? How many are there?"

"Twelve," Ahkinmai said, without thinking. He forgave Nachi for answering the friar's previous questions—Friar Diego's innocent questions went straight to the heart of the issue and couldn't be ignored.

Ahkinmai told Friar Diego the book about the temple was in another location. He thought Friar Diego would press the issue, but the revelation made the Franciscan withdraw into himself. The feathered man left the friar and Nachi, saying he was returning the books to their resting place. They fell asleep around the fuel-less fire, not knowing Ahkinmai had taken all the books from his repository at Mayapan and was moving them to another one, unseen by any Franciscan.

Nachi took Friar Diego back to Izamal, confident he had impressed upon the friar the quality of the Mayan culture and sure the Spaniard would appreciate their presence in the spiritual life of those living in the Yucatán.

Friar Diego wrote a frantic letter the second he got back to the monastery. In it, he told the Guardians of the other monasteries to identify the other eleven priests and to find out where they camped.

"Each man hides a trove of books about their worship of the devil," he said. "The Yucatán natives live on a steady diet of blasphemous words written in a cursed script."

CHAPTER TWENTY-TWO

A FIELD TRIP had introduced Cortez to the public library when he was in elementary school. The teachers and librarians had teamed up to provide every student with a library card, one that Cortez still kept, with pride, in his wallet next to his identification card and whatever cash he carried, when he had it. The occasion to use the card again had never emerged until now.

The library was a single-story old building made of bricks stained green from moss, with a metal roof with peeling red paint. An extraordinary amount of wires ran to the building from a nearby telephone pole, all connected to a single pole of Cortez's height perched at the building's corner. None of the wires were active. The operational telephone lines and electricity grid were all connected via underground cables, but since none of the workers who had laid the new infrastructure were told to get rid of the previous iterations, nobody did. Black birds of various sizes perched on the wires throughout the day, leaving a thick line of their droppings on the path beneath them. The library's few windows were reinforced with metal grates, protection from book thieves that never materialized.

Cortez pulled on the front door and found it locked. He

cupped his hands over his eyes and leaned forward, peering into the small vertical window. It was deserted, but not empty; leaning stacks of books were piled on every surface. His arm brushed against a laminated piece of paper taped to the front door that he hadn't noticed before.

THIS LOCATION CLOSED ON WEEKENDS. CITY'S MAIN LIBRARY (ACROSS THE PARK) OPEN 7 DAYS A WEEK.

So, for yet another time, Cortez set off across the park. He couldn't stay away from the other side of the city, a fact that he took as a sign he was meant to be with Alara Chel. Going to the library on the other side of the city allowed him to be closer to her, which added more fuel to the fire raging inside him, more strength to complete the day's mission. His feet returned to earth when he arrived on the other side of the park, at the moment he realized he had to ask for directions because he had no idea where the library was located. After he was ignored twice, a wrinkled woman rolling a basket full of groceries with small steps pointed in the opposite direction of Decant. He considered going to the coffee shop to see if Alara was working but decided he needed to be prepared for the next time they met, preparation he hoped would be complete by the end of the day, so he followed the woman's finger until he arrived at his destination.

The library held the key to Cortez's future. The building took up an entire block. It was built to stand for generations, a secure repository of the world's knowledge that the city's inhabitants could access every day of the week. Her sibling, the courthouse, stood blocks away; they were twin pillars holding up the virtues of the city. Dozens of wide stone steps rose from the sidewalk to the columns that ended beneath ornate carvings of books, dates, and animals, none of which were particular to the library but were there for decoration—the courthouse displayed similar images. Cortez found the entrance repugnant, an ostentatious display of power humble books didn't require. Despite his distaste, he climbed the front steps, walked through the columns, and went past the open dark-wood doors. A new world awaited him inside.

Multiple tables were set up, each overseen by an adult with a bright orange T-shirt. They were responsible for the hordes of children walking around the space, most with an adult close at hand but some roaming free. There were balloons, smiles, and books littered throughout. Cortez had never seen so many pencils; they were pre-sharpened and sitting in cups at the tables, ready to be taken by children along with accompanying index cards or forms for the children to fill out. On the far side of the lobby, past the bazaar, was a vast staircase that started wide and narrowed at the top with stacks of books visible beyond. The railings on each side were green, accented with brass, and prevented people from falling down into the aisles on either side of the staircase, where there were rooms with more book stacks.

There had never been many children in Cortez's adult life, and for the most part he deemed them frivolous. But that day, seeing the eagerness of their quest for knowledge, he smiled, wondering how his own life would be different if he'd been infected with their same sickness when he was young. He left the festival behind and walked up the staircase, ready to plunge headfirst into the pages. Vertigo took him in her clutches when he saw the magnitude of his task. The stacks went off far into the distance. With the name of Alara's book in his mind, he began walking around, trusting the divine would point him in the right direction. A few minutes went by without a single title registering in his mind, forcing him to walk back and begin once more. He passed a staircase with arrows that informed him there were more books on the levels above and below his current location, a revelation that made him stumble from the enormity of his task.

A librarian noticed the somber young man in her domain when he walked past twice without acknowledging her presence. Her glasses were green and pointed at the corners, connected by a chain of green beads around her neck, and they gave her an insect's appearance. Bushy red hair matched the shawl she insisted on wearing each day because she got cold and was scared of getting sick, one she left behind in the library each night when she got off work. It hadn't left the premises in years, even to be washed. When the searcher passed her for a third time, she cleared her throat.

"Looking for something, young man?" she said to get his attention.

"A book," Cortez responded.

The librarian first chuckled, then grew frustrated when she realized it wasn't meant as a joke. "Which book?" she said.

"It's called *Love in Time for Cholera*," Cortez said. He mispronounced the last word.

The librarian was taken aback by the patron's certainty, even though she knew the exact title he was looking for. "You mean: *Love in the Time of* Cholera," she corrected him, making sure to accentuate the correct pronunciation of the sickness.

"Yes, I think that's the one. Do you have it?" Cortez said.

"Follow me," the librarian said. She led Cortez through a series of twists and turns he couldn't have reproduced even if he had made an attempt to memorize the sequence. While walking, she tried to bring him out of his shell, treating him like other introverts who suffered from a love of books. "It's a wonderful book . . . he's a renowned author . . . one of the best love stories ever told . . ." None of her attempts at conversation had the desired effect.

She found the book, pulled it from the shelf, and handed it

to him. "You can check it out at the front desk," she informed him.

"Good to know, but I need to finish it today," Cortez said without a trace of humility. The truth was, he hadn't read a complete book since the last time he'd finished a picture book with his mother as a child. "Is there somewhere I can sit and read right now?"

The librarian tilted her head forward and looked at him from above the rim of her glasses. "Right over there," she said, pointing to the far side of the room. "Each floor has a dedicated reading area overlooking the park. It's what we're famous for," she said with pride.

Cortez thanked her before walking away. The librarian shook her head, thinking to herself that she had a lot to learn. She'd seen all kinds of God's creatures before, and it would have never crossed her mind that the young man she'd helped was the type to read an entire novel in a day.

The book was thicker than Cortez's Bible. The larger font was little consolation, because he'd never read anything more than the handful of passages he'd memorized. By the end of the first page he was beginning to lose steam, and after reading the first four pages not a single word registered in his love-addled mind. The words didn't go in and slip from his grasp; they never went in at all. The book in Cortez's hands kept lowering as if it was sinking through water, each time retrieved from the depths with renewed focus when he jolted awake. His ability to concentrate waned as his eyelids grew heavier, and soon after he turned the fifth page he fell into a deep sleep, his body starving after staying awake the night before.

He was shaken awake by what he assumed was an angel. She didn't have the same effect on him as Alara—no woman could—

but the haze around her blond hair and soft smile made him wonder how long until he met Peter.

"Tell him he can't sleep here!" Cortez heard the librarian with insect eyes say in the distance.

The young blond librarian closed her eyes and shook her head. "Don't worry about her. She's probably just cold." In the distance, the woman pulled the shawl tighter around her shoulders. "What are you reading?"

Cortez showed her the cover of the book. A page had bent when he was asleep. "Sorry about that," he said with a sheepish grin.

"Our little secret," the woman said with a wink, holding out a hand to take the book from him.

"I've got to finish it today," Cortez continued, maintaining his hold on the book.

"Why? What happens if you don't?"

Cortez grew embarrassed at the thought of divulging his secret. "It's for a friend," he stammered.

"You're reading an entire book in a day for a friend?" she exclaimed. "You're a good friend," she added. She indicated to Cortez that he had something on his face, below his lips.

Cortez used the back of his arm to wipe drool from his chin.

"Did you know they made this into a movie? It might be easier than reading the book."

Cortez's heart leapt at his sudden stroke of fortune. "They did? Do you know where I can get it?" Remembering he didn't have enough money with him to buy a movie, he realized he'd have to go home first.

"We have a copy here," the librarian informed him. She thought he was cute when the smile erased the melancholy from his face.

"Is there somewhere I can watch it?" he asked, timid. He didn't want his mother to ask why he was watching that particular movie. She was aware of Alara, yes, but she didn't need to know his plan.

"Here? Let's go find out." This time, Cortez handed over the book when she extended her arm.

The young woman led Cortez to the station she shared with the librarian whose shawl protected her from freezing to death. "Would it be possible to set him up in one of the private rooms upstairs?" she asked her colleague.

The frozen woman looked at her younger counterpart in shock. "No way, that's for educational purposes only."

"This is a library, Gert. Everything we do is educational." She rolled her eyes and looked at Cortez. "Could you give us a second?" she said, pointing to the side. Cortez waited a few steps away. Minutes later, the kind librarian led Cortez to another part of the library, talking the entire time.

"She's nice, once you get to know her," she said. They were among bookcases filled with DVDs. She found the one she was looking for, handed it to Cortez to carry, then led him to the staircase.

"The private rooms are on the top floor."

They climbed four flights of stairs and emerged in a shadowy corridor that had dark rooms along the entirety of its length. "These aren't used very often, so I don't know why she had to make a big deal of you using one."

The librarian opened the door closest to them—it was unlocked—turned on the lights, and ushered Cortez inside. It was small, wide enough for a single table surrounded by four chairs, and had an ancient television strapped onto a rolling cart with a DVD player beneath. She told Cortez to sit down and got the movie ready to watch.

"When you're done, do me a favor and turn everything off, including the lights, then just come down and find me. I'll be at the same station."

Cortez nodded, and she pressed play before leaving him alone, closing the door behind her. For the next two hours and nineteen minutes, he watched, enraptured. It didn't take long for him to realize his role in the love triangle. His destiny, like that of Florentino Ariza, was to wait, and he resigned himself to take up the sacred suffering with as much seriousness as he accepted the body and blood of Christ on Sundays. He grew to hate Dr. Juvenal Urbino for taking so long to die. When the movie ended, he was imbued with the certainty that Alara needed saving from Remy, more so than Fermina Daza needed saving from Urbino, because while their story had already been told, Alara's was just now being written.

The librarians were chatting while working through a stack of books on the counter in front of them. As Cortez approached, the temperature dropped a few degrees, and both women's arms were covered in goosebumps. His smile chilled them to the bone, freezing what little flesh had still been left intact.

"All done," he said, holding out the movie. The disc was covered with large red flowers visible through the clear plastic protective covering. When Cortez saw the bright petals in the well-lit part of the library, he grew certain he knew where to find the source of Alara's smell, the one he'd dreamt about two nights before. He'd smell every flower on earth if he had to, just to find the one that belonged to her.

The young librarian took it from his hands and smiled back, a brave attempt at normalcy in spite of the elements. "How did you like it?"

The bundled-up librarian was impressed by her colleague's ability to maintain cordiality while speaking to the strange visitor, and from then on never second-guessed any of her decisions.

"It was wonderful," Cortez said. "Best I've seen."

"I'm glad to hear it. Anything else we can help you with?"

"There is. Do you know of any gardens around here?"

She thought for a moment. "I think there's one in the park. Gert, do you know?"

Gertrude, looking at Cortez through her green glasses, would have said anything to get him out of the library and away from her. She told Cortez about the park's botanical gardens and where to find them. "Have a great time," she said, the last word clipped by a clack of her teeth.

"I will," he said, with a serpentine smile, before walking back out into the world.

CHAPTER TWENTY-THREE

In Friar Diego de Landa's opinion, the brothers of the Franciscan Order were underprepared and uninformed in the ongoing battle against the knowledge of the devil the Mayan priests possessed.

Friar Diego's meeting with Ahkinmai reinforced his belief in the importance of understanding the Mayan language. There was a wide gulf between himself and the other Izamal friars in the proficiency of their language, and Friar Diego knew their skill was more indicative of the abilities of the other Franciscans in the Yucatán. The lack of conversational ability by those who dealt with the natives every day meant information was always lost in translation. There was also a chance the natives had questions the friars couldn't answer with sufficient clarity, leaving gaps in faith the Mayan priests could fill with the devil. It wasn't lost on him that the newest members of the Franciscan Order in the Yucatán were sent to the farthest monasteries, putting the men with the least mastery of the language in charge of those who knew the least about Spanish customs and were therefore at greater risk of continuing to follow the Mayan religion.

An updated *arte* on the Mayan language was the first step in his fight against the Mayan priests. The original, used by every priest in the Yucatán, had been written by Friar Luis de Villalpondo years before. Friar Diego's own copy was covered in notes, crossed-out sections, and additional words and phrases—an incoherent jumble of all he had learned while stationed in Izamal. Creation of the updated document took over Friar Diego's life for two full years, during which time he forgot to cut a single hair on his body. Late 1555 found an aged Friar Diego emerging from his study with a full beard down to his chest and hair hanging below his shoulder blades, the top of his head made bald from then on by the intensity of his thinking.

Ix Cuatchel gave Friar Diego a haircut when he first emerged. She was growing into a young woman who possessed a beauty no man could ignore. Her chastity was never questioned, and her faith was beyond reproach. Her long black hair was rumored to cure everything from tiredness to broken limbs; worshippers stayed long after mass, combing where she sat, looking for a stray strand. A shiver traveled down the friar's spine and settled in his bowels as soon as Ix laid her hands on his shoulders, prompting him to run into the woods and relieve himself before she cut a single hair on his head. He was in a state of ecstasy while she cut his hair, losing sight of the world around him while her fingers worked over his scalp. Friar Diego fought through a strong urge to fall asleep when she announced she was finished, keeping himself awake with the knowledge that the other Franciscans needed the fruits of his labor.

Izamal's former top students were long gone, sent to remote parts of the Yucatán to teach the natives most averse to the Franciscan message about the Spanish way of life. Friar Nicolás de Albalate introduced the new top two students from among the crop of over a thousand, saying they were well on their way to joining their comrades in the field.

"You can write?" Friar Diego said to the displayed students.

Friar Nicolás answered for them. "Very well," he said, with a heaping scoop of pride.

"I was asking them," Friar Diego said with scorn. Living away from people for such a long time had made him forget how best to inspire confidence in his leadership.

The older friar closed his eyes and exhaled, giving a master class in patience that didn't escape the two native youths.

Both Mayan students answered yes.

"Good, come with me. I'm taking over your lessons."

Friar Diego led the two young men away without another word to Friar Nicolás. They were both wearing clothes common among the Spanish colonists: tan breeches and white tunics. Their hair was cut short and their skin was free of tattoos.

Friar Diego led them to his desk. Upon it sat a thick tome of handwritten pages on everything he knew of the Mayan language, written in Spanish characters. Ix had invaded the space in the short time Friar Diego was out in the sunlight, clearing up spilled ink and throwing away years' worth of trash.

"This will be sent out to the other monasteries—an updated manual about the Mayan language. First, I need the two of you to go through this and double-check that I got everything correct. Then, copies need to be made. Eleven more."

The students, eager at first, became disheartened. While reading through it would only take a matter of days, copying would take months. They didn't know if they should copy one book at a time, one page eleven times, or start from the back and allow the ink on the pages to dry before stacking the next on top. When Friar Diego provided no further instruction, leaving and telling them he was going to inspect his monastery, they sat down and started reading.

. . .

Nobody saw the two students for months. Everyone, including Friar Nicolás, assumed the timeline of their trips into the Yucatán, preaching to the natives, had been pushed forward, and that they'd left without saying goodbye. Everyone was too preoccupied with Ix's beauty to notice what she carried back and forth to Friar Diego's study twice each day: food and water for two. When the students were seen again, they each sported a spot of round baldness on the crown of their head. Every Franciscan but Friar Diego thought the two students, who'd come back after so long away, were making fun of them and their method of wearing their hair. The native men, after reaching their hands up and rubbing their scalp, said they knew what was happening when they had to pull hair from the fresh ink on the paper, leaving thin lines throughout each copy. These thin lines were the sole distinguishing marks in the replicas—if they weren't there, Friar Diego's original would have been lost in the group.

The *artes* were sent out right away, with instructions from Friar Diego that speaking the native tongue was of the utmost importance. "We are in a fight against the native priests for the souls of these people," he wrote, repeating the stance of the Franciscans since they'd first arrived in the Yucatán.

His treatise generated a lukewarm response of thanks in letters from the other monasteries throughout the Yucatán. To Friar Diego's surprise, Friar Lorenzo de Bienvenida, the *Custos* of the province, gave him the most support. The elder friar praised the comprehensive treatment of the language, saying he would urge the adoption of the text by all new and existing friars in his domain. His letter mentioned the pride Friar Luis must feel from beyond the grave, standing next to their Lord and watching the great strides Friar Diego was making for the good of the native people.

Another round of letters from the various monasteries

around the peninsula trickled in soon after Friar Lorenzo's endorsement. Each one heaped further praise on the work, with special mention of the quality of the replication. Before Friar Lorenzo's praise had reached the ears of the other monasteries' Guardians, each man thought the *arte* had been sent to them alone, a rebuke of their own mastery of the language—they couldn't imagine such a document was handwritten multiple times and sent to all. Their tepid responses had come from their distaste at receiving instruction from someone they deemed on equal footing to themselves; after they realized the great labor involved in the project, their appreciation of the effort increased by orders of magnitude.

While the friars were enjoying a resurgence in their battle against the Mayan priests, their past involvement with the *encomenderos* was bearing fruit. It was no secret that the friars were the object of scorn among the Spanish landholders. The *encomenderos* were powerless against the Franciscans' unified attack until the most powerful of their group, *Adelantado* Francisco Hernandez, experienced their holy eye inspecting his operation.

The *encomiendas* throughout the Yucatán were required to send their young men to the monasteries; it was an unquestioned part of their lives. The men, women, and children were available for labor, but the young men had to learn the Spanish and Christian customs taught by the Franciscans. Most *encomenderos* took the long view of the requirement—the indoctrinated youths were the next generation and could make their lives easier in future years. Among themselves, they joked that breaking the native spirit was like breaking a horse: do it once and reap the benefits of a docile creature.

The *Adelantado* busied himself with ensuring not a single pair of laboring hands was lost from his fields while Friar Diego rejuvenated the Mayan-language *arte* for his brothers. He took full advantage of the position of his land, centered between the Mani and Izamal monasteries. Whenever Franciscans from one monastery inquired about the young men in his care, he told them his charges were attending lessons given by the other. This situation lasted until one of the friars from Izamal, able to speak with the natives with more clarity thanks to Friar Diego's *arte*, spoke with the natives on the *Adelantado*'s land and discovered the young men weren't attending either monastery's school.

No Spaniard had dared such a blatant disregard for the Franciscans' mission to educate the young Mayan men. Friar Diego's blood rushed to his face when he learned about *Adelantado* Francisco's deceit. The pressure was so great that a number of capillaries popped on his face, creating red lines on his cheeks. The marks reminded the natives of the lines pregnant women got on their swollen stomachs, and amongst themselves they joked the Guardian of the Izamal monastery was carrying rage in his belly.

Friar Diego deliberated the best course of action for three days. He started dozens of letters to Friar Lorenzo, but each one burst into flames from the heat of his words before he could finish the first sentence. He couldn't use one of the native students to transcribe his words, because they didn't know Spanish, and Ix couldn't do it because she'd never learned to write. Friar Nicolás tried transcribing the letter, but the passion behind the words terrified the old man and he couldn't still his trembling hand long enough to get the words down on paper. In the end, Friar Diego did what he'd wanted to do in the first place: he marched down to the *encomienda* to talk to the *Adelantado* himself.

THE *ENCOMIENDA* HAD GROWN since he'd last visited the property. The central mansion was the same, but there were more small buildings surrounding the main house. A small village of permanent structures where the natives lived was within eyesight, the natives forced out of their traditional villages among the trees. Every building was made of the same bleeding red stone, each having dark streaks where water trickled down from the roof. The surrounding cleared land had expanded, encroaching into the undergrowth so that Friar Diego emerged under an open sky sooner than on his previous trip.

Friar Diego found *Adelantado* Francisco sitting at an outdoor table on a patio behind the massive main house, drinking tea from a stone cup. His breeches and tunic were bright white, and his shoes were well-worn brown leather with a short heel. Friar Diego inspected the property while approaching the man, looking at the post where the dead woman had been tied and remembering the native man who had been clubbed on his last visit.

Adelantado Francisco, following the friar's gaze, remarked how such barbarism was no longer required. "The natives learned their lesson long ago," he said, inviting Friar Diego to take a seat across from him without standing up. He turned to a native woman standing behind him, telling her to grab a cup for the priest. "He must be tired from his trip."

More capillaries popped in Friar Diego's face at the seated man's lack of courtesy, and he exhaled with purpose, hoping the Holy Spirit would take away his anger. "I'm fine," Friar Diego said.

The woman stopped. The *Adelantado* cleared his throat. "Who do you take orders from? Him or me?" *Adelantado* Francisco asked in a singsong voice.

The native woman scurried away.

"To what do I owe the pleasure of your presence at my humble residence?" *Adelantado* Francisco said.

Friar Diego looked around. His order, the Franciscans, lived in austerity; the *Adelantado* wouldn't know simplicity if it sat across from him at the table. "There's nothing humble about this place," he said.

"What brings you to my home? Is that better?"

"Much. It's come to our attention that you aren't taking care of your young men's education. Can you tell me why?"

"You're from Izamal, correct?"

"That's right."

"Then you wouldn't see my natives. I send them to Mani." The *Adelantado* took a sip of his drink as if the matter was settled.

"We both know that isn't the case," Friar Diego said, suppressing his anger. The native woman returned and placed a steaming cup in front of him before standing behind the *encomendero.* The smell of spices wafted from the liquid, a luxurious aroma Friar Diego cursed as a crutch of the rich.

"Should we go to Mani and fetch them?" the *Adelantado* asked.

"Stop playing games with me!" Friar Diego roared.

Adelantado Francisco's seriousness came with a foaming hint of murderous intent. He stared at the friar. "Who are you to raise your voice at me on my own property?" he said.

"I come to you as a man of God. No other Spaniard would dare lie in the presence of the Lord's messenger."

"And what can come of it? The Franciscans already took away half the labor of the other *encomiendas.* Now you're here to take mine too."

"Our orders come from God," Friar Diego said.

"God, the Pope . . . I don't care who it's from, the men are mine."

"They need a Christian education!"

"Not to dismiss your authority, but you're not even the man

in charge of the Yucatán. If this was important for the future of the Church, I would imagine someone with more . . . prestige would be seated across from me."

Friar Diego fumed, the acrid steam from his skin mixing with the spiced steam from the beverage.

"Get Friar Lorenzo if it's truly important," the *Adelantado* said with a wave of his hand.

"Friar Lorenzo can't be bothered with such trivial nonsense. Send the boys to the Izamal monastery or suffer the consequences," Friar Diego said through clenched teeth.

Adelantado Francisco stared at Friar Diego before erupting in a fit of laughter. "And what can you do? The Franciscans have no resources to enforce your decrees. Who do they rely on? The colonists. And who's in charge of the colonists? The *Adelantado*." The man took another sip of his tea, shaking with smug laughter, then set the cup down without making a sound.

"They'll throw you in jail if we tell them to. You forget we have the Crown's ear."

"Threatening me with jail on my own property? Your confidence in God has you tempting fate, my friend. What if I had you tied up to that post over there, taught you some respect?"

"In God's name, you'll regret those words."

"I'm God here," *Adelantado* Francisco replied, opening his arms wide. All of a sudden, he whistled loudly enough for all of his cleared lands to hear: two short, one long, then a lower short. The sequence had special meaning because, within moments, two large natives emerged from one of the buildings and ran to the *Adelantado*.

"Please escort this man from the property," the *Adelantado* said.

Friar Diego was stunned at the hubris of the *encomendero* and the depths to which the devil had penetrated in the Yucatán

—he was fighting with the Franciscans against the Mayan priest *and* the *Adelantado*.

The two natives and the friar conversed in the Mayan language while they walked to the edge of the property. It was confirmed that none of the Mayan youths ever left the *encomienda,* for education or for any other reason, except to accompany the *Adelantado* or travel with another Spaniard under the *Adelantado*'s orders. They reported that their treatment had improved since Friar Diego had last visited, due to their acceptance of their role on the land and unwillingness to fight back.

"It's better to get the work done quickly so he'll leave us alone," one native said. The other agreed.

"You won't have to live like this much longer," Friar Diego said, clenching his jaw.

The rage-inspired trip back to Izamal was made in half the time it had taken anyone before. Friar Diego stormed into his living quarters, wrote a letter outlining the *Adelantado*'s transgressions, then walked it to Merida himself to deliver it to Friar Lorenzo when he couldn't find a messenger willing to leave right away.

The *Custos* read the letter in front of Friar Diego, who hadn't slept for days. His habit was muddy at the bottom and reeked of stale sweat.

"These are very serious charges," Friar Lorenzo said after rereading the document's key points.

"He threatened to tie me up and have me flogged!" Friar Diego said.

"His lust for power has gone too far," Friar Lorenzo said. "Go back to Izamal, I'll take care of this."

. . .

Adelantado Francisco was arrested and thrown in jail in the summer of 1556. Friar Lorenzo himself marched onto the *encomienda* at the head of a retinue of secular forces who answered to the authority of Guatemala, the province who oversaw all of the Yucatán. Sending word to the faraway seat of power and awaiting their answer in the form of men to aid in the *Adelantado*'s arrest made Friar Lorenzo realize the distance between Guatemala and the Yucatán was too great for the peninsula to fall under their provincial control. The uninformed decrees Tomás López Medel made from Guatemala, out of touch with the native plight but still deemed effective enough when they were announced, were exploited by the Franciscans, but the distance's effect on the Franciscan cause made the *Custos* wonder about a better remedy for their political situation.

The secular officials in charge of Mani were told the *Adelantado* was to be imprisoned until his trial, which would be presided over by Franciscan judges within the month. There hadn't been a single scuffle in the entire affair, from the first time the forces stepped onto the *Adelantado*'s property through when the prison door slammed shut. In fact, *Adelantado* Francisco had had time to tell the natives to listen to his wife, or else there would be hell to pay when he returned, because he had every intention of coming back. He made sure to tell the men in Friar Lorenzo's service that they would soon find themselves arresting the friar because of the Franciscan's constant meddling in political arrangements in the villages.

Friar Lorenzo had laughed when he heard the *Adelantado*'s command and subsequent accusation, then stayed behind when the *Adelantado* left in the custody of the men from Guatemala. The Spaniards working on the property were dismissed back to Mani, and all the natives were called in from the fields. They didn't come at first, because of their fear of the *Adelantado*'s return, but when the friar convinced the *Adelantado*'s wife to stand next to him—she didn't possess the same anger towards the priests, nor his combative spirit—they started trickling in from every corner of the property. Each and every one had a visible scar somewhere on their torso, and they stared at the ground while waiting to hear their instructions.

"All young men between the ages of seven and seventeen! Step forward," the friar called out.

Thirty-seven boys stood in front of him, their skin darkened from long hours in the sun, which made the whip scars even more stark.

"You are going to school," he said.

The children looked terrified.

"Nothing will happen to you," Friar Lorenzo said, using his best soothing tones.

Taking a step back in the narrative, he explained to the natives how the former master of the property was going to jail, that there would be a trial, and how, in all likelihood, he would lose his property and all his holdings. "This means that, in effect, you no longer belong to him."

The *Adelantado*'s wife, a thin whisper of a woman with pale skin and jewel-covered fingers, collapsed onto the ground and wept.

"You're going to Izamal. There, you'll learn under Friar Diego de Landa. You've seen him; he's been here twice now."

The older men, stronger than the ones who would be leaving to school, nodded.

"Nobody's more passionate about the plight of the natives than him," Friar Lorenzo said. "You'll be safe there."

"And what about us?" a young girl said.

"Go back to your home villages. A new *encomendero* will come and tell you what's required. Don't worry, we'll have our eye on them!" Friar Lorenzo said. After making sure the schoolchildren knew the way to Izamal, he set out in pursuit of the men and the *Adelantado*.

When the friar left, the natives disappeared into the untamed land beyond the fields, going back to the villages they'd left behind when they were forced to move onto the property within sight of the mansion. The *Adelantado*'s wife, alone and with nowhere else to go, climbed onto the mansion's roof, tied a rope around her neck, and jumped off, her feet left tickling the top of the front door.

CHAPTER TWENTY-FOUR

Cortez had to continue in the opposite direction of Decant, aware that it was away from Alara, in order to get to the park's garden. It was surrounded by a dark gray chest-high barrier that absorbed the sunlight, with a taller wrought iron gate that served as an entrance. The people entering and leaving the garden were the relaxed sort who were out for an afternoon stroll, content with experiencing nature; they didn't pay attention to the feverish soul who joined them. Cortez walked in with the determination of a prisoner who had just learned his sentence and didn't want to give the judge the satisfaction of seeing him suffer. He walked past the examples of various trees, each one with a sign in front informing readers of the scientific name and characteristics typical of the species, and made his way to the section of flowers in the back. Alara's vapors reached him during a long whiff, one of many smells that filtered in through his nose. He got to work identifying hers, as if he was scanning a crowd for the one face that belonged to his beloved.

The faint sweetness of tulips didn't possess her vitality, and the hydrangeas were too heavy to belong to the lightness of her footsteps. He narrowed it down to the orchids, for they reminded him of her femininity, and the carnations, because their smell surrounded him the same way her memory did when he wasn't in her presence. Going back and forth between the two flowers, he became convinced he needed to mix them together to find the perfect concoction. Looking around to make sure he was alone before plucking a flower from each plant, he noticed a bush of red roses in the garden's corner. Not wanting to leave a stone unturned, he approached, leaned forward, and sniffed. The scent transported him away from reality, back into his dreams, and he stood tall, certain he had stepped outside of time. It was her smell. He wanted to lie in it, roll in it, bathe in it, and live in it. With nobody around him, he reached forward and tried to pluck the largest flower, not having seen the thorn hidden beneath the petals. It stuck deep in his thumb. He pulled his hand away and stared at the blood.

He had bled for her. To him, nothing was more sacred than suffering for the one he loved, for he knew Jesus had suffered on the cross for his beloved earth creatures. He licked the blood away and stared at the hole in his thumb. It was time for him to accept the crown of thorns. After lifting the rose petals and locating the largest thorn, he stuck it through his thumb until it hit the nail on the other side. He was smiling the entire time. The pain brought him closer to Alara, and he imagined she was on top of him with her hair, smelling of roses, surrounding his face.

Cortez pulled his thumb away and positioned his body between the lone rose bush and the rest of the garden before snapping the rose from the stalk. The other plants didn't need to know he was complicit in the destruction of their brethren, and he preferred to keep this secret from them so their flowers wouldn't seek revenge and cause his sinuses to revolt in the future.

The afternoon sun cast the shadows of the longest buildings

far into the park. Cortez left the garden with the souvenir of his visit in his pocket. As he passed walkers, sunbathers, and exercisers, he put his hand into his pocket, squeezed the petals, then sniffed his fingers. His thumb was still bleeding, and every so often he sucked the blood from the tip. He didn't know where he was going and couldn't think long enough to come to a decision, because every time the scent he associated with Alara hit his nostrils he became disoriented, lost in a dream. Step after step he approached her part of the city, and soon he plunged into the shadows that covered the sidewalks, the sun hidden by the buildings on each side.

His legs took him to Decant. He stood outside the front window, looking inside. Alara was behind the counter, unaware she was being watched. Cortez squeezed the rose in his pocket so tightly that when he withdrew his hand it was covered in red. He stared at his palm then put his hand back in his pocket. She would have to wait.

Remy's apartment wasn't far. It took Cortez a few tries to remember which block he lived on, but once he did, he leaned against the building across the street. According to the movie, he had to wait until Remy died. Cortez was driven by curiosity; he wanted to know more about the man, to know his lifestyle and habits, so he could have some idea of how long he might be stuck in purgatory. There was no plan other than to be in close proximity—murdering Alara's boyfriend had never crossed his mind. The heat of Remy's presence brought his hatred to a boil. Cortez stayed there until well after the sun went down.

On the opposite side of the city, Cortez's mother grew worried. For the last few weeks, they had spent Saturday nights out on the town, searching for lost souls to save. The people spending money, eating like kings, the fornicators: they all were worthy candidates to receive Christ's love. Both Cortez and his mother had no friends, and therefore no social obligations, and their evangelizing was the perfect use of their weekend night. A way to rush their salvation by growing the size of the Church, even though their fishing had been unsuccessful to that point. The lunch his mother had made earlier, chorizo and beans, was sitting in the refrigerator on a paper plate. Since Cortez never came home, she hadn't made dinner. At first, she assumed he was with the girl. Now, with the coming of the storm clouds in the distance, she wondered if he was all right, if he was safe, and she kicked herself for not asking more questions when he first mentioned his new preoccupation. She knew women made men do stupid things, but she had no idea what kind of trouble her son was capable of finding.

REMY APPEARED after the rain started. His broad shoulders and soldier-straight back made him easy to recognize. He had a black umbrella in his hand and was dressed in dark slacks, dress shoes, and a light blue button-up shirt. The light drizzle never reached his umbrella, the rain altering its path to avoid him. He set off down the street, taking long strides that cleared the puddles in his path.

Cortez didn't have the same power over the elements. In fact, he had the opposite effect. Instead of a light rain, he walked through a downpour as he followed Remy. Nothing was going to stop his pursuit. Curiosity about the man he had come to hate outweighed anything the world might throw at him. Block after block Cortez followed him. They passed by the fountain where Cortez had watched him dine with Alara. Remy continued until he got to a row of sports bars, where he went inside one without hesitation.

The bar Remy entered was one of five on the same block. They were notorious for being frequented by the city's younger inhabitants, most college-aged or within a few years of graduation. There was an Irish bar, a cowboy-themed bar, and a bar with a horse statue in front. None of the bars had windows separating their interiors from the street outside. Raucous noise spilled out of each, sports games and shouts Cortez thought had no place at dinnertime. Cortez had never seen so many people his own age concentrated in one area before, and the sight of them was another distraction from the hunger he had never gotten around to noticing. Even if he had, the establishments didn't serve anything but greasy bar food and numerous specials based on various mixtures of liquor and beer.

The crowd made it easy for Cortez to stay hidden while he watched Remy after following him inside. The young man was with three friends, the four of them cheering for the soccer team on the screen behind the bar. Cortez knew nothing of sports and made a mental note to ask Alara her thoughts on them. Since she wasn't there, he assumed she didn't like them either, and not watching them could be an interest they both shared. The back wall soon became Cortez's best friend. He was close enough to the bathroom that people would ask if he was in line, and each time he shook his head no and looked past the questioner, they stared at the young man who looked so out of place and miserable in his own skin.

A young woman, wearing a skirt and with a dizzy look in her eyes, leaned on the wall next to Cortez. It was obvious she had been drinking all day. Cortez ignored her. She asked him what his name was and he didn't respond. Not to be deterred, she said it again, louder.

"What's your name?"

There was no way Cortez could pretend not to hear. He looked at her and sized her up. "Cortez," he said, turning back towards where Remy sat at the bar.

The drunk woman leaned forward and whispered into Cortez's ear. "My name's Olivia."

Cortez pulled his head away. "That's nice."

One of Remy's friends stood up, turned around, and walked right towards Cortez. A momentary panic set in, one in which he wondered if Remy had sent his friend to confront Cortez. When the friend walked right by Cortez and into the bathroom, Cortez moved away, thanking God for sending him a sign to get out of the way before Remy's inevitable use of the restroom. The drunk woman, having decided she wanted to know more about Cortez, followed him to his new perch.

"Where's your drink?" she slurred.

Cortez told her he didn't drink in the most serious voice he possessed.

"Really? Then what are you doing here?"

Cortez looked at her. "I'm watching the game. What are you doing here?"

She looked at the television above the bar. "Me too, me too," she said. Together, they watched the game, until something distracted her and Cortez was left alone once more. He squeezed the rose in his pocket, whispering thanks for the inspired presence of Alara's ghost at his side.

REMY WENT to the bathroom when the game ended, unaware his every move was being watched. Cortez thought he'd be leaving the bar now that the game was over, but the energy of the people in the bar was escalating instead of dying down. Remy ordered shots when he went back to his friends. Cortez looked around himself in disgust. The people were sweaty, drunk, and touching each other way too much. Their behavior hadn't been so bad when he first got there, and their steady decline was never visible when viewed moment by moment, but now that he recognized it, he couldn't believe there were people who chose to participate in the debauchery. He thought about his plan to attend church the next day, about finding people who would join him in worship, and for the first time he understood what his mother had said about God not wanting "those kinds of people." His mother's expectation about their Saturday night activity never crossed his mind because, for him, it hadn't been a regular enough occurrence to be considered a part of his routine.

The second woman who approached him reinforced his opinion of the situation. Hours had gone by, and Remy had shown no signs of leaving. Cortez was standing still, ever vigilant, not wanting to miss any of Alara's boyfriend's actions, when the woman appeared in his vicinity. She was younger and drunker than the others, with red blemishes on her face and evidence of spilled liquid down the front of her green dress. Her black boots went up to just below her knees and were well-worn in a way that suggested her foot's heel didn't align with the heel of the boot when she walked.

"You're cute," she said. She stumbled against the wall next to him.

"Thanks," said Cortez. He was getting tired. His eyelids were held open through sheer willpower. He had never been called cute before, but since the compliment didn't come from Alara, he didn't care.

The girl's eyelids were held open just enough to make sure she didn't fall over. The whites of her eyes, streaked with red, were hard to distinguish. "Do you live close to here?" she said.

"Why?" Cortez said, defensive. He was confused, wondering if she could tell he was from the other part of the city by the way he dressed, how he stood, or some other characteristic he wasn't aware he possessed.

"Because I can come over and spend the night," she said, planting a wet kiss on his neck.

Cortez's heart raced at the thought of spending the night

with her. He had never been with a woman before, and he grew worried doing so would poison his knight's devotion to Alara. The repercussions of the action on his soul's ability to enter heaven never crossed his mind. Even God went to sleep past a certain point in the night, leaving his children to fend for themselves.

"That isn't going to happen," Cortez told her. "I'm taken." Cortez put his hand over his mouth and nose and inhaled the scent of roses. Somehow, he could still find the scent among the stale beer and sweat.

"Then what are you doing in a bar so late at night?" she said before walking away.

Cortez looked for Remy, wondering the same thing. It was past midnight, and Remy had been turning down women all night. He drank, but not enough to lose control of his senses. When Cortez looked back at the spot on the bar that had belonged to his target, the man had disappeared. A pit grew in Cortez's stomach, fearful his position had been discovered, and he examined his immediate surroundings. Remy wasn't close by. Relief washed over him, and Cortez broadened his search, finding his target walking out the front door with a beautiful girl under one arm. She was blond, thin, and used to being the prettiest girl in any room she entered.

The rain had stopped during their hours in the bar and Remy, no longer needing it, had forgotten his umbrella under the bar. Cortez knew but wasn't going to be the one to tell him. He walked behind the drunk couple as they retraced the path back to Remy's apartment, finding ways to touch each other while they walked. They would hold hands, then Remy would put an arm around her. Three separate times they ducked into the sunken threshold of a store and made out.

A pang of guilt ran through Cortez each time the couple disappeared from view, as if he was the one cheating on Alara.

He had to spit into the street multiple times to get the taste of bile from his mouth, thankful the street was already wet because of the rain. His body was exhausted, but he willed it forward with the stubbornness of a mule, certain this was the reason he had been called to follow Remy in the first place. High above them the sky was pitch black, but down on the streets the lights from the streetlamps illuminated every one of Remy's actions, and Cortez was certain God wanted him to see so he could test the strength of his devotion to patience.

Remy and his companion turned the corner a block ahead. Cortez maintained his pace, knowing they would be in the distance when he turned onto the new block himself. His eyes took the opportunity to shut, letting Cortez walk blind while they didn't have to keep the couple in sight. They commanded his hand to brush along the length of the building, promising to open when the hand detected open air. The building was rough stone and scraped his palm. At the building's corner, Cortez turned and his eyes opened. There, right in front of his face at the corner, stood Remy and the girl.

CHAPTER TWENTY-FIVE

Arresting *Adelantado* Francisco Hernandez was the final act of Friar Lorenzo de Bienvenida's role as *Custos* of the Order of the Yucatán. Soon after he arrived back in Merida, the rest of the Franciscan Order arrived in Merida for their third council. Friar Lorenzo de Bienvenida, in charge of all monasteries on the peninsula, had ordered the meeting of the priests to determine who would take over his position. He had been called by God to create a cycle of two-year terms, honoring Friar Luis de Villalpondo's two full years of service in the position, with the feeling no one deserved to lead their group longer than the great man who had laid the groundwork for the learning of the Mayan language. Friar Luis had served in the position from the end of 1549 until his death at the beginning of 1552, and, after the Yucatán had gone without formal leadership for a year and a half, Friar Lorenzo took up the post upon his return from Spain and served from the end of 1553 until the middle of 1556.

When asked by Friar Nicolás de Albalate why he didn't make the terms three years long, Friar Lorenzo said that, having served in the position, he knew two years was the most any man could hope to be effective.

"After that, you're waiting until the clock runs out," Friar Lorenzo said.

Friar Diego returned to Merida a hero. In addition to his great service in the creation of the *arte*, which every Franciscan found useful each day, it was also common knowledge that he had been instrumental in wresting the power from the *encomenderos*—his crowning achievement in the fight was his confrontation with *Adelantado* Francisco.

The friars met in the old Merida sanctuary—the new one built but not yet blessed—while the *Adelantado* sat in a Mani jail awaiting trial. Friar Lorenzo updated them on the status of their prisoner, saying the prisoner would have to wait for the new *Custos* before his case was heard.

"I'd also like to take this time, while all of you are here, to thank Friar Diego for his contribution to the advancement of our understanding of the Mayan language," Friar Lorenzo said.

Every friar in attendance turned to Friar Diego and thanked him for his service with a solemn nod.

"Not only will this help those of us called by God to serve in the Yucatán, it will serve as a guide for the natives on writing their own language in Spanish characters. The Maya owe you a debt of gratitude as well, whether they know it or not."

Friar Lorenzo then explained his reason for calling the council together—though every man in attendance already knew because of the rumors they'd waded through upon their arrival—and announced that they would be voting on who would be *Custos* until the end of summer in 1558. "Let's pray together for God to show us the correct path," he said, bowing his head. He led them in prayer before dismissing the group, saying he would see them again in a few hours for evening mass.

Friar Diego found his friend Friar Francisco Navarro, Guardian of the Campeche monastery, talking to a group of men who had arrived with him from the westernmost Franciscan establishment. At a nod from the Guardian, one of the priests in the group hurried away. Friar Francisco then excused himself from the rest of his retinue, turning his attention to Friar Diego. The two men started walking along the outskirts of Merida, letting their path unwind without initial determination. "There's always something," Friar Francisco said to Friar Diego as they set out. "As I'm sure you're aware."

"Always," Friar Diego replied. Friar Diego had ordered the rest of the friars from Izamal to take any decisions to Friar Nicolás, leaving himself out of any but the most pressing considerations. He had come to Merida for one purpose, and he didn't want any interruptions.

"What do you think about me becoming *Custos*?" he said, getting straight to the point.

Friar Francisco gathered his thoughts while they walked. A group of children, a mix of both Spanish and native, ran past, playing a game of their own design. "The lines drawn between them are already growing weaker," he observed. "The coming generations will have no distinction between Spanish and native; all will worship the same God."

"Let us hope," Friar Diego said, irritated at his friend's straying from the proposed topic of discussion.

"Let us pray. God gives no weight to the desires of man," Friar Francisco said.

"It was a poor choice of words."

Friar Francisco looked at his longtime friend. "Was it? If elected *Custos*, as you mentioned, you'll be tasked with the future of the province. Is this something you want, or is God calling you to the post?"

Until then, Friar Diego had never considered Friar Francisco a potent force among the Franciscan ranks. The directness of his question, a pious reframe, made him realize that together, the two of them represented the future of the Order in the

Yucatán: the next generation's Friar Luis and Friar Lorenzo. Without the slightest consideration of his own lack of contact with a higher power about the appointment, Friar Diego answered that it was in fact God who called him to serve.

"If you serve, you must look for God's path. Give your own feelings no second thought."

"Would you nominate me? And would the men from Campeche vote for me?"

"It's not a given," Friar Francisco said.

For a fraction of a second, Friar Diego considered demanding why not. The men from Izamal voted along the lines drawn by himself, the Guardian of their monastery, and he couldn't imagine a situation where priests didn't follow the orders of their direct superior. "Is your vote a given?" he said, unmasking the true nature of his question. After posing his question, a sense of awe grew inside his chest at how the weight of his friend's faith in God stripped away the external fruit of an issue and exposed the pit within.

"My vote . . . my vote is still undecided."

"We've known each other for years," Friar Diego asserted. "Those nights on the ship where we thought about our roles in the Church's future. Have you forgotten?"

Friar Francisco sighed. "That was a long time ago. But no, I have not forgotten. But I have learned during my years here that there's more at stake than just the issues of faith. The politics cannot be ignored."

"And who has done more to advance the Franciscans' power in the Yucatán than me? I want to preside over the trial of the *Adelantado,* finish what I've started," Friar Diego said.

"You play the game against the *encomenderos,* but there are politics within our ranks as well," Friar Francisco said. "We can't ignore what the current *Custos* wants—it's no secret he thinks Friar Nicolás's time has come."

"Friar Lorenzo didn't have faith in my governance of Izamal either," Friar Diego grumbled.

"Nobody can argue the quality of your time there," Friar Francisco said with a nod. "But your obsession with advancement also makes me question whether it's a personal desire or one of a man who has seen his path laid down for him by God."

"I told you all those years ago and I'll tell you again now: I was called by God to convert the natives. There's no doubt in my soul."

"I believe you don't doubt yourself. I do," Friar Francisco said. "What happens when the time comes for a new *Custos*? Will you be able to step aside?"

"Of course. Two years, in honor of Friar Luis. His memory still accompanies me from morning to night each day. Rewriting the *arte* was just one way of honoring his memory."

"The rewritten *arte* earned you a lot of goodwill. Let's say I vote for you, and tell the others from Campeche to help in your election. What will you do for us? You haven't been that far west, don't know our issues."

"They can't be much different from those I face," Friar Diego said. He thought for a moment. "What if, after my two years, I guarantee the Izamal friars vote for you as *Custos*? Any regional considerations will iron themselves out if we have leadership from both east and west in two successive terms."

Friar Francisco smiled. "God willing, this scenario could work."

The friars continued circling around Merida, and each went to their respective quarters at the conclusion of their discussion. Friar Diego was left with a knot in his stomach, feeling like he was a panther lying on a branch that could break at any moment. He hoped his reflexes were adequate enough for him to land on his feet.

. . .

Friar Diego sought Friar Nicolás after evening mass. Friar Francisco's mindset about trusting in God had rubbed off on him in regards to the vote from the Campeche men, and though he wanted to press the issue with the rest of the friars from the western location, he found an inner peace by leaving their vote in the Lord's hands. His discussion had made him aware of the possibility that Friar Nicolás would break away from the rest of the Izamal friars and vote for himself in the upcoming election. As long as Friar Diego had all the votes from Izamal and Campeche, two of the three largest monasteries in the Yucatán, he could become the region's next *Custos*. He could afford losing a vote from Campeche, if Friar Francisco's interpretation of God's message didn't materialize in a totality of the votes, but a dissenting vote from the Izamal monastery could spell doom for Friar Diego's chance at becoming *Custos*.

Friar Nicolás sat alone outside the Merida infirmary. He was often called to the service of the sick and dying. Praying over the afflicted men helped him sleep at night, his arms crossed over his chest, content with the knowledge he had done all he could to alleviate the total amount of suffering on the earth. Friar Diego sat next to the old friar as small flames were lit in the lamps around the city one by one.

"Counting sand again?" Friar Diego said. In Izamal, they joked that Friar Nicolás would collect grains of sand to save them from suffering in the ocean.

Friar Nicolás laughed.

"I've got a question for you," Friar Diego said, his voice adding to the totality of noise made by Merida's occupants, both humans and nighttime insects.

"You want to make sure I vote for you," Friar Nicolás said, staring off into the night.

"How do you know I'll be up for consideration?"

Friar Nicolás looked at Friar Diego sideways and chuckled.

"I've known you for years, Diego. Your desire for the position is as certain as the sun's coming tomorrow morning. I'm sure you've found a way to nominate yourself."

"And if I am up for consideration? Will you follow the other Izamal friars and vote for me?"

"Have you talked to the others yet?" Friar Nicolás said.

"Not yet, but all I have to do is give them a nod," Friar Diego replied.

"This is true," Friar Nicolás said with a nod.

"Your vote is the only one that concerns me. It wouldn't reflect well if a friar from Izamal didn't vote for their Guardian."

"Friar Lorenzo promised me the votes from the Merida monastery."

"And what do you want?"

"It doesn't matter what I want. It matters what God wants."

"Does God want you to serve?"

Friar Nicolás watched a bug flying around a nearby flame. It circled the light ever closer before being repelled by the heat. "I'm an old man, serving where I'm needed," Friar Nicolás said.

"And Friar Lorenzo wants you taking up more responsibility. Why don't I become *Custos*, then you can take over at Izamal?"

Friar Nicolás shrugged. "I'll withhold my vote and go where the wind takes me."

Friar Diego knew this was the closest to a concession the old man would give. He sat for a while longer, asking about the state of those in the infirmary, before leaving Friar Nicolás alone with his thoughts.

THE NEXT DAY, the friars gathered in the sanctuary to vote for the next *Custos*. Friar Lorenzo started the session with a prayer, asking God for guidance. Then, he reminded everyone of the rules for the vote.

"Once the candidates are nominated, we'll vote by a show of hands. The winner must have a majority, so we'll take as many votes as necessary. There are twenty-three of us here today, so whoever receives twelve votes will be the winner. Those still tending our flock will have to trust the decision made here today."

Friar Lorenzo examined the faces staring back at him; everyone nodded.

"So now, on to the nominations. If you don't mind, I'll start." He waited for any objections; none emerged. "I'd like to nominate Friar Nicolás de Albalate. He's been in the Yucatán since the beginnings of our mission and will bring a steady hand to the role."

Friar Nicolás stood up and gave a quick bow.

"Anyone else?" Friar Lorenzo said.

Friar Diego looked at Friar Francisco. His friend didn't move.

One of the friars from Valladolid stood up. "I'd like to nominate Friar Juan de la Puerta. With a similar record as Friar Nicolás and having overseen the most remote location in the Yucatán, we believe his leadership will be valuable in the coming years."

Friar Juan de la Puerta stood up, bowed, then rested his folded hands on his protruding stomach.

Friar Lorenzo scanned the crowd. Nobody moved. By now, Friar Diego was staring into the back of Friar Francisco's head, cursing his misplaced faith. He prepared to nominate himself and force the votes, taking his chance with the breach in protocol by calling in the favors owed to him by every Franciscan because of his years of work updating the language manual.

As Friar Lorenzo cleared his throat to speak, Friar Diego raised himself off the pew; at the same moment, as Friar Diego lost contact with his seat, Friar Francisco stood. Friar Lorenzo looked at Friar Diego, who pretended he was rearranging his habit before sitting back down.

Friar Francisco's voice rang clear in the sanctuary. "I nominate Friar Diego de Landa. His efforts creating the *arte,* now in use by every member of this order, and his handling of the *encomenderos* give me confidence he's the man who should lead our order for the next two years."

Friar Francisco sat back down, and Friar Diego stood up. He cast a smug glance to Friar Lorenzo as he bowed down.

"If there are no other nominations . . ." Friar Lorenzo said, his final word hovering in the air. "Let's vote. All in favor of Friar Juan?"

Four hands shot up, the four from Valladolid.

"All those in favor of Friar Diego?"

Seven hands shot up: four from Campeche, three from Izamal. Friar Nicolás's hand was down by his side. Friar Diego caught eyes with Friar Juan and looked down at Friar Nicolás, making it clear that the other nominee from Izamal needed to be watched.

"And all those for Friar Nicolás?"

Eleven hands raised, including Friar Lorenzo. Having seen the other vote totals, they all expected their nominee to win on their vote. But there weren't enough hands for a majority.

Friar Juan witnessed Friar Nicolás abstain from voting. He leaned over to the other friars from Valladolid and whispered to his huddled men.

"We need another vote," Friar Lorenzo said. He hadn't noticed Friar Nicolás not voting and wondered who among them didn't vote and who, in another round, might pick up the added vote.

Friar Juan stood up. "Before we vote, I'd like to withdraw my name from consideration. There's still a lot of work to do at Valladolid, and I want to be there to see the seed I've planted come to fruition. I appreciate the consideration."

Friar Lorenzo thanked the friar for his service and proceeded to another vote. This time, he started with Friar Nicolás. There were eleven votes once more, the same eleven men from Merida, Mani, and the surrounding satellite monasteries. This time, Friar Lorenzo saw Friar Nicolás not raise his hand. While their hands were still raised, his eyes questioned his old friend, fearing what it might mean during the vote for Friar Diego.

"Those in favor of Friar Diego?" Friar Lorenzo said when the hands were counted and lowered.

This time, the friars from Valladolid voted for Friar Diego, bringing the count for his ascension to *Custos* to eleven as well.

Friar Diego looked down at Friar Nicolás. They could vote again and again with the same results. It was clear that his vote was the one responsible for the future of the Franciscan Order.

Friar Lorenzo counted the votes out loud. As he reached eleven, he told the men to put their hands down. As they did, one solitary hand remained raised.

It was Friar Nicolás, throwing in his lot with Friar Diego. "Make that twelve, brother," Friar Nicolás said to Friar Lorenzo.

A murmur weaved through the seated men in the sanctuary. Each location's group converged, their Guardians discussing what the new elected *Custos* meant for them.

Friar Lorenzo stood with his hands behind his back, waiting for the men's attention to return to him. He hadn't raised his voice during his years as *Custos* and he didn't intend to start in his term's final moments. When the men's conversations died out, their attention trickled back to the front of the sanctuary, where Friar Lorenzo waited with his patient smile.

"Friar Diego is a wise choice. His tremendous efforts to convert the natives since his arrival demonstrate the energy and dedication he'll bring to the position."

Friar Nicolás urged Friar Diego to stand, whispering that now was the time to say a few words. For the second time during the council, Friar Diego raised himself from the seat before another man made his standing unnecessary.

"One moment, Diego. I want to tell everyone a story I heard, just last night, about how our new *Custos* has helped the Yucatán natives."

Friar Lorenzo continued once Friar Diego sat down.

"As you know, Don Francisco de Montejo Xiu is Lord of the natives of Mani. He wrote me a letter, transcribed by one of the priests, no doubt, about a written land treaty regarding territorial lines of some of the lesser lords. According to him, it's the first document written in the Mayan language using Spanish characters, and he's immensely thankful to the priests for educating his people."

Every Franciscan sat taller in their seats, their chests puffed out, swollen with pride at the great strides the natives had taken in their education. They all thought the treaty itself was the first one in existence, and a sense of relief washed over them knowing they'd prevented regional squabbles over land. In truth, Don Francisco Xiu had a long history of making treaties among the people within his domain—they were written in the Mayan script and held by the Mayan priests among their catalog of books. The treaty the Lord of Mani had referenced was similar to ones he had written in the past, but it included Spanish formalities and the language was written using characters the Franciscans had brought with them from the Old World.

"In addition, he wanted me to pass along his thanks to Friar Diego for creating the *arte,* which made the creation of the document possible. He says he hopes this becomes the standard for natives across the Yucatán."

"He should come tell the Maya in the area around Valladolid," Friar Juan quipped. The other friars from his region laughed. The natives in his jurisdiction hadn't been exposed to Spanish culture as long as those near Mani, and it was well-known the men had their hands full enforcing the Maya's adoption of Spanish customs.

"Regardless," Friar Lorenzo said, putting an end to the Valladolid laughter. "It's because of Friar Diego's contribution to the language that the natives can take the next step in the organization of their land and affairs."

Friar Lorenzo began clapping for Friar Diego, and the rest of the men joined in the applause.

Friar Diego stood up and bowed. He was about to address the council when Friar Lorenzo brought him forth.

"For the rest of the year, Friar Diego will remain here in Merida, where we'll work together to ensure a smooth transition at the beginning of the new year," Friar Lorenzo said while the two men stood together in front of the council.

Friar Diego's air escaped him. He assumed he'd be taking over as *Custos* right away, or at the latest, the following day. Since Friar Lorenzo was handling the transfer of power in the first place, and hadn't died or been ordered to a new location, it was up to him to determine the best course of action for the ascension.

"Friar Nicolás, you're in charge of Izamal until further notice," Friar Lorenzo declared.

Friar Nicolás nodded.

Friar Lorenzo dismissed the men without giving Friar Diego a chance to speak. He asked Friar Diego to stay behind. "What do you think?" he said to the *Custos*-elect when they were alone.

"I think that God has called me to perform my duty to the

Church. We've already seen a drastic reduction in the natives' worship of their primitive gods; under my watch I plan on eliminating their devil-worship altogether. I'm ready to serve."

"God had less to do with this appointment than your own plans," Friar Lorenzo said with a chuckle. "What do you have in mind that you couldn't do as Guardian of the Izamal monastery? Your skill with the natives will be missed in their day-to-day operations."

Friar Diego hadn't considered his absence from Izamal. In that moment, he decided he would stay in Izamal while *Custos*, continuing both duties. God had given him the energy for both, and he didn't want to waste the gift. "I want to preside over the trial of *Adelantado* Francisco," Friar Diego said, making his desire plain.

"Ever the champion for the natives," Friar Lorenzo said, smiling and putting a hand on Friar Diego's shoulder. "We'll hold off the trial until next year, when you've taken over complete control."

CHAPTER TWENTY-SIX

THE COUPLE WAS WAITING in line for a slice of pizza when Cortez appeared next to them. The small restaurant was famous for how late they served their signature dish, and at this time of night there was nothing else open. Even if there were other places to get food, the pizza was a tradition, the best way to cap off the night. It was the way Remy had gotten the blond girl to leave the bar with him, a trick he had used numerous times before. The restaurant was close to his apartment, and he then offered a space to eat the late-night meal. Once they were alone in his apartment, he could work his magic. His system didn't account for being followed.

It was hard to determine who was more surprised: Remy, Cortez, or Liza. She had met Remy for the first time that night and thought he was handsome. When he paid her tab and offered to buy her pizza, she accepted, even though she hadn't drank enough to make a bad decision. It wasn't like her to go off with new men on any night, let alone when she was still in full control of herself, but something about his confidence had convinced her to give him a chance. She wasn't disappointed, and soon found herself enjoying whispered conversations in shadowy corners along their walk, quick discussions that ended with his lips on hers.

"You followed us," Remy said when he saw Cortez. It wasn't said with an overwhelming amount of anger—which Liza would have thought off-putting—but as a declaration of fact, as if her new friend was prepared to fight for her honor.

Liza put a hand on his chest. "I have no idea who he is," she said. Men had followed her before. They had never been dangerous and convinced her they only wanted to talk. But the risk of being stalked was always present, which was why she never went anywhere alone.

Remy looked at the blond girl with sober eyes. His sobriety infected her, removing her sense of well-being and bringing her world into focus. "Why would you?" he said.

She pulled his hand from her chest. "I don't know," she said. She looked at the object of Remy's wrath. He was thin, his face sallow, and he was terrified. As she watched, Cortez put his hand into his pocket then withdrew it, holding it up to his face and taking a whiff that brought all the air in the city into his nostrils. His ritual transformed him, and he looked at Remy with a murderous stare.

Before Liza knew what was happening, Remy had left her side. He walked right up to Cortez and punched him in the stomach. Cortez doubled over but, to Liza's surprise, stood standing.

"Stop." A punch to the side. "Following." A pull on the shoulder, bringing Cortez to standing. "Me!" A punch to the face, accompanied by a sickening crunch of bones.

Cortez couldn't stay standing through the second onslaught. The crowd, who a moment before had been waiting for pizza, had made a circle around the two men and witnessed the beating. They parted when Remy took Liza with him to the front of the line, ordered two slices, and paid for them with a large bill, telling the employees to forget they saw anything in exchange for the massive tip.

A member of the crowd helped Cortez sit up. Another one went inside for water. Blood was pouring from Cortez's nose, and he couldn't breathe without a sharp pain in his side. "Are you OK?" the person helping him sit up asked. Cortez struggled to make out the brown beard that took up most of the man's face. The man held up two fingers.

"How many fingers am I holding up?"

Cortez turned away. "It doesn't matter," he muttered.

"That only works in movies, Ronnie," Ronnie's friend said from the crowd.

Two cups of water appeared in front of Cortez. He used them, along with a copious amount of accompanying napkins, to wipe as much blood as he could from his face. Cortez smiled when he realized how much blood he'd spilled that day in pursuit of Alara.

Liza looked back as she walked away with Remy after getting their slices. They wouldn't be followed anymore, that was for certain. She was also quite sure she'd imagined the terrified face, because now the victim of the beating looked delighted.

"Did that guy just attack you for no reason?" Ronnie, the one with the beard, asked while Cortez was struggling to stand up.

Cortez stood tall. "He has a reason," he said, laughing. "I'm going to take his girl."

As Cortez walked home, the pain in his side increased until he had trouble standing up straight. Every breath took an extraordinary amount of willpower to complete. He couldn't breathe through his swollen nose, and every swallow brought with it an awareness of his loose front teeth and the dull ache in his jaw. The employees had offered him a slice of pizza on the house, but he'd refused because he didn't think he could eat anything without losing a tooth. His maniacal laughter had died away when he left the crowd behind, leaving him gloomy, sore, and aware of how alone he was in the world. Walking through the park left him with an icy chill, and the one thing that kept him marching forward was the thought of his warm bed.

Being on his side of the city, in a familiar place, provided a measure of comfort. He knew to avoid the groups huddled in front of apartments, to keep his head down and ignore their jeers. Each of the two bucket fires he passed were surrounded by people either lying down or sitting at the edges of the provided glow. Nobody would have stopped him from warming his hands in front of the fires, a fellow night creature in need of their resource, but he kept moving, urged by his home's call.

His mother stood in front of their apartment building. She was like a lighthouse in a storm, her eyes scanning the horizon in every direction, looking for her son to emerge through the ocean's mist. When he hobbled up to her, the pain in his side affecting his gait, she rushed out to meet him, her mother's instincts on full alert. She didn't hug him, aware the pressure of her arms might crush what little strength he had left. Instead, she held his shoulders and kept him at arm's length, inspecting him. There was enough artificial light from the surrounding buildings for her to get a sense of the damage to his face.

"What happened to you?" she exclaimed. Cortez had never been a rambunctious child. There were no broken bones or stitches in his past. She doubted he'd ever even suffered a paper cut. Seeing his blood was one of the great fears of her life, and she always wondered how she would handle a situation when it emerged. From then on, she was always proud she had kept her composure in the moment she first saw him bleed, looking for a practical solution instead of growing faint at the sight of her son's condition.

"Nothing," Cortez said. He shrugged her away, trying to continue on his death march to his resting place. His mother could be dealt with tomorrow.

She wasn't willing to let him go. One hand on Cortez's shoulder twisted him back around, flooding his senses with the memory of Remy the moment before he had been struck in the face. His hands went up out of pure instinct. His mother let go and stepped back, horrified that he was scared of her.

"I would never," she said. Her eyes welled with tears.

Cortez dropped his hands and took a deep breath to steady his nerves. His mother was struck by how much time had passed from when he was still her little boy.

"I know," Cortez said. "It's been a long night. Can we just go upstairs?"

"Not until you tell me where you've been. I was worried all night! Do you think I like being up this late, standing outside, waiting for you to come home?"

"You could have stayed upstairs," Cortez said.

"I was going crazy upstairs," his mother whispered. Her moment of weakness, born from the fear she'd had to live with not knowing if her son was safe, or even alive, didn't pass unnoticed by Cortez. He closed his eyes and told her the truth.

"Alara's friend beat me up," Cortez said.

"Does he want to take her from you?" his mother asked. In her mind, Cortez was the crown jewel, the prince, and she couldn't imagine a world where a woman didn't recognize his greatness.

"Something like that." A tear slid down his cheek, a single drop of frustration, embarrassment, and pain.

"Let's go upstairs," his mother said. "You can tell me more when we're inside."

Cortez's mother stood behind him while they climbed the stairs. His reserve strength was depleted, and they had to stop multiple times before making it up the seven flights. She had never seen her son in such a vulnerable state, and she worried about what deed of her own had caused this situation to occur. Both mother and son shared the same unshaken belief that the world around them was the result of their own actions. It was an inherited delusion, passed down from generations, that caused each of them to carry the weight of the world on their shoulders. It wasn't a shared weight; they each possessed their own separate world.

Cortez got to the apartment first and found the door locked. He peeled himself away from the threshold and gave his mother space to access the lock.

"I don't have my key," he said. He kicked himself for forgetting, heaping more pain on his already fragile body.

At those words, his mother knew she had made a mistake. "I don't have my key either." She tried turning the lock herself. "It shouldn't be locked."

This one stumbling block was too much for Cortez. He leaned his back against the wall and collapsed in a heap. "I just want to be left alone." He pulled his knees to his chest, as close as he could without causing too much pain, then rested his forehead on them. His tears rushed out, and at the same moment the rain outside began again. It pelted against the window at the end of the hall, and down on the streets the downpour extinguished the bucket fires, causing everyone relying on their light and heat to scatter in search of cover.

His mother sat down next to him. "Why did her friend beat you up?"

Cortez started talking into his lap, telling his mother how he had met Alara at the coffee shop, about the free drink he'd received from her and their time spent on a bench discussing literature. He told her about walking Alara home, and about seeing her leave to spend time with a friend.

"This woman is leading you on, my son," his mother said when he finished his tale, tapping his shin three times.

Cortez lifted his face and looked at his mother with eyes so full of anguish it crippled her ability to enjoy romantic movies ever again. "Doesn't she know I just want to make her happy?"

His mother extended an arm around him and held him close. She ran her fingers through his hair, happy to be the one to console him. He was her independent boy, the one who always brushed off the world around him, and feeling needed, which she hadn't felt since he was a small child, was worth staying up late and getting locked out of her home.

"That woman doesn't deserve you," she said.

In an instant, Cortez transformed from her son into a viper. He pulled himself away, wiped his tears, and glared at her, ready to strike. "Don't talk about her like that," he said.

"She doesn't! You're all love, and she's throwing you to the wolves." They both stood up.

"You don't know the first thing about her," Cortez hissed.

"I know she's a fool of a woman."

Cortez looked at his mother. He wanted her to hurt. It was the first time he realized it was possible to share the weight on his shoulders, and he tried to share the entirety of his load with her. "You don't know the first thing about love," he managed to sputter. He never knew why he started with that statement, but it was the first crack in the dam before the water came rushing out.

Lightning illuminated the sky outside the window. "I love you," she said. The accompanying thunder shook the building down to its foundation.

"You can't keep anyone by your side who doesn't have to be there," Cortez spat out. Releasing his venom was like learning to walk for the first time; infinite possibilities awaited him in the world. "It's why dad left. He didn't have to be here anymore, so he took the first chance he got to leave."

"You're hurting," his mother said, wiping the tears from her eyes. "You don't mean what you say."

"I mean it!" Cortez roared. His proclamation woke the neighbors. Every door on their floor opened and faces emerged, looking for the source of the commotion. The neighbors shook their heads before going back to bed, not because of the yelling itself, but because it wasn't scheduled. Everyone thanked their lucky stars Ms. Roberts didn't have a male guest over that night.

"I have to stay here because I have nowhere else to go. Have you ever asked yourself if I really love you, or if I'm just stuck?"

Cortez's mother let her gaze fall to the floor. This venomous creature wasn't her son. The image of the boy she held on to with the iron grip of rigor mortis slipped away, replaced by an awareness of the full-grown man ahead of her. A man who didn't know his limitations, who was still stuck in the delusions of an adolescent. She lifted her eyes and stared at him, seeing what he had become for the first time.

"Why do you think you have nowhere else to go?" his mother asked.

The coldness of her tone dulled Cortez's fangs and transformed them back to human teeth. He sensed he had overplayed his hand, but he was committed to seeing his maneuvers through, even if that meant his own welcome destruction. He stayed silent while his mother widened her eyes and jutted her face towards him.

"Hm?" she said. When Cortez didn't respond, she continued. "I'm not keeping you hostage. I've never once told you not to leave. Since you know everything, why don't you tell me why you have nowhere else to go?"

Cortez was shrinking. At the height of his rage, his head had tickled the ceiling. Now, he was eye level with the door handle. He wished his mother would bring the guillotine down on his neck and end the torture. The rain continued to flood the city streets.

"Because no one loves me," Cortez answered. The admission released some of his pain into the world, creating room for more.

"Nobody but me. But keep going. Why do you think that is?"

By now, Cortez was the size of an insect. Animal instinct urged him to scurry away, to find a split in the wall where he could hide in darkness, but he was frozen to the spot. He stared at his mother, pleading with her to bring her foot down and put an end to his miserable existence. She didn't give him the satisfaction. Instead, she opened his eyes and showed him the fibers of the carpet his insect legs carried him through, a much worse punishment than the quick, painless death of being crushed.

"It's because you're not *normal*," she said when he didn't answer. "Who's going to put up with you and your ridiculous routines? Me. Who's going to make sure you have food you like to eat? Me. You think I don't want to eat eggplant? I love eggplant! But, since you don't, guess who never has eggplant. Us!"

Cortez didn't understand how routines were difficult—didn't it mean he was reliable? And he had never once asked her to make any type of food; she chose to do so under her own free will. Every complaint his mother had against him came out in a torrent of words that rivaled the water overflowing the sewers outside. She gained momentum as she spoke.

"Nobody else can love you because you're unlovable. Who

wants to live in fear of spilling toothpaste on the bathroom counter because you'll notice? Or pay attention to how high the bowls are stacked when they're put away, or making sure the spot where you keep your backpack is kept clear so that you're not in a foul mood the rest of the day? Do you know how difficult it is to live with you? No, you have no idea. And yet, I do it, day after day, year after year, because I love you. Nobody else will do it, Cortez. Nobody."

CHAPTER TWENTY-SEVEN

Friar Lorenzo de Bienvenida and Friar Diego de Landa were inseparable during the final months of 1556. Together, they attended meetings with local officials regarding resources for the monasteries, communicated with the Provincials in Guatemala about their ongoing efforts in the Yucatán, and said Sunday mass to thousands at the new Merida monastery. Though construction of the monasteries at Izamal and Merida had begun at the same time, the Merida location's was completed while Izamal's was halfway done because of the scope of Friar Diego's vision for the project. Friar Diego, now a few years wiser than his last time taking direct orders from Friar Lorenzo, learned to appreciate the measured cadence of the rhythms of the older friar's life and his consistency in judgment; what Friar Diego had thought was a slow decision-making process in the past was now seen as a patient chance for the emergence of God's message.

At the start of the new year, Friar Diego took over the myriad administrative duties while Friar Lorenzo stayed on as a guide. Friar Lorenzo saw himself become less and less involved once their roles flipped, and by the middle of 1557, the former

Custos could be seen walking through the halls of the Merida monastery like a ghost condemned to spend his time walking the same grounds after death he'd once frequented in life. One day, he woke up with the certainty that he was alone. Terrified something had happened to Friar Diego while they slept, he sought out the young priest and found him in the sanctuary performing his morning prayers, in the exact spot at the precise time as expected.

Friar Lorenzo waited for the end of Friar Diego's prayers, wondering why or how he had misinterpreted the feelings inspired by his dreams. Friar Diego smiled at his mentor when they met outside the sanctuary.

"I woke up with the feeling that I was alone," Friar Lorenzo said as a greeting. Spending so much waking time in direct contact opened the door for the sharing of their dreams and premonitions. Friar Lorenzo often said that making important decisions after sleeping was one of the best skills he had cultivated as *Custos*, and they got in the habit of sharing their initial feelings about a topic when they first saw each other after a full night's rest.

"You're never alone as long as you have your faith in God," Friar Diego said. Friar Lorenzo had also taught the new *Custos* the correct justification for his actions—inspired by God, or passed down from on high.

"It felt like you were gone," Friar Lorenzo said.

"Your dreams tell the truth, again," Friar Diego said. To him, Friar Lorenzo's power was too reminiscent of Ahkinmai's ability to infiltrate dreams, like the former *Custos* was sipping the same water Ahkinmai drank in gulps.

"You're leaving."

"Today. I'm going back to Izamal."

Friar Diego started walking back to his living quarters to straighten them up for the next friar who would inhabit the space. He walked faster than Friar Lorenzo was comfortable with, and the aged friar struggled to keep up. It was a habit he'd started when he first took over as *Custos* at the start of the new year, increasing his speed little by little as a way of signaling who was in charge. Friar Lorenzo didn't realize what was happening until one day he discovered he was out of breath just walking from the infirmary to the sanctuary, but he refused to mention anything to Friar Diego out of the same male stubbornness that had kept him alive for so long in the first place.

Friar Lorenzo caught up to Friar Diego when the *Custos* was making his bed. The small desk next to the bed, where papers were always kept in neat, organized piles next to the inkwell and pen, was cleared, the contents put into a cloth sack.

"The *Custos* has always stayed in Merida," Friar Lorenzo said from the doorway with conviction.

"That was their choice," Friar Diego replied without looking at the man.

"It was their duty."

"You decided to impose two-year terms. As *Custos*, it was your right—"

"Don't let your position get to your head," Friar Lorenzo warned.

"I'm not going to revert that aspect. I want to honor Friar Luis as well."

"Good."

"But I am going back to Izamal. You said it yourself: the natives there need me. The natives around Merida are already converted. All that is required here is management, something you can oversee. God calls me to oversee the conversions." The mention of God was the key input, and Friar Diego knew it.

Friar Lorenzo's pushback lost all steam. "Your intentions are well founded, but you see how much work there is as *Custos* . . .

you can't go back to worrying about the day-to-day operations of Izamal."

"I can and I will."

Friar Lorenzo shook his head. "I pray for you."

"And I for you."

"And what about the *Adelantado*'s trial? Whenever it's mentioned, you say the time isn't right. How will you being in Izamal affect your duty?"

"He'll stand trial. Let him sit in jail until next year."

"The colonists grow more annoyed with each passing day. They say it's cruel to leave him imprisoned."

"Let them!" Friar Diego said, turning on Friar Lorenzo. "It's the least he deserves for the cruelty he showed the people placed in his care."

"The people of the Yucatán, both native and Spanish, are placed in our care. One cruel act doesn't negate another; it starts a vicious cycle."

"That's one game they can't afford to play. We have the power in the Yucatán, and they'd be smart to remember."

Friar Diego left an exhausted Friar Lorenzo in the living quarters and made the trip back to Izamal alone. The first thing he did, before even announcing his return to the priests in the Izamal monastery, was inspect the construction of the new facilities. It had been four years since construction began. The foundation for the main building had been laid before he left for Merida, and now the four outside walls were being built. All of the massive stone blocks had been made into smaller bricks that lay in piles around the perimeter of the massive sanctuary. The land for the atrium, the planned open space surrounded by stone walls, had been cleared, the four corners marked with deep holes. Friar

Diego found the man in charge of the scores of Mayan laborers, a stonemason from Spain who had been brought by *Adelantado* Montejo to construct the first mansion in Merida and who had also built *Adelantado* Francisco Hernandez's mansion in Mani.

"How's construction coming along?" Friar Diego asked, as if he'd been down the street since they'd last seen each other.

The stonemason saw the brown habit and was about to give his stock answer, that they were working as fast as they could, but the man's entire bearing changed when he realized it was Friar Diego. He knew the man was *Custos*, in charge of the entire Yucatán, and could allocate resources as needed. Stammering, the man said the natives were lazy workers.

"I happen to know they are the most industrious workers on either side of the ocean," Friar Diego said. He slapped a pile of bricks, confirming their solidity.

"What I mean is, the language barrier makes it hard to communicate exactly what I need," the stonemason said. His low-cut shirt exposed the hair on his barrel chest, and his arms were the same diameter from shoulder to wrist.

"Allow me to help then," Friar Diego said. He called over the closest Mayan worker. The too-thin man was covered in stone dust. His tattooed skin stretched around his ribs, and his shoulders ended in sharp points. "What is it you need to tell him?"

The stonemason explained the entire process of building the monastery's walls, about where the stones would lay and how they would be secured. The Mayan man nodded as Friar Diego translated.

"Does that help?" Friar Diego asked, pleased with the update on the next step in the monastery's construction.

The Mayan man shrugged. "A little."

"Will it help you work faster?" Friar Diego asked. He

wanted his monastery done so nobody could question Izamal's prominence.

"Food will help the most," the Mayan man said.

"I give them everything possible, don't take any extra for myself," the stonemason said before he could be accused of corruption, displaying his understanding of the native language.

"You're given food once a day, correct?" Friar Diego asked the Mayan man.

The worker nodded. "It's not enough."

Friar Diego said he understood. "I'll take care of it," he said to the native man before telling him to keep up the good work. Addressing the stonemason, he said, "Let me know if you need any further translation. I'll be in Izamal from now on," Friar Diego said.

Both the stonemason and the Mayan man placed their hands together in front of their chests and nodded.

Friar Diego stormed onto the Izamal monastery's lands, looking for Friar Nicolás. It was the middle of the day and the students, friars, and infirmed were eating lunch in shifts, overseen by the new Guardian. Friar Diego didn't allow for a single nicety before getting straight to the point.

"Why haven't the native laborers been fed enough?" he asked without addressing his presence in Izamal.

Friar Nicolás, calm in his old age, took a tray of bowls filled with soup to the seated patients under his care. Friar Diego walked with him.

"They've been provided food once a day, just like you instructed," Friar Nicolás said. He noticed the *Custos* didn't ask in what way he could help with feeding the sick—it was a stark contrast to Friar Lorenzo's willingness to serve in whatever way possible.

Friar Diego sighed. "Make arrangements to double their allotment."

"We didn't do this before because there weren't enough funds," Friar Nicolás said, pushing back.

"I'll make the funds available. Just take care of it."

Up to that point, a large portion of the labor had been dedicated to the making of bricks from the massive stone blocks that had been used by the Maya who built the temple generations before. The very day Friar Diego showed up unannounced, the last of the stone was prepared for construction, and all the workers who had been working on brick formation were added to the crews making the walls. Friar Diego believed his interjection had increased the well-being of the natives, causing them to work at a faster rate, even though the monastery would have been completed at the same time regardless of how much food the natives were given just from the reallocation of labor.

Friar Diego let the rest of 1557 elapse without concerning himself with the *Adelantado*'s trial, letting the man suffer in jail with his pride keeping him company. With time to consider his own transgressions, the *Adelantado* might show up to his trial as a changed man. Friar Diego made sure no other man could be made *Adelantado* through repeated promises of a hasty trial, which would determine whether Francisco Hernandez would lose his title or retake his position among the *encomenderos*. His decision to begin the trial in the spring of 1558 was made after he received a nighttime visit from a man he hadn't seen in years.

In his dream, Friar Diego spoke to Ahkinmai, who sported bright red feathers the color of flames, outside the infirmary. Neither man wasted time with formalities. Ahkinmai shared his concerns for the people who were in the *encomienda* controlled by the *Adelantado*.

"Their *milpas* were destroyed by your prisoner. Now that they've lost their *encomendero*, nobody has anything to eat."

Friar Diego cursed the interlocking pieces in the Yucatán politics. "Nobody can give them food?"

"Neither monastery is close enough. Because of the situation your people have created, they need another *encomendero.*" Ahkinmai shook his head, saddened by the state of his people.

"My people are saving the natives from *encomiendas,*" Friar Diego shot back.

"Stop worrying about who gets the blame and start thinking about the starving people," Ahkinmai said. "It's bad enough the other *encomenderos* hold on to their laborers like a suckling baby, afraid they will be taken away. There are people starving with no place to go!"

"What do you want me to do?" Friar Diego said, chastened.

"Finish the trial. Either restore his lands or allow someone else to take over, then make my starving brothers and sisters their responsibility." Ahkinmai paced over the dirt. "It's pitiful they have to rely on you. We were once able to sustain many more without interference."

Friar Diego said he would consider expediting the trial. "If I can't think of any other options," he added.

Ahkinmai thanked Friar Diego and walked away. The *Custos* woke with a start and spent the rest of his sleepless night trying to come up with a solution for the situation the *Adelantado*'s elongated imprisonment had precipitated. Ahkinmai's solution struck to the heart of the matter and was the quickest way to save the native souls.

FRIAR DIEGO's arrival in Mani as leader of the Yucatán went unnoticed. There was little indication of the decision he would make in the city, which would reverberate throughout history, other than the small flames that illuminated the city in the darkness of twilight. The man in charge of the Mani monastery,

Friar Pedro de Ciudad Rodrigo, had just completed one final walk-through of the infirmary, blessing each patient for the night as he had every night for years, when he saw a man in a brown habit walking onto the monastery grounds as if he owned the place. The visitor, a Franciscan, wasn't one of his group stationed in Mani—the gait was foreign.

"Excuse me, brother," Friar Pedro said, shuffling forward to catch the visitor. Friar Pedro had arrived in the Yucatán with Friar Juan de la Puerta, around the same time as Friar Lorenzo. His back was bent from years spent praying over the sick, and his eyes had the peculiar ability of darkening during the day and brightening at night.

When Friar Diego turned, Friar Pedro let out a startled yelp. "Friar Diego! What brings you here at this hour?" Friar Pedro asked. He turned in the direction Friar Diego had come from, looking for others. "And alone?"

"The time for the *Adelantado*'s trial has come," Friar Diego said.

Friar Pedro ushered the visiting friar to the monastery's living quarters. "Rest tonight, we can take care of this in the morning," he said.

"I've already sent a letter to Friar Lorenzo; he should be here within a few days. Including you, the three of us will decide the *Adelantado*'s fate."

The entire city of Mani was eager for the beginning of the trial by the time Friar Lorenzo arrived. For the Franciscans, it was the opportunity to enforce their power over the region and strike fear into the hearts of Spaniards who didn't accept their authority. The *encomenderos*, the Spanish colonists with the most land and therefore the most power, kept close watch on the trial, knowing that if the *Adelantado* was at risk of outsized retribution, any of them could be next. The natives in Mani, made aware of the plight of the natives who lived on the masterless *encomienda* by Ahkinmai and a traveling Nachi Cocom, awaited word about what would become of their countrymen.

Friar Diego decreed that no witnesses would be permitted at the trial other than a government administrator who would ensure all formalities were obeyed. A disheveled *Adelantado* Francisco was dragged into the monastery courtyard by two broad-shouldered Spanish jailers. A table had been set up outside the sanctuary, where the three Franciscan judges sat in the sweltering sun. The charges were read out to the *Adelantado*, the main offense being his willful disobedience of the Crown's command that the native youths be educated in the Spanish customs and religion. There was mention of his treatment of the natives, and his threatening of Friar Diego, but neither of these were as detrimental to the Franciscans' authority in the Yucatán and were therefore glossed over.

Contrary to Friar Diego's expectations, *Adelantado* Francisco's time in jail had hardened him into a crust of a man. He made no apologies for his actions, saying the friars had gone too far in telling him what to do with his property. "The Crown provides the power over the land and everything in it," he said. "What I choose to do with my own property is none of your business." He spat on the ground, and his saliva's acidity killed the grass, yellowing it in front of their eyes.

Both the judges and the defendant believed the Spanish Crown justified their positions, but one held power over the other. After going through the motions of the court for the benefit of the administrator, which everyone present knew wouldn't affect the outcome a single iota, Friar Diego announced the three Franciscans would deliberate the *Adelantado*'s sentence.

The three friars excused themselves to the schoolhouse. Friar Diego spoke first.

"Let's take away his property and leave him rotting in jail," the *Custos* said.

"We can't leave him in jail," Friar Pedro said. His firmness surprised both of the other two judges. "There have already been whispers of escape from local *encomenderos*. Security will be a nightmare."

"Taking away his possessions won't sit well with other landowners," Friar Lorenzo said. "We risk a revolt if they think we can come for them too."

"I don't care about them," Friar Diego said, dismissing the other forces with a wave of his hand. "We have Spain's backing."

"Their support wouldn't arrive for months. Such a large fissure could set us back years," Friar Lorenzo said.

"We need to make an example of him!" said Friar Diego.

The three men grew silent, thinking. Friar Pedro suggested he pay a heavy fine.

"Even if he pays, he'll just go back to mistreating the natives once again," Friar Lorenzo said.

"Not if he's not allowed to go back," Friar Pedro said. "What if we exile him from the Yucatán?"

Friar Diego crossed his arms while glaring at the two men. "Exile him in jail," he said.

The other two judges ignored him. "A five-year exile and a heavy fine," Friar Lorenzo said. "That should get our message across. Nobody would dare cross the Franciscan Order again."

Friar Diego started pacing. He was a caged animal, his attacking ability taken away. "There has to be something the natives can see as well," he said, thinking out loud.

Friar Pedro looked at Friar Lorenzo and nodded at a nearby bench. The two men sat down.

"They won't care about a fine and his disappearance. We need to maintain our status as their protectors by showing them we're on their side, fighting for their cause. And what happens when he returns? He'll go back to treating the Maya the exact same way."

"We don't know that for sure," Friar Lorenzo said.

Friar Diego scoffed, dismissing the notion. "It's all but guaranteed."

"Let the man learn his lesson. We must give sinners the chance to prove themselves before God," Friar Pedro said. He still drew clear lines between political battles and the business of souls.

"What about a public humiliation? The natives here would see and spread the word to the rest of their brethren. Let him sit in jail until it's carried out." Friar Diego planned on delaying the public display as long as possible, in the same way he had pushed back the trial.

The other two judges considered the option.

"Look, you're right, taking away his property would create too much animosity among the other landowners," Friar Diego said, in a rare admission of error. "The fine and exile are a worthwhile solution. But neither of these options mean anything to the natives. Let's show them we are on their side in the fight against brutality."

Friar Diego's impassioned speech worked. Both other judges agreed before Friar Pedro asked what the *Custos* had in mind.

"Flogging is too harsh," Friar Diego said, thinking aloud while still pacing. "We could tie him to a post in the middle of Mani's market, hanging him by his hands."

"Humiliation, not torture," Friar Lorenzo said.

Friar Pedro marveled at the ease with which the two men discussed the sentence. The former *Custos* dismissed the barbarity as if he were a schoolmaster correcting a student's mistake.

"Keep his feet on the ground then. Barefoot and bare-chested, one full week where colonists and natives can see him."

Friar Lorenzo nodded. Friar Pedro said he thought the punishment was too harsh, that sitting on a raised platform alone in the middle of the market would be enough. "Though if you two agree, my vote on the method doesn't matter."

"That settles it then. Let's go inform the *Adelantado* what we've decided," Friar Diego said. His excitement was palpable.

The other two judges, having lived in the Yucatán much longer than the *Custos* and with knowledge of the initial battles for land, strode behind their leader lost in projections about the sentence's potential ramifications.

Back in the courtyard, seated at the table, Friar Diego relayed each portion of the sentence in a slow, measured cadence so the administrator could take note of the Franciscans' decision. When Friar Diego told the *Adelantado* he was subjected to a fine equal to half his worth, a five-year exile, and an upcoming public humiliation, the bedraggled man howled with rage, swearing on all in both heaven and earth he would get his revenge.

The jailers dragged him away, taking him to jail, where he would await the upcoming public humiliation. Friar Diego thanked both Friar Lorenzo and Friar Pedro for their help in coming up with a worthwhile solution in the matter, then excused himself and began the trip back to Izamal, knowing full well he'd drag this portion of the sentence out too, ignoring the plight of the starving natives and the reason he'd begun the trial in the first place.

Adelantado Francisco never went through the ordeal in the middle of the Mani market the friars had planned for him. Three days later, under cover of darkness, a group of *encomenderos* walked into the jail and, without a finger raised against them by the guards, released the *Adelantado* into the night.

CHAPTER TWENTY-EIGHT

CORTEZ STARED AT HIS MOTHER, fearful of the old age that appeared on her face. As he watched, deep seams emerged where her smile met her cheeks and around the corners of her eyes. Her hair turned from black to streaked gray, and she stooped, the hunch on her back pushing her head forward. Her laundry list of grievances wasn't finished.

"I've had to deal with finding the one brand of shirts you like because the tag doesn't scratch your back. Staying out of the bathroom at seven in the morning because that's when you use it—as if there's something special about the time! Not having friends, or meeting new people, because I need to be home to make sure the rhythms of your day aren't interrupted. The way you live isn't natural, Cortez, and you don't even know it. Haven't you ever wondered why you don't have friends? Or have never had a girlfriend before? Why do you think I was so excited to hear about Alara? Because it's never happened!"

Cortez wanted to say something at the mention of Alara, but his mother's onslaught didn't abate. All of her specific examples were obvious methods of existing in the world, and he didn't understand how any of them could cause her grief.

"Nobody else learns to talk to people by copying what they see on television. Nobody. Oh, don't think I didn't know. It's obvious when you slip into your *roles*. You do the same thing with people you meet. Your personality holds part of every teacher you've ever had. Knowing this, I get upset with myself, thinking I'm a failure as a mother because I didn't provide you with a better model. Did I not show enough examples of how to talk to people in different scenarios? Was I supposed to go through every possible situation, unaware that you wouldn't be able to use the lessons you learned from one in the other? The worst part of all this? It doesn't even work! You're no better at talking to people than if I had thrown you into the wild. You almost got yourself killed by that pimp the other day and you had no idea. You can't be left alone at any time, inside or outside the house."

The woman's age caught up with her and she started losing steam. "Maybe it's my fault. Maybe I babied you. But at the end of the day, you don't have anywhere else to go because nobody loves you like I do. You're not like other people, and the sooner you accept that the sooner you'll learn to be happy."

Cortez watched his aged mother turn and look out the window at the end of the hall. He was torn between wanting to run away and wanting to go home, between never coming back and pretending he hadn't heard her complaints. Her example demonstrated another lesson for him, one he would use just once in his time left on earth: to save up all his grievances and let them explode in a flurry of words. His bed called out to him from beyond the door. After listening to his mother reveal her issues with him and unsure of what else to do, he reached out for the door handle to try turning it once more, willing himself to grow until he was back to full size.

The lock had aged in the same way his mother had. The decades passed by while they were in the hallway, rusting the mechanism. There was a slight resistance to Cortez's turn before the lock gave way. He opened the door and a wave of stale air washed over his face, cool in the spots where tears had moistened his skin. He walked inside and went straight to the bathroom, his steps leaving footprints in a thick layer of dust. The mirror was grimy around the edges but clean in the center, and in it he saw how much damage Remy's single blow to his face had caused. His upper lip was swollen to the size of a fat red caterpillar, his nose was bloody but straight, and his teeth were all outlined by blood from his leaking gums. The water came out brown when he first turned on the faucet but became clear after he let it run. He washed the blood from his face, rinsed his mouth, and decided against brushing his teeth. When he was finished, he stared into the mirror again, wondering how he could change himself to be worthy of Alara's love. He smeared toothpaste on the bathroom counter, wondering how on earth the mess could make him easier to tolerate. No matter how hard he tried to ignore the stain it demanded his attention, and in a rush of perceived weakness he flushed it away with water. Maybe he was his mother's burden to bear.

His mother was in the kitchen when he emerged from the bathroom. She was looking through everything in the refrigerator, the open door releasing the smell of rancid food throughout the home. The floors were streaked with thin lines of remaining dust, the particles that had escaped her first attempts at sweeping. The beans and chorizo left for Cortez on a plate were covered in mold. Every vegetable had turned into a pile of mush that needed to be scraped from the surface and thrown away. She paused what she was doing and looked at her son. "There's a lot to clean up here. Why don't you go to bed and let me take care of this."

He knew they were going to act like her tirade had never happened. It was her turn to clean until he was done being mad at her, a tendency he had picked up from her in the first place. Without another word, he went into his bedroom. Time hadn't played tricks on the space—it was just how he left it. He turned on the lamp on his nightstand and was surprised to find no dust had accumulated on the surfaces of his furniture. His bed still smelled like him, like he'd slept in it yesterday and not years before. The floor was still spotless, and the clothes hanging in his closet were pressed for the next day's church service, free from moths.

From beyond his door he heard his mother crying. Cortez grew angry at every sob. She had no right to be upset. If anything, he should be upset, and yet there he was, thinking about ways he could change himself to be more worthy of love. He fell asleep wishing he could be more normal, confused about how his routines could ever be viewed as a burden, and, most of all, embarrassed that his reliance on learning to talk to people by mimicking television characters wasn't a secret.

Cortez awoke when the first rays of daylight trickled through his bedroom window. The clean and pressed clothes in his closet were cloaked in shadow, bringing the memory of the night rushing back. It was Sunday, and if his life hadn't been turned upside down, he would have turned back over and slept until it was time to get dressed for another day of worship. Instead, he sat up, a groan emanating from his aching body, and turned to the side, placing his feet on the floor. His mother's tirade still echoed through his mind. He had never considered how much of a burden he was, and finding out how much his most innocent actions affected her made him second-guess the organization of his life. Including going to church. This didn't bother him as much as seeing decades pass within minutes, his mother and their home both falling victim to the phenomenon. For some reason, he had been spared. Curious if it was a dream, he got up and went into the kitchen.

His mother had cleaned every speck of dust from the counters and floors. Their mustard-yellow couch, already old when they found it, didn't look any older than before. Cortez opened the refrigerator. It was empty, bare as if it was brand new, even though the exterior still showed evidence of the years. The open door released the smell of lemons into the room. The freezer was empty as well. There was no way his mother would have thrown away everything inside unless it had been spoiled; she kept tabs on their food cost with the diligence of a tax collector. The disappearance of the food was enough proof, for Cortez, that it hadn't been a dream, and after a shrug, he went to the bathroom to relieve himself.

His face's swelling had somehow gotten worse overnight. While looking in the mirror, Cortez inspected his gums, shook his loose front teeth, and poked his nose. There was a sort of masculine pride at his battle wounds. A soft chuckle brought the pain in his side into the forefront. He turned to inspect the site of the worst pain and found a dark bruise on his right side, closer to his back, from where Remy had struck him after the initial punch in the stomach. He reached across the front of his body with his left arm and poked the spot. The pain took his breath away and made his eyes roll back in his head. When his vision came back into focus, he looked again at the bruise, seeing if he could find a spot where a rib was poking out at an unnatural angle. Nothing stood out, other than the deep discoloration.

Seeing the results of the beating from the night before reminded Cortez of his discovery that Remy wasn't faithful to Alara. The hatred's heat spread through his body. Thinking of Alara, he remembered the rose he'd taken from the garden the day before. It was a lifetime ago; for the second time that morning, Cortez sensed the decades that had passed. He rushed into his room, found the pants he'd worn, and reached a hand into the pocket to find the flower, hoping it hadn't turned to dust. Its petals were still moist when he pulled out the crushed remnants, his own grip responsible for the damage. He held it up to his nose and breathed deep. Alara's scent reached him from far away, his swollen nose not letting her get any closer. He had to warn her about Remy, to tell her about his infidelity and beg her to end the relationship. With any luck, she would realize Cortez's value and leap into his arms at the revelation, thanking him with a shower of kisses. But, if he went to church, his entire day was spoken for, leaving him no chance to save her.

Alara couldn't wait until Monday.

Cortez decided to forego church with a resolve that surprised even himself, sacrificing his own salvation for the woman he loved in the same way Jesus had sacrificed himself for his flock. Cortez placed the flower next to his lamp on the nightstand and got dressed, leaving his church clothes on the hanger, instead choosing the clothes typical throughout the week: jeans and a T-shirt. Without anything to eat available in the kitchen, he decided he would wait until lunch. His plan was to warn her, receive her mountains of praise, which would ease the pain in his side, then make it back to the church in time for the post-service lunch and search for new members. There was no way he could know that she would ruin his appetite for good, and that he would never step foot in a church again.

Cortez shut the door behind him without making a sound. He thought the mechanism was silent because of his gentle touch, but the lock had been rendered useless by the passing years. The early morning sun was beginning to illuminate the streets outside his building, and in its light he saw the evidence of the flood. Piles of debris were accumulated in front of storm drains, and clothes were hung out to dry on every available surface, from both the homeless and the night creatures who'd refused to end their nocturnal escapades and escape indoors at the rain's arrival. Some parked cars were twisted, one side jutting into the street, and some were pushed up flush against the curb. The world had just been washed, the first time Cortez could ever remember it being cleaned. He was Noah walking away from the ark for the first time alongside pairs of every type of animal.

The park had welcomed the rain. Every tree sported new buds among their green leaves, and the grass had transformed into a field of flowers. Cortez could smell the sweetness in the air despite the swelling in his nose. It wasn't anywhere close to the power of Alara. He continued through the park, the lone person in Eden, and came out the other side, ready to fight the wilderness for Eve. Since it was still early, he assumed Alara would be at home; he headed in her direction.

Alara had worked the night before, closing the store late, and declined to meet Remy at a sports bar to watch his favorite soccer team, choosing instead to go home and read until she fell asleep. When the sky opened up in the middle of the night, well after her boyfriend had vented his frustration on Cortez, she was sound asleep and never heard the thunder and lightning. Her dreams included flowers. Not flowers from a budding romance, but funeral flowers, decorating an unmarked, open grave. When Cortez was walking through the park towards her home, she was lost in her dream, a ghost witnessing the lowering of a coffin, trying to figure out who was being laid to rest and having a sneaking suspicion she was witnessing the service celebrating her own life. She turned in her sleep when she discovered her specter was the lone witness in attendance.

Cortez walked onto Alara's block with his eyes scanning the sidewalks for signs of Alara's dog-walking neighbor. He spotted the tree outside what he presumed was Alara's window from the corner of the block, seeing it had also sprouted new buds like its comrades in the park. The branches looked too thin to support his weight, and he shook his head at what he had been prepared to do in the name of love—knocking on Alara's door in the first light of morning wasn't one of them. He was worried she wouldn't understand his intentions and her alarm at his knowledge of where she lived would override the quality of his information. Cars parked on the street across from the courtyard provided cover where he could observe without being seen, and he sat down to wait for his beloved to appear.

Alara left her home an hour later. Cortez grew excited when he saw movement outside her front door, and he watched her descend the steps certain she was an angel coming down from heaven. His belief was confirmed when she emerged on the courtyard in all her splendor. She wore a flowing floral dress that bared her arms and shoulders, and her hair was down, held back from her face with a thin golden headband. Her usual fabric bag hung from her shoulder.

"The queen of angels," he whispered to himself.

Alara didn't see the pair of darkened eyes watching her from behind a car as she walked across the courtyard in front of her apartment, turned, and headed into the part of the city where she worked. She was going to brunch with her friends, a Sunday tradition they held as sacred as Cortez considered church: to be missed at the risk of one's soul.

Cortez followed her. While doing so, he wondered if he could do it as a profession, imagining himself as one of the interchangeable detectives he watched on television. His track record wasn't stellar, having been caught by Remy twice now, but some hiccups could be expected for a beginner. He decided he'd look into what it took to become a detective, since he still didn't have a job, once he sealed up the case of Alara and the cheating boyfriend.

Alara's path led Cortez to a bistro with outdoor seating. She was recognized as soon as she walked up by two women her same age, both of whom stood up and gave her a hug. Seeing her with other women made her beauty stand out even more. Cortez couldn't imagine what they had in common with the delicate flower he was enamored with, and he attributed her presence with the other girls to Christian charity. There was a playground across the street with benches that provided a clear view of their table, and Cortez sat at one of them, his hunter's eyes not missing a movement.

Three more women arrived within minutes, all arriving by themselves: the rest of their party. As soon as everyone was seated, one of the group, a brunette taller than the rest with glasses, beckoned for the waiter, who came over and handed out menus. The waiter was new and didn't know the group was there every Sunday, rain or shine, the weather affecting whether they sat inside or in the sun. Friends from high school, this was when they caught up and came back together before they went back off in the directions of their own lives.

Cortez delighted in seeing Alara in her element. It was a different side of her, a smiling, happy side. His own shadow grew heavy beside him, knowing the information Cortez possessed would ruin her day. He grew restless. Sitting near the slide on a children's playground, Cortez steeled himself to walk over to her while she was with her friends.

Alara's group didn't see the man walking from the playground to the bistro, didn't notice when he tried to turn back twice before continuing while talking to himself, didn't dream the person pacing behind Alara's back was working up the nerve to talk to one of them. They were discussing one of their former teachers who had been caught up in an infidelity scandal when, from behind Alara, Cortez adopted an unaffected air and, leaning on the fence that surrounded the seating area, said, "Fancy seeing you here!"

He had seen this exact scenario played out on a sitcom whose name he couldn't remember, when a woman crossed paths with a man according to her own scheme. He imagined it would work just as well when the roles were reversed. His plan hadn't prepared him to be ignored.

Not one of the group paid any attention to him. He repeated the phrase, but louder. "Fancy seeing you here," he said, loud enough for everyone on the block to hear, before a lump of embarrassment choked off his voice.

Everyone seated outside the bistro, not just Alara's group, turned to see who spoke. Cortez stared at Alara with a sheepish smile, waiting to see her face lighting up even further when she recognized him. Instead, the light her face emitted dimmed with confusion, and she turned back around without the identity of the strange man registering.

If Cortez hadn't been sure of his mission, positive his message was of the utmost importance, he would have turned away, found a hole, and died inside. He fought the urge to run with every ounce of willpower he possessed.

"Alara," he said. He waited for her to turn around. "Can I talk to you?"

CHAPTER TWENTY-NINE

Friar Diego de Landa was livid when he heard about *Adelantado* Francisco Hernandez's escape from jail. The flames illuminating Friar Diego's study roared, fueled by an unseen source, as he read the letter from Friar Pedro de Ciudad Rodrigo.

"No word or sight of him since his escape," Friar Diego read aloud.

Ix Cuatchel, always nearby, heard the words and asked the *Custos* if he needed anything.

"Competent jailers," he said, throwing the letter onto his desk and leaning back. He reached up and rubbed his eyes with the heels of his hands.

"I don't know where to get those," Ix said. She had become Friar Diego's personal secretary when the man who'd saved her from sacrifice was elevated to *Custos*, foregoing her work in the infirmary and instead making sure the leader of the Franciscans in the Yucatán had everything he needed. The natives referred to the pair as husband and wife, and the friars all hoped the relationship stemmed from a quasi-paternal bond and not from primal urges. Since her beauty couldn't be ignored by any who crossed her path—and encouraged many young Mayan men's attendance at mass—the other Izamal friars all feared a slip into sin, but Friar Diego's consistent ill temper convinced them otherwise.

"You don't need to find me jailers," Friar Diego said. She had a habit of taking his words as literal statements. "Go to bed," he said.

Ix shut the door to his room and left him alone.

The letter from Friar Pedro had arrived after dinner, and Friar Diego had left it unopened until he could read it in peace. His blood boiled at the news, and he found sleeping difficult, not just for the night after he received the letter, but for months afterwards. Between the threat of Ahkinmai's dream invasions and perseveration of his thoughts about the escaped *Adelantado*, Friar Diego's sleep was reduced to the minutes he took in the middle of the day after lunch.

Adelantado Francisco didn't show up at his old house and never saw the skeleton of his wife hanging from the roof. The natives stood in a state of suspended animation, unsure of whether they should create their *milpas* once more and grow maize, await his return, or abandon their homes in search of better accommodations. Nachi Cocom took care of them. When Friar Diego told the Mayan leader that *Adelantado* Francisco was on the loose, Nachi walked to the *encomienda* near Mani, gathered the natives, and walked them back to Sotuta, where he made sure they had enough food by putting them to work in the fields near his village and covering the difference in their production with his own crop.

Friar Diego received another letter about *Adelantado* Francisco in the summer of 1558, as his tenure as *Custos* was coming to a close. It was addressed to him but had been sent to Merida, and by the time it got to him in Izamal the news had already been spread by others in the Yucatán who'd received the same message: the *Adelantado* was in Guatemala and had gotten himself a retrial.

The Guatemalan officials were well within their power to prescribe a retrial. The Yucatán had been in the custody of the Guatemala Province since the initial conquistadors claimed the land for the Spanish Crown. Tomás López Medel came from the faraway province and handed down his damning decrees, which ruptured the Mayan way of life. Friar Lorenzo de Bienvenida had come to the Yucatán via Guatemala and, as *Custos*, had taken advantage of the province's resources in his arrest of the *Adelantado* in the first place. His interaction with the officials in Guatemala had illuminated the disadvantages of being in the custody of a faraway seat of power—he never made the logical leap of equating the situation with Spanish rule.

Friar Diego was furious they'd rejected the original sentence but, besides the call for a retrial, there was little else the faraway province officials could do to check Franciscan authority. Dragging *Adelantado* Francisco into the courtyard at Mani, or any other courtyard in any other monastery in the Yucatán, and handing down the same sentence was still within their given rights. The sole problem was Friar Diego's role in the trial. As *Custos,* he had been the lead judge and had chosen Friar Pedro and Friar Lorenzo to complete the triumvirate. The planned ascension of Friar Francisco Navarro meant that his friend would be overseeing the trial of *Adelantado* Francisco; the best Friar Diego could hope for without intervention was serving as one of the two supporting judges.

"Francisco has powerful friends," Friar Navarro told Friar Diego when they saw each other again in Merida. The two men were sitting alone after eating lunch together.

"It's because of the rest of the *encomenderos,*" Friar Diego replied. "They don't want us involved in the management of their property. The authorities in Guatemala have the same concerns as we do here: managing the balance between the Church and state."

Francisco couldn't hide the annoyance in his voice. "I'm aware of the struggles in Guatemala, my friend. Campeche is closer than Izamal."

"That it is," Friar Diego said. Though he was still *Custos,* he was aware that within a few hours his friend would take his position, along with oversight of the trial of *Adelantado* Francisco. Knowing this, he broached a topic that had plagued his thoughts from the first reading of the letter from Guatemala. "What are your thoughts about letting me continue what I've started?"

"Elaborate," Friar Francisco said.

"I want to oversee the *Adelantado*'s retrial."

Friar Francisco crossed his hands in his lap, bowed his head, and closed his eyes. His breathing slowed as his thoughts coalesced. With a sharp intake of air, as if he had been woken up, he sat straight and agreed. "My one concern, if I'm being honest, is I feel like this could undercut my authority."

Friar Diego opened his mouth to speak but was silenced by his friend's raised hand.

"But what the officials in Guatemala are trying to do is a far greater infringement of Franciscan authority in the Yucatán. We can't let that stand."

"My thoughts exactly," Friar Diego said, nodding.

At the council a few days later, Friar Francisco Navarro was elected *Custos,* Friar Diego was given charge of Izamal once more, and Friar Lorenzo was sent back to Spain to both gather more friars for their Yucatán efforts and, as he put it, "To take control of the Yucatán away from Guatemala." The Yucatán Franciscans all agreed the Yucatán should be its own province, away from the restrictive oversight of faraway Guatemala.

Before Friar Diego went back to his home monastery, Friar Francisco sent a letter, as *Custos*, to Guatemala, saying *Adelantado* Francisco should return at once for his retrial. Then the friars all disbanded throughout the peninsula, taking the well-worn dirt paths to their respective stations.

Operations at the Izamal monastery didn't change. One of their friars, the youngest, was sent to Campeche after the council, making up the difference in manpower created by Friar Francisco's elevation to *Custos*, but the rest of the Franciscans stationed there were the same. Friar Nicolás had chosen Izamal again instead of going to an upstart location, saying he was too old and lacked sufficient energy for a less-established operation. Since Friar Diego had been in Izamal as *Custos*, overseeing the construction of his great monastery, natives, Franciscans, and colonists were accustomed to his overbearing presence throughout the area.

Ix continued her role as his personal secretary. The two were inseparable. It was as if she had a sixth sense about what Friar Diego needed, and she was there with food, water, paper and ink, or laundered habit before the necessity of the object even crossed his own mind.

Friar Diego was reminded of his time at the Toledo monastery in Spain, when he was a young man starting his education in Catholicism. He'd filled a similar role with his mentor as Ix did with him, making sure the older man was aware of his eagerness, always one step ahead of problems before they arose. Because of his own tenacity during his apprenticeship, when he would take care of small issues not worth bothering his mentor about, he wasn't surprised when he discovered Ix was responsible for dealing with an issue that arose from the Maya.

He discovered her hand in the care of the natives by accident. His morning prayers were always undertaken at the same time, and they always took more than an hour. On a morning at the end of 1558, while he was praying, a disturbance in his stomach pulled him from his reverie. He tried to ignore the sensation, adding prayers for the soothing of his bowels, but God didn't answer. When he could no longer ignore the churning, he promised the cross he would be back once he had relieved himself. He rushed off to the toilet, his feet splayed out and clenching his backside, pulling up his habit just in time for the expulsion and subsequent wave of relief. While walking back to the sanctuary, he heard Ix speaking in the Mayan language to a distraught woman.

"The baby was born dead!" the visiting native said. "Ahkinmai says I need to give the body to the gods"—the woman's words were interrupted by sobs—"but I don't want to burn him!"

Friar Diego stood next to the infirmary wall, peeking his head around the corner. Ix was standing with the woman at the edge of the monastery's lands, as if she was heading the native woman off before she could bother the priests. The woman was holding the dead baby against her bare chest as if she was nursing. The fact that a woman had run to the monastery, searching for guidance in direct opposition to Ahkinmai, gave him hope: the Mayan priest no longer held absolute power over the rest of his people. Soon, their devil-worship would die altogether, lost to time. He wondered if the other friars knew about Ix's involvement with Mayan visitors, if they had permitted it behind his back while he was busy with his duties as *Custos*.

"Well, first off, you know what God says about burial," Ix said. Her voice was soothing, tempered over years of dealing with people scared of death and disease in the infirmary.

"The body needs to be buried so he can rise up in God's land," the native woman said. Her voice was filled with sadness.

"That's right." Ix reached forward and withdrew the corpse from the woman's arms. Holding it with one arm, she pulled on the woman's top, which was gathered around her neck, using the other.

The woman finished covering her chest herself. "Isn't there anything you can do? Pray for my baby!"

Ix looked at the stillborn infant. The umbilical cord hung down to her waist. It was covered in dried amniotic fluid and the woman had the same substance crusted on her inner thighs. The native woman's hair was disheveled, as if she had run away from her people as soon as the body had left her womb. "There are no prayers that can raise the dead," Ix said, her gentle voice clipped at the final word, leaving the space around the two Mayan women filled with silence.

The would-be mother reached for her child. "If I could just get him to accept my milk," she said in desperation.

"He's gone," Ix said. The force of her words froze the frantic mother mid-reach. "If you can't bury him, I'll do it for you."

At this, the mother's arms dropped and she fell to her knees. Her chest rose and fell with her silent sobs. Ix reached down and helped the woman back to her feet.

"Spend the rest of the day with your child," Ix said, handing the baby back to the mother. "I'll come to you tonight and we can bury him together."

The mother nodded through her tears with the baby back in her arms. She looked down at his small face before reaching a hand up and stroking it with the back of her hand.

"Do you know the banana tree grove near the *cenote*?" Ix said.

The native visitor nodded.

"Meet me there at sunset and we'll find a suitable place."

With that, Ix reached an arm out, placed it on the woman's shoulder, turned her around, and escorted her down the dirt path that led into the jungle. She saw Friar Diego standing next to the infirmary when she came back.

"What did she want?" Friar Diego asked as she approached.

"Wants the friars to pray for her child," Ix said. She kept walking past him, not meeting his eyes.

"Did she just give birth?"

"Yes."

"A blessing is the least we could do," Friar Diego said to Ix's back.

Ix turned around. Tears wetted her eyes. "The baby was born dead."

"I see," Friar Diego said.

"And what did you tell her?"

Ix didn't bother hiding the details any longer. "I told her to bury the body. Ahkinmai wants it burned."

"Correct advice, but it's not your place to give it." Friar Diego's hands were behind his back when, all of a sudden, Ix rushed forward and hugged him. His own arms surrounded her and stroked her hair as she sobbed into his chest.

The moment lasted until Friar Diego remembered they were in full view of those walking outside. In the distance, he saw Friar Nicolás avoid looking in their direction. He pushed Ix away. Holding her shoulders and looking into her eyes, he said, "Next time, get one of us. We'll handle such matters." Whatever trace of anger he'd held because of her infringement on a priest's duties evaporated when he saw how much the situation had affected her.

Ix nodded, her eyelashes stuck together from crying. "I didn't want to bother anyone with their simple matters," she said.

"No birth or death is a simple matter. This is both."

. . .

THAT NIGHT, as the sun set, Friar Diego went with Ix to the banana trees near the *cenote*. While they waited for the arrival of the woman and her baby's corpse, Friar Diego went over the prayers she would say over the grave. They were simple, revolving around thanking God for sparing the child from suffering on earth, but Ix memorized them as if each word held immense power.

Friar Diego knew having Ix pray during the burial was pushing the boundaries of admissible duties, but the native students who went forth from Izamal into the remote lands far away from the monasteries performed similar actions during their evangelism. The sole difference was that Ix was a woman. The Franciscan assuaged his guilt about the situation by reminding himself that she would have overseen the burial on her own—at least this way, he could make sure the correct prayers were said.

The Mayan woman showed up with the darkness, just before Ix and Friar Diego would have assumed she wasn't coming and left. Her skin was wrinkled—her sobs having depleted her of water—and every muscle was etched into her stomach from the continuous contractions of her crying; except for the corpse, all evidence she had given birth was wiped from the earth. She carried it in her arms as if it was a fragile egg that could crack with a quick movement or stiff gust of wind.

"Let's find a good spot," Ix said.

Ix led the way, with Friar Diego following her and the native woman behind them both. The woman with the baby took slow, deliberate steps, and the pair from Izamal found themselves waiting for her multiple times, learning why she had been late to their meeting in the first place. She saw more of the area they walked through because of her slow pace, and she soon called out to the two, saying she'd found the spot for her child's eternal rest.

Moonlight filtered down from the cloudless sky, through the leaves, onto a small area of open space. Small shoots and grasses had sprung up in the space, but it was clear of larger trees and bushes. Without direction, the native mother handed her baby to Friar Diego and, together with Ix, began digging a grave. When the hole reached the mother's waist, Friar Diego said it was deep enough and handed her the corpse.

The baby was placed in the bottom of the hole, wrapped in a blanket. Ix and the mother started filling the hole with the displaced dirt, and Friar Diego contributed by kicking what he could with his sandaled foot, getting particles stuck beneath the sole of his foot, which bothered him until he returned to Izamal.

Ix said the memorized prayers over the grave, adopting the same composure she had seen from the friars during previous burials she had attended. Her words were said with the same cadence and intonation, rising and falling in a rhythm that soothed the mother and reminded Friar Diego of a song he couldn't quite remember.

"Amen," Ix said.

"Amen," said Friar Diego and the native mother, in unison. Her hysterics had lost their teeth without her dead child in sight.

Friar Diego blessed the woman, making sure she would come to mass on Sunday, before she disappeared into the trees. He walked back to Izamal with Ix in silence, each luxuriating in the memories of the burial: Ix dreamed of a future in which she could lead other Maya to God through prayer, and Friar Diego couldn't figure out the moment when Ix had become such a steadying force in his life.

Ix walked with Friar Diego back to his quarters, a small hut with a corner for his bed and space for his desk, asking if he needed anything else that night. The rest of the monastery was asleep.

She lingered at the doorway when Friar Diego said no.

A continuation of their shared company never crossed Friar Diego's mind. He eased the door shut while she stood there, removed his habit, then crawled into bed.

Ix went back to the infirmary, still elated from the responsibility entrusted to her by her mentor.

Friar Diego saw Ix in a brand-new light after seeing the burying of the stillborn child. He came to see her as not just someone capable of administrative duties, but as someone who could be his protégé within the church. He knew it would have to be secret, since she was a woman, but he couldn't help sharing the secret the priests in Toledo had shared with him.

During the next few weeks, he told her all about the prophecy of the third age of man, the age of the Holy Spirit. He described how the conversion of the Maya would lead to the conversion of the entire world, at which point the Church hierarchy would become superfluous. His explanation of how this would lead to the demolishment of the position of Pope left no room for controversy, and Ix accepted the upending of the Catholic Church as an institution in favor of a Christian unity spreading across the world without confrontation.

"That's why you want to convert the natives: it will save everyone on earth," she said, simplifying the matter.

During one of his lectures, Friar Diego tried to explain how the Maya and the Jews were similar. Ix had never seen or heard of the Jewish faith, so he drew numerous comparisons. He told her how the Jews and the Maya both had their own method of writing, a separate calendar, and their own religion.

"Their leaders are similar to the Mayan priests," he said. "They alone have access to their holy books, just like here. Both types of men are sworn to continue Satan's work."

Ix was struck with fear for Ahkinmai. "How do you deal with the Jewish leaders?"

"Well, we burned their books and removed their priests. If the people still didn't convert, we kicked them out of the country."

Ix thought about the treatment of the Jews and grew thankful she already believed in God. A nagging concern about the removal of the priests worried her, but she never brought it up.

The more Friar Diego talked about the connection between the Maya and the Jews, the more he believed the Maya were one of the ten lost tribes of Israel, spoken of in the book of Ezra. He puzzled through this revelation while speaking out loud, his words not directed at Ix.

"If this people really are one of the lost tribes, then the prophecy was still correct: the Jewish conversion will bring about the conversion of the entire world!"

Friar Diego couldn't contain his excitement. Ix pretended she understood.

"The natives' conversion won't *lead* to the Jewish conversion. It *is* the Jewish conversion!" he exclaimed.

His jubilation was short-lived.

Friar Nicolás walked in on the illuminating lecture, commanding both of their attention. "There's been an accident at the monastery," he said.

The three of them rushed to the construction site. Four men had been crushed by a fallen wall. Three had been killed in an instant, but one man's chest and head were exposed to the air—the fallen wall had crushed his body up to his rib cage. He was still spluttering blood when the group from Izamal arrived, and they stayed with him until he drew his last breath.

All four men were buried that night. Friar Diego himself oversaw the ceremony.

Friar Nicolás excused himself and went to bed when the exhausted group returned to the monastery. The infirmary where Ix slept was on the far side of the monastery's land, past Friar Diego's residence. For the second time, the mentor and protégé had gone through the crucible. Thinking their time together deserved continuation, Ix didn't hesitate outside Friar Diego's door. She walked in after the Franciscan and shut the door behind her.

Friar Diego lay down with his hands folded over his chest. He hadn't eaten all day. The distance of his thoughts was evident—between the discovery of the Maya–Jew connection and the accident at the construction site, he couldn't quite parse the information and found his thoughts scattered throughout space and time.

Ix thought he was upset about the dying men. She had known all four, prayed with them outside the sanctuary, and knew their families. In her soul, she believed death had tethered her to Friar Diego, creating an unspoken bond forged in sadness.

In truth, Friar Diego cared more about the setback in construction than the lost lives.

Ix extinguished the lamp and groped through the darkness before climbing into bed with the friar. He didn't resist; in fact, he made room on his bed for her.

That night, Friar Diego broke his vow of chastity. It was his first taste of a direct violation of the Catholic Church's directives, and by the time he was recalled to Spain, he'd have many more transgressions to his name.

CHAPTER THIRTY

ALARA HAD no idea who the person with the misshapen face was, or how he knew her name. His eyes were aflame with passion, and his whole body trembled with the strength it took to stand. She thought it was perhaps someone she had given money to on the streets by Decant; they knew her name, and her coworkers always told her they would keep coming back for more. Still unsure, she nodded, waiting for Cortez to continue.

"I'm listening," she said.

Cortez's eyes darted to the other members of her group. Some had pity in their eyes, the lips of others were contorted in disgust, but Alara displayed nothing besides divine patience for the man she didn't recognize.

"It's a private thing," Cortez said, looking down at her feet. Her toes were painted bright red, decorations on the most delicate, beautiful feet he had ever seen. He wondered what it would be like to wash them, then grew embarrassed with the primal stirrings the thought aroused. "Can we talk over there?" he said, tilting his head towards the corner.

Alara didn't miss the man's inspection, and she pulled her most visible foot back, hiding it beneath the folds of her long dress. "You can say whatever you want in front of them," she said.

"Trust me, you want to hear this alone," he said, still looking down.

"Trust you! I don't even know you!" It was the third time Alara didn't recognize Cortez.

These words stung Cortez more than any of Remy's strikes. He raised his eyes and looked into hers, pleading with her to acknowledge they had met before, begging her to admit that their interactions weren't a product of his imagination. "We talked on the bench, about your book."

An overwhelming wave of hatred for the sad man overtook Alara when she recognized the pathetic creature standing in front of her. Still mindful of appearances, and not wanting her friends to know she had a stalker—even though this was the first time she had viewed him as such—she stood and hugged Cortez, leaving him with a firsthand experience of the smell of her hair, which was better than anything he'd experienced during his feverish rose-filled daydreams. "What happened to your face? I didn't recognize you!" she said, with the grace of a seasoned actress.

"That's part of why I need to talk to you."

"Of course, let's walk over there," she said, the ball of anger in her stomach close to unbearable. She told her friends she'd be right back.

When they were a sufficient distance from the bistro that Alara could be certain her friends wouldn't hear, she turned and chastised Cortez. "You followed me again, didn't you!" she scolded. "Trying to pretend you just happened to be in the area, like I wouldn't see right through it."

Cortez wondered if every woman in his life harbored seeds of resentment deep in their hearts and were waiting for the chance to unload their burden onto his tired ears.

"What is it you have to tell me?" she said, capping another flurry of words where she called Cortez "delusional" and "creepy."

Cortez took a deep breath. "Remy's cheating on you," he said.

"One: no, he's not. Two: he's the one who did that to your face, isn't he? Did he catch you following him around too?"

Cortez told Alara the story of the night before, leaving out his reason for following Remy in the first place. He described seeing Remy at the sports bar and his own experience turning down the two women, hoping Alara would recognize his fidelity, before telling her about Remy leaving with the blond woman.

"I followed them to the pizza place, that's where Remy got me," Cortez said. He expected to be patted on the head and told he was a good boy.

Alara made no effort to hide her annoyance. "Remy already told me about helping his friend home who had too much to drink," she said.

"His *friend* was a girl!" Cortez said. He couldn't understand why Alara didn't see things from his point of view.

"Remy's got a lot of friends. Who am I to judge whether they're a boy or a girl?"

"Cheating is a sin," Cortez said, as if this explained the fault in her logic.

"A sin? Do you think I care about what *God* thinks? Priests came over from Europe, in the name of *God*, and destroyed my ancestors' entire lives. Where is my culture? Burned, because of *God*. What did *God* do when he saw the missionaries treating the Maya like *we* were the savages? *God* doesn't exist. And if he does, he's given up on us all a long time ago. What *God* thinks about sin makes no difference to me."

Cortez stood stunned. While Alara spoke, her hair levitated, surrounded her head, and turned to snakes. Serpents in the

Garden of Eden, sent by the devil to trick Adam and Eve into tasting the forbidden fruit. They disappeared at the conclusion of her speech. Cortez realized that she had exposed him to the secret seed hidden by the fruit's flesh: that the name of God was responsible for the deaths of countless innocent lives. He couldn't believe, he wouldn't believe—and he needed to save her.

"Come to church with me," Cortez said. "Listen to what the Bible has to say."

"Were you not listening to a word I said? The Bible is the problem! Men can do whatever they want, thinking they stand behind some ancient book. You know what I believe in? Love. My Bible? Whatever book I'm reading!"

"We meet every Sunday at—"

Alara cut him off. "I don't care when you meet! You all can meet in hell for all I care. Don't follow me again, don't talk to me again, I don't want to see you at Decant again. If you do, not only will I get Remy to soften you up, I'll come back and finish the job myself." She turned away and stormed off, her dress billowing behind her, leaving a trail of smoke.

Cortez didn't see his mother on Sunday. After talking with Alara, he had gone straight home, unable to stomach the thought of talking to anyone; finding more people to join his church was the last thing he wanted to do. Finding out Alara's views on God and the Church had left him deflated, exhausted, and hopeless. He had been certain she was the one who could turn his fortunes around, the catalyst that would bring his father back, and her outright rejection of his faith left him disillusioned and untethered. His bed was waiting for him when he got home, and he collapsed onto it, his silent tears wetting the pillow. The smell of the crushed rose on the nightstand wafted throughout Cortez's room, wrapping him in a constant reminder of his broken heart.

He had fallen asleep at some point in the afternoon. When he woke up hungry, he went into the kitchen, opened the refrigerator, and found a plate of food wrapped in tinfoil—leftovers from the church luncheon. His mother had come home and brought it with her. Her bedroom door was closed, and he didn't need to open it to know she was inside, disappointed he'd missed church. He ate the steak, rice, and beans cold with the television turned on for background noise. The rest of Sunday passed with Cortez staring at whatever show was playing, never changing the channel, and never registering what happened onscreen.

Cortez left Monday morning and his mother still hadn't emerged from her darkness. He wanted to give up on the charade, to stop pretending he had somewhere to be, but after missing church on Sunday he couldn't bring himself to disappoint his mother any further. Going to Decant was far from his mind. Alara's declaration against God had poisoned the well of Cortez's love, and after seeing her hair transform he was certain she was the same temptation Jesus had faced in the desert: the devil, there to test his resolve. Cortez hoped to break her spell by not seeing her anymore, but he couldn't even get close to the park without hearing temptation call out his name.

Cortez walked the streets on his side of town—passing by the school where his church was held without stopping—and found himself at a corner beneath the train tracks. After looking left and right, he sat down against a chain-link fence, with his backpack beside him, content with watching the world until it was time to go back. Everyone who passed that day assumed he was new to being homeless and didn't know the rest of his brethren came out at night. Drivers stared, walkers ignored, and dogs sniffed as they passed. Two of the five dogs were on leashes. They pulled against their owners' grip, trying to get closer even though Cortez ignored them. The other three dogs were strays. They traveled in a pack with their hair matted against their bodies, victims of neglect. Cortez wished they were feral, that they would tear him to shreds, but all three sniffed him from a distance before walking away.

His mother still hadn't emerged when Cortez got home on Monday night. There was nothing to eat, so he took some money from their shared jar and went out for a cheap hamburger. Using that little amount of money heaped more guilt onto his shoulders and he wanted to, yet again, apologize for his existence. Neither the white nor the blue pills took the feeling away. Not wanting to be around people in the restaurant, he ate the burger at home, on the couch, with the television volume as low as it could go while still being audible. When he threw away his trash and saw his mother's work uniform inside the bin, he knew this episode of darkness was unlike the rest and wouldn't be over soon.

Intent on maintaining his routine for his mother's sake, Cortez left the house at the same time again on Tuesday morning, going to the same spot against the fence. His morning was uneventful, besides the one time he had to get up and brush off the back of his pants because a procession of red ants tried carrying him away for lunch.

A group of four teenage boys found Cortez in the afternoon. They were walking back from school when they saw him sitting alone. Their leader, a cruel boy with a sharp face and messy hair, asked Cortez what he was doing. Cortez didn't answer, staring past them and pretending they didn't exist, hoping they would reciprocate and leave him alone.

"I'm talking to you," the boy said. When Cortez didn't

answer, he turned to his friends. "I think this guy's got a problem with us."

"Maybe he just wants to be left alone," the smallest in the group said.

"Well, he doesn't have to be rude," another chimed in.

The leader of the group walked up to Cortez and pushed a knee with the toe of his shoe. "You hear me?" he said.

"Maybe he's special, like the kids in that one class."

"Or maybe he doesn't like us."

When the leader of the group picked up the backpack, Cortez lunged to grab it back. He wasn't fast enough.

"So now you see us?" the leader sneered.

Cortez got up. He was taller than any of them but lighter than all but the smallest. "Give it back," he said, his voice heavy with the weight of defeat. The disappointment he'd caused everyone he cared about weighed heavy on his heart—these demons were there to punish him for his wickedness.

"You can have it back if you can catch me," the boy said a moment before running away.

Cortez didn't think twice before beginning his pursuit. They ran beneath the train tracks before turning onto a side street. The boy's friends were behind both of them, laughing. Cortez could feel his breath running out, the lack of oxygen making his legs heavy, but he kept going until he caught up with the boy at the end of an alley. He stood tall, using every inch of his height, and reminded himself he was older than them.

"Give it back," he said.

The boy thought for a moment. Cortez took a step forward. In a flash, the boy threw the backpack into Cortez's face. The backpack was empty except for his medicine, and therefore light, so it didn't cause more damage to Cortez's still-tender upper lip and nose. It did blind him long enough for the boy to rush Cortez and push him over. When he was on the ground, the leader started kicking. One of the blows landed right where Remy's fist had bruised his side; Cortez's vision flashed white with pain.

"Get him!" the leader said.

Two of the boys joined in, the smallest staying back, and the kicking stopped when they were out of breath. The leader bent down and pulled Cortez's shoulders up until they faced each other. He spit in Cortez's face, then rubbed it in.

"Shouldn't ignore people," the leader said before walking away with his friends. The smallest boy never went with them after school again.

Cortez held himself in the fetal position for a long time after they left. He was elated; the pain in his body matched his pain inside. Every breath was another reminder of what a deplorable creature he was, and he was certain God was taking steps to restore balance in the world. At some point he ended up on his back and watched the occasional cloud rolling through the blue sky, certain the angels of heaven were looking down on him and applauding him for taking his punishment like a man.

"Are you OK?" a woman's voice called out to him from the end of the alley.

Cortez didn't respond. He hoped she was there to inflict more pain on him for his sins.

The clicking of heels on pavement rang through the alley, growing closer to Cortez with each step. The approach ripped Cortez in half, his body screaming out to defend himself while his mind craved fresh punishment. His mind won, and he stayed still until the woman was right next to him. To his disappointment, she didn't strike another blow.

"Hey, aren't you the Bible kid?" the woman said.

Cortez looked into her face, crowned by the sky beyond. It was the sex worker who had taken him to her colleagues, the one his mother didn't believe God would want. "God doesn't want me anymore," he said.

The woman grabbed Cortez's arms and forced him to stand up. She brushed off his shoulders and face before inspecting the bruises on his arms. "Someone got you good, huh?" she said. "Were you trying to convince them to come to church with you too?" she said with a chuckle.

Her amusement disappeared when Cortez didn't laugh. "I was trying to get my backpack back."

"Well, you got it," she said. She looked at his face. "You're all skin and bones. When's the last time you ate?"

"Yesterday."

"It's four in the afternoon! Come on, let's get you something to eat."

She led him to a takeout Chinese spot with a window facing the street. There was no interior space available for patrons. She frequented the establishment, and knew the owner, and as soon as she approached the window he asked her if she wanted the usual.

"Make it two," she said, holding up two fingers.

The old man on the other side of the window looked confused when he saw her paying for Cortez. "You're paying for him? Now I've seen it all!" he joked.

"Shut up, Renzo," the woman replied with a smile.

She forced Cortez to eat, watching him finish every bite. "Now, what is this you were saying about God not wanting you anymore?"

"I don't want to talk about it."

"Then don't. Just listen. Look, it takes balls to walk up to a group of strangers and try to help them. You know you're the only one who's ever tried to talk to me about God? Most men are looking for a good time," she said with a chuckle.

She waited for Cortez to respond. When he didn't, she

continued.

"That kind of faith, it's not common. You have to hold on to it. Keep believing, even when things aren't going your way. I'd kill to believe in something the way you did when I saw you holding up your Bible to Bill. Did you know he still talks about it? He says, 'That kid had some balls.' Bill doesn't say that about just anyone, you know."

Cortez looked at her and saw her with fresh eyes. Past the makeup, past the hairstyle and choice of clothes, he saw a young woman who had a mischievous need to know what secrets the world possessed, and she was doing the best she could to support herself while she searched for answers to her unknown questions. She was beautiful, not in a sexual way, but in the way that emerges when someone knows who they are and has made peace with their existence on the planet.

The woman didn't withdraw or become embarrassed when she realized she was being seen. "Feeling better?" she asked.

"Yes," Cortez said. He smiled: not forced, not rehearsed, and not prompted by the suggestions and expectations of people who tried to impose upon him a way to exist.

"Good. Don't let your faith go to waste," she said. "And that includes wasting your time trying to get me and my friends to join your church!"

They both laughed before she tapped his thigh twice, got up, and walked away. Cortez watched until she turned the corner then began walking home, feeling better about his momentary lapse of faith but still smarting from the beating inflicted on him by the teenagers. Each breath stabbed his side, and every step exposed pain in a new joint, but the pains of his body didn't touch his mind, which viewed the world around him with a newfound certainty of purpose. His destiny was to save the Church—his mother had told him as much—and there was still time for him to figure out the best way to do it.

CHAPTER THIRTY-ONE

ADELANTADO FRANCISCO's continued freedom was a thorn in Friar Diego de Landa's side, bleeding his attention despite his best attempts at trusting God with the outcome. From the moment he got out of bed until collapsing at the end of the day —resting his body despite his inability to sleep—he wondered what the escaped Spaniard schemed in Guatemala. During his morning prayers he imagined a small army, led by the *Adelantado,* taking back the abandoned *encomienda*; his communication with God transformed into a warrior's call for protection before battle. The Franciscan's meals alternated between tasting too bitter and too salty, tainted with the thought of the *Adelantado* partaking in sins of the flesh in a tucked-away corner of a foreign city. He wasted the time he spent with Izamal's top students, busying them with rote memorization of baptismal prayers while he stared off into the distance at nothing in particular, lost in thoughts of how many, and which, of the Yucatán's *encomenderos* supported the *Adelantado.*

Friar Diego came crashing back to earth during one of his daydreams, sending a jolt up his spine from his tailbone to his skull. After a series of rapid blinks, he proclaimed that he was going to Guatemala. "I'll make them send him back," he said. The students looked at him; when they realized he wasn't addressing them they returned to memorizing their prayers with the fervent worry of future first-time practitioners.

Ix Cuatchel assumed Friar Diego's sullen mood was because of feelings of guilt for the night they'd spent together. She had tried continuing the nocturnal meetings the night after their first but was rebuffed by the door slamming in her face. Her days passed while she waited for an invitation that would never come. She was still as useful as ever during the day—an appendage Friar Diego didn't know he needed—but disappeared as the sun went down, worried about leading her beloved to temptation he would rather avoid. Though Ix had learned about the sin of adultery during her time in the monastery, and knew the friars prided themselves on abstaining from every form of pleasure and comfort most men couldn't resist, she never once experienced guilt for her own actions, knowing that the feeling among the Maya who worshipped at Izamal was that the pair was already together in every sense of the word. As she saw it, what had transpired when she spent the night with him was a natural furthering of their relationship.

"I'm going to Guatemala to bring back the *Adelantado*," Friar Diego told Ix the afternoon he made the decision. She had just brought him the water he had requested.

"By yourself?" she asked. She wasn't surprised he was leaving—there had been such a faraway look in his eyes that she had known he would be making a trip before he realized it himself.

"By myself."

"How are you going to bring him back? Even if he's in chains, you should have men there to help you."

"I don't see why they wouldn't send his jailers with him. They already agreed to the retrial."

Ix nodded. She stayed in case he needed something else.

"I'm setting off tomorrow morning," Friar Diego declared. "While I'm gone, make sure you give any letters that arrive for me to Friar Nicolás; he'll know what to do."

Ix told him she understood.

"Other than that, just keep an eye on things. Make sure the natives on the construction teams are being taken care of, and don't let the other friars find out you lead any prayers." Friar Diego paused. "As a matter of fact, forget you know them until I return."

"Nothing until you get back," Ix said. She turned around and walked out. When she was just beyond the door, Friar Diego called out her name.

"Yes?" she said in response, her heart fluttering. Was this the first daytime mention of their night together?

"Make sure nobody comes into my room while I'm away."

Ix stood still, waiting for gravity's normalization after a momentary spell of vertigo. Friar Diego dismissed her with a brush of his hand. "That's all," he said.

Friar Diego's trip to Guatemala took over a month. He wasn't alone, as he had told Ix he would be—he took with him two Mayan men who carried food, water, and his scant belongings. He hadn't lied to his protégé, but he'd assumed the true nature of her question: he was, in fact, the lone Franciscan making the trip. None of the other friars in the Yucatán knew where he was going, not even those in Izamal. He'd kept his travels a secret so the *Custos* wouldn't catch wind of his actions and prescribe patience. Deep in his soul, Friar Diego knew that the *Adelantado*'s imprisonment in Guatemala was more comfortable than what he deserved in the Mani jail, and the thought of the man relaxing while laughing at the Franciscans' attempts at justice provided enough sustenance that he didn't eat or drink until reminded to by his men.

The superior court was in a city called Santiago de Guatemala, which Friar Diego imagined was a place of splendor and sin. During the totality of his southward journey, he imagined a city like Seville, the last major city he had passed though in Spain before his journey west: the roads paved with stone bricks and a large cathedral where Catholics could worship. The cathedral in Seville had etched itself onto his memory with its numerous spires and the grandeur of its sanctuary. It was the largest in the world—having supplanted the Hagia Sophia for the title upon its completion—and inspired Friar Diego to leave his own mark on Catholic worship by creating the massive Izamal atrium, an open courtyard, knowing he could never rival the physical structure that had taken one hundred years to build.

A BONY FRIAR Diego limped into the central square of Santiago de Guatemala without realizing he had entered the city. The dirt paths through a sleepy hamlet led to a cathedral rising above all, obscured by thick fog that hid the structure until Friar Diego and his traveling party stood outside its wooden front door. The stone building was smaller than the Merida monastery but had a stand-alone bell tower adjacent to the main building. A small cut on the friar's foot had become infected, adding days to the trip's length. The Mayan men he'd brought with him, themselves bringing salt and cloths for trading in the city's market, showed no signs of their weeks of travel.

Friar Diego knocked on the cathedral's door and introduced himself to the priests. They took him to the infirmary, giving him one of six beds; the other five were empty. Friar Diego told the native men where to place his belongings before dismissing them, saying they should come find him later that night and he'd take care of their accommodations.

The head priest, a white-haired man with glowing, rosy cheeks and a sizable stomach, sat with the friar while the infirmary attendant looked at the traveler's foot.

"What brings you to Guatemala?" the priest said, sitting down on the adjacent bed.

"I'm here to bring back a prisoner."

"With the two who were with you?"

"The authorities here will take care of his transport. They're the ones who gave him another trial."

The head priest chuckled. "You're talking about Francisco Hernandez, aren't you?"

Friar Diego was stunned. "You've heard of him?"

"The whole city has. He's caused quite a stir since his arrival."

"What do you mean?"

"Let's just say, he doesn't come to mass on Sundays. He's aligned himself with a successful local trader, and every weekend they spend all they've earned the week before on women and drink."

"Sounds like the guy," Friar Diego said. He winced when one of the attending friars poked his swollen foot.

"Where can I find the administrators?" Friar Diego asked.

"They have a building south of here, a twenty-minute walk."

The attendant started wrapping Friar Diego's foot. "You aren't going to put any ointment on?"

"Ointment? It'll heal, just takes time," the attendant said, the first words he'd spoken. His Spanish was unpolished, as if he'd spent time as a sailor before deciding the priesthood was his true calling.

The priests left Friar Diego alone. His exhaustion magnified with his stillness, and his pain intensified with nothing else commanding his attention other than the consuming thoughts of the wicked *Adelantado*. When the Mayan men he had brought with him returned that night, they found him consumed by fever.

"Do you know about the ointment Ix uses? It's made out of red worms," Friar Diego said with beads of sweat on his upper lip.

The native men said they knew about it but had never made it.

"Bring me some of those worms. I'll make it myself."

The men left and returned hours later. The sun had gone down, and the priests had given Friar Diego a thin broth with cut-up vegetables, which he had finished with great effort. Using the bowl and spoon, Friar Diego crushed the worms, making a yellow paste flecked with specks of red skin. Then he sat up. Using the spoon, he applied the poultice to his unwrapped infected foot before collapsing back down.

The native men slept in two of the empty beds. Friar Diego spent the night in and out of consciousness, dreaming of Ix, Ahkinmai, his mentor in Toledo, and Friar Luis de Villalpondo. They were all together in front of a large conflagration. One by one, Friar Diego pushed each one in without the others becoming aware of the threat. He was left alone, staring at the fire, before the flames called out to him, urging him to jump. When he listened to the call and leapt, he woke up.

Morning had arrived. The attendant was next to his bed; the native men were gone.

"They said they'd find you in a few days," he said. "I don't think they like staying here very much."

Something about the way the attendant mentioned the natives gave Friar Diego the impression that his familiarity with their way of life wasn't shared by the Guatemalan priests.

The attendant pulled back the covers and exclaimed how the swelling had gone down despite the bandage coming undone during the night. "It worked!" he said, with a heaping dose of smugness. "This yellow stuff came out." He wiped away the ointment with the blanket.

Friar Diego knew the infection was gone. He didn't bother telling the attendant why, not trusting the man with the information, and allowed the rewrapping of his foot. Then, he set off farther south, looking for the administration building.

Any money the city of Santiago de Guatemala saved in the construction of its cathedral had been spent on the outsized building that housed the administration. It was a wide, flat stone building, with sharp corners free from additional adornment. Compared to other New World administration buildings, it was immense. All government power flowed through the stone building, and whoever was in charge inside was in charge of the Guatemala Province, which included the Yucatán.

In the building's shadow, Friar Diego took a deep breath and went inside. A young man, dressed in a matching orange doublet and breeches, stood from behind a desk as soon he saw the friar. Friar Diego's habit, in far worse condition than those worn by the priests at the cathedral, inspired a look of disgust.

"Who do I talk to about transferring a prisoner?" Friar Diego demanded.

The young man didn't bother hiding his annoyance. "Depends on the prisoner," he said, crossing his arms and shifting to one side.

"No business of yours. I doubt it has anything to do with you," Friar Diego shot back.

"I have no problem escorting you out," the young man said, pursing his lips.

The two men glared at each other.

"No, no, no, that won't be necessary!" an older gentleman

called out from behind the young man. He was running forward from a hall perpendicular to the entrance.

"Hello!" the gentleman said in a high-pitched voice. He was wearing similar clothes to the young man, but dark brown. "I'm Tomás López Medel. And you are?"

Friar Diego had never seen the man who issued the decrees that disrupted the Maya's way of life, but he and the other Franciscans had benefited from the intrusion by their increased importance within the Yucatán hierarchy. "I'm Friar Diego de Landa."

Both men's eyes grew wide. "You've been busy," López Medel teased, grabbing the friar by the arm and dragging him away from the entrance. He fired off a great many words while they walked. "First, I'd like to thank you for enforcing my decrees! They were designed with the good of the natives in mind, you know."

Friar Diego managed a nod of agreement while navigating the challenge of walking fast with a bandaged foot.

"And sounds like you and Señor Francisco have gotten into a bit of a mix-up! You are the one who handed down that harsh sentence, aren't you?"

López Medel looked sideways at the friar while he walked forward, turned left, then turned right, never looking where they walked.

"I did."

The hallway ended at a large door. "Everyone's already here. I was late, that's why I was passing by when I saw you." López Medel pushed open the door. "We'll make this the first order of business. This affair has gone on long enough!"

Dozens of men were seated at two rows of tables inside an expansive hall. López Medel ushered Friar Diego down the middle of the rows, past numerous pairs of curious eyes, and sat the friar in front. Then, he continued to the front of the room and sat down on a chair situated on a raised platform.

The men in attendance, all dressed in the same manner as the young man at the entrance to the administrative building, stopped talking and waited for López Medel.

"I'm adding an emergency deliberation to today's proceedings," López Medel said. He smiled at Friar Diego. "As President, I can do these things!" he said with a wink.

Friar Diego was tossed under waves of uncertainty and trying to find the surface. He had imagined his visit would be on more solid footing.

"Everyone, I'd like you to meet Friar Diego de Landa, from the Yucatán!"

Polite applause echoed through the chamber.

"Friar, why don't you come up and tell everyone why you're here," the President said.

Friar Diego stood in front of the men and cleared his throat. An awareness of his dirty brown habit entered his mind, followed by a repugnance at the seated men and their obsession with their appearance. He turned to look at López Medel.

"Go on," the President urged.

"I'm here to demand you send Francisco Hernandez back for trial," he said.

Murmurs erupted throughout the room.

Friar Diego continued. "I understand you've given him a retrial. It's within your right, but send the man back to the Yucatán so we can bring him to justice."

"Are you here under direction of the *Custos*? He could have sent a letter," one of the group said from halfway through the crowd. He had a luxuriant beard that continued through the curly hair on the sides of his head, framing his baldness.

"I'm here as judge," Friar Diego said.

"You were judge at the first trial, correct? The one who sentenced Francisco in the first place?"

"That's right. And I'm judge for the retrial too."

The President laughed. It was a deep laugh, coming straight from his belly; it didn't match his voice at all. The rest of the men joined in, adding their tentative chuckles to the din.

"We've already appointed his new judge."

Friar Diego looked dumbfounded.

"That's why Francisco is still here! He's under house arrest."

More laughter from the gallery.

"Well, technically. We've been arguing with your *Custos* about who will oversee the trial. He insists it be someone from the Yucatán. We say our head priest will determine the sentence."

"One priest is as good as the rest of them!" someone called out from the back.

Friar Diego's face flushed. He was furious at the situation and the new information, knowing the blame belonged to him for going to Guatemala without consulting the *Custos*. "He should stand trial where he was accused," Friar Diego said. Keeping his voice steady took every ounce of his willpower.

"Would it help if we sent our priest to the edge of the Yucatán?" someone called out from the back. The group around him cackled. Their delight ended when they saw Tomás López Medel not sharing in their amusement.

"That's the heart of the matter," López Medel muttered. He rested his chin on his hand, his elbow resting on the chair's arm. He spoke louder, so the group could hear. "We can grant the retrial, but the assignment of judges is out of our hands."

Friar Diego fought a sudden urge to turn around and bask in the men's reactions.

"It's what the *Custos* has been saying all along."

Methods of prisoner transportation filtered through Friar Diego's mind.

"But we also never said when the retrial had to occur. If Francisco stays here . . ." López Medel said.

A rush of wind from the assembly's collective exhale ruffled Friar Diego's habit.

"If you want the trial done with, let the priest here stand judge. If not, tell your *Custos* we won't get involved with the prisoner's transportation."

The gallery waited, curious about the friar's response.

"You called for the retrial. It's your responsibility to send him back," Friar Diego said.

"We won't get involved—"

"You already are!"

"—with his collection."

Friar Diego closed his eyes and exhaled. "Very well," he said.

The Yucatán Franciscans had no resources for the task and López Medel knew it. The official would let the *Adelantado* walk free before bowing to pressure from the region. Friar Diego imagined a group of Maya, with him at their head, collecting the prisoner. The idea dissipated soon after its arrival —no Spaniards in the New World would allow the seizure of one of their own by natives without interjecting on their countryman's behalf.

Friar Diego left the hall without saying another word. Tomás López Medel called the next item of business for the group's consideration, a water ration for the homeless, as the wooden doors shut.

Knowing the Maya who'd come with him were interested in trading their goods, Friar Diego went to the market. It was on a long strip of ground covered in stones, walled in with thick stone walls. Horse-drawn carts selling everything from fruit to cured meats passed through a stone arch and parked on either side of the paved path. At the top of the arch stood a magnificent statue of the Virgin Mary. She had her hands folded in front of her chest and was looking down and to the right with her head tilted at a slight angle: the perfect display of Christian piety. Friar Diego knew right away he wanted it for the Izamal monastery, a centerpiece for when construction was completed.

Friar Diego found the natives seated with other Mayan men. They were speaking their language, relaxing, when the friar found them and announced they were leaving. "I want to take the statue of the Virgin Mary over the arch." The other native men's eyes grew wide at the fluency with which he spoke their language.

"Which one?" one of his native companions said.

"Does it matter? They're both the same," the other man replied.

"Wait. There's two?" said Friar Diego.

"One over each entrance," one of the Mayan traders from the city said.

"Who do I talk to about buying them?" Friar Diego asked. With two, he could send one to Merida and not invoke anger over the spent money.

"They were donated by the Church."

Friar Diego waited for the native men from the Yucatán to conclude their trading before going back to the cathedral. There, he found the head priest and asked how much the two statues would cost. When the priest quoted what he thought was an exorbitant amount, Friar Diego agreed without reservation—it was still within his budget for the construction of Izamal, as long as he saved money by reinstating one meal a day for the native workers. He agreed the funds would be sent within the coming months, as soon as he returned to the Yucatán.

Over the next week, the Maya from the Yucatán and the Maya from the market prepared the statues for transport. Friar Diego hired extra workers for the trip back home, as well as carts and horses.

Traveling with the statues was slow, laborious work. During the entirety of the trip, Friar Diego walked behind one of the carts, alternating which one each day, making sure the cargo didn't crack or chip during transport. The trip to Merida took over two months, during which Friar Diego spent as much on the men and beasts of burden as he spent on the statues themselves.

Friar Diego wasn't sure how the *Custos* would react to the purchases. He hoped they would be appreciated, but he could foresee a situation where his friend decided the act was an overextension of power. One of the statues was sent on to Izamal with the two natives who had come with him and enough help for the statue's transportation; Friar Diego walked into Merida with the other, accompanied by the rest of the Maya from Guatemala.

Any fears of a negative reaction from the *Custos* faded away once the cloth covering was removed from the statue. Every Franciscan stationed in Merida agreed it was the perfect addition to their location. One of the first words the natives had learned was "Maria," and they believed the Maya would attend mass in droves for the chance to worship in the statue's shadow. Once the initial reception died down, Friar Diego announced he had purchased the twin statue for the monastery in Izamal.

"They're perfect," the *Custos* said.

In private, Friar Diego revealed the cost. "More than I'd like, but I had to have them," he said.

"We can allocate the funds for both. It was a worthwhile purchase," Friar Francisco Navarro said.

Friar Diego breathed a sigh of relief, thankful the costs wouldn't come from the allocation for the Izamal monastery. He never mentioned why he was in Guatemala in the first place, and his friend never asked.

CHAPTER THIRTY-TWO

Cortez knew something was wrong when he got home. The emptiness of the apartment was as loud as if it was crowded with visitors. It was Tuesday night, and even if his mother hadn't lost her job and had gone to work, she should be home by then. She wasn't supposed to be at church again until the following night, and she didn't go anywhere else. He opened her door and peeked in. During his walk home he had imagined he'd be opening the door to apologize. Cortez flicked on the light and saw she hadn't cleaned the decades of dust from her own room. There were lines in the dust on her empty bed's comforter and where her dirty clothes, thrown into the corner, had forced the dust into concentric circles. A thin pair of lines ran through numerous footsteps in the dust, some made by small bare feet, others by large boots. He closed the door, careful not to disturb the dust with the generated wind, leaving her room in the exact same condition as when she left.

With a full stomach, and with his mother missing, Cortez didn't know what to do. He should call someone but didn't know who to turn to for help. The former priest's number was written on a piece of paper in the drawer, a remnant from when his mother had needed to call him every night of the week during a crisis of faith a few years ago. But he was no longer their priest, transported to another country to serve a higher calling, and Cortez didn't have the number of the senior member who'd taken over the duty of shepherding for their flock. Cortez didn't know his mother kept the church directory, containing every number he could need, next to their dishes—she used it as a tray to transport plates too hot to carry.

Cortez's thoughts about who to call directed his gaze to the phone. There was a red flashing "1" on the device's tiny screen. His home never got messages because nobody ever called them. Cortez pushed play.

"Hey, Cort, how have you been? Look, I know it's been a few weeks, and you probably have another job by now, but I wanted to reach out in case there was any way you were interested in your old job. Turns out your friend Simeon is a thief. When we caught him, he told us all about how the drug deal was his idea, and he begged us to give you your job back. I think he felt guilty. At any rate, we'd love to have you back. Feel free to give me a call tomorrow or just show up; we'll hold it for you until Friday. Take care."

Cortez was left with the feeling that Simeon had another trick up his sleeve. He wanted to know why Simeon had chosen to tell the truth, and he didn't believe it was from guilt alone. Even though he sensed a trap, he allowed himself to have hope for the future; his faith was beginning to creep back and he had a job again, one that would allow him to support his mother now that she'd lost hers. He began dancing in the living room to the music in his head, and everyone looking into his apartment's window was sure the skeleton they saw dancing was death itself.

The movement and excitement shook the contents of his stomach, and the greasy food ran through his digestive tract, lubricated by copious amounts of low-quality oil. Cortez's eyes opened wide when the awareness of his body's needs became too much for him to ignore, and he ran into the bathroom, sitting down a moment before the eruption.

The phone started ringing; Cortez assumed it was his old boss once more. He tried to get up and answer but was forced to sit back down when another wave of nausea struck. The ringing stopped and the answering machine clicked on.

"You've reached the Vuscars. Please leave a message," his mother said, her voice recorded years ago.

Hearing those words from the bathroom without difficulty made Cortez's stomach drop—he would've sat down if he wasn't already seated. The number of messages displayed by the answering machine had been blinking, so he assumed nobody had heard the message from his boss. Now he had no doubt his mother could hear the answering machine from her room and had heard the message as it was being left.

"Hello, this message is for Cortez. This is the head nurse at Mercy General calling on behalf of your mother. She's in the cardiac unit, room four-eleven. Goodbye."

The answering machine clicked off.

When Cortez finished in the bathroom, he ran to the machine and listened to the message he had already heard. He repeated it twice more, feeling worse about his failure as a son each time. He convinced himself that his mother, after hearing the message left by his boss from inside her bedroom, had suffered a heart attack, and now she was in the hospital. He imagined, and was correct, that she had been lying under the blankets in her room, surrounded by darkness, too weak and exhausted from carrying the weight of the world to even get up and answer the phone when it started ringing. She had let the phone's noise pollute the apartment, hoping whoever it was would leave her alone, and had grown annoyed that they stayed on the line until the answering machine was called into action.

She hadn't recognized the boss's voice at first, but it hadn't taken her long to understand her son had lost his job, that he had hidden it from her, and that the new woman in his life, Alara, was to blame. Her heart had beaten her eyes in a race to bursting; she had found enough strength to call an ambulance before passing out.

Every decision Cortez had made over the past week replayed in his head, all of which had led to his mother's broken heart: pretending to go to the factory, not being by his mother's side at church, and obsessing over Alara. He cursed himself for eating lunch with a sex worker while his mother lay in bed because of his poor behavior in the first place.

Cortez went into his room and grabbed his Bible from the dresser. He knelt on the ground, resting his elbows on his bed, and prayed. Prayers for his mother, asking him to heal her, and prayers for the woman who had bought him lunch, that she would recognize the wickedness of her ways, change, and one day see the Lord's light. He prayed for Simeon, asking that he be punished for lying and costing Cortez his job. As soon as he uttered the words, he was struck by a twinge of uncertainty: he would never have met Alara if he hadn't been fired.

He crushed his reservations as if they were a spider creeping towards him on the floor.

"And I pray that you make sure Alara is never, ever happy for what she said about you." He didn't say, but God knew, that he wanted to make sure she was as miserable as he was about his rejection.

"Amen."

Cortez put his Bible into his backpack then opened the door to his mother's room, checking for anything she might need. Finding nothing, he left for the hospital. It was the last time he ever looked inside her space.

. . .

"It's all my fault," Cortez repeated to himself as he walked to the hospital. He couldn't shake the mantra from his head, a reminder of his guilt for being the cause of his mother's inevitable last breath. To him, hospitals meant death. The institution had the same connotation for him that others reserved for "hospice," a word Cortez didn't possess in his lexicon. He had been in a hospital once before, a visit to a former member of his church who had late-stage cancer. The patient, Mr. Eckles, had been one of the few men who paid attention to the timid shadow clinging to his mother before and after the service. He was a white-haired black man in his late seventies who had relied on God's grace to preserve him from major illnesses until his sudden diagnosis and subsequent decline. Cortez's mother had dragged him to visit the man on his deathbed, drilling into his head that it was the right thing to do, disregarding Cortez's lack of resistance to the excursion. Since Mr. Eckles was a widower, the church had created a schedule so not a day would pass when he didn't have a visitor. They never said he was dying; they referred to his ultimate fate as "going home." Cortez's mother had chosen a time when nobody else from the church would be there, knowing her son's muteness would resurface if it wasn't just the three of them.

Cortez had first opened up to Mr. Eckles when he was a young boy. After Cortez's mother shared that her son was interested in joining a soccer team, and mentioned the challenges of finding a coach considerate of his lack of athletic ability—taking care to call it his temperament—the wrinkled man looked around for a piece of paper, settled on a church pamphlet, got down on one knee, and asked for an autograph.

"Sign your name so I can say I knew you before you were famous," he said with a smile, pulling a pen out of his shirt pocket and holding it at arm's length.

Cortez looked at his mother. A thin-lipped smile emerged

on her face, and she nodded. Cortez took the pen and wrote his name in big block letters, in the best handwriting he could manage. The old man brought up the signature when they saw each other at church every week, year after year, along with the question, "How's the dream going?" Cortez never had the heart to tell him that the first practice had been a complete disaster and he'd vowed to never go back, and his mother always covered for him by saying they were looking for the right situation.

Mr. Eckles hadn't mentioned the autograph when Cortez visited him in the hospital. He hadn't mentioned anything, because he didn't talk. Cortez remembered the clear plastic tube running down his old throat, the two tubes plugging his aged nose, and his own confusion about how the man was able to breathe.

"His lungs need help," Cortez's mother had told him.

The patient managed a weak smile and nod.

Cortez's mother had brought her Bible. After informing Mr. Eckles about their lives, which didn't take long, since each week was the same as the one before, she began reading various passages from the holy document. Upon completion of her selected verses, and with nothing else to talk about, she opened to random pages, reading aloud whichever passages she turned to, believing their selection was inspired by the Lord. Her fears about Cortez's silence were prescient: without the old man's urging, Cortez had nothing to say, other than "hello" when they arrived and "goodbye" when they left.

Mr. Eckles died soon after their visit. Cortez's mother sat him down and broke the news of the death with rehearsed lines meant to spare her son from pain. Cortez didn't feel anything. To him, the news of the death was like a canceled television show that wouldn't return, one enjoyable enough to watch when it was on but not addictive enough to miss. He remembered his mother's tears and, thinking about how many other people there were in the world, wondered why she was struck by the loss of a single one.

Now that his own mother was in the hospital, he understood.

The hospital was over an hour's walk from Cortez's home, a trip taken with the stoicism of a flagellant, blame his implement of choice. The facility was the kind of place that never slept; those responsible for its design went to great lengths to remove the building from the surrounding city's timeline. Bright lights on tall towers lit up the asphalt moat, illuminating every parking space, the lone shadows in existence beneath parked cars. Enormous angled lights on the ground and at various heights on the building banished all darkness from the building's face. The light leaked into the rooms and polluted the night, making sleep impossible for the doctors and nurses who worked too many hours on too little rest; the impact on the health of their patients, in particular the prolonged duration of their stay due to lack of sleep, was never investigated.

A screaming ambulance screeched to a halt behind another as Cortez walked across the brightened parking lot—there was no respite from people requiring medical attention. The doors swung open and the patient was rolled in, passing by two men returning to the first ambulance with their empty gurney. The first ambulance pulled away and passed Cortez on its way back into the wild, two ragged men out to retrieve more people in need, the driver talking into a handheld device while the passenger rested his eyes.

Two pairs of automatic doors opened for Cortez as he approached. He walked into the well-lit lobby and headed straight for the front desk, proclaiming that his mother was inside. After giving the receptionist the relevant information, he was directed to a set of elevators down the hall. Taking one to the fourth floor, he then found the correct room. He peeked inside the same way he would have if he was entering her space in their shared apartment: slow, cautious, and afraid of disturbing his mother.

His mother didn't hear him come inside. She was alone, despite the presence of a second bed, staring out the window at the dark sky beyond the hospital grounds. Cortez had never seen her in such a pitiful state, and she wore her age without realizing the results of the passing years; it was the first time he saw what she looked like when she went through periods of darkness hidden in her room. Her hair was in a tangle, her cheeks were sunken, and her shoulders sagged as if she had never sat up straight a day in her life. "It's all your fault," Cortez thought to himself.

Cortez absorbed her appearance before he spoke. "Hi, Mom," he said, cautious about how he proceeded. He didn't know if she was still upset at him for missing church, if she was mad because he hadn't told her about losing his job, or if she was embarrassed her retreat into her room had caused her to lose her own.

His mother turned to him, registered his presence, then said, "Hello," letting the word linger in the air.

Cortez didn't know what to do. With her, there was always a clear path forward, a way she expected him to act and a role for him to step into. Her lack of direction meant Cortez was adrift in a sea of possibilities about what to do next, what to say, and where to go. The uncertainty was unwelcome. "How are you?" he said.

"The doctor tells me it's my heart," she replied. "I'll have to be here for a few days."

Cortez looked down and waited for her to divulge that he was the reason her heart was broken.

His mother sighed. "Sit down, Cortez," she said, pointing to a lounge chair by the window. It was beneath a tiny television, the screen black, the layout designed so patients and visitors couldn't watch together.

"You'll have to feed yourself, of course. Though you've got no problem figuring things out for yourself nowadays," his mother said with a sigh.

Cortez nodded, accepting the veiled swipe with decades of practice.

"Don't even need God now," she added.

"I'm sorry I missed church. I had to go—" He cut himself off.

"Where'd you have to go?" his mother said with scorn, her words sharp.

"I had to tell Alara her boyfriend is cheating on her," Cortez said. Confessing removed the weight from his chest. He took a big breath and waited for the attack's continuation.

"A woman keeps you away from church and you're worried about *her*? What about your soul? Or mine! Throwing me away like yesterday's garbage."

"I'm not throwing you away," Cortez whispered.

"Sure seems like it." His mother looked out the window again, letting the silence settle between them like mud to the bottom of murky water.

After she was convinced her son had suffered her silence long enough, she looked back at him and asked about the message left by his former boss. "Why didn't you tell me you lost your job?"

Cortez was prepared. "I didn't want you to worry. I thought I could get another one before you found out."

"Where did you look?"

"Nowhere," Cortez admitted. He didn't elaborate, not wanting to disclose that his new occupation was unpaid and involved following around two people on the other side of the park. It struck him that all he had done since losing his job was spend money on unneeded beverages and acquire a range of bruises, scrapes, and cuts.

"Of course not. I got you the ice cream job, remember?" she said. She had asked around at church if anyone knew of any low-skill jobs, and a member of the congregation had put her in touch with his brother, the boss at the ice cream factory. She had called the contact herself, begged him to give her son an interview, and coached Cortez on what to say.

"I thought that if I could find another job, I could make Dad proud and he'd come back for you. For us," Cortez said. He viewed every action, past and present, through the lens of his own inadequacy in causing his father's absence, and he forgot he hadn't told her about losing his job because she was lost inside her room when he got home and hadn't emerged before he left the following day.

His mother sighed. "He's not coming back, Cortez."

Cortez shook his head, not believing his mother's words. "He will, once we get ourselves settled. You said so yourself!"

"Your father only cares about one thing: the Church. He's obsessed with finding new members, bringing more people into the fold."

"And once we show how we grew our own church, he'll come back!"

"He's not coming back!" she said, her statement followed by a fit of coughing. She continued when she calmed down. "He's not coming back because I'm the one who left."

CHAPTER THIRTY-THREE

ALMOST THREE MONTHS had elapsed since Friar Diego de Landa first left the Izamal monastery on his way to Santiago de Guatemala. After leaving the first statue in Merida, he had caught up with the Mayan men transporting the twin statue on the road, and together they went straight to the construction site of Izamal's new facilities. By then, construction of the exterior of the monastery's main building was completed. It was taller than the cathedral in Guatemala, broader than the monastery at Merida, and deeper than the schoolhouse that had been built years ago. Friar Diego commanded the horse-drawn cart go right through the center of the doorless building, where the Mayan men he'd brought were helped by the construction workers in getting the statue off the cart. It was the first and last time an animal was brought into the sanctuary. Under the watchful eye of the stonemason, the men moved the statue to where the altar would sit and erected it vertically. Friar Diego then pulled the protective cloth off himself, proclaimed the area blessed by the Virgin Mary, and commanded everyone in attendance, both natives and Spaniards, to bow down before the image.

The Mayan men, scolded about their idol worship from the

moment their education in Christianity began, wondered why the appreciation for the gods in the form of sculpture had taken so long to materialize. It was as if a weight was removed from their souls, and they could demonstrate their love for the deity without fear of retribution.

Friar Diego led an impromptu mass, a full hour of prayer, song, and bestowed blessings. The natives were dismissed after the service, but Friar Diego's searching eyes found the stonemason and called him forth.

"Can you construct a shelf on this wall"—Friar Diego pointed to the wall behind the altar, on the opposite side of where the congregation would sit in the future—"and put the statue there?"

All of a sudden, a large beam fell off the roof and landed flat between six Mayan men, dividing the group in two. None of the men were injured, though a shift in any of their positions would have meant their death. The men, eyes opened wide, all stared at the statue, knowing it was by the Virgin Mary's intercession that they were all unscathed. They fell to their hands and knees, their foreheads close to the ground, and thanked her holy hand for saving their lives. It was the first of many miracles attributed to the statue, earning her the nickname "The Virgin of Izamal."

"I can do that," the stonemason said, answering Friar Diego's question. Looking at the six thankful men, he said, "I imagine there will be a lot of people coming to visit her in the near future."

"Then let's get this finished up so we can lead them all in prayer!"

An elated Friar Diego left the stonemason behind and went back to the old monastery: home. His first order of business was finding Friar Nicolás de Albalate and making sure the native men who'd helped transport the statue were paid. Then, he went to his room.

Stale air rushed out when he opened the door. Inside, nothing had changed. Looking at the barren desk, he made a mental note to ask Friar Nicolás about any correspondence, knowing if it was pressing the *Custos* would have mentioned it during his stop in Merida. A layer of dust had gathered on the desk, the small stand next to his bed, and the lamp, and he removed his habit and wiped every surface with the soiled garment, spreading bits of the road from his travels throughout his room. Then, after taking a clean habit from a shelf high off the ground next to his desk, he sat down on his bed.

The totality of the frustration of not bringing back *Adelantado* Francisco Hernandez hit him with full force. The feelings had been kept at bay while he traveled, replaced with fear for the statues' safety and the potential consequences of the purchase, but now that he was alone and the statues were deposited in their final locations, he cursed his luck and impatience at going to Guatemala in the first place. He hit the mattress with his fist, wondering how he would ever get the *Adelantado* back into the Yucatán to stand trial without the government's support. Although the natives didn't give the punishment of the *encomendero* a second thought, the fact that the escaped prisoner still had a claim to his land and held his title filled Friar Diego with so much anger that the dry mattress beneath him started smoking. It would have caught fire if he hadn't been pulled from his reverie by a knock at the door.

"Hold on!" A harried Friar Diego threw on his clean habit and opened the door.

Ix Cuatchel stood in the doorway, staring at him with large, shining eyes. Her skin radiated warmth and her cheeks were fuller than he remembered, with an added reddish hue. Her hair, dark black and shining, hung down to her lower back. "You're back," she said.

Friar Diego turned around, giving Ix space to enter behind him. She walked in and closed the door.

"How was your trip?" she said.

"Longer than I'd hoped, and, in the end, worthless," Friar Diego said, still seething.

The pair looked at each other in silence. Friar Diego hadn't thought much about their night together once he'd prayed to God for forgiveness, thinking the matter behind him.

Ix, on the other hand, hadn't thought of anything but for the entirety of their time apart. "I have something to tell you," she said.

"What is it?" Friar Diego snapped.

"I'm pregnant."

The news struck Friar Diego like a thunderbolt. He sat down on the bed, his stomach tied in knots. Breathing took his full concentration.

When Ix tried grabbing his hand, Friar Diego inched it away, shoving both hands beneath his thighs. He took a staggered breath through his nose and let out a slow exhale.

"Whose is it?" Friar Diego said.

"What?" Ix asked. The question caught her off guard.

"Who else did you sleep with?" Friar Diego said through clenched teeth. There was a frozen edge to his voice, a cold harshness that frightened Ix when she heard him speak.

Ix pulled away. "Nobody," she said.

"How am I supposed to know that? I've been gone for months and when I come back you're pregnant. You've had plenty of time to seduce another."

Silent tears streamed down Ix's face. In recent weeks, she had cried for everything beautiful, anxious for the time in the near future when she would share the world with her child. Friar Diego made her cry from sadness for the first time in her life, and the strange sensation of her intestines coiling beneath her unborn child was the precise moment the child inherited his solitary disposition.

"It's yours. I've never been with another man," Ix said.

Friar Diego couldn't handle the information. As far as he was concerned, once his prayers had escaped his lips, asking the Lord for forgiveness, the deed had been erased from his soul. Hearing Ix refer to their night created an untenable situation in his reality, one he couldn't permit while battling *encomenderos* for the future of the native souls. The future of Christianity depended on him; Ix was a distraction.

"Leave the monastery," he said in a harsh whisper. "Leave Izamal. Leave the Yucatán. Don't ever come back or I'll tell everyone about the devil in your soul."

"The devil?" Ix said, choking on the words.

"Who else would come tempt me with the future of the world at stake?" Friar Diego stood and began yelling. "I'm close to the final conversion, and he sent his seductress to pull me from my path!"

Ix tried stifling her cries. It didn't work. Her wailing transformed into a fight for her survival.

Friar Diego had the taste of blood in his mouth and couldn't temper his emotions. Ix, as she had done so many times before, sat in his presence and took the responsibility for his support on her shoulders.

"There's nothing here for you! These are good people, ready to accept the true God. No wonder they prepared you for sacrifice, you are filled with the devil! If you love your people, you'll leave this place and never return."

Ix floundered, struggling to breathe. Friar Diego sat back down on the bed, pulled back Ix's hair, exposing her ear, and said in a lowered voice, "I never should have saved you."

All resistance evaporated. Obeying his commands, Ix stood

up and ran from his room, not stopping until she reached the ocean.

THE ENTIRE IZAMAL monastery heard Friar Diego yelling and Ix's sobs, though most didn't know what the commotion was about. Friar Nicolás alone knew Ix was pregnant, not because she'd told him but because he had been helping the sick for so long that he'd noticed the telltale signs before she even knew herself. The old friar couldn't imagine when conception could have occurred, since the monastery's underling, having been there for years, went nowhere else. Friar Nicolás prayed every night it wasn't one of the men tasked with spreading the word of God throughout the Yucatán. He had no question about the cause of Friar Diego's explosion.

Friar Diego witnessed the end of Friar Nicolás crossing himself when he emerged from his quarters.

"What was that about?" Friar Nicolás asked, knowing the answer.

"She won't be coming back."

"Oh?"

"God has called her somewhere else."

"God called her, or you sent her?"

Friar Diego lashed out at Friar Nicolás. "I've got enough on my plate between the *Adelantado* and Ix. I don't need you adding to my problems!"

Friar Nicolás bowed his head and walked away.

Friar Diego wallowed in his own self-pity for months. The conversion of the natives was the sole bright spot in the collapse of his entire world—they showed up to the construction site in droves, hoping for a glimpse of the statue of the Virgin Mary. The stonemason, instead of navigating the visitors while finishing the structure, created a temporary pavilion in the center of the planned atrium, where he placed the statue. The Maya were heard shouting "Maria" as they walked by, reaching out a hand and brushing the statue with gentle fingers and open mouths. There were reports of the statue shedding real tears for sick children, its surface being ice cold during the sweltering heat of midday, and twice open wounds stopped bleeding in her presence, though the wounded died in the end both times.

As the year 1559 drew to a close, two letters from Spain arrived that shook the Spanish New World to its foundation. The first provided a glimmer of hope in the fight against the *Adelantado*, and the second reaffirmed Friar Diego's zeal for converting the natives and drove Ix from his mind.

Friar Lorenzo de Bienvenida, who had returned to Spain in hopes of separating the Yucatán from the Guatemala Province, sent the first letter the Yucatán Franciscans received. Though it was addressed to the *Custos*—with language that specified that he assumed it was still Friar Francisco Navarro—it was in fact for the benefit of the entirety of the Yucatán. In it, Friar Lorenzo laid out how he had been given ten more friars and one hundred pesos for books. Then, he shared that the Yucatán had been made its own province, free from the yoke of Guatemala.

Entire outposts cheered when each monastery's Guardian read the news for their friars. Because of the lag in delivery times, natives who were used to the silence of the trees found their tranquility interrupted by cheering friars at random intervals. The interruptions continued for a period of ten days, sometimes twice a day, sometimes with a day between.

Friar Diego's first concern was what would happen to the *Adelantado*. Alongside the letter from Friar Lorenzo was one from the *Custos* about that very topic. In it, Friar Francisco laid out how the Guatemala Province now harbored a fugitive, how he'd sent a letter to them telling them as much, and that the new Yucatán Province would respect the orders for a retrial because it had been made while Guatemala was still in charge. The *Custos* added that it could be years before they had enough resources to tie up the *Adelantado* affair without support from Guatemala.

Friar Diego clenched his jaw so hard while reading the letter that he cracked a tooth, and he preferred soft foods and lukewarm liquids for the rest of his life. If the leaders of the province hadn't sent the prisoner back when the offense was committed in their jurisdiction, there was little chance they would send the man back now that the Yucatán had separated itself.

The second letter from Spain came from Princess Joanna of Portugal, who was serving as regent to the Spanish Empire. She was the most religious member of Spain's ruling elite, known for founding a convent supporting barefoot nuns. Her letter was addressed to all Franciscans in the Yucatán, though it affected Friar Diego the most. She thanked the friars for their service, their piety, and their previous successes while at the same time imploring their further action. According to her, Catholicism in Spain, and therefore Spain itself, was in danger. The attacks came from all sides, she said. From the east and south, up from Africa, came the threat of the Muslim incursion under the banner of the Ottoman Empire. Despite their attempts at expelling or converting Muslims within their borders, Spain still suffered from the threat of pockets of resistance rising up in support of their brothers across the Mediterranean.

"The thought of which kept me up at night," she wrote.

Her list of threats to the empire continued, outlining the threat from Protestantism from the north. She recounted the capture of men smuggling Protestant teachings into the heart of Spain and their subsequent burning at the stake, justifying the actions by saying they were preserving the purity of the faith.

"The only place left for Catholicism to flourish is in the

west. Therefore, take great care of the things of faith of Christianity because in Spain there was a great perdition."

The letter, reproduced and distributed in the same manner as the letter from Friar Lorenzo, reinforced the Franciscans' resolve. The importance of their mission reinfected their bones, knowing the Maya were the souls that would strengthen Catholicism's numbers. Friar Diego took the sentiment a step further: he knew, deep in his soul, the coming of the New Age was upon them. He read secret meanings in the Princess's words, hidden calls to action, and he suffered under the weight of the world pressing down on him as he wondered if she was privy to the same secret prophecy. The Catholic Church in Spain was the last holdout, the westernmost tip of the true resistance in the Old World. The New World was their final crusade.

Friar Diego thought about the Popes who'd organized the previous crusades. He became convinced their gaze, towards Jerusalem, had faced the wrong direction, obscured by their pride over a past long gone. A new man was needed, one without the ostentations of the Church, the desire for riches, or a subservience to a position within the Church that would be extinct in short order. While the rest of the Yucatán Franciscans read the letter with renewed vigor, Friar Diego came to grips with a small darkness inside his soul that pulled him inward and convinced him he was the man who would lead this final crusade, a Pope without being given the title.

The signs of the prophecy's fulfillment were lining up. Without the Church politics prior Popes had faced, he could act in the Maya's best interest. The Maya who, according to the revelation he'd had when talking to Ix, were one of the lost tribes of Israel; their conversion would, in fact, be the Jewish conversion spoken of hundreds of years ago. The Yucatán would flourish without the yoke of Guatemala holding them back.

The one question Friar Diego had after reading the two letters was how he could position himself as the leader of the Franciscans and receive the title of Provincial for himself. There were whispers about Friar Lorenzo's natural assumption of the role, though every man spoke about the need to listen to God's message during deliberation. The veteran was the longest-serving friar in the Yucatán, the man responsible for their support from the Spanish Crown, and the one who had convinced most of the men to journey across the ocean in the first place.

Friar Diego found his answer in the Mayan priest, Ahkinmai.

On a nondescript Sunday in the dry season's peak, Friar Diego set about getting ready for mass. The numbers of attendees had swollen past the point of fitting into neat rows in the courtyard outside the old sanctuary, and now both Mayan and Spanish colonists stood wherever there was room. The friars, instead of sitting in the front of the service while one of their number preached, were forced into action each week. Three were given notes on the same sermon, and they preached from one of three locations: in the sanctuary proper, and on each side of the courtyard. Someone in the middle of the gathering could turn in any direction they wished and hear the same message spoken, in Spanish, out of sync with the other friars and with varying levels of skill in translating the important portions into the Mayan language. They had tried delivering all Mayan-language sermons in the past but found the natives' mimicry of the Spaniards during mixed services helped teach the natives proper methods of behavior.

Friar Diego had created the notes and distributed them to his two comrades. As Guardian, the altar was his. The congregation trickled in while the friars sat on the altar alongside Friar Diego. The other two were sent outside at the appointed time, where they took up positions on each side of the crowd in the courtyard.

Halfway through the service, while Friar Diego was leading the group in a prayer that reminded the natives of their new year's chanting, a wave came in from outside and crashed onto those in the sanctuary. One row at a time, men, women, and children turned around, looking outside. Each turning person continued praying, saying the memorized words despite their lack of attention.

As Friar Diego said, "Amen," a display of color caught his eye at the entrance to the sanctuary. There, in full ceremony attire, was the man who invaded his dreams as a large bird: Ahkinmai. The Mayan priest didn't walk inside, content with leaning on the doorway, casting a bird-shaped shadow into the center of the room as if he stood in the middle of the doorway.

At a nod from Ahkinmai towards Friar Diego, both Mayan and Spanish worshippers turned back to the altar. Friar Diego did his best job continuing the service despite the feeling his authority was under direct attack. While he read from the Bible, he had the peculiar sensation of understanding the Princess's fears about the threats faced by Catholicism in Spain—it was not a rallying cry; he felt like a shepherd fearing for the loss of his flock.

Ahkinmai stayed through the end of the service and dismissed all the Maya who approached him after the benediction. The Spanish colonists from Izamal stared at the man, not understanding why feathers covered his body. The feathers were inspired by the toucan: jet black on his lower body, bright yellow on his chest, and a mixture of green and orange crowning his head. Friar Diego approached the Mayan priest at the first chance, greeting him with a compliment on his plumage.

"The colors are beautiful," he said, certain he had never seen this permutation of Ahkinmai's ornament, not even in his dreams.

"Appropriate for the occasion," Ahkinmai replied.

"And what occasion is that?"

"I've come to worship your God. The others came before me, and now it's time I entered the room."

The next breath Friar Diego took was his first free from worry since Ahkinmai had arrived. He bottled his excitement. "We're honored you're here."

"I won't be here for every service, but I'll attend the ones I can. Are there different rituals?"

"There are different prayers."

"But the worshippers sit and listen each time? They never get involved?"

"Yes, they listen to me each week. Different than what you're used to!" Friar Diego said, attempting a joke.

Ahkinmai stayed serious. He rubbed a cape feather between his thumb and forefinger. "You hold a lot of power over these people," he observed.

"God has the power."

"Right, your God," Ahkinmai said. After a moment, he added, "Could I see your sacred text?"

Friar Diego showed the man the Bible, allowing him to leaf through the pages. Ahkinmai's fingers scanned a number of pages as if absorbing the writing through his skin. He spent the most time flipping through the pages in the Book of Revelations, his hands moving down the page while his unfocused eyes stared into the shadows behind the altar. He slammed the book shut.

"Stay for a meal?" Friar Diego said, playing the part of host.

Ahkinmai declined, saying he was needed elsewhere.

Friar Diego watched Ahkinmai disappear down the dirt

path that led out of Izamal, wondering if there was any way the Mayan priest could have read the Bible's pages. They were written in Latin, not Spanish, and not the Mayan script, and without an education within the Church there was no way the man could know what words the pages contained. Still, Friar Diego couldn't shake the sense that the place the priest said he was needed was among his own books, where he would transcribe what was in the Bible into the Mayan script for the coming generations.

Chuckling, Friar Diego convinced himself he was giving the priest far too much power, even though a small part of him wondered if the priest had learned the Bible's language while dream-walking. Despite the questions surrounding Ahkinmai, Friar Diego knew the Mayan priest's presence at mass was a major victory in the quest for native conversion. The last step was Ahkinmai's renouncement of the old faith—once that occurred, saving the world was a matter of time.

Ahkinmai left the monastery certain he was right about the friars: they didn't care about any gods other than their own, and without the appreciation for the rest of the pantheon they would always be fighting a losing battle for the hearts of men.

CHAPTER THIRTY-FOUR

Cortez was stunned. Everything he thought he knew was turned on its head, and his tenuous grip on reality was slipping away. A dull ache began at his brain stem, and its tentacles spread over the back of his skull.

"You're old enough to know the truth," she said. She took a deep breath and allowed herself a long exhale before she continued. "I met your father when he saved me from a religious ceremony. He was in town to spread the Gospel and grow the area's first Catholic church. None of us had ever heard his kind of message before, talking about how we were all equal before God. Some rejected it, others embraced it, and a few listened one day then forgot the next. I knew from the moment I first heard him speak that I had found the reason I was put on this earth.

"Now, it's hard to call where we lived a town, or even a village. There was a centralized location for the leaders, but the people who worked the land never stayed in one area for very long. The views on women weren't progressive, to put it one way. By interrupting the religious ceremony, your father had unknowingly taken responsibility for providing for me; I was no longer welcome in my own family. He let me sleep in a small room near the church. In return, I made myself useful in any way I could. I helped with the sick, helped prepare food, and helped ready the church for Sunday service. Those were good days.

"Your father was the most driven man I'd ever met. It was like he could think of nothing else but how to spread the word of God. The native religion made him furious. I respected him, I feared him, and in time, I grew to love him. I like to think I kept my sinner's desire a secret, but it's hard to know for certain. As the years passed, we grew into a rhythm. I was a young woman before long, my head filled with questions and passion in equal measure. I was the last person he saw before going to bed, and the first person he saw when he woke up. In hindsight, I knew what I was doing, but at the time I convinced myself I was serving him and therefore serving God.

"One night he was upset over the death of three men in an accident. I walked him back to his room and went inside. That's the night you were conceived, Cortez. He left to Guatemala, saying he needed to retrieve a statue, promising to return. By the time he came back, I knew I was carrying you in my stomach. He flew into a rage when I told him, banishing me from the church and from his side. I took one last look at the town that had grown up around the church, while I was growing up inside its walls, and started walking. When I got to the ocean, a captain took one look at me and pitied me: it was obvious I was pregnant.

"Crossing the ocean was an experience I'll never forget. The captain said he had never been in, or heard of, the kind of storm we passed through. Not a single drop of rain fell while the boat was tossed around by wave after wave of foam. Balls of lightning ran along the deck like billiard balls, bumping into each other and the rails, making it impossible to stand on deck. I was in bed, my stomach aching, praying I wouldn't lose you in the ship's hold with nothing but men around. At some point in the storm I passed out, and when I woke up I was alone in the unmoving ship. We were docked in a harbor, and seemed to have been there for some time, because there was a connected walkway for people to come on board. A tourist found me in a daze without a single possession. They spoke English and I didn't, but we found someone I could talk to and they took me to the hospital, where I had you.

"The truth is, you were born here because I immigrated while I was pregnant with you. Your father kicked me out of the church, his church, and didn't want anything to do with you."

Cortez's mother buried her face in her hands and began to sob, releasing years of pent-up frustration. Since she always hid herself in her room when she cried, away from Cortez, he didn't know what to do. He took a white pill, sat back, and watched her, waiting.

"Those pills don't do anything," his mother said, her voice catching in her throat.

"What do you mean? The doctor gave them to me."

"The doctor gave you the blue pills; I gave you the white pills. They're sugar pills. I thought you'd outgrow them, but you never did."

Cortez inspected both bottles, ashamed at falling for the false medicine. "I'm sure he'll come back if I can find more people to come to church," Cortez said after a moment, putting the pills back into his backpack. "It's what he wants. We can work together."

"He's not coming back because he never left. He doesn't know where we are!" his mother said, grateful her duplicity was ignored—she had lived with the guilt for far too long. "Unless all of Christianity knows your name, he'll never hear of you. And even if he did, he'd never know you were his son."

Cortez wondered what he would have to do for everyone to know his name. He knew it was more than getting people to come to the small church that met in the bottom of a school, but that was a good place to start.

"Did you ever hear anything else about him?" Cortez asked.

"Never. I always wondered if there was another woman I didn't know about, one he loved more than me, and that was the reason he made me leave. There's nothing else I can come up with. I helped in the church, I stayed out of his way, I was a bridge between my people and him, useful whenever conflicts arose . . ."

"Another woman?" The memory of Remy's infidelity kicked open the door to Cortez's mind and walked in. "But that's a sin."

"Men have needs, Cortez. You'll learn one day, if you haven't already. Your father's vows didn't allow for us to be together, but we still found a way, didn't we? It's a moment of weakness like any other. God understands, and forgives; as long as you go to church each week and confess, your soul is safe."

"So you think he got rid of you so he could be with her?"

Cortez's mother curled her lips between her teeth and bit down to stop herself from crying. "It was just so abrupt. I don't see any other reason."

His mother's once-black hair—now gray—square jaw, and disconsolate eyes provided Cortez with a vision of Alara Chel's potential future, after discovering Remy was cheating on her with another woman. Cortez thought it was a fate no woman deserved, and now he understood the long-term damage rejection could accomplish. He made a vow to himself to save Alara from Remy and to bring her to church, not having given up on making his father proud.

"You're growing up too fast, my son," Cortez's mother said

to him. "I think that's why I got so upset when you missed church, because it feels like you're slipping away. Then when I heard you lost your job, I couldn't take it anymore. My body broke down."

"I'm sorry," Cortez said. He wished there was something to clean.

"Don't worry about making your father proud. He doesn't care about you, or us. Know that you've already made me proud, and there's nothing you can do to change that."

Cortez's mother opened her arms and used her fingers to beckon him to her side. Cortez stood up, walked over to her bed, then leaned over and gave her a hug.

"I love you, you know that?" his mother said.

"I know. I love you too."

"Now that you know about your father, don't bother trying to impress him anymore. He's not worth having you as a son."

Cortez nodded into her hair. She pushed him away, inspecting him at arm's length, then fixed where his hair stuck up at odd angles.

"It's late. Why don't you go home? You've been up long enough because of me."

"Well, I don't have work tomorrow," Cortez said, testing the waters with a joke.

A flash of anger, followed by disappointment, were illuminated by the bright outside lights. "You're right, you don't. Do you think you'll go back by the end of the week?"

"Maybe."

"And what happened with Simeon? He's your friend, right?"

"I'm not sure. I'll find out more when I go back."

Cortez was shooed out of the room by the back of his mother's hand. "We can talk more about everything when I get home," she said, assuming his world was turned upside down.

Her words didn't register. Cortez was lost in thought, wondering how he was going to save Alara from sharing his mother's fate, and the years of uncertainty about his father fueled the rage directed towards Remy. Balls of lightning trailed in his wake while he walked, leaving dark burns on the sidewalk from the hospital to his home.

Remy woke up at dawn on Wednesday morning with no idea Cortez was waiting for him to emerge from his building. He had checked the sunrise's projected time the night before and set his alarm to the same minute, typical practice during the week. His stretch routine, designed to eliminate the resulting soreness from the previous day's workout, took place in front of the large window that faced the building across the street. It took twenty minutes, and after he finished he was ready to face the day's challenges.

As a financial advisor at his father's firm, getting dressed and making himself presentable was a necessity. The job was his from before he went to high school. Each university year—where he studied finance—had been paid for in advance. His wardrobe had transitioned to a full assortment of button-downs, slacks, and dress shoes after graduation, outfits Cortez considered "church clothes." A suit jacket was reserved for days he met with his most important clients.

Remy's breakfast never varied, a quality Cortez would have appreciated if he knew of its existence. Two hard-boiled eggs, a bowl of oatmeal, one glass of orange juice, and one glass of water. He always ate in the same order: one bite of half an egg, one bite of oatmeal, half the orange juice after each egg, finish the oatmeal, then wash it all down with the water. Appearances were everything in his line of work, and he considered the care of his body a part of his job. This view was opposite from that of his father, who declared with pride that his large belly showed customers that he ate well, and that he could ensure they ate well too.

The television was on while he ate breakfast, and he turned to the sports channel. He watched the highlights and news from the day before, valuable talking points he used when he met with male clients, their typical sexual preferences making them immune to his charms. The women he met with never listened to what he said; their primary concern was the way he said it, and he had figured out from an early age that smiling while he talked was the key to winning them over.

Remy rinsed his dishes and put them in the dishwasher when he finished eating. He took a look around, making sure his marble countertops were clean and his floor spotless. In essence, his goal was to keep the place looking like nobody lived there and therefore ready for visitors at any time. He was proud of what he had accomplished in life, accomplishments he had been set up to achieve by a loving father and obedient mother, and he had never questioned the role privilege played in his life.

With a banana in one hand and his briefcase in the other, Remy left his apartment and took the elevator down to the ground floor. He told the worker at the front desk, one of five who rotated throughout the week, good morning, stopping to ask if she was just starting or just finishing her shift.

"Been here since midnight, I'm about to go home," the woman at the front desk said.

"Well, enjoy the day." He looked outside. "Looks like it's going to be a nice one."

"You too!" she replied.

Remy walked into the day's sunshine, appreciative of the morning's cooler temperature before the sun rose high in the sky and baked the city. He didn't see the man watching him from across the street.

. . .

Cortez had been staring at the entrance to Remy's building since before the sun rose. He had gotten home from the hospital late at night, thrown away his stockpile of worthless pills after staring at them for so long the instructions lost all meaning, and managed to sleep for a few hours before his eyes opened in the early morning. Nobody bothered him when he crossed the park and walked the now-familiar path to Remy's. Everyone continued ignoring him as he stood across the street from the luxury apartment building, assuming that anybody awake so early was a productive member of society. He was worried he would miss Remy leaving the building when delivery trucks parked in front of the building's entrance two separate times. His eyes darted to each side of the trucks, watching for his target. For an instant, Cortez thought one man was Remy, but when he stood up from against the wall and began following him, he realized he didn't recognize the gait. The possibility of Remy escaping through another door never occurred to him.

Remy started walking to work, thinking about the client meetings he had scheduled for the day. After an upcoming relaxed morning, he had a meeting before lunch, a lunch meeting, then two more before the completion of his day. As he got to the corner of the block, thoughts of the end of his workday trickled in, and while he waited to cross the street with the other walking commuters, his day's first thoughts of Alara appeared. They were logistical in nature, a study of whether there was time for her that night and if he could still get his workout in. He remembered his friends had asked him to play soccer and decided on a call to Alara around lunchtime to discuss the evening's plan. All of a sudden, he became aware of another's eyes on him, a specific gravitational pull that forced his gaze to the right.

Cortez stood next to him, a few paces behind. Remy tilted

his head back and closed his eyes. Dealing with Cortez was the last thing he wanted to do that morning. There was too much work to devote even a second to the creature who insisted on appearing in his life at the most inopportune times. He had never once feared retaliation for the beating he'd inflicted the last time they met because he didn't respect Cortez enough to think him capable of causing any real damage.

"Didn't I tell you to stop following me?" Remy said, exasperated. Confronting someone during the morning had a much different flavor than confronting someone after a night of drinking.

Cortez got straight to the point. "I have proof you're cheating on Alara." He had wondered what would come out of his mouth until the very moment the words appeared and was proud of himself for not beginning with a declaration of love for Remy's girlfriend.

"Oh you do, do you?" Remy knew he had been careful, both in his exploits and in his language with Alara, having never promised his own fidelity. It was how he could sleep at night, knowing he'd never lied to her. What she chose to believe was another matter—he knew she expected him to be faithful.

The light turned red and the signal to walk flashed on. The people who were waiting with them crossed the street, leaving the two men alone.

Cortez nodded, fearful Remy would lash out but not caring about his own well-being.

Remy had no intention of raising his heart rate before work, worried about potential perspiration. Prioritizing his occupation was a trait instilled in him by his father, and since the man was also his boss, Remy knew he was held to a higher standard. "And what about it?"

Cortez thought Remy would beg him to hand over the proof

or command him not to show it to Alara—at the very least, to pretend he cared about his relationship with the most magical human Cortez had ever encountered. The fact that Remy didn't waver in his nonchalance sent Cortez over the edge. "You're ungrateful," he said, suppressing the urge to rush Remy and tackle him to the ground.

"What can I say? I don't believe you." Remy looked at his watch, a gold timepiece his father had given him when he moved out of the house. He wasn't late. Yet.

"Oh, I have it," Cortez said. "Meet me in the library tonight and you can have it back." Getting Remy to agree to a meeting on the top floor of the library had been his plan all along.

"What is it, a picture?" Even if it was a picture, there was nothing wrong with being seen with someone. Unless Cortez had been able to snap a shot of him alone in the doorways with Liza before pizza. He was curious what the evidence consisted of, and he was also curious how he would explain away the situation to Alara if she ever got hold of what Cortez claimed to have.

"You'll have to wait and see. Tonight, top floor of the library. The light will be on in one of the rooms."

"I can't go tonight, I have a meeting I can't miss." Rescheduling meetings at a time more favorable for him was a trick he'd learned in his earliest days in the office. It was the first step in establishing power over his counterpart during negotiations.

Cortez grew annoyed at Remy's lack of appreciation at the potential loss of Alara. What could be more important than preserving her love? "Tomorrow?" he asked.

"I can be there tomorrow. What time?"

"Six," Cortez said.

Remy nodded, then turned away. By now, the light had turned back to green, and Remy had to wait for another chance to cross the street. For a moment, he feared Cortez was heading in his direction. It would lead to an awkward wait and an awkward crossing; with any luck, the thorn in his side would turn left when he turned right. His fears never came to fruition; Cortez turned around and walked away.

CHAPTER THIRTY-FIVE

Friar Diego de Landa created reasons for visiting the various monasteries in the Yucatán Province during the year 1560. He traveled to Mani under the auspices of checking on the natives left in limbo after the *Adelantado*'s arrest, visited Merida as if he missed his old friend, called on the friars in Campeche while arranging a supplies exchange, and even traveled to Valladolid with two of his top students, leaving them there in a support role for the friars stationed in the western location. During long conversations with the Guardian of each monastery, he reminded them of his work on the *arte*—they all used the resource so much the pages were bent and torn. He made sure he told them about his crowning achievement: the conversion of Ahkinmai.

"If we can convert the priests, the rest will follow," he said. He never outright told the Guardians he was seeking the title of Provincial.

His conversations weren't just with the monastery's leaders. During meals, after services, and before bed, he cornered the other friars and told them about his accomplishments at Izamal.

"You should see how well the Maya work under my direction. The new monastery is near completion as we speak!"

If their reaction was positive—which it always was—he would let slip that he was the leader the Franciscans needed now that they had become their own province. "Who showed the *Adelantado* who was in charge in the Yucatán? Me, as *Custos*," he said, playing the politician. He trusted the underlings would relay the message to their superiors, planting seeds from inside that would grow into crops ready for harvest when the time for the election came.

The separation of the Yucatán from the Guatemala Province wouldn't be official until the paperwork was completed and brought back to the Yucatán, at which point the election for Provincial would take place. Friar Lorenzo de Bienvenida assumed he would be the one taking the title, after securing the separation in the first place, and he went about making arrangements for the ten friars who would accompany him back to the New World without knowing about Friar Diego's whisper campaign while he was predisposed.

One of the issues that arose from the restructure of their organization was what to do about the upcoming election for *Custos*, which was scheduled for September 1560. With the changing of the Yucatán from a custody of the Guatemala Province to a province in its own right, the position wouldn't exist once Friar Lorenzo returned, replaced by a Provincial as head of the region. Friar Francisco Navarro, the current *Custos*, told Friar Diego during his visit to Merida that he feared the other friars would assume he was seizing power in the void left by the reorganization if he suggested a delay in the elections. "I want to propose we keep current appointments until Friar Lorenzo returns," he said.

Friar Diego derived a mischievous joy from his trusting friend's sharing of his concerns about seizing power, when he was traveling the Yucatán looking for his own promotion's support. "I don't think anyone will question your motives, Francisco," he said with a soft tone of understanding. "In fact, let's write the letter right now."

Together, the two friars wrote to the rest of the Franciscans that they would postpone elections until Friar Lorenzo came back with the necessary paperwork for their province. The *Custos* mentioned Friar Diego's guidance and support, hoping the weight of the former *Custos* would assuage all fears about the decision being made from the desire for authority.

When they received the letter, the rest of the friars in the Yucatán were glad the trip to Merida for another council was put off until further notice.

FRIAR DIEGO's campaigning came to a sudden stop at the conclusion of the harvest season, early in the year 1561. Word reached Izamal that *Adelantado* Francisco Hernandez was back in Campeche, which was the closest Franciscan monastery to the Guatemala Province, causing an uproar within their ranks. According to reports, the *Adelantado*, who still retained his title because of the delay in his ultimate judgment, had come back to the Yucatán with a full retinue of men and natives and was throwing around money, buying whatever he pleased. This news stoked the flames of Friar Diego's vengeful passions—the brashness of the man!—but his hatred turned into a full-blown inferno when he heard about the attacks on the Franciscans.

The attacks weren't physical; they were verbal. The *Adelantado* accused the friars of entering the Order so they could get out of work, saying they weren't real priests but liars. He claimed all their teachings were false and their baptisms were no more than sprinkles with water. The worst accusation, which Friar Diego couldn't forget and couldn't ignore, was that the friars were entering the villages under the pretext of spreading Christianity so they could get their hands on the native women.

"The Maya in the market listen to him for hours," the friar from Campeche wrote. "No doubt they spread their misgivings to the others in the area. We've seen attendance at mass decrease three weeks in a row."

Friar Diego tasted metal in his mouth as he read the letter. A drop of blood escaped his lips and splashed onto the page, onto an added message from the *Custos*.

"This is a problem," Friar Francisco wrote.

Trembling hands placed the shaking letter onto the desk. A clenched fist wiped blood from pursed lips before a worn habit was brought up to Friar Diego's face, blotting the sweat from his brow. He thought of Ix Cuatchel for the first time in months, wondering where she was, about how succumbing to their primal desires had never been the intention.

In a rage, Friar Diego overturned his desk.

The *Adelantado*'s other accusations were false and the friar knew it. But the one about women, the one about Ix, hit the target so dead center the man who uttered it couldn't walk free without consequence.

Friar Diego paced his room, wondering how he could imprison the blaspheming man. At a fundamental level, imprisonment was forcing an offender to move, giving him a new place to live. He remembered the Maya's relocation, and how Tomás López Medel had made money available for the enforcement by guaranteeing payment with the power of the Guatemala Province.

The Yucatán was now a Province too, and once he was in charge he could guarantee payment. What difference did the order of events make?

Friar Diego, blood trickling from the corners of his lips, went to the portion of Izamal where the Spanish colonists lived.

There, he found the men who had gone with him into the jungle and forced the Maya out of their homes years ago. Within days, the three dozen Spaniards who'd helped the Franciscan in the past were ready for the warpath once more. Friar Diego, in charge of their ranks, at first wondered if it was enough men, but his blind rage, sustained with great effort over the days since reading the letter, forced him into action despite his misgivings.

No Spaniard, let alone a group of them, had ever made the trip from Izamal to Campeche faster than Friar Diego's troop. The mercenaries woke each day thinking it was the morning when they would rest, or at the least slow down, but the friar, feeling rejuvenated at the age of thirty-six, rushed them out of camp and made them stay on the trail until well after the sun went down.

CAMPECHE, on the coast, was very different from landlocked Izamal. For one, the dock provided easy access to the broader world, bringing a host of unsavory characters the local Franciscans warned the natives about each week. The second reason was the market, the largest in the Yucatán. The transient lifestyle of the Mayan traders made consistent attendance at mass impossible. These natives didn't have the same ties to the Franciscans at their local monastery, whether Campeche or the one where they traveled from, and *Adelantado* Francisco's words took root in more fertile ground—or at least that was Friar Diego's fear.

The friar led his men, filled with promises about their service to the province, right into the market in the middle of the day. The salty smell of the sea was heavy throughout, fueled by winds from the coast that swept away the smell of rotting fish and plant matter. The Spanish colonists in the market and the

Spaniards with Friar Diego exchanged menacing glances, both parties clutching knives, clubs, and the occasional gun.

"There's no room for hesitation," Friar Diego had told his men before they entered the city. "We can't afford giving him any time to get away and gather his men."

Knowing the *Adelantado* was speaking out against the friars to the natives, Friar Diego led his men through the market to where the Maya sold their goods. There wasn't a physical landmark differentiating the two spaces; at one point, the stalls and carts were manned by Mayan men from the surrounding region instead of by Spanish colonists and sailors. Inquisitive native glances followed Friar Diego's men as they walked through the market in tight formation, searching for the *Adelantado.* They came to the end of the stretch of road that held the market without finding him.

Friar Diego asked a native man at the end of the market, an old man selling a variety of collected fruit, where he could find the *Adelantado.* The man pointed to the docks in the distance. There, a number of men were unloading a ship.

"Let's go," Friar Diego said, leading his men.

The dockworkers didn't pay any attention to the friar when he shouted he was looking for the *Adelantado.* It was as if they weren't speaking the same language. From the ship, a spectacled man looked down on the friar.

"Quit bothering them!" he said in Spanish. His head was covered in tight curls and his glasses made his eyes take up more of his face than an owl's.

"We're looking for someone," Friar Diego said.

"Look somewhere else!"

When the man on the ship disappeared from view, one of the native men unloading the ship whispered the *Adelantado* was staying at a nearby house.

"He's probably eating lunch right now, if I had to guess," the man said in broken Spanish. He set the wooden box he was carrying on top of the others, turned around, and waited in line to get back onto the ship.

"The widow Cortés," the native man added before turning away for good, looking at the back of the head of the man ahead of him in line.

Friar Diego wasted no time pursuing his quarry. After twice asking for directions, he came to a large stone row house. He knocked on the door with all three dozen men behind him. A native servant girl answered the door. She was young, her hair braided, and wearing a Spanish-style dress—ornamented with lace, narrow at the chest, and sweeping below the waist. Friar Diego told her the Catholic Church had arrived; two of his largest men accompanied him inside.

"Wait here while I announce to the lady you're here," the girl said, in Spanish.

Friar Diego was amazed at how well she spoke. He didn't obey her command, instead following her until they were in a hall leading into a courtyard. There were two voices. One, a patient woman. The other was a rough snarl that Friar Diego recognized right away: *Adelantado* Francisco.

"All I'm saying is that they pretend their entire existence is according to God's will, when in reality they are liars and thieves. They took my property without thinking twice about how it goes against the Ten Commandments!"

Friar Diego burst onto the patio ahead of the apologetic servant. His two men were behind them.

The courtyard's walls were covered with flowering ivy. In the center was a modest table and four chairs, two of them empty. *Adelantado* Francisco stopped eating as he was bringing a fork laden with red meat to his lips. He set the food down and stood up. His dining partner, the widow Cortés, demanded the intruders leave her house. Nobody paid her any attention.

"You made a mistake coming back here," Friar Diego said.

"Why? There's nothing you can do the Provincial won't overturn." The *Adelantado*'s bravado was, in part, a show for the widow. The lines on his face were more pronounced than when Friar Diego had last seen him.

"Your friend didn't tell you the good news? The Yucatán is a province in its own right, no longer subject to Guatemala's oversight."

The color drained from the *Adelantado*'s face. "That's not possible."

"Not only is it possible, it's true. The paperwork is coming from Spain as we speak."

"It's not official until the paperwork arrives! You have no authority."

Friar Diego walked over to the table, took a pinch of the pulled red meat, and ate a bite. "Delicious," he told the widow.

The widow Cortés imagined strangling the friar, then grew distraught at the thought of harming a priest.

"What did he tell you?" *Adelantado* Francisco said to the two sentinels standing behind Friar Diego. "He has no power!"

"Their friends outside beg to differ. It's all about who you know," Friar Diego said with a wink. He turned to the two men with him. "Take him."

The two men strode forward and grabbed the furious Spaniard. "You can't do this!" he screamed, writhing in their grasp. He was about the same age as Friar Diego but carried much more muscle. During his youth, he had waged war on the Maya in the region then spent the peaceful period afterward working the land. The two men, though large, struggled while leading him out of the house; binding his hands took the help of another two men when they were outside the residence. Their prisoner screamed the entire time.

"This is illegal!" Adelantado Francisco said. The few people who heard his cries ignored him, knowing the Franciscans were dangerous enemies in their own right, let alone a Franciscan with three dozen men at his disposal.

The road the group and their prisoner were on would take them out of Campeche. They would pass right by the Campeche monastery and offer a lesson about the proper response to the *Adelantado*'s behavior. Friar Diego thought the friar's witnessing of the *Adelantado*'s arrest would be a worthy addition to his case for becoming the next Provincial, but displaying his captive to the misguided natives in the marketplace was a siren's call he couldn't ignore. Despite his initial misgivings about resistance to the *Adelantado*'s arrest, he told his men they were going back the way they came.

"Through the market," he said.

Seventy-two eyes glittered with delight. These men, hardened by the cruelty shown during the native relocation, had come ready for a fight, and the potential offered by the marketplace made the hired Spaniards smile, chuckle, giggle, and laugh. They all withdrew their weapons.

Friar Diego walked at the head of the procession, head held high, looking for dissidents. Behind him, hands tied behind his back, was *Adelantado* Francisco, prodded on by a short, thick club held by the largest man. Behind them, the other thirty-five men walked, each one of them looking outward and begging for an intervention.

The *Adelantado* screamed as he was led through the Campeche market's Mayan traders. "They want me silenced so you don't know the truth!" he roared. "The Franciscans aren't real priests, they're lazy, power-hungry beasts! You'll suffer the same fate if you ever go against what they say!"

Friar Diego laughed at the absurdity of the claims. The native traders ignored the procession. They were making money in the market, not getting caught up in religious squabbles. Their passivity did not go unnoticed.

"Save your words; they don't care either way," Friar Diego whispered to the *Adelantado*.

The Spanish traders cared even less, if possible. Who held the power and in what province didn't affect them in the least, as long as they could trade their goods without interference. By the time Friar Diego's group left the market, the *Adelantado* realized he had overplayed his hand, relied on his benefactors beyond their protection's capability, and left himself to his fate.

Friar Diego decided the *Adelantado* should go back to Merida. Along the way, he spent a lot of his time talking with the captured man, asking questions about why he'd risked coming back to the Yucatán in the first place, regardless of the power of his protection. "You had to know this was possible," the friar said.

At first, the *Adelantado* didn't respond to Friar Diego's overtures. But traveling across the Yucatán without using anger as fuel took days of walking, and his silence couldn't hold out forever.

"I came to get my house back," *Adelantado* Francisco said, cracking the silence while they sat next to a cooking fire near the end of their trip. "I ran out of money months ago and the creditors in Santiago de Guatemala cut me off. For a while, Tomás López Medel sponsored me, but even his goodwill ran out."

Friar Diego chuckled. "Of course you came back because of money. The reports said you came back like a king."

"You ruined me," *Adelantado* Francisco said. There wasn't enough fire in his blood to inspire anything more than a whisper.

"Your cruelty to the natives ruined you."

"They were my property, I could do whatever I want with them. And I wasn't cruel."

"You'll confess before this is all over," Friar Diego said.

Adelantado Francisco was thrown in jail as soon as the group set foot in Merida. Friar Diego chose three volunteers as guards, not trusting the local guards after what had happened in Mani—there was no way he would lose the *Adelantado* again. The rest of the men would go back to Izamal with him.

Friar Lorenzo had returned to Merida by the time Friar Diego arrived with his prisoner in tow. With him, ten new friars had come to the Yucatán from Spain. Instead of walking the countryside and acquainting themselves with the New World, as Friar Diego had done, the new friars were tasked with studying Friar Diego's *arte*. The prevailing thought was that the new recruits could become better spreaders of the Christian faith if they had a mastery of the Mayan language before they went to their assigned monastery.

Friar Francisco, the current *Custos*, called a meeting between himself, Friar Diego, and Friar Lorenzo—the first time three men who had held the title of *Custos* met in one place. It took place in an assembly room that had been added to the Merida monastery for future council meetings.

"Now that we're a new province, thanks to Friar Lorenzo's great effort," Friar Francisco said. Friar Lorenzo closed his eyes and dropped his chin in a slight bow. "We need to decide when our next council will be to elect our first Provincial."

"As soon as possible," Friar Diego blurted out. He wanted the election held while his campaigning was fresh in everyone's mind, and he planned on using the second arrest of *Adelantado* Francisco as proof for why he should be the man who would protect their province's best interests.

"September, just like the other elections," Friar Lorenzo said without hesitation.

"I must confess, I was leaning towards September as well. Continuing with tradition," said the current *Custos*.

"Of course, you get to stay in power longer," a pouting Friar Diego said.

"That isn't fair," Friar Lorenzo said. "These are extraordinary times. Friar Francisco has been God's mouth during the transition."

"You know that's what I feared," Friar Francisco said, hurt infiltrating his voice.

Friar Diego apologized. "You're right. I know it isn't true. I've gotten used to talking with the *Adelantado* and I've allowed it to affect my judgment."

"Besides, it's no secret one of you two will assume the role. It's just a matter of time. Then, you'll only answer to Spain and the Pope, no longer having to deal with Guatemala."

Friar Diego and Friar Lorenzo spoke at the same time.

"I'll serve wherever I'm needed," the older friar said.

"God willing," said Friar Diego.

The *Custos* looked at Friar Diego, the hurt from a moment before having evaporated. "When do you plan on holding the *Adelantado*'s trial?"

"After the elections," Friar Diego said. "I don't want there to be any doubt about where the authority lies."

"We are our own province now," said Friar Lorenzo.

"But without a direct equal for Tomás López Medel, the man might be able to sway Spain in the *Adelantado*'s favor," Friar Diego responded.

"We already agreed the retrial will take place as ordered by Guatemala," Friar Francisco said.

"And it will. After the election. I was given charge of the case, and I say he sits in jail over the summer."

Friar Lorenzo cast a pitying glance on Friar Diego. "Your cruelty will be your undoing," he said.

"Is it cruel for us to allow him to live unmolested in Guatemala all these years after passing his sentence? Cruel to allow him to spew his vitriol to the natives in the Campeche market? He has to learn."

"An eye for an eye makes the whole world blind," whispered Friar Lorenzo.

"The natives have to see how we fight for them. This will help earn their trust and, in turn, their conversion. We saw the letter from Princess Joanna, and I'm sure you know what threats Christianity faces in Spain. Our goal isn't fair treatment of treacherous Spaniards; it's conversion of Maya to Christianity."

Though Friar Diego had changed the argument on them, neither man had the energy or desire for conflict.

"You've become cruel and spiteful," Friar Lorenzo said. "But you are in charge of his fate, so do as you see fit."

Friar Diego ignored the criticism.

Friar Francisco concluded the meeting by saying he would send out word to the other monasteries about the upcoming council, the first chapter of the Yucatán Province.

Friar Diego began the trip back to Izamal with the majority of his mercenary force, walking apart from the others and not talking to anyone now that no orders were necessary. The *Adelantado*'s words in the market plagued his thoughts: "You'll suffer the same fate if you ever go against what they say."

"No," Friar Diego whispered. He thought about how the *Adelantado*'s statement had lumped Friar Lorenzo and Friar Francisco in with him. "What *they* say doesn't matter. You'll suffer if you ever go against what *I* say."

CHAPTER THIRTY-SIX

Cortez left his conversation with Remy feeling like he was grateful to even get a meeting. Alara's salvation depended on them being alone, and he didn't have a plan in place if Remy declined the invitation. He walked back through the park thinking about a future with his beloved by his side, sitting between him and his mother at church because the two women in his life had become so close. Let his father stay gone, he thought, they had no room for him in their lives. If he did show up, wanting to be a part of his life after hearing about him and Alara saving the Church, he would slam the door in his face, tell him his chance was left in the prior years. Thoughts of his absent father had filled his head ever since he learned about him from his mother. Before, whenever the man was mentioned, an inflamed void opened in Cortez's heart. Now, that space had closed off, solidified, and been made impenetrable by anger.

The one thing that stuck with Cortez from his mother's confession was her suspicion about another woman. There was no pride about his lineage's responsibility for spreading the Christian message, no sympathy for the trials his mother had endured; instead, his mother's attempt to find an underlying reason why she had been tossed away haunted her son. The mother's story was Alara's story, a relationship with a man who didn't deem her special enough to swear off others. Anger at Remy had been with Cortez from the moment he left the hospital, and he'd woken up with the certainty that his prayers had been answered, that his dreams revealed what he had to do.

In the dream, Cortez had been seated on a wooden platform looking down at a fire. Brown-skinned bodies hung off to one side, tied by their hands, with their heads limp against their chests. He knew they were nonbelievers. Sinners. All around the growing fire stood his own men, their backs to the blaze, armed with thick wooden bats. They wore dirty brown priests's robes and were protecting the fire from more brown-skinned nonbelievers who stood watching the fire in horror. Anguished cries rang out from the witnesses, tears streaming down their faces. A sense of pride grew in dream Cortez as he watched the fire burn, certain the sinners would go to church after the flames of their passion died down, their introduction to the faith leading him to prominence. Maybe, if he was lucky, he had saved enough souls to convince his father to come back and welcome him with open arms, a welcome Cortez would reject, making his revenge complete.

When Cortez awoke, he knew the library would have to burn before the people of the city would come to church. His father would hear about the swelling of their ranks, try to come back into his life, then be shunned for what he did to his mother. It all made perfect sense in Cortez's head, and Remy agreeing to meet him on the top floor of the library was the piece of the puzzle that would guarantee Alara was one of the people whose souls he was responsible for saving.

Back at home, Cortez sat down on the couch, waiting for the

day to pass. He had nothing to do, nowhere to go, and didn't want to see Alara again until after Remy was out of the picture. His mother was still in the hospital. Being alone as an adult for the first time he could remember offered numerous possibilities, but he didn't change a single thing, pretending instead it was a Saturday morning and his mother was still in bed—a Saturday morning that would last all day.

Cortez watched mindless daytime television: first a game show, then a talk show, then he stumbled upon a show about a small claims court, which he ended up watching for multiple episodes. When he grew hungry he ate spoonfuls of peanut butter, one of the few items in his house that hadn't expired during the weekend's storm. The setting sun cast long shadows into his apartment, throwing reflections onto the screen overtop the plaintiff. When the distraction could no longer be ignored, Cortez stood up and closed the blinds. A knock on the door at the same time made him jump.

Nobody was visible through the front door's peephole. Cortez looked left, then right, before a second round of knocking began. Confused, he looked down and saw Simeon, sitting in his wheelchair, his fist pounding on the door. Cortez unlocked the door and opened it enough to look his former friend in the face.

"What do you want?" Cortez said, trying his best to sound angry. It didn't work, and his words came out giving the impression he was constipated.

"I heard your mother's in the hospital and I came by to visit," Simeon answered.

Cortez inspected his slimy eyes and lying tongue, not trusting him for a second.

"And to say I'm sorry. Can I come in?"

Setting boundaries wasn't a part of Cortez's skill set. He

frowned, nodded, then opened the door wide. He walked away, letting Simeon roll in and leaving him to close the door himself.

"How did you get up here?" Cortez said as he retook his position on the couch. He took the stairs every day and couldn't imagine how Simeon had navigated seven flights.

"The elevator. Smells terrible in there," Simeon said. He rolled next to the couch and looked at the television. Cortez turned down the volume.

"Right, the elevator. That's why I don't take it."

"No choice for me," Simeon said, tapping one wheel with his hand.

A moment of silence passed, both trying to come up with something to say.

"Your mom called the boss from the hospital," Simeon began. "She said you would come back by the end of the week, but that you'd be dealing with some extra stress."

"He left a message on the machine," Cortez said, pointing to the telephone mounted on the wall. "He said you don't work there anymore though, so how'd you find out about my mom?"

"Well, I called earlier today to see if there was anything I could do to get my job back. There isn't. But, the boss said since we were friends before, I might like to know your mom was in the hospital, in case I wanted to send a card. I just decided to show up to your building. The mailboxes downstairs told me your room number."

"You should've just sent a card," Cortez said. He looked at the muted television.

"I'm sorry, I didn't know how all this would turn out."

"Well, it's all your fault. If I hadn't lost my job, she wouldn't be in the hospital in the first place!"

"How is it my fault? I got fired too, remember?"

"Her heart couldn't handle finding out I lost my job. *That's* why she's in the hospital. And why did I lose my job? Because of you. Because you had to sell drugs."

"I was just trying to get some extra cash, for both of us!" Simeon said, raising his voice. Then, he deflated. "They caught me taking pints to sell for cash, that's why they fired me."

"That's fair. Unlike mine, where they fired me because you lied about me."

"You shouldn't have left me behind for the cops!"

"Well, you shouldn't have said anything to the boss in the first place for your own idea!" Cortez stood up, looking down at his former friend. After a moment, he said, "You should leave." It was the first time he'd ever kicked someone out of his home, and the first time he'd had to; before then, the apartment had never had visitors.

Simeon turned himself around then rolled to the door. The door opened inward, and Cortez watched Simeon struggle to navigate the confined space while pulling the door open, one hand on the doorknob and one on his wheel. A malicious joy grew in Cortez's heart, the delight of revenge. Simeon turned around after he managed to cross the apartment's threshold.

"One more thing," Simeon said, holding up a finger to Cortez from the hallway.

"What."

"Can you put in a good word with the boss for me?"

Cortez's hand took control of the situation, taking the initiative to lash out and strike Simeon in the nose. A second punch glanced off Simeon's face because, by then, his seat was already tilting back. Simeon's head hit the wall behind him, but the blow didn't knock him out. He propped himself up with his elbows and crawled forward, pulling himself away from his overturned wheelchair. A swift kick to the gut took his breath away, and he curled up into the fetal position.

"There's something wrong with you," Cortez said, looking

down at Simeon. His hands were on the wall opposite his front door, supporting his body for when his leg decided Simeon deserved another strike.

"I could say the same to you," Simeon sputtered. In response, Cortez stomped Simeon's flaccid knees with his right foot. Simeon laughed, knowing his legs hadn't registered a sensation since the day he was born.

One of Cortez's neighbors, a middle-aged man with thick glasses and a mustache, poked his head out and asked if everything was alright. Cortez took one look at him with a maniacal look in his eyes and he shut the door.

"What's so funny?" Cortez demanded.

"My legs are already useless," Simeon responded with a pained chuckle.

Mrs. Wyatt, who lived on the opposite side of the hallway from the middle-aged man, emerged from her apartment. Her youngest child, shirtless but wearing a diaper and turquoise socks, stumbled out and held onto her leg. "What are you doing, young man!" she screamed, beginning to rush forward.

Cortez turned to her. Something in his gaze stopped her in her tracks. "Mind your own business," he said. He looked down at Simeon and got a sense of being Remy, looking down on a weaker victim with disgust.

"Don't let me see you again," Cortez said, doing his best to say the words the way he imagined Remy would say them. He turned around and went back into his apartment, slamming the door behind him. Watching through the peephole, he saw Mrs. Wyatt right Simeon's wheelchair and help him into the seat. While she brushed off his shoulders, Simeon looked right at the peephole and smiled.

No matter how hard she tried, Cortez's mother could never scrub away the shadow that Simeon saw in the space between the bottom of the door and the floor.

. . .

THE NEXT DAY, Cortez got to the library early in the afternoon. The sun was still high in the sky, and the people enjoying the weather, the ones whose jobs didn't tie them to a desk from nine to five each day, partook in a collective laugh at the expense of those who lived and died by the clock. He stood in the park, watching the flow of people he didn't care for going in and out of the entrance, past the pillars and through the massive wooden front door. The enormity of the wide steps in front of the library overwhelmed him. The proximity of the books to the trees, whose sacrificed cousins contained millions of knowledge's words, created dozens of leafy witnesses who stared at Cortez as if they saw the flames in his heart. He couldn't ignore their gaze, and, to settle his soul, even if for a moment, he walked around the building and entered through the rear door.

Compared with seeing the entire library bustling with children during his last visit, the rear entryway was suffused with loneliness. The few people present were silent, their steps muted, as they walked through the smaller lobby. A person at the desk asked for his library card when he approached.

"Nobody asked for my card last time I was here," he remarked as he handed over his card.

The young man at the desk assumed the statement was a complaint. "They should have," he said while he scanned the card.

"There were a lot of kids here," Cortez added.

"Oh, you came during the festival," the library worker said, his attitude changing. "It's a nightmare trying to get everyone to scan then." He handed Cortez's card back to him. "But, according to the rules, we still should've."

Cortez took the card and continued past the desk. He passed a man and woman walking out, each with a book in their hands, keeping his eyes down so he didn't have to acknowledge their presence. In his pocket, bulging against his leg, was a can of soup. It was the heaviest thing he could find in his house, and he hoped it was enough to get the job done. The lighter his mother kept for birthday candles was in his other leg's pocket.

He found the librarian's stand on the second floor of the library, abandoned. He milled about, waiting for someone who could help him. A book about military helicopters on the counter caught his eye. He picked it up, began turning through its pages, and was pleased at the numerous pictures. The timeline of helicopter technology ran from early drawings by Da Vinci about the theoretical machine to modern sand-colored war helicopters. The librarian arrived as he was skimming through the various weapon systems.

"Can I help you?" the librarian asked. It was the woman with green glasses who always wore a shawl.

Cortez remembered the woman's name: Gertrude. He wished he knew the name of the other librarian, the nice one, the one who had helped him despite Gertrude's reluctance. He thought she'd be a good woman for him, if he wasn't sold on Alara.

"I need to check out a book. *Love in the Time of Cholera*," he said, smiling while putting the book about helicopters back down on the counter.

Cortez's cheap impression of a smile stirred something in Gertrude's memory, and she remembered their interaction the weekend before. It had been a busy day, so busy she'd almost forgotten the man who took the warmth from the room. She got goosebumps when she recognized him, shaking her head as she wrapped her shawl tighter around her shoulders. She had never associated Cortez's presence with the temperature change since she lived in a state of perpetual cold.

"I helped you find that a few days ago," she said. She looked beneath the counter. "Elisabeth still hasn't put it back," she said, annoyed.

"Thanks," Cortez said, staring at the cover.

"Did you need anything else?" Gertrude asked.

"Yes, I'd like to watch a movie on the top floor," he said, holding the book by his side.

"Those rooms are for educational purposes only," Gertrude replied.

"I've done it before," Cortez said.

"What did you want to watch?" Gertrude acquiesced with a sigh, wanting to rid herself of the visitor. She would have made Elisabeth handle the man and the problem her charity had created if the woman had been working that day. As it was, she cursed her coworker for showing Cortez sympathy in the first place.

"I don't care," he said. He traced the helicopter on the cover of the book with his index finger. "Something long."

The librarian's eyes pierced Cortez through her green spectacles. She waited for him to notice her glare, but he never looked at her face. Giving up, she told Cortez to follow her.

Together, they went to the selection of movies. Seeing his interest in the military helicopters and assuming his tastes included all facets of war, she chose a four-part documentary about World War II. "This one is long, especially if you go through all four parts," she told him, handing him the first installment.

"Can you give me all of them?" Cortez asked.

Gertrude almost said no, almost confronted him about what he was running away from that he wanted to spend hours watching television at the library, but instead nodded and handed him the discs in their plastic containers. "Hours of entertainment," she said.

Cortez didn't pick up on the sarcasm. He thanked the librarian and confirmed he could use any room on the top floor.

"Some of the rooms don't have TVs," she said. "The rooms on the other side of the stacks just have desks. You won't be able to use those."

"Stacks? I didn't see any when I was up there last time."

"Magazine stacks. They're behind the first hall of rooms. If you didn't walk very far down the aisle you wouldn't have seen the cut-through."

Cortez thought about the stacks, considered the ways he could use them. "Filled with magazines, huh?" he said, his plan coalescing.

"And bundles of newspapers. The stuff nobody uses except the journalists." Gertrude started walking back and Cortez followed. "The library saves what everyone ignores," she said with pride.

"Good to know," Cortez said. He turned into the staircase as they walked past it, leaving Alara's favorite book on a shelf near the break in the bookshelves. The librarian was left describing the various magazine and newspaper subscriptions the library had collected over the years, and the task of cataloging the numerous volumes, to the air around her. When she turned around and noticed her words were wasted on thin air, she shook her head and cursed Elisabeth once more for empowering the strange young man.

Cortez walked up the stairs and past the room where he'd watched the movie that taught him Remy had to die before he could be with Alara. He found the space between the rooms that led to the stacks that Gertrude had mentioned and, walking through, found a vast expanse of metal bookshelves. They all reached to the ceiling, each one holding a different number of magazines, depending on the width of the spine. An entire collection of thin magazines about the advancement of chemical processes was on a single shelf, while the collection of landscape architecture magazines, thick with pictures, took up all the shelves on two full bookcases.

Cortez found the newspaper bundles behind the rooms near the entrance, at the farthest point from the access point that ran through the rooms. Newspapers from every major city in the country, with small placards beneath each stack of bundles, were all tied up with twine and a neat bow on top.

After his inspection of the area behind the rooms, Cortez returned to the aisle and chose the room farthest from the staircase, turned on the light, inserted the movie, and began waiting.

CHAPTER THIRTY-SEVEN

THE SUMMER SUN bore down on Ahkinmai as he approached the new Izamal monastery for Sunday mass. He walked up a sloped stone path among a throng of fellow Mayan worshippers to the immense open courtyard in front of the sanctuary. The courtyard was surrounded by a paved covered walkway; the walkway was bordered by two layers of repeating stone arches supporting the roof. These arches stood upon stone walls that elevated the courtyard above the level of the settlement—anyone approaching the church from the town saw stone walls with arches on top. Walking up the angled stone path revealed the immense courtyard it bisected; it ended at the enormous sanctuary. Three crosses looked down on the courtyard from the sanctuary's three peaks, and beneath the middle cross were two openings in the wall filled with three bells each. Beneath the bells, cut into the stone, was another space, this one filled with stained glass—a colorful rendition of the Virgin Mary.

"It's the same as the statue inside," Ahkinmai heard the worshippers whisper among themselves, their eyes squinting in the sunlight reflecting off the colored glass.

Ahkinmai had heard about the statue and all the rumored

miracles it performed. Despite his fellow Maya's certainty regarding the strength of the idol and the underlying strength of the religion from where it drew its power, he believed the true source of the power was the holy location Friar Diego de Landa had chosen for his monastery nine years ago. In his books were numerous examples of successful sacrifices held at the destroyed temple, detailing how droughts had been ended and crops rejuvenated when the old gods were shown their proper deference.

Friar Nicolás de Albalate admitted worshippers into the space in waves, creating a line that stretched across the courtyard. The heat was stifling; Ahkinmai was glad he had foregone wearing his feathered cape and headdress. Beads of sweat trickled from his forehead and underarms and, judging from the smell, the rest of the native Maya were sweating as well. The space on each side of the path was covered with grass shoots, small green dots on dark black dirt. Ahkinmai had heard about Mayan men transporting dirt from the most prosperous *milpas* and regretted where the life-giving soil had ended up. While many of the natives found humor in the relocation, seeing the discontent with the original soil as childlike, Ahkinmai was saddened by the second-guessing of what nature had deemed the correct spot for plant growth. Seeing the way in which the Franciscans wasted the vitalizing potential in the dirt by growing grass and knowing how many natives had starved after being forced from their homes filled him with a sense of pity for the foreign men who didn't appreciate the natural rhythm of his homeland.

Ahkinmai still wore bright green feathers on the piece of fabric hanging from his waist. Friar Nicolas spotted them then looked at him, inspecting his face. It was the first time any of the friars had seen Ahkinmai without his ceremonial garb. Out of respect, Friar Nicolás gave Ahkinmai a deeper nod than most, which the rest of the natives didn't witness because their gaze was transfixed on the altar and what sat behind it: the statue of the Virgin Mary.

The statue sat in an indentation in the back wall, high off the ground. The bottom of the space could be accessed by a full-grown man reaching up. An array of candles on the ledge were burning bright, flicking light on the statue's face and making the woman's face alive. Light spilled in from two enormous windows in the right wall, illuminating rows of wooden pews. Halfway along each side wall was a pair of doors, leading to the rest of the building and all the attached facilities the Franciscans in Izamal required: the infirmary, the school, and the living quarters. The friars had moved their base of operations from the original location as soon as construction was completed, leaving behind their facilities for the students. Ahkinmai questioned the students' abandonment of their old encampment and its traditional structure, knowing their overtaking of the previous monastery was another step forward in the eventual complete adoption of the Spanish way of living.

None of the other Maya sat next to Ahkinmai, leaving a space on each side of him during worship. He couldn't decide if it was out of respect or because they wanted distance between the old religion and the new, but regardless of the reason he sat up straight, mimicking more seasoned worshippers, taking in the majesty of the space while wondering who had been the first people to decide worshipping higher powers should take place indoors.

The service Ahkinmai attended was for the Maya, spoken in their language except for the traditional prayers and Bible verses. Though the Franciscans preferred mixed services, in both Spanish and the Mayan language, the outsized crowds they expected at services in the new facility made them shelf their own preferences in service of practicality. The Spanish colonists had worshipped earlier that day, flooding the town with words of praise about the new space's perfection after the conclusion of their mass. Continuous awed chatter from rows of seated Maya filled the sanctuary until the right-side door opened and Friar Diego emerged with the rest of the Franciscans stationed at Izamal. A silence radiated out that was so pervasive even babies who still relied on their mother's milk turned their attention to the priests, mesmerized by the pageantry.

Each of the four friars walked in carrying religious paraphernalia in their hands. The first friar led the way with a golden incense burner swinging from a golden chain. The smoke diffused into the rows closest to the procession, where the seated Maya drank the aroma with deep inhales through their nostrils. Next came a friar holding a golden bowl filled with water; he dipped his fingers in the liquid and alternated splashing to his left and right. The natives sitting on the wooden bench nearest the priests stuck their feet out, hoping droplets would land on their skin and wash away their sins. Friar Nicolás came third, carrying an enormous golden cross mounted atop a dark wooden pole; he was followed by Friar Diego, clutching the Bible.

Over the next hour and a half, Ahkinmai listened as Friar Diego led the group in a series of memorized prayers and songs, then interpreted the message for the congregation. Though he didn't know any of the words, he bowed when necessary, kneeled when commanded, and stood when invited. Paying attention took his full stores of energy; he reminded himself about the strength of the Franciscan God, the one that inspired Friar Diego's hornet-like fearlessness. Despite his best intentions, he couldn't help comparing their worship to the ceremonies he held for the Maya, outside and in nature's presence. The enclosed space made him long for the outdoors. The stifling of his soul, the abandonment of his fervor, and the disgust for his impulses were all galvanized by the droning Friar Diego in the summer heat.

Ahkinmai withdrew into himself while the rest of the Maya around Izamal lost themselves in worshipping the Christian God. He thought about the recent ceremony, his least-attended in years, where they'd had just enough men for the Dance of the Warriors. The incantations he had spoken that day rang clear in his mind, and he repeated them to himself during Holy Communion, while Friar Diego reminded everyone they were eating their savior. Ahkinmai declined the ritual, thinking how sacrificing a human wasn't as gruesome as eating one; in particular, the consumption of the alleged savior of their souls didn't sit well with him. He recalled the Mayan prayers for ending droughts, the ones he read about in his ancient texts that had been written before him and would be read by those who came after, and recited them to himself, knowing the land where he sat still possessed some of the power despite the missing temple.

It was the first and last time the Mayan gods were worshipped in the new Izamal sanctuary.

By the end of the service, Ahkinmai's legs were filled with so much restlessness that each of his ten toes wiggled with impatience. He struggled with staying seated while the friars walked down the sanctuary's middle aisle, then shifted from left to right and rocked back and forth while he stood with the rest of the Maya waiting for the post-worship blessing. Those who saw him thought the bathroom was calling him, or a scorpion had crawled up his leg, never knowing he was repeating the footsteps of the Dance of the Warriors alone, in miniature, under the watchful eye of the Virgin Mary.

Friar Diego gave Ahkinmai his blessing, asking the Mayan priest what he thought of the new church.

"It looked better before," Ahkinmai said, still dancing.

"Before it was painted?" Friar Diego said, smiling.

"No, before it was destroyed."

Ahkinmai left the stunned friar behind, walking straight across the courtyard and down the stone path back to ground level. He continued walking until he was deep in the surrounding wilderness, where he found the oldest tree he could find and sat down with his back against it, his hands buried in the dirt and clutching its roots.

A perturbed Friar Diego didn't let Ahkinmai's reaction diminish his elation. The rest of the worshippers that day, both Mayan and Spanish, were more involved than ever. Despite Friar Nicolás not yet having calculated the day's attendance, Friar Diego knew they had set a record for a single day. Even if it was because of the novelty of the new facility, the Lord's words now had the chance to crack through the shell surrounding the hearts of the people of Izamal and salvage the soul within. Ahkinmai's criticism, Friar Diego thought, was understandable; after all, they had destroyed his religion's temple when making the new monastery. The man would need time before accepting the new location, and the fact the Mayan priest had showed up at all was still a step forward in the Christian faith.

The Izamal monastery made waves within the Franciscan community. Before long, members of the Order started showing up unannounced, saying they were curious about the facility with the highest average attendance. Friar Diego had kept the size of the atrium a secret during construction, but now that word had spread that it was second in size only to Rome's, Spanish settlers from all over the Yucatán came and worshipped alongside the visiting Franciscans. Even the *Custos* showed up, saying he was proud of the facility and how the statue of the Virgin Mary now had a resting place worthy of her splendor.

Friar Diego seized on the opportunity given to him by the visiting friars. Most of the men who visited him were the Guardians of their facilities, having left their men behind during their trip. Friar Diego made no secret about his desire for the position of Provincial at the upcoming council, using the success of his monastery in leading large numbers of worshippers to God as a springboard into a conversation about his true desire: the oversight of *Adelantado* Francisco Hernandez's punishment. No matter how much success Friar Diego had, the man's continued existence proved a splinter he couldn't extract. The accusation of friars stealing native women struck too close to home, cut a hole too deep, and Friar Diego still seethed as the wounded part of him, which he kept hidden with great effort, oozed hate into his blood, carried into his extremities by his furious heart.

This was how everyone in the Yucatán, with the exception of Friar Francisco Navarro and Friar Lorenzo de Bienvenida, knew who the next Provincial would be without a single vote yet cast. Friar Diego rode the wave of good fortune into Merida and found himself seated at the first chapter of the Yucatán Province as Friar Francisco de Navarro began the election process. The *Custos* had already announced Friar Lorenzo and Friar Diego as the two candidates up for election and had waited in case any others were put forth. When none came, the process began.

"First, a show of hands for Friar Diego de Landa."

Two people's hands didn't shoot up; both had once held the title of *Custos*. Everyone else knew Friar Diego was a force in the Yucatán, his election all but guaranteed, and even if they thought Friar Lorenzo would be a better Provincial, they didn't want their vote cast on the wrong side of history. Friar Diego accepted the role of Provincial with a dignified word of thanks to his peers. Showing the proper amount of deference to Friar

Lorenzo, and not wanting him assigned to any specific monastery, the chapter bestowed upon him the title of Definitor, an advisory role still above the fray of traditional monastery activities.

The rest of the chapter's decisions concerned shuffling friars around the Yucatán. None of the Guardians were changed, just the friars under them. The new recruits brought from Spain were assigned to established monasteries, and veteran friars were sent to new locations as reinforcements to those having trouble converting their Maya population.

Friar Lorenzo congratulated Friar Diego and, with a dejected nod, left the room. Friar Francisco, who was going back to Campeche by his own choice, asked Friar Diego for a word after the council. The two men ended up alone in the assembly room, where they sat down in the row of wooden benches closest to the door.

"You already talked to everyone before the vote, didn't you?" Friar Francisco said.

"I simply reminded them of the services I've rendered the Yucatán Province. Their vote was their own."

"You could have told me so I could soften the blow for Friar Lorenzo."

"And what, have you whisper to the others in his favor?"

Friar Francisco pursed his lips together and the skin on his cheeks sagged around his jaw. His watery eyes gave him the appearance of a sad dog. "All these years of friendship and you still scheme behind my back," he said.

Friar Diego leaned forward, turned, and surrounded his friend's hands with his own. "It's not personal. All I care about is the conversion of the natives. To do that most effectively, I have to be Provincial. This was not an indictment of you, or of Friar Lorenzo."

Friar Francisco pulled his hands away and stood up. "Imagine how he feels!"

Friar Diego patted the spot next to him. "Sit down, there's no reason to get worked up about this," he said.

Friar Francisco obeyed. "Imagine how he feels," he repeated, less impassioned. "He went over to Spain, secured our independence, and isn't even trusted with its stewardship. The man was one of the first in the Yucatán and has done more to support our men here than anyone else, including you."

Friar Diego nodded. "You're right. There's no denying his support of the Franciscans. But I've been the one most concerned with supporting the Maya in their understanding of the Christian faith. That's what won the votes."

"Still, you should have told me. We've been making plans about the church's next steps."

"What kind of next steps?"

"A standardized school curriculum, increased Mayan presence within our order. We think a native could become a priest, in time."

Friar Diego thought about his own students and their work converting remote natives. Then, he thought about Ix and the prayers he had taught her. Her memory filled him with an immeasurable sadness; between wetted blinks, he bottled the emotion and buried it deep inside.

"Those are worthwhile tasks," Friar Diego said. "I'll want both of your input in due time."

"You'll get his. I'm going back to Campeche. I need a break from all this," Friar Francisco said, waving an outstretched arm to the room.

Both men laughed.

"Make sure you keep Friar Lorenzo involved. He loves the Yucatán, and will provide a steady voice of reason," Friar Francisco said.

"We named him Definitor, didn't we? He'll have his chance for input. There are some things I need to take care of first."

"The *Adelantado.*"

"Correct."

"That poor man. He should have never crossed you."

"He'll learn that lesson if it's the last thing he does on this earth."

Before Friar Diego took care of the *Adelantado*, he made sure the men who'd helped secure the prisoner were paid. They had hounded him in Izamal like amateur tax collectors during the weeks between the prisoner transport and Friar Diego's assuming of the role of Provincial. None of them threatened outright violence, but Friar Diego could tell some of the angrier men, hard-pressed with debts, were close to losing their temper. He made sure every man involved in the operation was paid, minus the few loans he'd arranged for the ones who needed money for necessities. Friar Diego took the money for the prisoner's transportation from the portion of the church's funds dedicated to helping struggling colonists. He believed the church shouldn't provide any money or services to the Spanish, that all available resources were better served going to the Maya. After all, their conversion was what mattered; the Spanish, born into religious indoctrination, were already Christian. However, by taking resources from struggling Spaniards and giving them to the Maya—or in pursuit of aims that would further the conversion of the Maya, which he believed he was doing with the trial of *Adelantado* Francisco—he'd created a generation of Maya-hating Spaniards, young men left to their own devices by the Franciscans' lack of support who also ended up hating the church more than any of the men who were discontented by Friar Diego's delay in payment.

. . .

Adelantado Francisco was in a miserable state when he saw his captor return as Provincial. Large sores had emerged on his backside from living in his own filth; they'd multiplied until they covered his back and legs. Most of his teeth had fallen out, yellowed victims of his meager diet of watered-down chicken broth and bread crusts. When his guards wanted entertainment, they threw in pieces of dried meat and watched as the starving man attacked the scraps, chewing them with bleeding gums before giving up and swallowing the hard piece whole. The guards said he looked like a pelican, gulping down a large fish.

Friar Diego was pleased the same men he'd left as guards were still there, and arranged for extra pay for their quality service. He covered his nose with his habit because of the stench emitted by the *Adelantado*.

"What's going on with him?"

"He's rotten, through and through," one of the men joked.

"It's his soul," Friar Diego said. He was on the lookout for smells similar to the *Adelantado*'s from then on, hoping he could find sinners before they caused trouble for him or his flock.

Friar Diego ordered a stool placed in front of the bars. He sat down, still holding his habit over his mouth and nose. There was no regret for the *Adelantado*'s condition; after all, the man had brought his treatment upon himself.

"Are you ready to confess?" Friar Diego said, getting straight to the point.

The *Adelantado* looked surprised. "Confess? Without even a trial?"

"Correct."

"Why would I do that?"

"You may have heard I'm Provincial."

"I can't hear you. Show me your mouth."

Friar Diego dropped the habit with a look of disgust. The *Adelantado*, knowing his wretched condition, smiled.

"You were saying?"

"You may have heard: I'm now Provincial. As such, I can delay your trial indefinitely. The trial that, I'm telling you right now, I'll judge and come to the exact same sentence."

The *Adelantado*'s expression remained unchanged, but his eyes betrayed an impotent rage.

"So, confess here and we can skip all the steps in between."

Adelantado Francisco shook his head no.

All of a sudden, Friar Diego stood up and picked up the stool. "Very well. Call me when you're ready."

Friar Diego's election had taken place at the end of September 1561, and he had met with *Adelantado* Francisco during the first week of October. Over the next three weeks, news of the *Adelantado*'s worsening condition reached Friar Diego via the Merida monastery's other friars, who were concerned for the prisoner. Then, Friar Lorenzo intervened.

"He's dying," said Friar Lorenzo. "The smell of death is heavy around him."

"It's his own stubbornness. He doesn't have to stay in there; all he has to do is confess."

"You could start the trial. It's his right."

"And it's mine to make him wait."

"At least reduce his suffering," Friar Lorenzo pleaded. "His treatment is inhumane."

"Would you rather I tie him to a post and whip him until he dies? Or maybe I club him in the head, send him away running scared and helpless and defecating all over himself?" Friar Diego said. He was breathing heavy, having relived the experiences of the *Adelantado*'s treatment of the natives and feeling the associated revulsion.

"Eye for an eye," Friar Lorenzo said, leaving Friar Diego alone with the smell of excrement in his nostrils.

Adelantado Francisco told his guards he was ready to

confess as October drew to a close. Friar Diego arrived soon after with a scribe, and together they heard the *Adelantado* admit to mistreating the natives, withholding them from Christian education, and attempting to undermine the Franciscan authority by slandering their members.

Friar Diego focused on the question of Franciscan authority, and by extension his own, wringing a number of confessions out of the *Adelantado* about his attempts to circumvent their oversight. The *Adelantado* even confessed to a number of made-up charges, such as sleeping with native boys and girls, further damaging his reputation and making it clear to any *encomenderos* who thought they could undermine the Franciscans' power what could happen in response.

Francisco Hernandez, stripped of his title and half his land, was released into the custody of local Merida *encomenderos* who had fought alongside him in the initial conquest of the Yucatán. Having received the *Adelantado*'s confession, thereby solidifying his own power, and not wanting death on his hands, Friar Diego decided the man wouldn't survive public humiliation in his current state. It was postponed until Hernandez's health returned.

It never did. Francisco Hernandez died one week later, penniless and ruined, at the age of forty-two. When Friar Diego heard, he shrugged—all he cared about was that the Yucatán now knew that his power to protect the natives from the Spaniards was absolute.

CHAPTER THIRTY-EIGHT

REMY WAS STILL at work while Cortez was in the library. He had scheduled meetings all day, and not once did he give any consideration to his day's final meeting, the one with Cortez. After Cortez's initial confrontation, when he'd learned evidence of his cheating existed and was in Cortez's possession, he decided that, regardless of the outcome, he would deny it if confronted by Alara. It was his duty, as a man, to hold his ground, not to admit his sampling of other women, in order to preserve his honor. Denial would also be helpful for her, would give her peace of mind, and the last thing she needed was to second-guess her own quality as a woman because Remy wanted to taste other flavors. His day had started the same way every other day began, and his meetings ran like clockwork, efficient chunks of time where he could say anything and still collect money. He told his father about his success after each meeting, where prospects transformed into clients; the man then congratulated him, told him how proud he was of him, and urged him to keep up the momentum.

When Remy looked at his calendar and saw he had no more work meetings that day, he tilted his head back and succumbed to the dread of meeting Cortez. He was annoyed the man was taking his time, his most precious asset, and he had to tell Alara he couldn't pick her up from work before dinner; their date had been planned before Cortez approached him on the street, and he had forgotten about it when he agreed to the time. When he left the office at quarter to six, the secretary told him to have a good night.

"We'll see about that," he said, letting the pronouncement hang in the air.

Remy didn't know the library's location because he'd never been there before; his father had bought any books he needed for school brand new. He looked up his destination's address before he left the office and was surprised the institution was in prime real estate, next to the park in the heart of the city. His surprise doubled when he approached the imposing stone building, with its wide staircase and extravagant carvings atop broad pillars, and he wondered why he had never been there before. For the first time in his life, he experienced a twinge of regret for never having visited the library as a child, and for not reading any books as an adult. The grandeur of the design betrayed its power, and Remy vowed to return under different circumstances to investigate what the city's planners deemed important enough to devote such vast resources to keeping safe.

After walking up the front steps and feeling his legs burn, he looked around and wondered why nobody was using them for exercise. His head was filled with the ways he would train in the space when he pushed open the immense wooden doors and entered a lobby that rivaled any in the city.

"Hello," the women at the front desk said in unison. Both had on glasses, wore their hair tied back, and had on no makeup —the type of women Remy expected would be drawn to work in a place full of books.

Remy nodded and kept walking, intent on getting his meeting over with as soon as possible.

"You have to scan your card," the woman closest to him said, her cheeks flushed.

"Card?"

"Your library card. We can issue you one if you don't have one."

This was how Remy got his first library card. He used it once.

Remy left the women behind, giggling, telling them he'd be back to say goodbye before he left. He went in search of the way to the meeting's location. Climbing the main staircase in the lobby brought him to the second floor. Once there, he approached the librarian and asked about getting to the top floor.

Gertrude shook her head, annoyed that, for the second time that day, a young man had requested access to the area that was reserved for educational purposes. But one look into Remy's eyes erased her reluctance and spread tentacles of warmth throughout her body. "The staircase is back there," she said, pointing to where Cortez had disappeared and left her talking to herself. "What do you need help with?"

"I'm meeting someone up there," he said, scowling.

Remy turned away and left Gertrude wondering what kind of arrangement the two very different young men had that required them to watch a long movie. She reminded herself that love takes many forms. She got the urge to check on them if they didn't come down soon, then decided against it because she didn't want to walk in on them in an embarrassing situation. She assumed the charming young man's smile hid his secret, and if he didn't need her help with books, she could at least provide a measure of privacy.

. . .

The only illuminated room on the fourth floor was at the far end of the hallway. Remy shook his head, frustrated at Cortez for making his life difficult and not choosing the first room. The walking wasn't what bothered him, it was the extra time; he wanted the confrontation finished. A sliver of trepidation entered his mind while he walked through the unlit darkness, wondering what kind of proof Cortez could have. Why had Alara ever brought the pitiful creature into their lives in the first place? He toyed around with the idea of letting Cortez give her the evidence and inflict pain on her heart, as punishment for giving a parasite access to their lives. Lost in thought, Remy didn't notice the space between the rooms that led to the magazine stacks and bundles of newspapers, or the eyes peering at him through the darkness.

Remy stood outside the closed door. The blinds were drawn closed. From seeing inside the other empty rooms, he knew the enclosed space was small. He snorted and shook his head, thinking about Cortez's foolishness—the man was no match for him and posed zero physical threat.

Cortez watched Remy stand in front of the closed door from the aisle that cut through to the stacks. He'd never imagined his target would stand still for so long. It was as if he was waiting for Cortez to sneak up behind him and attack. The moment before Cortez made his move, Remy reached forward and walked into the study room, leaving Cortez alone in the dark hall.

Opening the door released the sound of the playing documentary into the top floor. The narrator was talking about German propaganda efforts leading up to and during the Jewish population's internment. The room was empty, and Remy thought perhaps this was a message from Cortez. He spent the next few moments staring at the screen, wondering how his situation was similar and what Cortez implied by showing him this material. His best guess was that Cortez thought he was leading Alara on in a similar way to how the Germans led its citizens to believe their lies about the Jewish population, but he dismissed the comparison as ludicrous. As the narrator continued on about the power of words to shape the future, Remy was struck in the back of the head by a can of soup.

The way Cortez had imagined it, the blow would knock Remy out. It was how it was always done in the movies, except they used the butt of a gun. When Cortez tried to recreate the scene in real life, his victim stumbled forward, his hand on the back of his head, annoyed.

"What was that?"

Knowing it would have been safer to hit a beehive than to stay in the small room, Cortez turned and ran into the rows of magazines. He had a head start on Remy, and while he ran he looked down at the can in his hand. It was dented on the side because Cortez had held it sideways when he struck. The new dent made it easier to palm.

"What the hell's the matter with you?" Remy yelled from the aisle that cut through the rooms. He didn't know where Cortez was, but he knew he was among the shelves. He started walking forward, peering down one aisle at a time.

Cortez was on the far side of a long bookshelf, hoping his heavy breathing wouldn't give him away. Fear rose from his legs, urging him to flee, but he suppressed the feeling with the certainty that he was saving Alara. God would smile down on him as long as he did what was necessary for love. His love for her made everything manageable, the whole world—even its distasteful parts—palatable, and Remy was the one thing standing in their way. In *his* way.

When Cortez heard Remy's voice pass from his right to his left, he ran down the aisle on his right. He didn't notice Remy had stopped speaking, calling his name, or asking him questions that would never be answered. Cortez clutched the can in his hand and peeked around the corner.

Remy had guessed Cortez would try sneaking up behind him. It was just the type of thing the coward would do, catch him when his back was turned instead of facing him like a man. When he was walking forward, looking down the aisles, he was laying a trap, always certain the true threat was behind him, not ahead. Once he got close to the far wall he stopped talking, certain it was a matter of time before Cortez emerged to finish the job. Remy wouldn't let him. He snuck from bookshelf to bookshelf, slow when he turned the corner of each, ready for Cortez to emerge. He didn't have a sense of what he would do when he caught him, since hurting him with his fists hadn't produced the desired results, and he couldn't imagine any amount of pain would stop Cortez's pursuit.

Both men saw each other with an entire aisle's width between them—Cortez crouched, Remy standing tall. After a breathless moment where neither man made a move, Cortez pulled back and Remy ran after him. The chase didn't last long; although Cortez ran for his life, Remy exercised every day. Remy tackled Cortez, knocking the soup can from his hand.

Remy's firm grip held Cortez fast when the pursued tried scrambling away. Remy climbed to his knees and his first punch landed right in Cortez's stomach. All of his anger towards the interloper came out in a flurry of body strikes, leaving Cortez with a sore liver, bruised kidney, and swollen spleen. Before Remy exhausted all of his anger, he stood up and pulled Cortez to standing. "You're going to show me this evidence you have," he said, pulling Cortez by the shirt back towards the room now educating the hall's air about the German treatment of the Jewish population.

Cortez allowed Remy to drag him the length of the aisle. Through watering eyes he saw they were about to reach the end of the bookshelf and turn back towards the cut-through and the room. Thoughts of Alara, of how grateful she would be when she found out he'd saved her, trickled into his mind, replacing the pain. When Remy turned the corner, Cortez pushed with all his might, twisting away. Remy's grip never faltered; Cortez's shirt ripped. He ran back down the aisle, in the direction from where they came, and dove for the soup can.

Remy, in close pursuit, had reached out to grab a hold of Cortez the moment he dove. Reaching through thin air caused him to lose his balance and he fell. He got back onto his knees and scrambled towards Cortez when a blow struck him in the mouth. He tasted blood and discovered stones rattling in his mouth.

"My teeth," he said, his hands under his chin, catching both blood and pieces of chipped tooth.

That moment was the opportunity Cortez needed. With all his might, he wound up and smashed the edge of the soup can against Remy's skull, behind his ear, knocking him out.

Remy woke up with a throbbing headache, the pain radiating down to the base of his neck. He was seated with his chin down against his chest, the weight of his skull too much to bear. His eyes fluttered open then closed when they realized full exposure to the room's light was overwhelming. Unable to focus, he saw what looked like throw-up on the left side of his shirt through the blur. He took a deep breath, allowing the internal air pressure to lift his chin while keeping his eyes closed. In the background he heard about the German war strategy: blitzkrieg. Strike fast, with power, to break through the opponent's defenses. The smell of tacos reached his nostrils. Once he identified the smell, he couldn't ignore it. The vapors surrounded him, emanated from him. He didn't remember eating Mexican food. Thinking about what he ate that day jogged his memory: leaving work, going to the library, and Cortez. He opened his eyes wide, ignoring the pain, forcing them to take in the world around him as he came back from the darkness.

Seated in front of Remy, his back to the television, was Cortez. His hands were folded on the table, patient hands matching his patient face. He was waiting for Remy's return from unconsciousness with pleasure.

Remy lunged forward, and sharp bites cut into his wrists. Leaning back, he found his legs tied to the chair, each one lashed just above the ankle. He stared at Cortez, enraged.

"What did you do?" he said.

Something in Cortez had changed while Remy was unconscious. The man seated across from him was both disconnected and alert, like a puppet master watching his performance from above. His hair stuck out at odd angles, his shirt was stretched and torn; nevertheless, he exuded the tranquility of someone who had accepted their purpose in life and was committed to seeing it play out until the end. Each breath Cortez took produced a smiling grimace, the pain welcome, a reminder of his sacred duty.

"I tied you up!" Cortez said in a singsong voice, as if nothing could be more obvious. His pupil had asked a frivolous question that produced a wonderful teaching moment.

"Why?"

Cortez grinned, followed by an almost imperceptible tilt of his head and batting of his eyelashes. "So you couldn't come after me anymore! You were going crazy." Cortez held an index finger to his head, swirling it around his temple.

Remy tried to pull his hands apart. His wrists received a second biting sting for the effort. "Where did you get the rope?"

"Oh, there's *tons* of it," Cortez said in an offhand manner. "The library uses it for the newspapers."

The library. Remy thought about the librarians below, wondering if any of them had heard their skirmish. He looked at Cortez, inspected the smiling face.

"Help!" he yelled out as loud as he could. "Help! I need help!"

Cortez made no effort to silence his prisoner. He stared at Remy, delight in his eyes. "The door's shut, Remy. They can't hear you."

Yelling created an unbearable pressure behind Remy's eyes. He shut them and bowed his head, trying to calm himself with deep, even breaths. Immobilization in the chair produced a sense of helplessness he had never before experienced in his entire structured life, and he couldn't ignore the agitation in his gut the state produced. The smell of Mexican food reached his nostrils once more. He opened his eyes, looking at the remnants on his chest. There were pieces of cubed chicken, corn, and beans, all unchewed. "Did you pour soup on me?" he asked.

Cortez pulled his lips away from clenched teeth, looking sheepish. "Sorry about that," he said, standing up. He walked around the table and brushed the food from Remy's chest, then wiped his wet hand on his pant leg. "Chicken tortilla soup. I just picked a can from the house. It exploded."

Remy shook his head, unable to believe what Cortez was telling him. The ridiculousness of the confrontation made him chuckle, then laugh. "You're telling me . . . you asked me to come to the library . . . so you could knock me out with a can of *soup*?" Remy said, howling with laughter.

Cortez sat back down and laughed along with him. "That was the plan," he said. "I got lucky with the newspaper bundles."

"Lucky?" Remy said.

Cortez pulled the lighter from his pocket and flicked it, creating a small flame. "I would've had to act faster if I couldn't tie you up." A dark shadow passed over Cortez's face, making his face, with its sunken cheeks, look like a skeleton with two glittering chunks of anthracite in its eye sockets.

Remy choked on the awareness of Cortez's ultimate plan. On the television, the narrator started discussing the creation of the concentration camps.

"Why don't we forget this ever happened?" Remy said. "We can go our separate ways, put the whole thing behind us."

Cortez slammed his fist against the table. "I don't want you to forget, Remy. That's all you do, forget about everyone else but you. Like you're the only one who matters around here! You forget, Alara forgets; everyone forgets about me!" He stood up and started pacing the room, talking to Remy as if he were a member of a vast crowd of listeners who, now that he had their attention, Cortez wouldn't let go without them hearing what he had to say. "My whole life I've done the *right* thing. Done what people expected of me. And what do I get for it? Nothing! I get left behind, ignored—" He turned to Remy. "Forgotten. It's time people like you learn you aren't untouchable."

"People like me?" Remy said, lashing out with his own anger.

"People on your side of the city! You all act like we don't exist on the other side of the park. The part that needs to stay hidden—out of the limelight, away from the world. Well, I have news for you, *Remy*. We aren't all drug dealers! We aren't all insects hiding in the shadows, scurrying around at night. What if we want to see the daylight too? What if I want to be seen? Did you ever think about that?" Cortez punctuated the final word with a slap on the table.

CHAPTER THIRTY-NINE

THE MONTHS after Friar Diego de Landa's promotion to Provincial were the most fulfilling he had ever experienced in the New World. He declared Izamal as the seat of his office, making his new monastery the central location of the Yucatán Province. Both Spanish and Mayan worshippers continued coming from all over the province for mass in the awe-inspiring facility, and the Virgin of Izamal, the statue of the Virgin Mary, was venerated by all who laid eyes on her sculpted face. The Franciscans at Izamal held multiple services a day, with many more on Sundays, accommodating the vast numbers that descended on their town. An entire industry of temporary housing sprang up, giving the Maya around Izamal a money-making opportunity in taking care of the town's guests. Friar Diego took full credit for their increased prosperity.

The other Spanish landowners in the Yucatán took care of the *Adelantado*'s abandoned lands. They decided a young man who had been born in Mani to Spanish parents would take over the lands, and they made sure the decision was approved by Friar Diego, acknowledging his role in the peaceful coexistence between Mayan, Franciscan, and Spanish inhabitants of the province. Friar Diego consulted Nachi Cocom before giving his approval, who in turn consulted the Maya around Mani who had interacted with the family in question. The family was renowned for their humane treatment of the natives on their *encomienda*, a fact that Friar Diego took as a further nod to Franciscan authority. Nachi himself took the natives who had once lived on the *Adelantado*'s lands back home, helping them pull down the *Adelantado*'s wife's skeleton from the mansion, airing out the buildings, and preparing the grounds for the new *encomendero.* The landowners chose the most powerful Spanish landowner in Merida as their new *Adelantado*, hoping his proximity to the former Franciscan seat of power would offer favorable conditions for collaboration, not knowing Friar Diego had transferred all power from Merida to Izamal.

The early months of 1562 passed with a consistency Friar Diego had dreamed of since first arriving in the Yucatán. The students attended school, the adults attended mass, and there were no reports of Spanish mistreatment of the natives on the numerous *encomiendas.* But then, in early May, Friar Diego received troubling news from Mani. Two native youths, students at the Mani monastery's school, had been hunting in the countryside when they discovered a cave with human skulls and idols within. They told Friar Pedro de Ciudad Rodrigo, the Guardian of the Mani monastery, who ordered all the bones and idols brought to the church.

"We examined them and found evidence of their recent use," Friar Pedro wrote to Friar Diego.

The news was troubling. The Franciscans knew some natives had continued worshipping their idols but assumed the practice was relegated to the distant corners of the Yucatán, far away from the monasteries. Years ago, when he was *Custos,* he'd received word from Friar Juan de la Puerta about idol worship among his charges. The man who owned the idol was sentenced to three lashings—a light sentence. In response, the Guardian of Valladolid had gathered the Mayan lords and chiefs together, had explained the necessity of worshipping the Christian God and no others, and had extended a pardon, according to the letter. There had been no further reports since then. But now the idols had been found in Mani, which was very different from the faraway Valladolid. Filled with dread about what the discovery suggested, Friar Diego left for Mani straightaway.

Friar Pedro met Friar Diego on the road into Mani. "We've collected all the Maya who live around the cave where the idols were found," he said.

"Good and proper steps," Friar Diego said. He still couldn't quite wrap his head around the situation. Evidence of the continued practice close to one of their principal locations made no sense. According to all Friar Diego had seen, the natives, in Izamal and at other nearby monasteries, were committed heart and soul to the Christian God.

Friar Diego inspected the evidence as soon as he arrived in the town. In the accumulated pile were a number of wooden statues of lizards, cats, monkeys, and fish—similar to the ones he'd seen all those years ago at the festival for the Mayan new year—and bastardized versions of the cross. Wooden masks, painted blue and black, were made in the image of humans, cats, and monkeys. Clay vessels were painted with bright-colored animals, or shaped like animals, and held charred bones. In a separate pile, a number of jeweled human skulls lay in a pile.

"These were arranged in front of the idols," Friar Pedro said.

There was no doubt about what was happening outside the monastery's view: the Maya were still worshipping their old gods. Still, Friar Diego couldn't parse the information. In all he had seen, there was no question about the fervent passion with which the natives worshipped God during mass at Izamal. There was no reason the natives in Mani should be any different; in fact, they should be further developed within the Christian faith, having lived near the oldest monastery in the Yucatán.

"Perhaps this is the work of a lone holdout. Maybe one of the Mayan priests?" Friar Diego said. "It wouldn't surprise me if Ahkinmai kept a similar store of his old religion's relics." Friar Diego decided the time had come for Ahkinmai's baptism—this would ensure the natives saw his abandonment of their old ways.

There were thirty-seven Maya held captive by the friars at Mani, too many for the prison where Francisco Hernandez had once sat awaiting trial. The young men were stuffed into the cells, the old men held in the infirmary, and the women of all ages were held in a series of houses and shops belonging to Spanish traders that had the unfortunate fate of being located next to the monastery. One by one, the Maya were brought from their holding places to face Friar Diego and Friar Pedro outside the sanctuary, in full view of the piles of idols and bones. The first person brought forth was an old woman; the Franciscans wanted the houses and shops cleared and returned to their owners.

Friar Diego, with his superior command of the Mayan language, took control of the interrogation. "Do you have any idea what these are?" he asked her.

The old woman looked at the idols and bones. "Yes?" she said, asking a question herself with the way she said the word. Her confusion was evident.

"And do you know who they belong to?"

"Various gods," she answered.

Friar Diego sighed, then turned to Friar Pedro and flashed a smile. The Guardian smiled back.

"No," Friar Diego said, turning back to the woman. "Who worshipped them?"

"We did," the woman said, still not understanding the point of the questions.

Friar Diego sat up in his chair. "You worshipped these idols?" he asked, wondering the likelihood of finding the culprit on the first try.

"Yes," she said. "What's going on?"

Friar Diego closed his eyes and waited for the dissipation of his momentary rage. "What about the Christian God?" He turned to Friar Pedro. "Does she attend mass?"

"Oh yes, I worship him too," the woman said, turning Friar Diego's attention back to her. With a sense of the danger she was in, she added, "I pray he saves my soul." She smiled after saying this, displaying several missing teeth framed by wrinkled cheeks, proud of her remembrance of the Christian message.

"God doesn't save devil-worshippers," Friar Pedro said with disgust.

"What do you pray to the idols for?" Friar Diego asked.

"Rain," the woman responded, her scared eyes trained on Friar Pedro.

Friar Diego shook his head. "Take her away," he said. Friar Pedro led the woman from the room.

"Should we continue asking the others?" Friar Pedro asked when he returned.

"Of course, she wasn't worshipping them alone. There are too many idols for one person's personal shrine."

Friar Pedro turned but was stopped by Friar Diego. "How widespread do you think this idol worship is?" he asked.

"We're about to find out," Friar Pedro said before retrieving the next native woman.

Friar Diego asked thirty-six more natives if they worshipped the idols and he received thirty-six more answers in the affirmative. Not a single person tried denying their involvement, not understanding the severity of their transgression. They all acted like adding the Christian God to their pantheon was the most natural thing in the world, a different higher power that served a different purpose—none of their gods specialized in saving souls from eternal damnation. During Friar Diego's interrogation of the women, he discovered that they were also praying for high-yielding corn harvests and bountiful deer, in addition to asking for rain. He abandoned asking why the men were praying to the idols during their interrogation, because each time the frivolous requests for prosperity were disclosed another flash of rage welled up in his chest.

One of the last men questioned said something that struck panic into Friar Diego's heart. According to the young Mayan man, the surrounding villages also prayed to their idols for fruits of the earth while taking care of their souls by attending mass. At a look from Friar Diego, Friar Pedro said he would tell the constables to gather the Maya in the nearby villages.

"We'll get to the bottom of this," he said.

Friar Diego paced his room in Mani while the men retrieved the local Maya for questioning. He was a fool for not seeing their treachery taking place right in front of his face. Everything he'd done for them, protecting them from the worst Spanish *encomendero*, learning their language, teaching their children—it was all for nothing! They were playing him, using him for their own ends, betraying his trust. Worse, far beyond his own wounded pride, was the delay in the fulfillment of the prophecy. The entire world rested on his ability to bring about the age of the Holy Spirit, which would begin after the native conversion spilled into the traditional Jewish population and, in time, to the rest of the non-Christian world. Their conversion had been so close; now, the sinners must face the consequences for their deception.

That night, Friar Diego dreamed he was on the ship coming to the New World. His friend Friar Francisco Navarro was asleep next to him when a mighty crash rang out. Friar Diego jumped out of bed while Friar Francisco slept. In fact, no one else woke but him. He ran to the boat's deck and stood watching water rush up one side of the boat, tilting the craft. Friar Diego screamed for the others, but they still didn't awaken. As the ship's angle increased, he was left clinging to the mast so he wouldn't fall into the dark black waters swirling below. Looking up, he saw the shadow of a large bird illuminated in the moonlight, perched on the end of the boat high in the sky. It was Ahkinmai, watching him struggle. As his feet, body, then his head were submerged in the water, he took one last look at the bird as it took flight before the water took the entire ship into the depths.

Friar Diego woke up and turned to the side, water bursting forth from his lips. He was freezing cold, and for hours before the sunrise he sat next to the fire, hell-bent on revenge.

The monastery was bustling with activity when Friar Diego emerged from his room. There were over one hundred Maya brought in for questioning. The women and old men sat leaning against the monastery's various buildings with their hands tied behind their backs, while the young men, those who could pose a threat if inspired, were placed behind locked doors, their hands bound as well.

Friar Pedro found Friar Diego walking to the sanctuary for morning prayers.

"Time to find out if they worship idols too," Friar Pedro said.

Friar Diego, still upset from his nighttime vigil, lashed out.

"We already know they do! We need to find out how many they own."

"I'll let you take charge of the questioning."

"Give them the *garrucha*. It'll make the confessions come faster."

Friar Pedro stood with his mouth open.

"What didn't you understand?" Friar Diego asked. "We all paid the price for your input on the restrained punishment of the former *Adelantado*. Either do what I say or I'll find someone who will."

Friar Pedro rushed off. Friar Diego walked past the mound of idols and jeweled skulls and into the sanctuary, where he prayed for God to give him strength for the task ahead.

Friar Diego didn't question any natives that day. Instead, he oversaw the construction of thirty thick posts dug into the ground, with a short post attached at the top of each, parallel to the ground. Using his role as Provincial, he made the funds available for the lumber and for the large amount of rope needed. As the sun set, he looked over the field of posts with rope hanging down, grateful for the opportunity to bring about the New Age of man. He didn't sleep that night, fearing Ahkinmai would visit him once more, and the sunrise saw him huddled in front of the fire in the exact same position as the morning prior.

Thirty natives were hanging from their hands when Friar Diego emerged from his morning prayers. Friar Pedro walked with him from the sanctuary to the field of posts. Some Maya were crying; others had their eyes closed. The sturdiest of the victims—it was a mixed group of individuals in age and gender—was focused on steady breathing while their shoulders screamed.

"Taking it easy on them?" Friar Diego said.

"Easy?" repeated Friar Pedro.

"This isn't the *garrucha*." Friar Diego commanded the closest Maya brought down, a middle-aged woman with pregnancy scars on her stomach. The rope hung slack while he untied her hands then retied them behind her back.

She cried, begging for forgiveness, saying she didn't know why she had been brought from her home.

Friar Diego ignored her and slung the rope over the post. At his command, two men, constables from Mani, pulled her off the ground. She screamed. Her torso was close to horizontal and her legs dangled below her.

"This is the *garrucha*," Friar Diego said with pride, patting her shoulder while it strained in its unnatural position.

"Now, how many idols do you own?" he said.

"Idols?"

"IDOLS!"

The woman would have said anything in exchange for the end of her torture. "Three," she said.

"Three? Is that all?"

"Yes, that's all!"

"Good." Friar Diego nodded to the two men holding the rope. They lowered the woman, making sure her knees were under her before letting go altogether. "Devil-worshippers don't deserve your mercy," he told them when he saw their gentle treatment of her return to earth.

Friar Diego leaned down and pulled the woman's head up by her hair so she could see his face. "Go back to your village and bring the idols here. Add them to our collection."

The sobbing woman nodded and collapsed. Friar Pedro helped her off the field as Friar Diego told him the confessed number of idols should be written down and confirmed when they brought the contraband back to the monastery.

The next native questioned also said she had three idols without Friar Diego imposing the true *garrucha* on her already aching shoulders. Friar Diego let her down, with the same command: bring the idols back to the monastery for destruction.

A curious pattern emerged as Friar Diego continued down the line: every native had three idols in their possession. The Maya being questioned when he realized the trend were older, and he feared subjecting them to the true *garrucha* would cause irreparable harm. When a square-jawed young man, tattoos of Mayan script covering his lower legs, said he had three idols, Friar Diego had the constables untie the rope holding him up. Then, he turned the man around and subjected him to the true treatment.

"I'm going to ask you again: How many idols do you have?"

The man said three once more as his shoulders screamed in their sockets.

"For some reason, I don't believe you," Friar Diego said. Turning to two young friars standing nearby, he said, "Bring me a large stone."

The friars returned and held the stone beneath the man while Friar Diego tied a piece of rope around it; he then tied the other end to the tattooed native's legs.

"Before they let go, I'm going to ask you one more time. How many idols do you have?"

"Three," the native man cried.

"Wrong answer." At a nod from Friar Diego, his men dropped the stone. It jerked to a stop just above the ground. Moments later, with a chilling scream from the native, the stone hit the earth as the man's shoulders dislocated.

"Still have three idols?" Friar Diego asked. "I'm just getting started."

"Six," the Mayan man said, his head hanging down and tears rolling from his eyes. His labored breathing shot pain through his shoulders until he passed out.

"Take note of his six. Untie him and send him to retrieve them."

The rest of the natives all said six, a high enough number that Friar Diego believed was in the ballpark of the true amount in their possession. He regretted letting the older Maya off with claims of three but still had too many natives to question to return to those already let off the rope.

Four total groups were brought in for questioning—Friar Diego had refined his process by the final group. With a scribe close by, he would go through all thirty natives once while they hung from their hands overhead in front of their body, asking them how many idols they had. These numbers would all be written down and double-checked on the second pass, where every single native—no exceptions—was given the true *garrucha*. Then, while they all still hung with their shoulders bent up behind their back, a third pass was taken, under the threat of the added stone. A handful of people's shoulders dislocated when they were first strung up by their hands behind their back; nobody's shoulder withstood the added rock, and most of the time the first jerk was enough to wrench the shoulders from their socket. The strongest man held both his own weight and the rock for close to ten heaving breaths, but in the end the added weight won.

The Maya's screams were heard throughout Mani. Their tears muddied the ground. As the friars and constables left the field of torture, and the Maya were escorted away, their footsteps made loud squelching sounds that reverberated off the monastery and reminded the Spanish townspeople of a man loudly chewing cured meat. The salt from the Mayan tears killed all vegetation on the field for centuries, and it wasn't until Friar Diego's final descendant died that the first green shoots of grass sprouted forth.

CHAPTER FORTY

REMY STUCK a finger in Cortez's open wound. "You're just mad Alara doesn't want anything to do with you."

"She's never had the chance! Poisoned from living on this side of the city, from being around *you*." The words dripped from his tongue. "I'm the one who can save her, the only one." Cortez lit the lighter and stared at the flame.

"Save her? What are you saving her from, me?" Remy asked, fueled by impotent rage.

"Saving her soul! You don't deserve her." Cortez extinguished the flame then paced while he gathered his thoughts; Remy waited for him to continue. "She needs to learn about Jesus, to study God's word. She reads all those books but doesn't read the Bible. She's going to hell, Remy, unless she changes. And you don't even care."

Remy's mouth opened but no words came out. He wasn't prepared for another battle to add to the numerous wars caused by religion throughout history.

"You know she said she doesn't believe in God?" Cortez said. "She said she believes in love."

"She's told me. She blames your God for murdering her ancestors."

Cortez ignored the attack on his faith. "Believes in love but doesn't believe in Jesus's love. He loved humanity so much, he sacrificed himself to erase our sins."

"I don't think that's what she meant when she was talking about love." Remy tried to wiggle his hands, seeing if he could find any slack in the rope. By putting pressure on one hand, he could create more space for the other.

Cortez turned on Remy. "Of course that's not what she meant! Because she doesn't know any better. And I can't show her the right way if you're still around."

"So what, are you going to kill me?" Remy said, his jaw locked in defiance.

"I won't." Cortez looked down at the lighter and flicked on the flame again. "The flames will."

Remy worked the rope down his hands, gaining slivers of freedom one hand at a time. His shoulders shifted in a way that created suspicion in Cortez, who walked around to inspect the knots.

"You almost got them out," Cortez said, laughter in his voice. He tightened the knots, making the rope stab Remy's wrists. "Even if you did, your legs are still stuck."

Remy shook back and forth on the chair, alternating slamming the front and back legs in frustration. "If I get out of here—"

"You won't," Cortez said, cutting him off. He reached into Remy's pocket and took out his cell phone. He looked up Alara's name and called her before putting the phone up to his ear.

There was no answer.

Reaching into his own pocket, Cortez withdrew a slip of paper. "I wrote down the number before I came, just in case," he explained while dialing. "Hello? Hi, yes, is Alara working today? . . . She is? . . . OK, can you tell her the library is on fire? . . . It doesn't matter who this is, I just know she'd want to know." With that, he hung up and put the phone back in Remy's pocket, returned to the opposite side of the table, and sat back down. With his hands folded on the table, he looked at Remy, smiling. "Now, where were we?"

Alara was making a latte when her phone vibrated in her pocket. Strict company policy prohibited use of phones, citing sanitation reasons, but every barista at Decant kept theirs stashed on their person for when the line of customers receded and gave them a moment to communicate with the world outside the coffee shop. A quick vibration meant a message, continuous a phone call. Everyone who had Alara's number knew not to call her, ever, because she wouldn't answer. When her phone continued vibrating while she lidded the drink she had made and handed it to the waiting customer—this particular customer always got the same sized latte, at the same time, every day—she sensed the continued vibration's significance. With a line of drinks still to go, and a cluster of customers waiting for those drinks across the counter from her, she risked a peek, withdrawing her phone just enough to see the front screen and discover that her boyfriend was calling her.

She had been cold towards Remy ever since Cortez informed her about the other woman. Her woman's intuition, deep down, confirmed that the pitiful creature had been telling the truth, though his pained, awkward delivery rankled her to the core. She had seen Remy just once since Sunday, at dinner on Tuesday, where she listened to him go on about work problems, exercise accomplishments, and sports news, never once asking her about herself. She had mastered the art of listening long ago. Remy never suspected her shadow had turned away from him and was searching for a way out. They'd spent the night together at her place, sleep preceded by physical satisfaction that turned her thoughts away from her situation for the duration of their love, but, once he finished and gave himself over to sleep, she lay awake, wondering how many women had experienced the thrusts of his passion since they had first started dating. Remy was gone the next morning, off to work, leaving Alara alone to unravel, in the light of day, how she would untangle herself from the mess she was in.

The coffee shop's phone rang right after the vibration in her pocket stopped. The supervisor, a man who made the hairs on the back of Alara's neck stand on end, answered, looked at her, then nodded while saying, "Yes." Alara poured milk into the next drink on her docket, a mocha, topped it with whipped cream, and handed it off with a smile that disappeared as soon as she turned around and looked in the landline's direction.

The supervisor was balding despite being in his late twenties but insisted on growing what hair remained to shoulder length, tying it back in a ponytail while on the clock. His skin possessed a constant sheen, a combination of sweat and oils that had resulted in consistent acne for over a decade, with the associated scarring to match; there was too much junk food and too little physical exertion outside his time spent at work for him to outgrow the affliction. He was a tall man and wide in both directions; whenever the baristas worked with him, providing enough navigable room for him behind the counters was an added part of their job. Shifts with Alara were circled on his personal calendar, looked forward to until they arrived and relished during their execution.

Alara, on the other hand, dreaded shifts with this supervisor. She could never shake the sensation that he was staring at her, taking in the shape of her body during every trivial movement. Now, she watched him approach, knowing the phone call to Decant was for her, that Remy had called the store when she didn't answer her phone.

"The library's on fire," the supervisor said. His chapped lips were outlined by a thin red line.

The floor fell away and Alara put a hand on the counter for support.

"They didn't say who it was," he added.

Alara knew it was Remy. What she didn't know, and couldn't figure out, was how her boyfriend had knowledge of the library fire in the first place, and why he thought she should know. He hadn't shown the least interest in books as long as she'd known him, and she stopped talking about books she was reading with him long ago. Her heart warmed one degree towards Remy, a trapped woman impressed by the slightest gesture of goodwill in a frigid relationship. She leaned back and looked at the register, taking note of the time.

Forty minutes remained on her shift.

In the library, Remy knew the end was near. There was no uncertainty in the crazed man's voice, no second-guessing during the entirety of his tirade. "She'll never love you."

"You're wrong. I've already seen this story played out!" Cortez said. His childlike delight had returned in full, banishing the anger to the shadows. Anyone who entered the small room on the top floor of the library at that precise moment wouldn't have believed the man was capable of the vitriol that had spewed from his mouth moments before. Pictures of different medical experiments performed on Jewish people during the Holocaust flashed on the television.

"Where, in the *Bible*?" Remy sneered.

Cortez closed his eyes and shook his head. "No," he said with an exhale, calming himself. He opened his eyes. "You think you're *so* smart, don't you? It's actually a book Alara is reading now. Her favorite, in fact. She said so herself."

When Cortez stopped talking, Remy jutted his chin forward and raised his eyebrows, encouraging Cortez to continue.

"*Love in the Time of Cholera.* Have you ever heard of it?"

Remy shook his head no. "I don't read," he said with an outsized dose of pride.

"You should try it sometime." Even though Cortez hadn't read the book himself, watching the movie was just as effective in his view, a way to get the information much faster than reading permitted. "Anyways, in the book, the main character falls in love with a girl. Of course, right, that's why we're here in the first place!"

Cortez wanted Remy to acknowledge his assessment of the situation; he continued after a nod from the captive man.

"Well, here's where it gets good. And why it relates to us! In the story, the girl rejects the first guy, who truly loves her, and marries another man because of his money. That's you and me!"

"You don't have money," Remy said.

"No, you're the one with money. I'm the one who loves her!"

"You're the rejected one."

Cortez glowered. "Yes. The rejected guy waits years for the guy she married to die, so they can be together in their old age." Cortez looked at Remy, waiting for recognition of his quality analysis. It never came. "I figured, why wait, you know? Why not get rid of the guy so I don't have to wait all that time?"

Remy stared at Cortez. "You sat here talking about how you wanted to save Alara's soul, how you wanted her to learn about God, but really you want her for your own selfish reasons! And you're willing to kill to get her."

Cortez's eyes welled with tears when faced with his own hypocrisy. "No, that's not it at all!"

"You just said so yourself," Remy said, calm in the face of mania.

"Stop confusing me!" Cortez whimpered. He lowered his face between his elbows and joined his hands behind his head.

"Look, I'm just trying to understand," Remy said. "I'm sorry that I wrote you off, ignored you. I shouldn't have done that. You're worth more than that, and Alara would be lucky to have a guy like you."

Cortez lifted his red, tear-streaked face. "You mean that?"

"I do. I think she'd be very happy with you. Good luck getting her to church though."

The two men shared a laugh. "I think she can help me save the Church," Cortez said.

"Save the Church?" Remy knew the time for his final request was coming. The timing had to be perfect; he couldn't rush because Cortez could be scared away. His strategy was the same as catching a butterfly without a net: wait for it to land on his arm.

"Our church needs more members. I go out every week but never convince anyone to come with me," Cortez said, meek as a lamb. "If I could get Alara's help, I could save the Church."

"I'd go to church with you," Remy said. It was almost time.

Doubt crept into Cortez's mind. Misjudging Remy would turn his holy act of killing to save the Church into murder, in direct opposition of the Ten Commandments.

"We could save it together," Remy added.

Cortez was blindsided by the proposition. It was an option he'd never considered, not in his wildest dreams. In a flash of jealousy, he imagined his father hearing about Remy's exploits to save the Church, ignoring Cortez's contribution. Thinking about his father reminded him of the man's suspected infidelity, enraging Cortez and reminding him why he hated Remy in the first place. His prisoner was lying about saving the Church, the same way he'd lied in his other relationships. Remy was cheating on Alara, making a fool of her, the same way his father had done to his mother. He couldn't forget, he wouldn't forgive, and Remy's kind smile sowed suspicion in Cortez's heart.

"We won't save it together, because you won't be around to help," Cortez said with finality.

The distance Cortez traveled in the space of a few breaths made Remy scramble for a hold on a situation that was slipping away from his grasp. A moment before, Remy had been certain he was close to gaining Cortez's confidence. Now, he knew he had to take his long shot, that soon there wouldn't be another chance.

"Why don't you untie me so we can go find some souls to save?" Remy said.

Cortez laughed. "And share the glory with you? You've had your chance, and you squandered it. You had Alara and she wasn't good enough for you! You run around with other women, acting like you're untouchable. It's time for someone else to have a chance, someone who won't ruin the opportunity because they actually appreciate it!"

"Look, I don't know what else to tell you. I underestimated you and how much you care for her. Let me go and you won't see me again."

"You'll run to the police the second you leave here; I'm not dumb."

"No I won't, Cortez, we've got work to do."

Cortez stood up, paced the room, then told Remy he needed to think before leaving the room. Remy strained against the ropes on his wrists and ankles, using every ounce of strength he had accumulated during his years of training. For his efforts, he was left with four patches of torn skin and bloodless extremities.

Defeated by the knots, Remy looked at the television. The narrator was discussing the chemical properties of Zyklon B and talking about the delivery mechanism, how the masses were told they were being deloused and washed off. The victims died in twenty minutes.

Cortez walked in carrying two bundles of newspapers. He put them on the ground before turning around and leaving the room. Once Remy realized what was happening, he used each opportunity to plead with Cortez to let him go, telling his captor he could help him save the Church, that he wouldn't tell the police, and that he would let Alara go without a fight.

Any doubts Cortez had harbored evaporated when he heard Remy's last offer. She was too precious to be discarded, and the fact that Remy was willing to do so meant the man didn't appreciate what God had given him. He was saving Alara by eliminating Remy, and once he convinced her of the power of God's love, they would be able to convince many more, together, through the power of her angelic grace.

When enough bundles of newspapers were in the room to line the interior walls, Cortez began stacking more bundles around Remy. He didn't hear Remy's apologies, or tears; he was lost in daydreams of the future, when his role in the Church's salvation would be beyond question. He imagined all the eyes on him and Alara when he entered their place of worship, basking in the warmth of their gaze. His sudden shift from the shadows to the light, from staying hidden to being seen, was empowered by the strength of his love for Alara, the woman he was certain God had put on earth, in his path, for a reason. One small bump in the road remained, and he would soon be taken by hell's flames for his sins.

Cortez separated the newspapers at the top of the piles

surrounding Remy. The pages were thrown on the floor, some crumpled, some floating through the air on unseen breezes, until the floor was covered in gray and black. As he worked, Cortez would find an eye-catching headline, then read it aloud to Remy.

"Five dead in terrorist attack."

"Cowboys are Super Bowl champions!"

"Markets recover after days of turmoil."

Remy waited for the end with the smell of chicken tortilla soup and the morning newspaper in his nostrils. For some reason, the scent reminded him of his father. He wished he could tell him goodbye, thank him for sticking around, and ask him if he'd ever regretted being a father in the first place. When it was clear that Cortez was pleased with his preparation, Remy began praying, talking to a God he had never known but hoped would still listen.

A description of the liberation of Buchenwald by American forces played on the screen behind Cortez when he pulled out the lighter. He pulled a *Money* magazine from his back pocket.

"I saw this on the shelf and thought it was perfect," he said with his childlike voice filled with innocence.

Remy recognized the cover; it was a subscription his father had kept for years. "I'm sorry," Remy said. Not to Cortez, but to his father—an apology for leaving his family behind without an explanation.

Cortez sparked the flame and held it to the corner of the magazine. It wouldn't light. He tried different edges, different corners; none of them worked.

Inspired by the Holy Spirit, Cortez brought the lighter to his face, breathed on it, then kissed it before lighting it again. He held the flame to the magazine and it erupted into flame, the dry sheets of paper accepting the heat like a thirsty traveler in the desert.

Remy and Cortez met eyes with the flames between them. Remy dropped his gaze and let his chin rest against his chest. Seeing this gesture of defeat, Cortez stood tall, took a deep breath, and dropped the magazine. He walked out, closing the door on the growing inferno.

CHAPTER FORTY-ONE

The prevalence of the natives' deceit convinced Friar Diego de Landa to expand their operation beyond the villages around Mani. Together with Friar Pedro de la Ciudad Rodrigo, they formulated a plan involving the systematic interrogation of the entire population in the triangle formed by Merida, Izamal, and Mani, three of the most established Franciscan strongholds in the Yucatán. Thousands of Maya were within the search area, the increased density of their numbers courtesy of the relocation campaign in 1552. When they were drawing the map, Friar Diego saw it included Sotuta, where his friend Nachi Cocom lived.

"What should we do with him?" Friar Pedro asked when Friar Diego pointed out the fact.

"Leave him for now. Let him watch his neighbors confess their sins."

The logistical problems faced by the interrogators became apparent while Friar Diego was still in Mani. The construction of enough posts to perform the *garrucha* for so many interrogations wasn't possible. Friar Pedro and Friar Diego—both men terrified at the thought of allowing the idol worship to continue any longer—decided the initial questioning could take place with flogging as encouragement for the Maya's confessions.

The pile of wooden and clay idols, painted clay pots, charred and jeweled bones, and wooden masks outside the sanctuary at Mani grew larger each day. The confessing natives were sent back home, escorted by constables and trusted armed older students, where they collected their relics and brought them back to the monastery. Many of the natives were charged with returning more idols than they in fact owned, after their initial confessions were deemed unsatisfactory. Under the watchful eyes of their escorts, they scoured their homes, nearby caves, and former festival sites looking for enough material to fulfill their quotas. Some even ascribed everyday objects ceremonial status, making the friars believe the idol worship was more rampant than first imagined when the Mayan transgressors returned and added these wares to the pile. Upon their return, they faced sentencing for owning the idols—the torture that had encouraged their confessions was deemed separate from the punishment for the ownership in the first place. Their aching shoulders—some still dislocated—had a companion in pain: whipped backs, their lashes received while tied to the posts where they'd experienced the *garrucha* days before. The skin on the back of the Maya whose confessions had been encouraged by flogging in the first place was so torn from their initial questioning that there was no intact surface for their punishment. The friars, before whipping native backs already peeled open, proclaimed inflicting the punishment hurt them more than those receiving the blows.

Friar Diego returned to Izamal while the search was underway. His fellow Franciscans at Mani didn't need the power of the Provincial during the interrogation process. Before leaving, he made sure Friar Pedro, the man in charge of the operation, knew the full resources of the Yucatán Province were at his disposal, under the belief that their religious order had faced no greater peril to its existence up to that point. Friar Diego arranged for the involvement of younger friars from the surrounding monasteries in the search, in particular those fresh from Spain, thinking they should know the kind of deceitful people they were tasked with converting.

Life at the Izamal monastery continued as if the nearby trials weren't underway. None of the natives around Izamal had yet been targeted for questioning, and they thought the problem was outside their region, despite reports of interrogations originating ever closer to their homes. They still showed up in droves, listening to Friar Diego speak, praying before the statue of the Virgin Mary, and believing their displays of piety kept them safe from the growing wave of terror from Mani. Friar Diego let them luxuriate in their perceived safety, knowing full well he wouldn't raise a finger in their support when Friar Pedro's forces landed on their doorstep.

At the end of May, mere weeks after the first idols were discovered in the cave, Friar Lorenzo de Bienvenida visited Izamal unannounced. He showed up on a Sunday and begged the Izamal friars continue with their standard preparations for the day's masses, not wanting his presence affecting the planned worship services. The ancient friar sat in the back row during the six hours of services, watching with pride as his younger brothers in faith preached to both Spanish and Maya alike. His heart was heavy with the knowledge of the upcoming conversation, knowing the Provincial wouldn't like the topic.

Friar Lorenzo joined the Izamal friars at their afternoon meal, during which he ate but didn't taste a thing. The food was consumed for his continued strength, knowing full well that he needed every advantage he could get at his advanced age. His seat was far from Friar Diego, to avoid the reason for his visit being exposed before they were alone. Friar Diego asked Friar Lorenzo what had brought him to Izamal after everyone finished eating.

"Let's walk," Friar Lorenzo said.

Friar Diego led the pair around the immense atrium. As they walked between the stone arches, Friar Lorenzo heaped compliments on the monastery's design.

"You didn't come here to look at the monastery," Friar Diego said, his impatience evident.

Friar Lorenzo took a deep breath. "What you're doing to the Maya. It has to stop," he said.

"Friar Pedro is leading the questioning," Friar Diego responded.

"Let's both call it what it is: an inquisition. Your inquisition."

Friar Diego bristled at the term. They continued walking in silence, rounding the corner in step. At the sanctuary entrance, Friar Diego said they should sit down. Then, under the watchful eye of the Virgin of Izamal, they discussed the sensitive subject.

"Even if it is an inquisition, I have every right."

Friar Lorenzo was incredulous. "By what authority?"

"By my own. According to the papal bull *Exponi Nobis Fecisti*, I have all the authority of a bishop."

"A bishop!" Friar Lorenzo couldn't believe what he was hearing. "We have a bishop in the New World. He's in New Spain."

"Ah, but he's farther than two days away. Therefore, his full powers are granted to me, as Provincial in the Yucatán."

"You've bastardized the point of the decree," Friar Lorenzo said.

Friar Diego smiled. "It's the law."

"Regardless of the extent of your power, this has to stop! It's counterproductive to the conversion of the Maya. They could assemble and rise up against our order. You would have the blood of your fellow Franciscans on your hands."

"If they do, I'll squash that too." Friar Diego patted Friar Lorenzo's leg. "Don't you see that I'm doing this for their own good? They still worship the devil. What kind of father would I be if I allowed my children to continue sinning without setting them along the correct path?"

"They're dying under torture!"

"Dying? If they didn't withhold information they wouldn't suffer. It's their own doing."

"The rules of inquisition are clear, outlined in *Ad abolendam*; they have to involve an investigation and a trial. None of these people are given the chance to prove their innocence or repent!"

"Don't quote church law to me, Lorenzo," Friar Diego said, glaring at his former mentor. "*Ad extirpanda* makes it very clear that torture is allowed to coerce confessions from heretics when the evidence against them is certain. The process works: not a single native has been innocent."

"Because they are being tortured! The papal bull you speak of also says torture can only be used once, and can't cause loss of life or limb."

"It has only been used once, to get their confessions," Friar Diego shot back. "And who's lost a limb?"

"Don't pretend you don't know about the destroyed shoulders. Their arms are worthless! And the others, with hands like hooks, frozen in place from the damage to their wrists."

"But the limbs are still attached."

Friar Lorenzo's mouth hung open and his head jutted forward. "You're being willfully manipulative. What about those killed in the process? There's already been reports of nearly one hundred dead."

"Their stubbornness got them killed. If they confessed sooner they would still be alive."

"Or maybe they're truly innocent and have nothing to confess!" Friar Lorenzo said.

"What about those who commit suicide to escape being caught? We've found nearly twenty bodies of men who don't want to be questioned."

"They could be innocent too! Your brutality is past anything the *encomenderos* ever did. They see what could happen to them and they'd rather escape through death, God rest their souls." Friar Lorenzo crossed himself.

Friar Diego grabbed the man's hand. It was a spur-of-the-moment action taken in frustration, but as soon as he did it he knew he had crossed the line.

"Let go," Friar Lorenzo said, his tone severe.

Friar Diego released his hand.

"If you don't stop your inquisition, I'm going to Guatemala. My heart is here, in the Yucatán, but I can't stand by while you murder innocent people."

"You don't think this hurts me too? I care deeply about the natives. Think of all I've done for them," Friar Diego said, his first display of any remorse.

"Then look into your heart and forgive them. They didn't know any better. Their complete conversion will come, in time."

"They did know better! This was planned! Deceit fills their hearts; they sit with us in mass then go back to their idols, making us look like fools."

"Nobody feels like a fool but you, Diego."

"And why wouldn't I! They betrayed my trust. After everything I've done for them, protecting them, making an example of the *Adelantado* so no *encomenderos* would dare harm a hair on their head . . ."

Friar Lorenzo thought he saw tears forming in Friar Diego's eyes. Seizing the opportunity, he grabbed the younger man's hands. "Let us pray for the strength to forgive them."

Friar Diego ripped his hands away. "No!" he screamed. The sound reverberated off the walls of the empty sanctuary. "I won't let their duplicity go unpunished. In fact, I'm going to round up all their priests and bring them to justice, just like our forebears did to the Jews in Spain."

"The Maya aren't the Jews. They don't know any better!"

"That's where you're wrong. They are one of the lost tribes of Israel that departed from Babylon."

Friar Lorenzo was taken aback. "Who told you this?"

"Nobody, I figured it out myself. Their conversion is the first step in the conversion of all the world's Jews. And I'm not going to lose the opportunity to save the Christian faith because the natives refuse to abandon their old religion."

"You're not making any sense," Friar Lorenzo said, shaking his head.

"It all makes sense! Who propagates the Maya's religion? The priests, with their ancient texts filled with the devil's script. They're the reason we've been losing the fight for the Mayan souls; they're the ones who need to be brought forth for confession!"

Friar Diego stood up, filled with energy and looking like he wanted to run from the sanctuary.

Friar Lorenzo tried getting through to the Provincial one last time before he got away, a final plea before the Provincial fell into the abyss of madness. "The New Laws require you to take care of the well-being of the natives. How does what you're proposing contribute to their preservation?"

"Don't bring up the New Laws to me! They were overturned in 1545. Go to Guatemala then. The last thing we need is someone within our ranks questioning my methods. I have a mission, handed down to me by the Crown, the Pope, and God himself, to convert the natives. And I'll make sure it happens if it's the last thing I do on this earth."

"God willing, the end comes soon," Friar Lorenzo said.

Friar Diego's long strides carried him out of the sanctuary, his habit trailing behind.

Friar Lorenzo looked up at the Virgin of Izamal, crossed himself under her watchful eye, then left the sanctuary. After gathering his belongings in Merida, he continued on to Santiago de Guatemala, where he prayed night and day for the preservation of the Mayan people.

Friar Diego, after leaving the sanctuary, ran into his room and wrote eleven copies of the same letter. In it, he outlined that school was suspended until further notice and that the students now had a new task, more important than learning the Spanish customs and Christian faith: finding the priests. There were twelve total priests and twelve monasteries in the Yucatán, a fact that Friar Diego saw as a showdown of equal forces both tugging on the Mayan souls. There was little chance the boundaries of the Mayan priests aligned with the Franciscan delegations, but knowing the boundaries of the different Mayan provinces provided some rough insight about where the Mayan priests could be found. The army of children would soon find the Mayan priests, regardless of where they hid. There were well over three thousand students within the Franciscan education system, and Friar Diego informed the Guardians of the Yucatán monasteries that the priests should be brought to Mani straightaway once taken into custody. He added, as an afterthought, that any and all books recovered should be brought as well, since they were the main repository of the knowledge the Mayan priests carried among themselves.

"Tell the students not to worry about entering the space where the books are held, which has been refused to them before now. The devil holds no power over them when they go out in service of the Lord," he wrote, remembering Nachi telling him the book's resting place was off-limits to the Maya who weren't priests.

The letter was sent out Monday morning, and by Wednesday the Yucatán Peninsula was crawling with searching youths like ants scattering from twelve independent anthills. Finding some of the Mayan priests was easy, since they made no effort at concealment, and by the end of the week there were already seven priests imprisoned at Mani, two of which had come under their own power because of their conversion to the Christian faith. Their handwritten books, made of folding sheets of bark paper, forty-seven of them in total, were brought alongside them and thrown into the pile of idols and skulls.

Finding Ahkinmai wasn't easy—he wasn't one of the men who surrendered under his own power. The Mayan priest Friar Diego had met when he first came to the Yucatán, who had visited the Izamal monastery for worship services, was by no means converted. Friar Diego told his students about Mayapan, and the stash of books in a small stone building at the edge of the city, but his students returned empty-handed. He thought about asking Nachi but dashed the thought from his mind, deciding he would rather not face his former friend's criticism. After days of unsuccessful searching, Friar Diego imposed structure on the search. First, he sent the oldest students out far away, having them search the farthest edges of the land surrounding Izamal that could be traversed in one day. Then, according to age, he created smaller circles, where the youngest stayed closest to the monastery. He doubted the youngest students would find the man, but a mixture of caution and pride made him wary of another instance of deceit in close proximity.

Friar Diego, for his part, came up with a plan for luring the Mayan priest to the Izamal monastery: he would sleep. His days were built around going to bed, convinced that if he could grab the leg or rip off the feathers of the bird in his dreams, then Ahkinmai could no longer evade capture. Before his plan, his sleep time had been mere hours each night for years. He'd convinced himself there was always work waiting for him; the truth was, if he wasn't sleeping, he couldn't dream, and if he couldn't dream, the large bird wouldn't visit him. Unaccustomed to so much sleep, he stayed awake tossing and turning, praying for calmness of mind so he could hunt for his prey. Then, one week after he sent the letter about the new assignment of the native students, sleep visited him soon after his head hit the pillow.

Friar Diego didn't dream of Ahkinmai. Instead, he was visited by Ix Cuatchel.

They were walking along the same beach where he'd first landed in the New World. Ix wasn't pregnant. Friar Diego got the sense their son was nearby, though he never saw him. No matter how much the friar talked—and he talked a lot—Ix didn't say a word. She would nod, she would smile, but her mouth never opened, so it was impossible to tell if she even knew how to speak or if she had lost her voice. They walked past the same stretch of shoreline over and over without turning around; the section's end was the beginning. Friar Diego released all his pent-up complaints onto Ix, telling her about the Maya's continued idol worship, Friar Lorenzo's unappreciative attitude towards the cleansing of the Yucatán, and, at the end, chastising her for crawling into his bed.

"The rest of your people are just like you!" Friar Diego

snarled. "Pious and respectful in the church, then sinful behind closed doors."

Ix just smiled.

"Are you even listening to me?" Friar Diego said, grabbing her hand. It snapped with a loud crunch, leaving her hand bent at an awkward angle, fingers turned inward.

Still, she smiled.

Friar Diego raised the hand as gently as if it was a newborn child, inspecting the wrist while supporting her forearm with both hands. When he poked the hand, Ix's shoulder separated with a loud pop. Horrified, Friar Diego dropped the arm, where it hung loose from the socket.

Ix looked at Friar Diego with wide-open eyes, still smiling.

When Friar Diego brushed her shoulder with the tips of his fingers, not believing what he saw, the other shoulder dislocated with a loud pop. Her other hand bent into a claw. Then, unprompted, her neck bent forward as if she had hung herself by jumping from the roof of a mansion.

Friar Diego leaned forward, inspecting her face from below. Smiling.

Shouting from the atrium woke him up. The sun was bright; he guessed he'd slept more that night than the last few weeks combined.

The students were carrying Ahkinmai on their shoulders. He was gagged and tied up like a wild deer. The feathers on his cape, his headdress, and the fabric hanging from his waist were all bent at odd angles. The students deposited him in a heap in front of the sanctuary.

"Did you find any books?" Friar Diego asked the students. Eleven young men shook their heads no.

Friar Diego removed the gag from Ahkinmai's mouth. "Where are the books?"

Ahkinmai turned his face away.

"Go look around the villages he frequented," Friar Diego said. "If you don't know, ask your parents."

The youngest boy of the bunch looked down. "Our parents were all taken in for questioning by the priests."

"All of them?"

The students confirmed they were left on their own.

"Well, there has to be someone who knows." Friar Diego thought for a moment, then realized everyone who had the requisite knowledge would be in Franciscan custody. Ahkinmai's favorite spots would be one of the first questions. "Never mind, I'll find out and let you know. Now leave us alone," Friar Diego said.

The children ran off.

Friar Diego sat on the grass with his legs crossed next to Ahkinmai. The Mayan priest, his hands and feet still tied, turned to his side, facing away from the Franciscan.

"You almost had us fooled," Friar Diego began. "Here I was, thinking I was playing a secret game, when in fact you were doing the same to me."

Ahkinmai rested his head on the grass.

"I learned about your language, your festivals, your way of life—even about your books!—in my attempts to convert your people to Christianity. It seems you knew the rules of the game as well."

Friar Diego continued when Ahkinmai stayed silent.

"Is that what your presence in the church was? Gathering information so you could undermine our efforts to save the native souls? It almost worked," Friar Diego said with a laugh.

Ahkinmai turned over. "I urged acceptance of your God,"

he said. "I was the first one to do so, when you stormed into the clearing and interrupted our ceremony."

"The first mass conversion," Friar Diego said, daydreaming.

"Conversion? I told them not to kill you. Your outsized bravery interested me, like a hornet unafraid of death. If I knew then what I know now, I would have killed you myself."

Friar Diego laughed. "And look at us now."

Ahkinmai glared at Friar Diego.

"Why don't you tell me where your books are? We already have a sizable amount of your devil-script in our pile at Mani, so I hear. Yours would be a welcome addition."

Ahkinmai spat on the ground.

"Talk now or talk later. I was trying to save you the trouble, friend."

"I'm no friend of yours."

"You're right. My mistake. I'm going to tell you something, but you can't tell anyone else, OK?"

Friar Diego waited for a promise that never came.

"OK, tell everyone you want, just not the Pope. Deal?"

Still, silence.

Friar Diego leaned close to Ahkinmai's ear. "You're going to be the first native man to suffer the *garrucha* twice. Better yet, I'm going to hoist you up myself," he said. Then, he leaned back. "Congratulations!"

Ahkinmai was left tied on the ground for the rest of the day. The sun glinted off the new monastery's stained glass as night fell, magnifying onto the feathers on his chest. They started smoking. He breathed on them with whispers of their name, urging the ignition of a spark. The sun went down beyond the horizon before he caught fire.

CHAPTER FORTY-TWO

THE SUPERVISOR SENSED Alara's purpose for checking the time and reminded her of how much time remained before she could leave. For him, these were precious moments, ones he wouldn't release from his vice grip, even under the most pressing instances, because he held the strictest certainty that once she left the premises she was beyond his reach; he would have to cross another chasm of time before another scheduled shift together.

Alara went back to the line of waiting drinks with renewed determination to find the end. The customers that day had never seen, and never saw again, someone work with her haunted intensity of a madwoman, her insides aflame with the knowledge of the burning books. Pots of steamed milk and shots of espresso were pulled from thin air, as if there were twice as many machines and baristas operating them, and the entire operation took on the cool efficiency of a special forces mission. With the line of drinks eradicated, and before more could be added, she cleaned the floors, wiped the tables, and stocked the sugar packets customers used for black coffee. While Alara was in the lobby, her specter started the production process when a new customer placed their order, replaced by her physical form when the time came to hand off the drinks, so the waiting customers wouldn't have their corporeal sensibilities offended by her spirit.

By ten minutes after the call, Alara had taken care of behind the counter as well: the cups were stocked, syrups replaced, counters cleaned, and new milks behind old in the refrigerator. She swept and mopped the floor where the employees stood without any of her coworkers taking a single step from their positions. In short, there was no work left for the other employees before closing, other than taking care of the customers, and she told the supervisor as much when she requested to leave early, her myriad tasks completed.

The supervisor licked his lips. Beads of sweat glistened on his forehead. "You've still got another half hour," he said.

Alara, staring at the sweaty face, became aware of her own perspiration. The rapid work had been difficult but wasn't responsible for her shirt sticking to her skin; her skin dripped from the effort required to be in two places at once.

"Come on, I've done everything," Alara said. She looked at him with the stare generations of beautiful women had perfected over years of bending men's iron will. "Can't you let me go, just this once? I never ask for anything." She blinked twice and softened her expression, accentuating her good looks.

The supervisor wasn't the type of man who shied away from the truth. He knew, without ever being told, that he had no shot with Alara. Her feminine charms had the opposite effect on the possessive supervisor: his heart hardened with a fierce determination to wring every second of her presence from her that he could. Being a practical man as well, and lazy, he also enjoyed the work she had saved him from, and he grew inspired to squeeze still more from his desperate employee.

"The bathrooms still aren't done," he said with a sadistic

smile. The thought of degrading Alara by having her clean the bathrooms he himself frequented did more to awaken his slumbering genitals than any of her curves.

Alara didn't wait for a promise, or for a direct request. Leaving her ghost making drinks at the counter, she took the mop, the window cleaner, the toilet cleaner, and the disinfectant and proceeded to make quick work of the bathrooms. When she returned to the employees' side of the counter, she found six drinks waiting to be handed off. She washed her hands before giving the drinks to the waiting customers, who would have rushed out if they were handed drinks from anything but a flesh-and-blood human. She checked the clock and found that there were still twenty-five minutes remaining in her shift.

At that exact moment, unknown to her, Cortez was struggling to light the magazine. The fire hadn't started, yet, but she imagined thousands of unknown pages throwing inked ash into the air and couldn't bear another moment away from the blaze. The flurry of work helped her escape the gravity of the situation, but without any tasks left, her thoughts had nowhere to hide. Her stomach twisted like a slug sprinkled with salt.

She took off her apron and went into the back room to clock out. The supervisor, his hungry eyes always watching, blocked her path back to the lobby with his enormous frame.

"Where do you think you're going? I didn't say you could leave."

"I did the bathrooms," Alara said, exasperated. She stared at him. "I need to go. Fire me if you want."

The supervisor said, "I will!" the way a child might claim he would stay awake until midnight on New Year's Eve.

Alara knew he would fall asleep well before the ball dropped. "OK, I'll worry about that when it happens," she said. She grabbed her purse, flung it over her shoulder, and tried to walk out.

The supervisor didn't move. Still acting a child, he didn't recognize the ramifications his continued overbearing behavior could produce on his career, instead believing it was his divine right to rule, and his subject's subservience had been decreed by a higher authority.

Alara tried to squeeze past but he blocked her with the bulk of his frame. She stood back, frustrated, and he smiled with delight.

The employee at the register, the sole person dealing with customers, yelled to them, saying one of them needed to come make drinks.

The supervisor's beady eyes focused on Alara, his heavy eyebrows cinched together. "That's all you," he said.

Alara took a deep breath. She had better things to do than argue with a child. Books were burning, and while there was nothing she could do to stop the conflagration, she at least wanted to be there to pay her respects.

The emergency door in the back room had a bright red handle with numerous warnings about the attached alarm. The entire store would hear, customers included, and disturbing Decant's operations would harm her chances of continued employment more than upsetting a supervisor nobody liked. Left with no other options, she turned around and walked towards it.

When the supervisor realized the lengths she was willing to traverse in order to leave, and knowing the store's manager would hear about the alarm, the supervisor told Alara to wait.

Alara turned around with one hand on the handle and glared at the sweating supervisor.

"Don't! You can leave this way," he said, moving out of the way and holding out an arm, courtesy replacing obstinacy.

"Too late," Alara said. A blaring siren erupted overhead at the exact moment she pushed the bright red handle, accompanied by flashing white lights feared by epileptics. She drank in the chaos of the scene inside Decant, the stunned faces of the supervisor and her coworker in the store's main area, then turned, letting the door close under its own weight, and headed to the library.

She tried calling Remy as soon as she left Decant. It went straight to voicemail. Her own memories of the library weighed heavily on her mind as she walked as fast as she could to its location, just short of breaking into a jog. Her father—an immigrant who'd had trouble reading himself but was convinced of the written word's power—had taken her to the city's library on Saturdays when she was young, walking hand in hand with her through the aisles while she chose three books for the week. Over the years, that number had grown to four, then four to five. There were many weeks she selected more than her allotment, but her father was adamant about the predetermined number, her first lesson in not receiving everything that she wanted.

If the crowd ahead hadn't been stopped on the corner, waiting to cross, she would have kept walking through the intersection without pause, lost in her memories.

The number of books she read had dwindled once she hit puberty and realized attention from boys could be just as enthralling and required little work on her part. Her pleasure reading ground to a halt during high school, when her scholastic demands combined with her social life to sap every ounce of free time from her life, often taking time away from her sleep as well. She received books as birthday presents each year, gifts she requested, and she added them to her collection, deliberating their placement on her shelf with care, with every intention of reading them as soon as time permitted.

Alara didn't see the automatic doors of the grocery store on her right open wide, and she almost ran headfirst into a woman with a load of groceries in each hand rushing out to a waiting car with its hazards on.

"Watch where you're going!" the woman yelled, the effort further straining her laboring body.

"Sorry," Alara said.

Reading time hadn't materialized until she moved out of her parents' house after graduating from high school. She never second-guessed her decision to bring her piles of books into the city with her, even while carrying the heavy boxes up three flights of stairs. Without her parents' expectation that she read, and subsequent disappointment, she rediscovered her passion for reading and began working through the volumes she'd collected over the years. Dating Remy provided her with a reason for ignoring men, which provided her still more time to catch up on years of neglected words.

Cortez assumed that Alara would care about the burning library because she loved reading books. He was wrong. Alara cared about the burning books because the library was the one place where her father had been proud of her, pride that was replaced by a creeping disappointment that spoiled their interactions during her teenage years.

Smoke rose between distant buildings. Alara quickened her pace, the fire's evidence extracting her from swirling memories. One lingering question remained, a small sliver of a fact that stuck to the back of her skull like gum on a shoe: How had Remy known about the library fire?

Alara was among the first people standing transfixed outside the library. She stood in the building's shadow, staring up at the smoke, wondering how much damage the stone building would suffer. Someone bumped into her while her eyes were skyward, yelling that she should keep moving as they strode past. Words escaped her when she attempted a reply, incinerated as they rose from her stomach to her throat. The overwhelming desire to be alone took hold of her and wouldn't let go. Though her soul wanted to witness the fire and luxuriate in the resultant pain, her body was called to escape to the park, to the trees, and to her bench. Her mind, the arbiter between her body's two forces, put forth a compromise, and so she relocated to the park opposite the library's front doors to watch the destruction unfold.

The crowds outside the library grew piecemeal. Most people took one look at the smoke issuing from the library's roof and hurried past, or crossed the street and hurried past, certain that their destination was more important than the fire. The drivers, after seeing onlookers staring into the sky from the sidewalk, leaned low so they could see the building's top—none of them stopped. The people who congregated outside the library, the ones who couldn't ignore the destruction, stood in solemn reverence of knowledge's cremation. They each wanted to scream at the people who passed, to question them about what was worth stopping for, if not the burning of something as pure as books.

Alara wondered if any of the books her fingers had touched were already gone. It had been so long since she'd been in the library that she couldn't remember if the children's books, the ones she devoured with the tenacity of a dog with a bone, were on the bottom levels or were closer to the top, where the thickest smoke issued from the building. She shook her head at her false assumption, that the books on top were the ones burning, knowing that smoke rises and therefore the books on the bottom floor could just as well be on fire and the smoke would still appear in the same location.

. . .

Cortez chose that moment to leave the side of the building, where he had been watching Alara from a distance, and approach his beloved. He did his best to stand tall despite the shooting pain every breath produced in his aching ribs, walking forward with the certainty that everyone watching the fire was also aware of his holy steps. He'd had enough of hiding in the shadows and was glad to have an audience. They would soon get to see what he was prepared to do for Alara's love.

Alara didn't notice the broken man scuttling across the street from the library until it became obvious she was his destination. His shirt was torn on his leaning torso, which was misshapen from favoring one side of his rib cage. She recognized Cortez out of the corner of her eye while still staring in horror at the smoke issuing from the roof of the library. Dealing with him was the last thing she wanted while the pages inside were burning. She prepared herself for his arrival by imagining she had a twin and swapping places with her counterpart, a useful strategy for ignoring men she had often employed in the past whenever one of their ranks grew too familiar for her taste.

Cortez walked right up to her and stopped mere steps away. His ravenous eyes sparkled with a newfound confidence, a mania Alara sensed without seeing his face. She looked at him, pretending not to know who he was. When it became obvious he wouldn't be deterred, she lit the lighthouse of recognition hidden behind her eyes.

"What are you doing here?" she said, annoyed.

"The library's burning," he said. He didn't elaborate.

"I can't believe it," Alara said, filling the silence. She continued staring at the library, and Cortez continued staring at her, unwilling to peel his eyes away from her beauty and look in the direction of her gaze.

He turned around at the arrival of the first fire truck; its siren cut off as it pulled to a stop in front of the library. Its chipped paint and rusted ladder matched the firefighters who trickled out with aged equipment that had seen better days. A moment later, two more fire trucks, newer than the first, screamed around the corner and skidded to a stop. Without hesitation, a driver of one of the newer trucks told the first truck to move. With the space occupied by the first cleared, the two trucks positioned themselves in front of the library's wide steps with the older truck behind.

The street in front of the library transformed into a hive of activity. The road running between the library and the park was closed off, forcing cars to stop. Some drivers climbed out of their cars, watching the unfolding attempts to save the library, and others turned down side streets, frustrated and searching for a way around.

"Remy's in there," Cortez said.

Alara looked at Cortez in disbelief, studying his face, searching for hints of a lie. Cortez didn't waver in his certainty. Her boyfriend, the notorious nonreader, was in the library; she couldn't piece together a single reason why. "Remy?" she said.

"Uh huh," Cortez said, his voice suffused with laughter that didn't transfer onto his face. This confirmation was said in the same manner as a child who knows the end of a picture book but doesn't want to share the knowledge with the adult they are reading it with for the first time—it was a joke to him.

Despite her disgust at Cortez's delivery, Alara weighed the information. There was still a chance her boyfriend was alive. In that moment, she forgot about her recent displeasure with him, ignored the alleged time spent with other women, and wanted him out of the fire, safe by her side. "What's he doing in there?" she said. "How do you know?" Turning away from Cortez, she looked for the closest firefighter, deciding between reporting his presence in the fire to the worn-out firefighters from the first truck or telling the haughty, gleaming men who'd arrived in the second wave.

"Relax," Cortez said, stretching out the word. "There's nothing to worry about. God brought me here for a reason."

Alara would've expected Cortez's tone if she were badgering him about leaving for the airport earlier than necessary; in their current situation, his delivery was cold, detached. Alara didn't put any stock into his proclamation. She imagined this was yet another childlike fantasy, and she cursed the men in her life who refused to grow up. In that instant, and for the first time, she realized why she was drawn to Remy, alongside numerous other women: he acted like a grown man.

"Of course there's something to worry about! Remy's inside a fire!" she said, her words erupting on Cortez. She hoped her urgency would pull Cortez from his uncaring attitude.

Cortez looked around at the people watching the library fire, the ones who were about to witness his sacrifice. With a nonchalant air, he informed her that he could save him.

"And what are you going to do?" she snapped.

Cortez looked at Alara with a heart full of love and an overwhelming sense of larger purpose. This was the moment he had been waiting for, his chance to prove to her, and everyone around, that he was a great man destined for great things. It was the first step in his ascendancy, the domino to begin a cascade of events that would result in Alara by his side at church.

"I'll go in and get him," Cortez replied. A great weight evaporated from his shoulders now that his body was on the line, filling him with lightness. He imagined Jesus felt the same way after refusing to defend himself before Pilate.

CHAPTER FORTY-THREE

Nachi Cocom had been running in the dark for hours. His feet were ripped and torn, leaving blood on the ground with every step. Four Mayan texts were hanging from a fabric sack slung over his shoulders, taken from Ahkinmai's hiding place near where the celebration of the new year's festival occurred each year. The pain from Nachi's feet shot up through his calf, ending at his knee—he deserved it, for entering the sacred space where the books were kept. Those spaces were reserved for the priests.

Friar Diego de Landa's capture of Ahkinmai had sent shock waves through the Yucatán. Ahkinmai was the most powerful Maya, a man with mystical talents no ordinary person understood. Nachi had thought his capture by Mayan children would be impossible when he heard the schools had closed. He was wrong.

Stealing the books became a thought-worm burrowing into the base of Nachi's skull when he found out about Ahkinmai's transport to Mani. Guilt paralyzed him, knowing he was the one who'd shown Friar Diego the books in the first place. He had heard about the imprisoned priests bringing their books to the pile of idols, depositing them with the Franciscans, hoping they were buying leniency for themselves and their people, and the hoisting—what the Spaniards called the *garrucha*—of the prisoners, always in search of more. Soon, Ahkinmai would suffer the same torture, and, despite Nachi's faith in the feathered man, Nachi knew the hiding places of the ancient books were under threat of discovery, if not by Ahkinmai's revealing of their location then by the students who wriggled over the countryside like maggots on a carcass.

The new year's festival temple was the third place Nachi looked, the last place he knew where books rested. The other two spaces he'd looked, the stone room at Mayapan and a cave, had both been empty. Nachi had paced outside the hidden entrance to the stone chamber beneath the new year's temple, knowing there was no reversal of his trespassing. As he passed over the threshold to the space, he was struck by a vision of his ultimate fate. His knees buckled, but he accepted his sentence without question. He hoped there was enough time left in his life to save the books. The space inside the chamber was barren; dried leaves scattered at the wind created by Nachi's steps. The books were inside a wide clay vessel, itself sitting atop an overturned clay vessel, covered by a wide piece of bark. A number of spiders scurried away when Nachi lifted the bark. He grabbed the four books and started towards Mani.

Friar Lorenzo de Bienvenida's flight from the Yucatán had given the Maya hope that not all Franciscans believed in Friar Diego's methods. Some even hoped for a Franciscan revolt, the friars standing up to their leader. Nachi knew Friar Diego's determination and knew no such mutiny would occur. Despite knowing his life's road ended at Izamal, courtesy of his vision, he made the trip to Mani, running as much as he could, walking when he needed rest, arriving in Mani as daylight emerged over the horizon and hoping Friar Diego hadn't taken his last hope into custody. Nobody else knew where he was or what he was doing.

The Lord of Mani, the Mayan man baptized Don Francisco de Montejo Xiu by the Spanish conqueror of the Yucatán, was surprised when a distraught Nachi arrived at dawn. The Cocom and the Xiu had been rival families for generations. His home was on the outskirts of Mani, one of the few Mayan men who lived among and as the Spanish. He knew about the questioning of the natives and had been spared from the inquisition by his own years of service to the Franciscans—in particular, to Friar Lorenzo de Bienvenida. Many of the natives thought he was complicit in their torture because he wasn't arrested, not knowing Friar Pedro de la Ciudad Rodrigo had given him strict orders prohibiting him from leaving his home.

"The only reason you aren't strung up with your friends is because of your friendship with Friar Lorenzo," Friar Pedro had said.

Now, Friar Lorenzo had left the Yucatán, and each day the Lord of Mani expected the friars would collect him too. He thought his time had come when Nachi knocked on his door. With a wave of relief and aware of the family rivalry, he invited Nachi inside. His young family was still asleep.

Nachi deposited his cargo on the man's wooden table, pulling open the fabric and exposing the books.

The Lord of Mani's eyes grew wide—no Maya but the priests ever carried the texts. "Why did you bring these here? The friars are looking everywhere for them. They call them the devil's script." He threw the fabric back over them.

"These are all I could find," an exhausted Nachi said, collapsing into a chair.

"Get them out of here! If they find out I have them, I'll be hoisted like everyone else."

"Then don't tell anyone else they're here," Nachi said.

The Lord of Mani weighed his options. His boy was already learning the Christian ways from the Franciscans; there was no question he would tell the friars if he saw the books. Before the child woke up and walked in, the Lord of Mani took all four books, bound the bundle with string, then put them in a trunk given to him by *Adelantado* Montejo before the man had been removed from office.

"Why me?" the Lord of Mani asked.

"I can't trust any of the Spaniards, and you're the closest thing I know to one," Nachi said.

The Lord of Mani glared at him.

"And if Friar Lorenzo trusts you, then so do I."

"Friar Lorenzo left us to our fate," the Lord of Mani said with sadness.

"He did, after leaving Izamal. I imagine he tried stopping Friar Diego and the man wouldn't listen."

The Lord of Mani thought for a moment, then agreed. "He'd never let this happen if he could help it."

"And now it's time for you to play your part. The friars will never expect the texts in Mani."

"Why are you clinging to the past? Our children already don't know the old ways."

"For the future. The knowledge in these books could help during the next cycle."

"Everyone who can read them is being rounded up as we speak!"

"Someone will figure it out."

The Lord of Mani paced the room.

Nachi heard his own future's call and stood up. "I'm going back to Izamal," he said.

"They'll catch you and interrogate you with the others!"

"The trees will protect me."

Nachi left a speechless Lord of Mani behind, walking out into the daylight. Don Francisco de Montejo Xiu was disgusted at himself for relishing the knowledge that the most powerful member of his rival family had put their ancient feud aside for the good of the Maya and turned to him for help. If it wasn't for the selflessness of Nachi's act—which ended the feud in a single blow—the Lord of Mani would have turned the books over to the friars, cementing his place in their good graces. Knowing Friar Lorenzo disagreed with Friar Diego's inquisition made hiding the books easier. If the aged friar had stood up to the Provincial, he could too.

Long after the torture ended, when Friar Diego was sent back to Spain to stand trial for his Maya inquisition and before he returned as Bishop of the Yucatán, the Lord of Mani got rid of the books after years of worrying his family would discover them. He sent two to Spain, one to the descendants of *Adelantado* Montejo and one to the descendants of Hernán Cortés, the conqueror of New Spain. One book was deposited in Merida, left in the care of an old native librarian working for the Franciscans, when a new friar was in charge of the Yucatán who didn't persecute the Maya. The Lord of Mani took the final book, the smallest of the four, with him on a trip to New Spain—before it was called Mexico—and hid it in a cave far from his home when he realized the continued erasure of the Mayan culture wouldn't reverse in his lifetime.

Nachi's trip back to Izamal was slow, painful, and exhausting. Straying from the main paths made for difficult travel with bleeding feet. Despite growing up in the Yucatán and spending his formative years fighting the Spanish colonizers, he found he had grown too old for hacking his way through the foliage. He stopped often, daydreaming while resting of an impossible future in which Friar Diego called off his search. The outskirts of Izamal emerged through the trees at the end of his second day walking. He slept while waiting for nightfall, ignoring the ants crawling over his body. A tongue licking blood from his feet woke him up. It was night, the darkness cut by the full moon. Lifting his head and looking down the length of his body, he saw two luminous yellow eyes looking back at him. A panther, jet black, lying on its belly. Powerful muscles stretched the skin where the creature's four limbs met its body. Nachi wasn't scared—he had seen his fate and knew his life didn't end there. He lay down and let the creature continue. In time, the panther stood up and sniffed Nachi's whole body, starting with his toes and ending at his head. Nachi stayed still, his eyes open. He had never seen a living panther up close and was surprised at how clean the animal looked, its coat reflecting the moonlight. The massive jaws and head inspired awe, not fear, and its golden honey eyes looked straight through him.

Nachi sat up when the panther walked away. The bottoms of his feet no longer screamed in pain. He inspected them, finding they were healed. He stood up, left the cover of the trees, and walked into the night surrounding Izamal. He found a length of rope after scouring the area surrounding the monastery. Then, he went into the courtyard in front of the sanctuary, the atrium Friar Diego had designed to be second in size only to Rome. He stood staring at the stained glass image of the Virgin Mary, wondering why worshipping the statue of the woman was permitted while other idols were deemed as coming from the devil. Shaking his head, convinced he would never know, he found a way to the top of the monastery. The sprawl of Izamal could be seen from the roof, along with vast amounts of forest surrounding the settlement. Forest where the Maya had lived, and prospered, before the Spaniards arrived. There was so much more wild forest than inhabited land, but the cleared spaces held all the power—drops of poison in otherwise clean water. Knowing what he had to do, his fate revealed to him by crossing into areas reserved to Mayan priests, Nachi tied one end of the rope to the middle of the three crosses, the tallest point of any structure in the Yucatán. He tied the other end around his neck. Taking one last look into the forest, imagining the moon as one of the panther's glowing eyes, he jumped.

The cross atop the monastery snapped from his falling weight. In his vision, his body had been left hanging above the stained glass image of the Virgin Mary as a final memento for Friar Diego. Instead, his body hit the paved path leading to the sanctuary, shattering his pelvis and spine. The final image he saw was the cross falling from the sky, backdropped by the moon, before it crushed his skull.

Friar Diego never found out what happened to Nachi, the man who had educated him about the Mayan way of life, revealed the books, and given him the knowledge of who could read the script. He assumed his friend had left town, escaping into more remote areas of the New World, the same way he had helped other Maya escape during the great relocation. The Izamal priests threw Nachi's body in the woods and arranged for the remounting of the cross atop the monastery, so when Friar Diego returned from his affairs in Mani he had no idea anything had transpired while he was away. The panther, who had started digging a hole as soon as he walked away from Nachi, dragged Nachi's broken body to its final resting place and covered the man with dirt.

Ahkinmai revealed the locations of his seven books under torture. Friar Diego assumed there were more than what

Ahkinmai admitted to having, and he almost killed the feathered man who had infiltrated his dreams for years before accepting the truth. The fastest runners among the older students were sent out and returned with three books and heads hanging in disappointment.

"The other hiding place was empty," they reported.

Friar Diego walked to the field of torture. Ahkinmai was hanging from his bound hands, his arms lifted up from the front instead of from the back, though it no longer mattered—his shoulders had separated during the *garrucha.* Friar Diego grabbed Ahkinmai's hair and lifted the man's head so they were eye to eye.

"You lied," Friar Diego said. His anger bubbled deep below the surface.

"I don't have any more," Ahkinmai said.

"The four weren't where you said they were."

"That's where I left them." He knew Nachi had cleared the cache.

Friar Diego threw Ahkinmai's head down and spat on the ground. "Torturing you more won't do any good."

The final priests, their books, and their idols were brought into Mani during the second week in June. The pile of Mayan contraband was as wide as the Mani sanctuary, and taller than any man. There were over seventy Mayan books; most of the twelve priests had seven, but some showed up with six, claiming they'd always had that number despite Friar Diego's application of the heavy stone during the *garrucha.*

"We need to teach the natives the importance of repenting," Friar Diego said at a meeting of the friars in Mani. In addition to those stationed in Mani, there was a handful of the new recruits, their eyes squinting as they fought back tears. "They need to see our power."

"What do you have in mind?" Friar Pedro asked.

"Something like what we did to the heretics in Spain. A great *auto de fé*."

An audible gasp erupted from the gathered friars, followed by murmurs throughout the assembly.

"You want to burn them at the stake?" Friar Pedro said, his voice quavering.

"We don't need to go that far," Friar Diego said, considering himself lenient. "But we will burn everything they use to worship the devil after their punishments."

Friar Pedro nodded.

"The natives need to see the power they are up against. They worship the devil in secret; we punish devil-worship in public."

"They'll see the wisdom in repentance," Friar Pedro said, nodding.

The preparations began in earnest. Fabrics needed dying—in particular, the rough yellow fabric with a red cross all the native devil-worshippers would wear. Banners that would be carried by the procession as they entered into the courtyard outside the sanctuary were dyed yellow and red as well, and more lengths were dyed black for hanging over the crosses.

A wooden platform was erected on one side of the courtyard outside the Mani sanctuary, where the friars would sit and watch the completion of the punishments handed down on the offending natives. Twelve holes were dug and fitted with twelve posts in a semicircle around the pile of contraband, where the Mayan priests would hang and watch the ceremony. One final post was installed between the platform and the pile of books and idols, where the native offenders would receive their lashings.

The natives completed the necessary work for the *auto de fé,* the ceremony of their own punishment. The women dyed the cloth, and the men built the platform. The old and sick were left sitting behind locked doors, waiting for the sentencing for worshipping idols.

The ceremony was scheduled for July 12, 1562. The new *Adelantado* and local *encomenderos* declined their invitations, still seething at the way Friar Diego had handled Francisco Hernandez and not wanting their attendance seen as a show of support. The *encomenderos* around Izamal and Merida jumped at the chance to show their support for the Franciscans, fearing the wrath of the priests turning on them in the future.

EVERYTHING WAS ready by the morning of the ceremony. There wasn't a cloud in the sky, and the morning mist hovered over the Franciscans, Spaniards, and one hundred male offenders at the edge of the town—the rest of the offending Maya had to watch the men take the punishment for them all. The friars led the procession. Friar Diego came first, holding the Bible high above his head. Friar Pedro followed with holy water, and one of the friars from Mani swung the burning incense. The rest of the friars carried large crosses draped in black fabric. The Franciscans were followed by the two young boys who had first discovered the idols in a cave, dressed in new Spanish-style outfits—their reward for reporting the discovery. The Mayan men on trial came next, wearing their yellow garments with a large red cross. Scattered among them were individuals tasked with carrying the yellow-and-red banners. At the rear were two Spanish *encomenderos* on horseback, both ensuring no Maya ran away and also showing the Spanish secular support for the ceremony.

Friar Diego led them through streets lined with crowds of Spanish settlers and natives. So many Maya were on trial that every single one of the natives in the crowd knew someone facing trial, and they stood both thankful it wasn't them and fearing for their friends and family. Friar Diego had allowed Friar Pedro to spread word that the idols would be distributed after the punishments were doled out, and many of the natives who had already been punished for their ownership thought they were coming to claim their seized property.

The people in the courtyard stood outside the semicircle created by the priests hanging from the posts. Every priest had a large stone tied to their feet, placed there when they had experienced the *garrucha* in the early morning hours. Twenty-four shoulders had separated; their bodies now hung limp. Of the twelve, three were conscious, including Ahkinmai. Friar Diego wanted them to see the results of their leadership in worshipping the devil.

Friar Diego, Friar Pedro, and the rest of the Mani priests joined the *encomenderos* already seated on the platform. The line of natives dressed in yellow snaked out of the courtyard and into the street beyond. Friar Diego said mass, a solemn affair filled with references to eternal flames. At a nod from the Provincial, Friar Pedro stood and announced the sentencing would begin.

As each Mayan man was brought forth—the Franciscans believed the women followed the men in questions of faith—Friar Pedro read their charges aloud and proclaimed how many lashings they would receive. Each time he said a number, Friar Pedro would look at Friar Diego, checking if the number was acceptable. When Friar Pedro said fifty, Friar Diego disapproved. At one hundred, Friar Diego looked away. One hundred and fifty received a shrug from Friar Diego, and two hundred earned a nod.

Giving almost one hundred men two hundred lashings each took hours. Most of the men had been whipped during their questioning, meaning they were receiving their punishment on backs still raw, split, and scabbed from dozens of prior whips.

One prepubescent child, no older than Ix had been when Friar Diego saved her from sacrifice, was brought forth for not revealing his father's stash of idols. When Friar Pedro started saying fifty, Friar Diego said two hundred louder. Everyone turned away while the child received his punishment, not seeing but hearing his cries, which continued until he passed out well after one hundred lashes.

The sweating young friar who had given out the thousands of lashings, his right arm now aching, looked at Friar Diego. "That's all of them."

Friar Diego shook his head. "We still have twelve more."

The young friar looked at the street where the Maya had been lined up. The two Spaniards on horses sat alone, their mounts pawing the paved street.

Friar Diego pointed at the priests when the young friar looked back up at him. The young man took a deep breath, massaged his right forearm, and nodded.

"Two hundred for them too!" Friar Pedro said.

"And make sure they feel it," Friar Diego added.

The Mayan priests, their bodies already broken, were subjected to the worst lashings of all. Some were awoken from their exhausted slumber by an eruption of pain, while others set their jaw as they saw the young friar walking towards them. Regardless of whether they were conscious when the lashing started, they all passed out before their two hundredth lashing—all except Ahkinmai. No matter how much he begged his gods, and the Christian God, to put him into the dreamworld, he stayed awake for every painful strike. Blood trickled down the backs of his legs, down his heels, and onto the rope supporting the rock hanging from his feet. He never dream-walked again, cursing every god in his pantheon for withholding access to the other world when he needed it most.

Everyone in the square was anxious for the end of the *auto de fé*. They had witnessed blood, screaming, and suffering for hours and wanted away from the turmoil. The Maya stayed in hopes they could help the twelve priests after their ordeal, and the Spanish colonists stayed because they considered the ceremony a church service.

Friar Diego rose from his seat. The sun was high in the sky and his habit clung to his body. "Heretics have no place in the Christian Kingdom!" he proclaimed.

His words were met with lukewarm applause.

"And neither does devil-worship. Let today be a lesson for everyone in the New World: the power of the church is absolute!"

The friars and Spaniards all crossed themselves.

"And now, to wipe this from the earth," he muttered.

Friar Diego descended from the platform and approached the pile of wooden idols and masks, bark-paper books, and bejeweled skulls: the entirety of the Mayan culture in the densest part of their civilization, all in one place for the first time. The pile had been doused in lamp oil the night before. Friar Diego grabbed a long pole fitted with a wax-covered wick and put the tip into the flame of a nearby candle.

The flame didn't catch.

Friar Diego, furious at nature's revolt in front of the mass of gathered witnesses, brought the wick to his face, breathed on it, then kissed it before putting it into the candle flame again. It caught fire in an instant. Pleased with the sign of a higher power's aid, Friar Diego walked to the pile of Mayan artifacts and set them on fire, plunging them into hell's inferno.

Every Mayan priest woke up and struggled against their bindings at the eruption of the first flame. Their shoulders, already torn apart inside, clung to their bodies through the strength of their tattooed skin. They jerked and twisted, but none could get free. The natives who had been whipped, blood still pouring from their backs and tears from their eyes, tried running into the flames but were held back by the Spanish constables who stood guard over them. The Maya in the courtyard cried out, screaming for the lost knowledge of their ancestors and out of fear for what the future would hold without the prosperity bestowed upon them by their gods.

Friar Diego laughed when he saw how the burning relics affected the Maya. "And still, they cry for the devil," he said without taking his eyes from the flames.

A shift in the pile allowed for a deeper glimpse into the assembled collection. There, among the burning Mayan texts, was a book he recognized. Friar Diego didn't blink as the flames licked the edges of the Bible; it was a small price to pay to get rid of the words written by the devil's agents on earth.

CHAPTER FORTY-FOUR

Cortez stood on the sidewalk between Alara and the library. She moved him to the side with the back of her hand and proceeded to walk towards the firefighters, determined to report her boyfriend's presence in the fire. It was her duty to tell a professional about the potential victim, something Cortez should have done himself. She knew Remy was Cortez's perceived obstacle to her, so it came as no surprise her stalker would leave her boyfriend to his fate, but she second-guessed both his knowledge and his intentions. The absolute certainty encapsulated in Cortez's words sent chills down her spine. How did he know beyond a shadow of a doubt?

Alara's myriad thoughts ran on parallel tracks in her knotted stomach and her aching heart. They arose as a sudden awareness, with little processing required, and emerged in their final form before she took two steps. She was stopped by Cortez's firm hold on her arm before she could step down from the sidewalk and onto the street.

"I'll be right back," Cortez said. He waited a breath for a response, and upon receiving none, listened to his body's urges to touch her. He reached an arm up and brushed her cheek with the back of his hand, certain this was the part of the movie when the woman realized the identity of the man destiny had decided should be hers.

The library's collapsing floor created a loud crashing noise that blanketed the streets; Cortez's delusion continued, self-propagating. Alara, frozen, couldn't find the strength to pull away. At last, Cortez knew the time was right to put his plan into action.

He positioned himself between Alara and the library then took two steps backwards, still staring at Alara, drinking in the angel placed on earth for him with his eyes, and said, swelling with pride, "If God has put me in a position to help, I can't look the other way."

With his final words, Cortez turned around and ran past the worn fire truck, then between the two new ones. The firefighters, still close to the trucks and wearing their heavy gear, tried stopping him. One managed to grab a hold of his shirt but the garment ripped further, exposing all of Cortez's chest. Past the barriers, he bounded up the wide stone steps two at a time, ignoring his aversion to the front door, in full view of the trees, because there wasn't time to run around the entire building. Cortez ignored another crash that issued from inside the library; nothing would stop him from completing his holy mission. He was a man possessed by a power greater than himself, and he rushed into the library as the inferno raged overhead.

A MOMENTARY AWARENESS of a memory that didn't belong to her, a mere flash of a vision, transported Alara through time. Her father had mentioned his family's history many times, under many circumstances, and the legend of her ancestors—which had influenced her opinion of organized religion, in particular Catholicism—appeared to Alara as she watched the growing fire. He'd told her all about the clergy burning the Mayan-language books in the 1500s, urging her to remember so she could one day pass the knowledge on to her own children. There were people in Mexico who could still trace the date based on the Mayan calendar, so he claimed, and he made her promise she'd remember to do her part to preserve the memory, saying their culture had been taken from them and that one day they'd have their revenge against the priest who'd instigated the destruction.

While fire truck sirens pierced the air in the distance, growing louder as they sped through the city streets, Alara stood beneath the trees in the park, staring without seeing at the base of the library, trying to preserve what she saw in her vision. She was in another place, at another time, staring out from among the trees, watching a circle of men dressed in brown habits, holding thick wooden clubs, surrounding a fire. Behind the men was a raised wooden platform with a man seated in the center, his face obscured by shadow. Next to the platform, also protected by the club-wielding men, was a series of wooden structures supporting men hanging from tied hands—men she sensed she knew. Without introspection, Alara knew her grief came from both the men and the fire. It was the burning books of the Mayan people, the flames her father had urged her to commit to memory until the day she died, and the hanging men were her ancestors.

Raising her gaze and watching the smoke, Alara couldn't help but think that the people of the city deserved to lose their culture in the same way her ancestors had centuries ago. The library fire wasn't the punishment they deserved, because no fire would ever be enough—all the books that would burn in the library fire could, and would, be replaced. There was no one to replace the tomes her ancestors wrote, nobody to print another edition; they were lost to time, erased from human history by a priest who'd decided the power for his judgment had been bestowed upon him by God.

Swinging open the library's massive wooden doors released a wave of heat that dried Cortez's mouth and singed his hair. The noise was deafening, the roar from a waterfall of flames. He smiled as he stormed over the threshold. The belief that Alara would recognize what he had done for her, the beginning of their future together, created enough euphoria for him to face down the fires of hell if required by fate.

Thick black smoke, pungent with the smell of burning paper and ink, obscured the top of the grand staircase on the far side of the lobby. Cortez experienced a momentary pang of guilt for lying to Alara—Remy was dead on the top floor. He remembered his mother's words, that a man's soul is safe as long as he goes to church each week and confesses. Nothing would keep him from attending church the upcoming Sunday. There was a lot the Lord needed to hear.

Cortez couldn't wait to see the look on Alara's face when she discovered he had saved her favorite book. It had been his plan all along: get rid of Remy and impress her by emerging from the fire with *Love in the Time of Cholera* safe and sound, held high in victory. Even if she needed time after losing Remy —time Cortez would give her—she wouldn't be able to deny Cortez's value, evidenced by his grand gesture. In the end, she would be his.

The heat and smoke in the lobby obscured his vision, and Cortez relied on the knowledge of previous excursions to navigate through slitted eyes. He ran past the main staircase and into the stacks on the first floor. The books were all still intact, untouched by flame, but the overwhelming heat meant combustion could occur at any moment. Cortez's eyes watered from the smoke, moisture that evaporated as soon as it hit his cheeks. Even squinting was difficult. He turned right and closed his eyes, running down the length of the wall, his hands guiding his path. He stopped when his breathing became heavy then looked around through narrowed eyes, trying to get his bearings.

If he could find the smaller staircase that led to the second floor, he could dart into the black smoke to where Alara's gift waited for him.

Knowing he was close, Cortez closed his eyes again and ran through a row of books, crossing to the other side of the first floor. His right hand located the end of the bookshelf he ran along, and he shot out his left hand to find the book-covered wall across the aisle. He dared another peek and found the staircase in its expected location.

Cortez crawled on hands and knees up the stairs. The smoke was stifling, the heat oppressive, and the noise of the fire was magnified, no longer muffled by the ceiling. He lifted the bottom of his torn shirt up to protect his face, taking deep breaths through the fabric. His ordeal was almost complete. He crawled forward with an awkward three-limbed stance, one hand reserved for keeping the shirt over his mouth. When he thought he'd gone far enough and was at the correct bookshelf, he used the shelves to hoist himself to standing. Finding the book he'd left behind, he then crouched back down, inspecting the title.

It wasn't the right book. He had grabbed *The Universe in a Nutshell.*

Cortez groaned. His head started to ache as the power bestowed upon him by the thought of a future with Alara receded into the past, and his senses started fading from the lack of oxygen. He stood once more, grabbed another title, and didn't need to read the title to know it wasn't the correct book. On the third try, he attempted to open his eyes while standing. He couldn't register a single title in front of his face through the smoke.

In a rage fueled by inadequacy, he swiped the entire shelf of books down. Lowering himself to the ground, he felt for books that were the correct size, the right thickness, and when he found a candidate, he forced his screaming eyes to open, making them scan the cover.

None of the books were the one he was looking for.

Some of the books had fallen further into the stacks when they were tossed from their shelf. The third and fourth floors had collapsed onto the second floor, scattering debris among the shelves that filled the spaces where Cortez searched. Cortez crawled into the mire, his hands leading him along trails of pages that would soon be incinerated. Growing desperate, he scanned cover after cover, searching, despite the searing pain in his eyes. He spun around when he felt more books under his feet, then spun again when his movements knocked more books down from their shelves. All the while, the fire raged above him, around him, licking the room's walls and approaching his position from above.

Still without the book he came for, he felt himself suffocating and panicked. It had never occurred to him that the fire he'd started out of love would ever turn against him. He turned, looking for the staircase, and felt himself kick one final book, lying atop charred remains. The feeling reverberated through his bones, sending a shock of recognition through every nerve in his body. Ignoring his suffering lungs and blistering skin, he crawled to the book, the farthest one from freedom. He lowered himself when both hands were over the book's assumed location, sunken in the debris. Prone against the floor, he opened his eyes as best he could. Through his squint, he saw it: *Love in the Time of Cholera*. With renewed drive, he grabbed the book with his left hand and tried turning back to the staircase.

He was stuck, his right arm trapped.

Cortez, frantic once more, leaned close to his arm, inspecting what held it fast. His hand was trapped inside a rib cage, Remy's rib cage, and the skeleton wouldn't move. He twisted and turned his arm, believing the man he'd sentenced to death had escaped from the room and was now returning the favor by making sure Cortez was incinerated alongside him. Cortez, now on his knees, pulled and pushed, straining so hard he thought he'd break bones, though the force he produced was nowhere near enough. His vision narrowed, and through smoke he saw the skull, its jaws open. Laughter surrounded him; farther away, tortured screams. Terrified, Cortez poured every ounce of strength into a final pull.

It was enough to send him bowling back. He collapsed onto his back, still holding the book tightly against his chest. Sputtering, he turned over and found his right hand carried extra weight—the rib cage, detached from the skeleton. With his eyes closed, he crawled in the darkness, one slow elbow at a time through the deafening whoosh of consumed air, in the direction he believed was the staircase that would lead to his salvation. The noise of the vortex produced by the hungry flames soon faded away, leaving him senseless while he wormed along the second-level floor.

Cortez never arrived at the staircase. His last crawl didn't have enough strength behind it to move him forward, and he lay down with Alara's favorite book beneath him, a thin smile on his blistered lips from the knowledge that he had died for love.

Alara had recovered control of her body as soon as Cortez ran into the library. She rushed forward, following in his footsteps, until she got to the firefighters, their backs turned around as they watched the crazed Cortez running into the flames.

"You have to help my boyfriend! He's inside!" Alara said.

"That nut was your boyfriend?" a firefighter responded when he saw her.

"We saw. He ran right past us," his comrade added.

"No, he's not my boyfriend. There's another guy in there!"

"Look, there's nothing we can do. They're in charge now." The two firefighters, both from the first truck, spit on the ground at the mention of the men who had taken their place in front of the blaze and forced them to the rear.

Alara ran forward. Before she could utter a word, the firefighter holding the hose told her to stand back.

"My boyfriend is in there!" she yelled over the combined noise of the fire, water, and general pandemonium.

"There's nothing we can do until we get the blaze under control. Stand back!"

Alara looked around, unsure. Reality was slipping away from her, the world a blur as if she were spinning around when, in fact, she was standing still. Two lingering questions remained, sticking into her like hooks and refusing to let go.

Why was Remy inside the library?

How did Cortez know?

Stumbling back beneath the trees, she sat down with her back resting on a trunk, her elbows on her knees, head buried in her arms. When she called Remy's phone it went straight to voicemail again. She tossed the phone back into her purse and cursed Cortez, the one person who might have the answers, for running back into the blaze. His words echoed in her head, his declaration that God had put him in a position to help, and an ancient anger rose up in her. In an inspired flash of understanding, she knew Cortez's face belonged to the man seated on the wooden platform presiding over the conflagration in her vision, the one hidden in shadow. He was responsible for the burning books of her people, he was responsible for the burning books in the library, and without being told, she knew he was responsible for Remy's presence in the flames.

Even with this knowledge, she couldn't wish him dead. Death was too quick an exit. He had to suffer, to hurt, to beg for his life in exchange for what he'd done to her ancestors. Her own loss of her boyfriend was minuscule compared to the generations of suffering caused by his actions.

The minutes dragged by. Curious onlookers came and went, staying for various lengths of time, as night descended on the city. Few stayed until the blaze was under control, and fewer still stayed once the firefighters entered the burned building, searching for survivors. At some point, portable lights were brought, illuminating the fire trucks and the area in front of the library. Bugs flew around the bulbs, calling out to their brethren to come forth from the park into the continuation of the daylight. Their counterparts in the park responded, creating a cacophony of buzzing wings and various clicks, pops, and whirls.

Alara stood up when the first firefighters entered the building. She didn't have to wait long until they came out nodding their heads, indicating no survivors had been found. The rescuers went in a second time, returning minutes later. They grabbed a stretcher then rushed back inside. After tense minutes that crawled past like hours, the firefighters reemerged with a charred and blistered body covered with a white sheet. Alara ran forward, taking stock of the size of the remains, wondering if she could tell the difference between the shape of Remy's body and Cortez's.

"Can't come over here," a firefighter said, holding a hand up to her. Behind him, one of the men told the other how the body they'd recovered was holding a book. "Guess he was trying to save this one from being burned," he said, holding the book up. It was charred but intact.

"Did you find any other bodies nearby?" Alara called out, her voice betraying her anxiety. She wanted to know if Cortez had even made it to Remy in the first place, thinking the two of them might have been caught while they were exiting the blaze.

"Nope, just a bunch of books. His hand was caught in part of a bookshelf," the firefighter responded without a second thought.

"Which book was it?" Alara asked. It was an odd question.

The man looked at her, then looked at one of his comrades. The comrade shrugged. The man with knowledge of the book looked back at Alara, then told her it was the Bible.

"It was burned too," he added.

Alara knew it was Cortez. She guessed that when he realized he wouldn't make it out alive he'd clung to his faith like a life preserver, hoping his God would save him from the flames.

"Good," she said.

The book crumbled in the firefighter's hand. Cortez had run into the flames but hadn't been able to save the sacred text.

COULD YOU DO ME A FAVOR?

Please help other readers learn more about this book by leaving a rating and review!

Then head over to my website authormarcoshernandez.com and subscribe to my email list. You'll hear about upcoming releases and deals you don't want to miss!

ALSO BY MARCOS ANTONIO HERNANDEZ

Android City Chronicles

The Return of the Operator

Before Anyone Finds Out

Good Enough in a Pinch

The Edited Genome Trilogy

Awakening

Alternative

Absolution

Hispanic American Heritage Stories

The Education of a Wetback

Where They Burn Books

They Also Burn People

Demons in the Golden Empire

Indigenous Magic

Jesus Chan and the Return of Mayan Magic

ABOUT THE AUTHOR

Marcos Antonio Hernandez writes from the suburbs of Washington, D.C. An avid reader of both fiction and non-fiction, his favorite authors are Haruki Murakami and Philip K. Dick — in that order.

Marcos graduated from the University of Maryland, College Park with a degree in chemical engineering and a minor in physics. Since graduating, he has worked as a barista, a food scientist, and a CrossFit coach.

Where They Burn Books, They Also Burn People are Marcos's seventh and eighth novels.

authormarcoshernandez.com

www.ingramcontent.com/pod-product-compliance
Lightning Source LLC
LaVergne TN
LVHW012338100826
845148LV00018B/2706

9781736806708